TANGLE OF CHAOS

TANGLE OF MAGIC
BOOK TWO

J.E. NEAL

To Chelsea—

*For listening to my wild ideas, believing in dreams, and helping to make them
a reality*

CONTENTS

CHAPTER 1

CATS AND DOGS

DAN VINDICO

The Gifted papers and news networks were out in force as Dan pulled onto Venton's campus. He ground his teeth. This was going to be a disaster.

Dozens of flash bulbs went off in his face as he slowly traveled Venton Drive to the faculty parking lot. He exited his car into a mob of reporters.

"Mentor Vindico, can you give us your take on your father's decision to suspend Chancellor Wilshire and take over Venton himself?"

"Mentor Vindico, how do you feel your father should proceed as chancellor?"

"Dan, can you describe in your own words what led to Chancellor Dean Wilshire's suspension?"

Scowling, Dan shot an incredulous glare at the man in a cheap suit that asked the last question. "My father is stepping in, adding to his own responsibilities as a Realm governor, to make certain that Venton remains the outstanding Gifted academy that it has always been."

To his shock, the reporters suddenly raced away from him. His stomach twisted as they surrounded Katherine Bryant as she edged out of her car. Dan couldn't see her face as she attempted to force her way through the throngs of reporters desperate for any word from Wilshire's mistress.

He shook his head. He felt genuinely sorry for her, but terrible choices had terrible consequences.

As his first act as chancellor, Governor Vindico had moved all of the Predilect heads' offices to the admin building. He was determined to make certain that each Predilect department was working just the way it was supposed to. He was going to run a tight ship.

Wilshire may have used his time to fool around and cheat on his wife, but Governor Vindico was going to work. The staff was going to toe the line as well.

"I'm sure as hell not sitting in the man's chair, so find me another one. I don't care if it's from a student's desk," Dan heard his father command one of the maintenance staff.

Dan, Fionna, and Aida had joined Governor and Mrs. Vindico, along with the Haydenshires and the Willows, the evening before, to help rearrange offices and begin trying to discern why Wilshire was putting so much money into the academy, why he'd called a blocked number right after Katherine Bryant's custody trial, who was breaking into the test vaults, how drug tests were being altered, and who was behind all of the scandals at Venton Academy.

Dan left his office door open. He was mildly curious to hear his father's next few commands.

"I want a cash flow and balance report on my desk every morning by eight o'clock," Governor Vindico ordered the head of accounting, Ron Clover.

Ron cleared his throat. "Sir, Chancellor Wilshire didn't begin finance meetings until ten. We haven't had one since September of last year. I don't have any balance sheets."

"I don't recall asking you what Wilshire did. As I am standing here and he is not, it does seem fairly obvious to me that bringing up anything that Wilshire used to do might not put you in the best light as I am the man that suspended Wilshire," Governor Vindico snarled.

Dan choked back laughter. This was going to be fun.

"We are going to figure out where all of that money is going, and we are going to make certain that each and every penny this academy takes in is being used to further the education of the students that attend here. So, you will make certain that I have a cash flow and balance report from every department on my desk every morning at eight o'clock."

Still chuckling, Dan gathered his things for his first period class. He locked his office door behind him and met his father in the corridor.

"Where are you going?" the governor demanded.

"Since you are currently paying me to teach, I thought I might go offer my wisdom and sarcasm to my senior defense class."

The governor laughed as he nodded. "Sorry. I've just yet to find anyone who actually wanted to go do their job since I arrived this morning."

"That might be a slight case of when the cat's away. Only in this case, I'm pretty sure he's a dog."

"Yeah, well, the cat's boss is back, and he's angry."

"I picked up on that."

"My sweet girl is still coming over tomorrow night, right?"

"Yes, and thank you again. Garrett has a shift. It's a Non-Gifted drug bust, and he wants to be there to make sure everyone's okay. We have to be at Georgetown at six thirty. The class goes 'til eight."

"You don't need to thank me. I'm thrilled. I'm determined to get this mess cleaned up, and then I'm going to spend time with my grandkids. I've missed too much."

"You're doing great, Dad." Dan slapped his father on the shoulder and headed down the corridor.

Jeff grinned as Dan entered the class. He looked eager to begin. All of the students in Dan's senior defense class were vying for positions either in the National Iodex office or in one of the Iodex branches in every major city across America, and they'd all impressed him so far.

They worked hard, asked intelligent questions, and most had turned their assigned papers in on time. They'd even done extra research and then asked Dan about their findings.

Two hands shot up as soon as he began class. Smiling, he nodded to Ben Cobson.

"Do you think, as the former Chief of Elite Iodex, that Iodex should have provided Mentor Bryant security this morning when she arrived on campus and was mobbed by the press?"

"Mr. Strenton, would you care to field that one?" Dan directed Jeff.

He nodded. "Iodex can't just decide to offer anyone security unless they've made the request themselves and then the chief agrees to the protocoled response or they're sent out by one of the governors or a Senteon Representative."

"Right, I know that," Ben huffed. "I'm asking do you think that policy should've been changed in light of the public persona involved in this particular affair?"

Dan seated himself on the edge of his desk. "Truthfully?" he quizzed the class. Everyone nodded. "I can tell you that Mentor Bryant could certainly have used a little help getting in the building this morning, and Iodex could have cleared the way. But Mentor Bryant's need of security is of her own making. Remember, every time Iodex teams are sent out, it costs the Realm money either in personnel or even gasoline for the vehicles. I do not feel that the Realm should fund the consequences of her incredibly poor decision-making."

He grimaced as he realized that he'd left the classroom door open as Katherine Bryant happened to be walking by.

"So you're more of a no mercy kind of guy?" Ben insinuated. He looked extremely intrigued.

"No, it's not that at all." Dan considered. "I don't believe that Mentor Bryant was ever in any physical danger. Because of that I don't believe Iodex should've gotten involved."

Shaking that off, he summoned on his laptop. They had a lot to cover.

"Building on what we've covered so far this year, today we're going to dive into the criminal mind. Can anyone tell me the six foundational reasons people break the law?"

Monique Thomas's hand shot up, and Dan nodded to her.

"Poverty, position, pity, privilege, peace of mind, and power, either their own or power someone holds over them," she replied dutifully.

"Excellent, Ms. Thomas."

"All right, knowing those foundations, let's go over a few ways that criminals think differently than law-abiding citizens. Raise your hand if you've already met the object of your shield. You're already in a relationship you consider to be the one your shield seeks constantly, the person you would stop at nothing to protect."

About a third of the class raised their hand, and Dan smiled. That was what he assumed. Once Ioses Predilects met their mate, it was generally instantaneous and forever life-changing.

Jeff's hand had been the first one up. Dan grinned. "All right, Mr. Strenton, if you, or more specifically your shield, had a preference, where would Becca exist constantly?"

"Inside my shield," Jeff responded.

"Any idea why that is?"

"She's safe there. Nothing can hurt her. Keeping her safe is the most important thing to me. I'm *her* Shield."

"You are an outstanding Shield, and what you just said is completely correct. But let's expand out a little farther. You prefer for Becca to be inside your shield with you because she is no longer at…?"

"Risk."

Dan nodded. "On the whole, Ioses Shields are the most risk-averse Predilect. We do not like chances. We cannot stand for someone we care about to even potentially take a chance where they might be hurt, and I don't just mean physically. Our shields are equipped with a distinctive, honed radar. If our shields sense even the potential of danger, we're generally out. It doesn't matter how commonplace something in society is. Once we've detected potential risk, we are particularly bad at ever reassessing it. That's something we can learn. Flexibility and adaptability are required to be excellent Iodex officers, and they are not skills that we come equipped with.

"Now, based on the reading I assigned you over the weekend, what does risk aversion have to do with the criminal mind?"

Jada Yadav's hand was up before anyone else's. Dan nodded to her. "Overall, criminals are not risk-averse. In fact, according to the latest research, they tend to take risks that most law-abiding citizens would never even consider taking. They'd rather lose significantly more just for the chance to win a little."

"Outstanding. Now, can you tell me why it's so important that we understand this? What does our understanding of the criminal mind do for society?"

She thought for a moment. "Laws and public policy would better serve criminals and law-abiding citizens alike if we understand where people are coming from. So, knowing that someone has exhibited risky behavior and understanding if they are already at risk of breaking the law because of the foundational reasons you taught us can help us mitigate criminal activity. It can help us potentially intervene."

Dan grinned. "Could not have given you a better answer, class. Excellent work, Jada."

She beamed. "Thank you, sir. The research you gave us was so interesting. I'm actually thinking of withdrawing my application to the Atlanta Iodex Precinct. I think I want to work in criminology instead."

"And that is why it is so important for you to learn this here. What we're learning will affect the rest of your lives. I'm sorry it wasn't presented to you before I got here. It really should have been."

The entire class nodded their heads.

"All right, so we've got a person who has no issue with risk. They'll take a gamble they have a very small percentage of winning without a second thought. In fact, for more than half of people with a criminal mindset, the slighter the chance they have of winning the more appealing the gamble becomes. What does that tell us about consequences?"

"They won't work," gasped from Xavier Reston.

"They do work," Dan corrected, "but not in the way we like to think. So, why don't they work to prevent crime?"

"Because to criminals there's always a chance they won't be caught."

"Precisely, so who do they actually work for?"

Xavier considered. "They protect people *from* the criminals' activities."

"Good. So, when Crown Governor Lawson rewrote the constitution and reworked our entire justice system, what did he include for people who've been incarcerated?"

"Therapy," Jeff answered.

Dan nodded. "One caveat to that—just because criminals don't tend to be dissuaded by consequences doesn't mean that they won't do what they can to try to turn the odds in their favor. That's part of what drives a criminal and a large portion of why they can be difficult to apprehend. They tend to like a big chance that they believe they can outsmart." Dan chuckled at the rapidly flying clicks of keyboards.

"Another thing, once a criminal has gotten away with their gamble once, they are all the more likely to make the same gamble again. They believe that if they outsmarted the system once, they can certainly repeat the odds. That's why criminals tend to stick to the same patterns. It is extremely rare for someone who believes themselves skilled in white-collar crimes to suddenly become a perpetrator of violent crime. Their lack of risk aversion and the thrill they get when they gamble and win to some degree means they're lazy. Once something works and they achieve the outcome they want, they don't change their stripes. From that knowledge, what can we deduce about criminal organizations?"

Ben Cobson raised his hand again. His brow furrowed for a moment. "So, you're saying, if a criminal believes that he can outwit Iodex with a specific kind of crime but they need other crimes committed, they're more likely to recruit someone they think has the skills they need rather than trying to do it themselves."

"Excellent, Mr. Cobson. Typically the other crimes they need committed are ones that cover the original crime. They may not mind risk, but they do not like to worry over what they think they've already gotten away with. They typically want to move on to the next chance.

"In our next class, we're going to go over the other half of the makings of a criminal mind. But before the bell rings, let's bring it back to our Predilect as a whole. There are a few Shields serving time both in Coriolis and Felsink Prisons. If we know that Shields are almost universally risk-avoidant, how can that possibly be? What else makes a Shield tick?"

Everyone stared up at him. No one seemed to have an answer, so he explained, "Shields tend to have a deep and abiding thirst for justice. That hunger for righting what we perceive as wrongs can take over your entire shield, and then your shield can take over your mind. Believe me, I've lived what I'm explaining to you."

He got a few sympathetic nods.

"It is imperative that you understand that your thirst for justice can force you into situations where you are willing to take risks, even criminal risks, often for no other reason than to serve your own ego. That is a dangerous place to exist. Don't let your shield sell you on a risk because you're seeking a specific outcome or punishment for someone else. Which leads us to...empathy. There may be a few Shields in prison, but there are no Receivers. There is a reason for that. Read chapters six and seven from your textbooks on why a lack of empathy is the other necessary ingredient for crimes to be committed. Be prepared to discuss and for a quiz on why Receivers are far and away the most powerful Predilect."

That earned him several discreet eye rolls and huffs. He smirked. They had to learn somehow, someday that Shields couldn't and shouldn't rule the world.

CHAPTER 2
EARNED NOT GIVEN

D an returned to his office for his off period.

"Daniel, could you come here a minute?" his father called.

Moving into the chancellor's office, Dan chuckled. There were numerous pictures of Mrs. Vindico situated on the desk along with all of the governor's children and grandchildren. His father was making a point. That much was obvious.

"What can I do when these kids are brats?" the governor sighed. He'd clearly forgotten that being chancellor meant that if a mentor couldn't handle a student, he was the heavy.

"I personally assign more work," he offered. "You can do detention. Saturday morning works well, or refuse them passes to upcoming events. You can send them home for the day, week, month, your choice. Or they can do manual labor around the school, which I happen to know is a personal favorite of yours when it comes to discipline."

His father laughed. "Why, yes it is. Remember that, do you?"

"Yeah, I remember." Dan rolled his eyes as he recalled the Monday afternoon after he, Garrett, and Will had spent the weekend regurgitating pure alcohol they'd stupidly snuck to their campout when Dan was eighteen. They'd been made to empty every trash can in the entire Senate and then to scrub the dumpsters. Doing yard work was another common punishment in the Vindico household.

Just then, a knock sounded on the chancellor's door. "What now?" He opened it to reveal a student who was sporting quite a smirk. He handed the governor the pink slip from the mentor who'd sent him to see the chancellor.

"Sit down," Governor Vindico barked.

Dan leaned against the wall. He wondered what the kid had done that he was so visibly proud of.

Rolling his eyes, the governor clenched his jaw. "What did you do?" He didn't bother to read the pink slip.

"See, Mentor Bryant decided on her first day back to rearrange everybody's seat. So, I told her I like to sit in the back of the class. She said, 'not in the back, Mr. Coggin.'" He could hardly contain his laughter as he concluded, "So, I said, 'betcha never said that to Wilshire.'" He cracked up as Governor Vindico's eyes goggled, and Dan bit his lips together to keep from joining in the laughter.

"Given how delighted you seem to be with your incredibly rude comment, why don't you compose an apology letter to Mentor Bryant? You can do that after you scrub all of the urinals in the men's restrooms in the Adminis building."

"Seriously?"

"Do I appear to be joking?"

"No, sir," he huffed, not quite so full of himself.

"Go get started."

He flung the door open dejectedly.

"How was that?" Governor Vindico lost his menacing growl as soon as the kid made his escape. Dan cringed. "What?"

"If his parents are on the 'Katherine Bryant deserves to be burned at the stake' bandwagon, you may hear about the letter, but other than that, it was good."

"I don't really care what his parents think of Mentor Bryant. I can't say I have a tremendous amount of respect for her myself, but he has to respect her role as his mentor even if he doesn't respect the woman holding it."

10

"That's not true, Dad, and quite frankly, that's a dangerous way to think."

"What do you mean?"

"Respect should be earned not given. These kids don't trust a leader without a limp, and I think they're right. A lot of shitty things have been done by people who decided they deserved respect for the title they have instead of the work they've done. Deciding that some people are universally entitled to respect because of their last name, or their job, the color of their skin, or how much money is in their bank account, is how we got the board that you helped overturn."

Governor Vindico nodded his acceptance of that.

"These books are insane." His father settled back at Wilshire's old desk with ledgers, spreadsheets, and bank statements strewn everywhere. Numerous windows on the computer monitor displayed the Venton books. "Dean has been making those payments every month for a year and a half. I can't figure out what he was thinking."

"I'm telling you it was a negotiation with his conscience."

"I should fire him for the state of these books alone, but I just can't bring myself to do that to Ellen."

"How's she doing?" Dan wondered if his parents knew anything about Mrs. Wilshire.

"I'm not certain. Lillian took her out to lunch. Her sister's staying with her. Lillian would certainly never share with me what they discussed, not that I'd want her to betray that confidence. Stephen says she was doing as well as could be expected. I just hope the press isn't hounding her. She's been through enough, and truthfully, I don't think she even knows the half of it."

"Has she filed for separation?"

"To everyone's shock, no, but as far as I know, Dean still has a room at the Holiday Inn."

"Fi would bury me under the Holiday Inn. Rightfully so."

"Yeah, well, when she finished with you, then I'd take my turn," Governor Vindico assured him.

Pride welled in Dan's soul. He was proud to have been raised by the man that sat before him trying desperately to clean up another man's disaster.

"Thanks, Dad."

His father raised his head. His brow furrowed. "For what?"

"For everything," Dan offered sincerely. "I'm gonna go teach my senior lab, but how about if we eat lunch in here, and I help you try to make heads or tails of all of this?"

"Thank you, son, and you're welcome—for everything."

Completely exhausted an hour and a half later, Dan fell back into his father's new office carrying his lunch that his loving wife had prepared for him. After she'd read over his lesson plans for the day, she'd prepared enough for five, but Dan was about to inhale each and every delectable bite.

"Are you okay?" Governor Vindico looked extremely concerned.

Dan nodded and downed a protein shake that he'd shaken up quickly. "I was teaching them to siphon shields today."

Understanding lit Governor Vindico's face. "And you let them try to siphon yours to show them just how much they still had to learn and how much muscle they needed to add before they could complete that task."

Dan nodded as he tore into Fionna's homemade macaroni and cheese which was astounding. "Yeah, and Jeff Strenton failed to mention that Portwood and Rainer Lawson had already given him a few lessons, so he knew what the hell he was doing." Jeff hadn't quite been able to conceal his pride as Dan had visibly weakened under his cast.

The governor laughed. "He's a good kid, and there's always something appealing about even coming close to upping your hero."

After Dan ate his weight in macaroni and cheese, two Reubens, and two apples, he could think clearly again. He began reading over the stacks of different reports on the desk. "When was the last time all of this was reconciled?"

Governor Vindico's eyes closed in defeat. "Three years ago."

"What?!"

"It seems about three years ago, Dean let a whole lot of things fall by the wayside."

Dan shook his head in disbelief. "What about all of these extra mentor seminars and conferences? It wasn't just him and Bryant that were going. A lot of the staff went as well. He tried to get me to go to one in Philadelphia when I signed my contract. It was all to be at the expense of the school."

Governor Vindico nodded. "And that was never approved through me or even the budgetary committee, but that still doesn't explain him dodging me on the books or why he's been paying the school. What he was adding back in wouldn't cover a fraction of all of the conferences. What did you tell him when he asked you about Philadelphia?"

"We'd just found out Fi was pregnant again. I was still a disaster over everything that had happened. We'd just adopted Aida. I told him that I wasn't coming home early from Kauai, and that I wasn't going anywhere overnight without my wife and my daughter. No questions asked. He informed me that spouses were not included and that absence made the heart grow fonder. Oh, and that me getting away would be good for both me and Fionna." Dan growled from the thought alone.

"I told him Fi was pregnant again and that I wasn't leaving her overnight. I was *not* polite. I was still insane over what happened to her and terrified that something would happen to Halia because of the gunshot wound," he confessed to his father in a choked whisper. "He dropped it when he realized that he wasn't getting anywhere."

Governor Vindico didn't comment. He went back to the computer. "I can tell you that there was a conference in Philadelphia, and one in Chicago that I never approved and had no knowledge of," he sighed. "They took twenty-five mentors to Vegas for a week, but that was approved by the budgetary committee. There is a healthy allotment for furthering the mentors' education, but he's well over budget." His father narrowed his eyes. "So, the bottom line is that he *was* robbing the general fund for his out of town conferences."

Dan eased away from his dad. He'd seen that look a few times growing up, and if he were being perfectly honest, it still made him uneasy. "No, the bottom line is that the academy *was* paying for his affair."

"I doubt Wilshire sees it that way, and I'm certain the mentors that were there to actually learn something gained some benefit from them. I need you to go back to the information you have and try to tell me if Wilshire and Bryant actually attended classes at these seminars. Did they surface long enough for that, or was Venton quite literally paying for their weekend getaways?"

With a defeated sigh, Dan nodded. "That's not going to be easy to prove."

"I know, but I'm not messing around with this anymore. I want to know the truth. I want to get to the bottom of this black hole, so I can fix what I let slide."

Dan hated that his father was taking this on himself, but he knew he would do the same thing.

"I'm sure they attended most of the classes. Otherwise, the staff would have talked long before the story broke."

With another impressed grin, the governor nodded. "That's true, so, is it my job to legislate another man's morality? If he went to the classes and learned something, in terms of me governing the Gifted academies, other than the overages he used, can I really tell the mentors and administration of this school what they can and can't do in their off hours?"

Dan considered that. "I don't know."

"Me either, so help me figure this out."

Dan glanced back at the bank statements in his lap. "I guess if Wilshire had been single or even just dating someone and had gone on a company expense-paid trip, attended what the company wanted him to attend, and then decided to hook up with a woman at night, you and I wouldn't be sitting in this office."

"That's true."

"But it's never quite that clear-cut. He did misuse appropriated funds to go on the trips. Whether or not he had sex on the trips is irrelevant. I'll tell you this too—the day I got the call that Wretchkinsides was in DC and planning to attack Haydenshire Farm while half the Realm was there, nothing could've prevented me from doing what I did. I'd sat day in and day out watching my relationship with the woman who means more to me than anything in the world fall completely apart because I knew she was pregnant and I knew she was scared to death."

Governor Vindico nodded. His expression was heartbroken over all that his son had been through.

"Nothing could have stopped me. Not you, not Governor Haydenshire, not Will, not Garrett, not even Fionna. In fact, the last thing Fi said to me before I took Marlisa and locked her up, was 'stop, you're scaring me.' I didn't stop, and I wasn't going to stop until I had what I wanted. Was that immoral? Hell yeah. Was it wrong? Absolutely. And, I'm sitting here today without a badge because of it. I'm certain I could drum up some support under the fact that I killed a mass murderer and ended his outright evil organization, so I shouldn't have lost my job. But Governor Haydenshire didn't see it that way and neither did you.

"All the other reasons aside, I'd already broken protocol and I'd already proven that I was perfectly willing to bend the rules to get what I wanted. You don't get to come back from that. You leave it to burn because Wilshire might not have out and out stolen money from the academy, but he's proven that he's perfectly willing to make the money work for what he wants instead of him working for this academy."

His father smiled. "All right, tell me this, since you apparently went and grew up on me at some point. A few years from now, my granddaughters are attending here, along with any others you and Fionna decide you might like. You find out the chancellor's been having an affair with a mentor, and all of the details are played out online. As a parent, how do you feel? Because I can tell you that Stephen and Lillian are furious that this was going on while Connor, Logan, Rainer, and Emily were here."

Dan knew that his father felt like he'd let one of his best friends down on top of everything else. He tried to envision the scenario. "I'm not sure. I can tell you that some of the students knew what was going on. Wilshire would show up in her classrooms at the end of her classes, so anyone paying attention generally picked up on something.

Fi was so disappointed. I was as well, I guess. He's the guy that told the Angel owners to come see Fionna challenge, that she was good enough for the pros. He signed me into special ops. He came to Amelia's funeral and guided Rainer after Governor Lawson died. You can't work up here with the kids and not become a part of their lives. It might ultimately only be between him and Ellen and Mentor Bryant and her husband, but they let a lot of people down. More than they'll ever realize."

Deep concern etched the beginnings of wrinkles on his father's face.

"But,"—Dan stood—"I have to go teach History of Defense to a bunch of freshmen, and since I no longer have to teach Mentor Bryant's sub-freshman creative writing class, I'm going home to my beautiful bride. Aida has open house at McCarron tonight, but after we get her to bed, I'll see just how many classes Wilshire and Bryant missed during their trysts."

"I really do appreciate your help with this."

"Pretty sure I owe you, Dad."

CHAPTER 3

INSECURITIES

A broad grin spread across Dan's face as he eased in the door to his home that afternoon. Fionna was sound asleep on the couch under her favorite quilt.

He debated walking down to the bus stop to meet Aida when Fionna stirred.

"Hey, baby doll." He kissed her cheek.

"You're home!" A broad grin formed on her face.

"On time for once. Want some coffee?"

"Yum. You're home and making me coffee. I don't deserve you."

When he returned with their mugs, she yawned and stretched. "I saw you on the news this morning."

He grimaced. "Did you see when Bryant arrived?"

Fionna drew a long, restorative sip of coffee. "That was awful. They kept asking her these horribly offensive questions. I feel sorry for her despite what she did. On the television screen, it's so surreal though."

Dan was well aware that the majority of the American Realm was getting the flat screen image of the affair. Most people would never know how it all began or the illicit and often haunting details. And most people would only ever see it the way they wanted to see it anyway. Only one dimension was ever displayed on their television screen.

The door pushed open, drowning out that topic of conversation quickly.

"Daddy!" Aida gasped. "You're home!"

There weren't many sweeter sounds in the entire world. Dan lifted Aida up into his arms.

"Hey, baby girl." She hugged him fiercely. He set her down, and she flew to Fionna and hugged her as well.

"When do we go to open house?"

Fionna took Aida's hand and guided her into the kitchen. "First, we have to have a snack, and then you can watch TV or read or play, then we're going to eat dinner, and then we go to open house." She provided Aida a bowl full of grapes and a squeeze pack of yogurt.

"And I have to do my homework." She bit her lip and sounded worried.

"You have homework?" Dan wondered if Aida was struggling with something and needed a little extra help. He'd been bracing himself for this. Aida had never been in school before. She was bound to be behind the other students.

Aida returned to her backpack and handed Dan her purple folder. Fionna moved to read over his shoulder as he pulled out the stapled packet of worksheets and read the note from Mrs. Powell.

*Dear Parents, The school board
has now decided that the seven hours your young
children have spent in school is no longer enough
and that each second grader should complete
at least thirty minutes of homework each night as well. As I
myself feel, after thirty years of teaching,
that their time after school would better be spent playing, or spending time
with their families, or using their imaginations, I feel that spending a little
time reading each night out of a reading level appropriate book and then
perhaps drawing a picture or sharing with you what they've read will be
quite adequate. If you disagree, which*

"She has the best teacher in the whole damn school," Dan decreed under his breath.

Fionna nodded her adamant agreement. "This says that you need to read each day and then draw a picture about what you read or tell me and Daddy about your book," Fionna soothed over Aida's tension about having homework.

"It does?" Aida's brow furrowed. "But there were so many sheets."

Dan smiled. "Mrs. Powell says you do enough sheets at school, so you can play and read and spend time with Mommy and Daddy when you get home."

"Those are my favorite things to do and to feel baby Halia in Mommy's tummy."

Fionna smiled. "Baby Halia has been wearing me out today." She rubbed her hands over her belly.

"More contractions?" Dan tried to quell his nervous energy before Fionna caught it, but he wasn't quick enough.

"Yeah, not as painful—just for a long time."

"Did you call Adeline?"

Fionna nodded. "She wasn't as worried as last time because they really weren't painful. She said they were normal to some degree. If it weren't for the other problem, she wouldn't be concerned. But for now, more rest and more water and less standing. She still thinks going back to Kauai in a couple of weeks will probably help reset my energy and Halia's."

"Sweetheart, if you want to go back now..."

"Not without you and not without Aida."

"Fi," Dan started to argue. "I can stay here with Aida. I'll make certain I'm home every afternoon before she gets home."

"Please don't make me cry." Fionna effectively ended his arguing.

"Then Daddy's in charge. Mommy's going back to sit on the couch, and Aida can finish her snack and go read. And then we're all going out to eat before open house."

Fionna grabbed her water bottle and flopped back on the couch.

After burgers from Big Buns, Dan drove his family out to the elementary school. He was astonished at the sheer number of cars.

After insisting that he drop Fionna and Aida off at the door, Dan pulled in behind a line of cars parked along the edges of one of the playgrounds. Rushing into the school, he rolled his eyes as he took in his extremely pregnant wife standing in the cafeteria.

The lunch tables were folded and put away, and chairs were arranged in rows enough to accommodate most of the crowd of parents and students. Dan glared at the sheer number of men all seated comfortably.

Shaking his head, he moved to the remaining cafeteria chairs that were stacked near the kitchens. He lifted one off the stack and added it to a row near the back.

"Mrs. Vindico." He added the chair to the row where Meredith and Olivia were seated and directed his wife into the seat.

"Thank you."

The woman that had called Dan out for entering the school in an attempt to pick up Aida on the first day stepped up to the podium. Her entire being appeared to have been attacked by faded denim.

She had apples appliqued all over the denim vest she was wearing and apple-shaped buttons made a line down the front of her long denim skirt.

"Thank you, everyone, for being here tonight at McCarron Elementary's Have a Beary Good Year Open Cave night." She giggled at her own play on words.

Fionna and Dan shared a mischievous glance. Open cave night could be construed many different ways, but none of the other parents seemed to see the humor.

"My name is Cindy McBeechum, and I'm your school board liaison this beary good year," she announced in a high-pitched squeal that made Dan's skin crawl. "Now, I know I've met some of you and many of our returning bears, but if I haven't gotten to know you, I'll either be stopping by your homes or you can make an appointment here for a brief conference about your little bears."

Fionna's head shot back as she scowled at Dan. He tried not to laugh at her disdain that someone from the school might take it upon themselves to just show up at their home.

Dan was certain the woman was exaggerating, so he continued to listen. "Our first beary exciting bit of news tonight will be our first school fundraiser of the year." She clapped and leapt up and down as Dan and Fionna both laughed outright. They halted abruptly as they received odd stares from the people around them.

"We've decided to pair two of our most successful sellers from the past few years," she trilled. "It is my distinct honor and pleasure to announce the esteemed head of Bingham Cheeses and Holiday Gift Wrap, Tipton McClain." She began applauding as a man in a polyester suit moved to the microphone.

Thirty-three minutes later, Dan rubbed his temples and considered just writing the school a check so that Tipton would shut the fuck up about how amazing the opportunity selling processed cheese food and severely overpriced wrapping paper would be for their children.

Fionna was shifting uncomfortably in her chair and had briefly exchanged texts with Dan making fun of the esteemed Tipton McClain, but they'd stowed the phones when Meredith shook her head at them.

Mrs. McBeechum returned to the podium, patting tears from her eyes as she blew kisses to Tipton. "Now, let's remember, all of my mama bears and papa bears, we're working this year to fund a committee that will be in charge of removing inappropriate or harmful materials from our curriculum and library."

Dan narrowed his eyes. "She wants us to fund a committee for her bigotry," he spoke between his teeth. Several parents nearby gave him a nod. They all looked equally disgruntled.

The school counselor stood next to go over the standardized testing that the children would take in the spring.

The school nutritionist was after that. She began going over how, despite parental concerns, McCarron's lunch system did provide the children with a complete meal. Breakfast and lunch menus were then passed out to everyone.

McBeechum returned to scold, "And for all of our mama and papa bears who have decided that you'd prefer to make your little bear's lunch each day, please remember that you are creating more work for your child's teacher and more work for the lunchroom staff."

"How is my making Aida's lunch more work for them?" Fionna huffed under her breath.

Almost in answer to her question, McBeechum continued, "The children have to be reminded to get their lunchboxes, and it provides a much smoother lunch line if everyone is getting a tray.

"Moving on to the library issues." She produced a poster board list of books she was urging parents to write the school board to have removed from the library.

Who the hell voted for this moron?

All of the children appeared to be just as aggravated as Dan, and the staff was losing control of the room.

Aida, who carried a book with her most everywhere she went, was leaned up against Fionna reading. Dan added her a chair when he realized that she might be graduating from elementary school before they were allowed to leave the meeting.

The principal went to the mic to explain disciplinary procedures should a student do something deemed inappropriate.

Aida would beam and pat Fionna's belly whenever she felt Halia move. Fionna seemed to have decided that bonding with her girls was a vastly better use of her time, so she was showing Aida where to touch when Halia moved. The delighted grins stretched across his girls' faces, and the twinkle in their eyes as they giggled quietly and nodded to each other had Dan much more interested in his family than in the meeting.

Mrs. McBeechum had returned to the mic, and Dan leaned and

popped a kiss on the top of Aida's head. Suddenly, every head in the room turned toward him.

"Mr. Vindico," Mrs. McBeechum drawled with a complementary scolding sigh. "My eye just landed on you, what with your just standing there so tall and well built—you must work out." Dan scowled. "But being built like a strapping stallion won't keep you from the red rule violation list, will it, Mr. Vindico?"

Meredith sank down low in her seat and covered her face with her hands. Fionna's mouth fell open in fury.

As no one was speaking, Dan decided to say his piece. "I was unaware, since my daughter is new to McCarron, that my wife and I were not allowed to have our child once school was over. Seeing as how she is our child, we should be able to access her at any time."

To Dan's relief, the crowd seemed to agree.

This was, however, not the response Mrs. McBeechum was hoping for, and she began to pout. "It is our job here at McCarron to keep your little bear and all of our little bears safe."

"Does she want to see mama bear?" Fionna threatened. Dan clasped his hands on her shoulders. This would be a particularly bad time for one of her pregnancy mood swings that would most definitely end with Fionna shoving McBeechum's apples down her throat.

"From her father?" sneered from a dad on the other side of the room.

"Yeah," was echoed from various spots around the lunchroom.

"My daddy just wanted to pick me up because I'm his baby girl, and it was my very first day at school ever, and he missed me," Aida sweetly explained.

Every parent in the room melted and swooned. Dan tried to wipe the smirk off his face without much success as the crowd stirred and began discussing the two o'clock rule.

A man near the front stood. "I suggest we form a subcommittee to discuss reworking the policy that children have to be picked up before two o'clock if it is a parent that is picking them up." The crowd, now worked into a frenzy, cheered. "And Mr. Vindico will be the head of our committee."

Dan shook his head. "I'm sorry, I can't. We're busy all the time." He gestured to Fionna's stomach and then realized what he'd just said. Fionna grimaced in horror as parents began to chuckle. "Not like that." He cringed and started once more, "I am all for disbanding the two o'clock rule, but I cannot head a subcommittee."

"Attention back to the front." Mrs. McBeechum went so far as to snap her fingers. "I do encourage everyone to join our PTA. With your membership, you will each get a car sticker for our beary great school. And now, I believe it is time for your little bears to lead you to their classrooms. If you have more than one little bear here at McCarron, please take your time as the teachers will be available until eight thirty. If you happen to have a student in our Gifted program,"—she rolled her eyes and then shot a vengeful look at Dan—"you may also stop by and meet Mrs. Willow, our Gifted teacher." She stomped away from the microphone. Dan helped Fionna out of the chair, certain he'd died and gone to some kind of PTA hell.

"You're busy all the time." Meredith cringed as she and Olivia made their way over.

"That is not what I meant."

Fionna began to giggle but it quickly turned to full-blown laughter as she laced her arm through Dan's. They were herded out into the entryway of the school where tables had been set up for parents to pay to join PTA and to purchase school memorabilia.

"Now, would you like a McCarron T-shirt or sweatshirt?" the PTA president chirped to Fionna.

"Oh, uh…" Fionna looked horrified as she took in the crayon-red sweatshirt that read, "My little bear learns to care at McCarron." It had a brown bear on the front sticking his hand in a honey pot.

"You know, I'm not really able to wear sweatshirts right now," Fionna fumbled for an excuse.

"How about a McCarron bumper sticker, Dad?" She flung a car magnet at Dan.

He shot Fionna a pleading look. "I am not putting an *I'm a caring Papa Bear* magnet on my Ferrari. That is disturbing on so many levels." He shuddered from the thought alone.

"You could get a sticker for your helmet or for the Agusta." She could hardly get the words out before she was giggling hysterically.

"Uh, no." Telling everyone where your child went to school was incredibly dangerous, not to mention that putting a sticker on his custom Agusta would be almost blasphemous.

Dan discreetly slipped the magnet back on one of the tables and followed Meredith down the hallway. He was pleased to hear that Tim had volunteered to stay home with Oliver and have a guys' night, so that Meredith could take Olivia to open house.

His comfort that his sister looked happier than he'd seen her in years was short-lived, however, as a brood of mothers from Aida's class sauntered toward them.

"When are you due, Mrs. Vindico?" one sneered. Dan wondered how a relatively innocent question could sound so smug. Fionna drew from Dan suddenly. Her internal Receiver's shield set around her as she pulled herself away from what she clearly saw as a dangerous situation.

"Oh…the end of November." She tucked farther behind Dan.

"I suppose when you start out as young as you must have been when you had Aida then you feel you can space them out. But you'll find that, if you put too many years between them, older children ask lots of uncomfortable questions and then they just aren't close as siblings that are less than two years apart like my Mindy and Michael."

Fionna forced a smile. "It's so kind of you to have opinions about my children and my life despite the fact that I've never met you before."

Dan was so damn proud of her he beamed.

"Will Aida be signing up for softball, lacrosse, soccer, and cheerleading? They all start next week, and I didn't see her name on the forms," another mother edged in.

"No, Aida wasn't really interested in playing a sport after school, and we're about to have a baby obviously." She gestured to her midsection. "Aida wanted to be in the reading group at the library on Fridays," Fionna explained as if she had to prove her worth as a mother to these horrible women. "And that's something the baby and I can do with her," she offered almost mutely.

"You're still young, so you'll learn the more they're involved in the better. You have to begin preparing for college now."

Dan's blood began to boil as he stared at a group of women all older than Fionna by at least five years who were standing in the hall outside of their children's classroom making his wife feel like she was incompetent.

"Come on, Mommy." Aida tugged on Fionna's arm.

Fionna followed her into Mrs. Powell's classroom on the koala second grade hall.

Mrs. Powell grinned as they entered. "Well, hello, Aida, how are you this evening?"

"I'm very well. Thank you." Aida responded perfectly. "Come and see my desk."

They followed her to her desk. "She's a lovely child. She makes each and every day a delight. She's so thoughtful of everyone. Thank you so much for giving me hope that perhaps not every parent has completely lost their sense of themselves and of the understanding that just because something is good for Susie doesn't make it good for, well, Aida," Mrs. Powell whispered.

"Oh, thank you." Fionna blinked back tears as she hugged Mrs. Powell.

"Don't let them get to you, my dear," she soothed. "Aida is a product of a wonderful, loving, caring home. She is confident in herself and in your love, and at seven years old that's really all she needs. Worry about test scores, dance recitals, and homework when she's older. Right now, just enjoy her."

Fionna nodded and wiped away the few tears that had escaped as Dan kissed the side of her head. Mrs. Powell smiled at them and then gestured her head to the collective mob of women that had attacked Fionna. They appeared to travel in a pack like some kind of fungus.

With a dramatic eye roll only Dan and Fionna were privy to, Mrs. Powell moved and greeted their children.

"This is my reader." Aida pulled out a well-worn book with a picture of an eagle flying high above the mountaintops. As she showed Dan all of her textbooks, Haley approached with her mother.

"Hi, Aida, this is my mommy."

Aida beamed. "Hi, Haley."

Fionna extended her hand. "It's so nice to meet you. I'm Fionna Vindico." Dan saw Fionna's smile falter as if she was reading something from Haley's mother though Haley and her parents were not Gifted.

Judging from Haley's mother's exhausted expression and downtrodden demeanor, Dan guessed that life had taken its toll and that Fionna had immediately picked up on that.

"I'm Ruth," the woman explained. "It's nice to meet you as well. Haley's told me all about Aida." She grinned sweetly at Aida though exhaustion plagued her.

"This is my husband, Dan," Fionna introduced.

"Nice to meet you." Dan shook the woman's hand, giving her a kind smile.

"I really appreciate…" Ruth choked, "Uh…."

Dan assumed she was trying to thank them for making Haley's lunch.

"Oh, it was no trouble at all," Fionna rescued her.

"It means more than I can ever tell you." Ruth looked thoroughly embarrassed.

"Please don't worry about it. I love doing it."

"My husband was just hired on as a security guard at a bank at nights."

"Has he worked in security before?" Dan tried to sound nonchalant.

"He's trying to work his way through the police academy. It's just gotten a little tight so he picked up a night job. I work days at the grocery store out on Clark, but they won't ever give me forty hours so I don't have any benefits," she confessed the strain. "My son had to have emergency dental surgery and…" She shrugged.

Dan nodded. "I have quite a few connections to the local precincts. When will your husband graduate?"

"Hopefully in December."

"Why don't I make a few phone calls and see if we can't get him started at the precinct while he finishes training? That would get you insurance."

"Really?"

"Of course." It certainly wouldn't be a difficult thing for him to do. Fionna smiled up at him proudly.

"He's a real hard worker," Ruth assured.

"I have no doubt."

Mrs. Powell gave a formal greeting and encouraged the parents to look around the classroom. Haley dragged Ruth to see her spelling test that was hanging on the board full of children's work. As soon as they moved away, the bitch committee made a rapid reappearance.

"Hi Saran, Hi Jessica," Aida offered half-heartedly. She reached and took Dan's hand. She seemed to have no more desire to deal with the offspring than Fionna had to deal with the mother pods.

Jessica rolled her eyes at Aida as Dan narrowed his. "I noticed you talking with Ruth Tribble a moment ago," Jessica's mother tsked.

With Mrs. Powell's assurances that she was a good mother coupled with Fionna's abject disdain of any person thinking that they were better than someone else, she glared. "Why, yes, we were. Haley and Aida have become such good friends. We're hoping to get the girls together to play."

"I'd be careful. You know Haley's father is out of work." Jessica's mother mouthed the words as if the man had consciously decided that he'd prefer his family go hungry rather than understanding that he was trying desperately to work them out of a bad situation by the sweat of his brow.

"And that means she shouldn't have friends?" Fionna menaced.

Jessica's mother's mouth hung open. "We were only trying to make certain that you ended up in the right kind of groups here at McCarron."

Fionna offered a hate-filled smile. "Thank you for your concern, but I think Aida is perfectly capable of picking her friends." The implication was quite clear. Aida hadn't chosen Jessica and Saran, and by Fionna's estimation, she'd chosen well.

Dan certainly knew there was much more to it than either Saran or Jessica's mother, but he shared his wife's opinion no matter the reasoning. Aida was a Receiver, not nearly as strong as Fionna but a powerful Receiver nonetheless. They could feel the emotions of those around them.

Receivers would never put themselves in a group whose goal was to make others feel bad about themselves. It simply wasn't in them because they could feel the responses to their hurtful words and actions. This often meant that Receivers were the target of abuse as they would rarely strike back. It was the very reason that most Receivers developed such strong internal shields. It was no coincidence that Receivers and Ioses Predilects tended to make very strong couplings.

The protector was driven to protect those he loved above all others but often needed to be reminded to feel emotions the way their mates felt them. They spoke with Ruth once more and then headed down to Mrs. Willow's classroom.

One day a week, Aida would attend Gifted classes taught by Governor Willow's wife. They would learn about their energies and how they would be able to use them once they developed.

"Dan, Fionna, I was hoping you'd stop by." Leah Willow smiled as they entered the small classroom.

"Hi, Mrs. Willow, how are you?" Fionna grinned.

Dan was given a hug. Governor Willow had been Dan's boss when he was Chief of Iodex, and he'd been on the governing board with Dan's father for decades.

Wes Willow, an old friend of Dan's, was in his mother's classroom with his wife and his sons, Kendrick and Clayton. Aida was wary. She hadn't begun her Gifted class day yet. She would go on Fridays with all other children of the Gifted Realm that were second-grade students at McCarron, but they didn't start until a few weeks into the school year.

She kept tight hold of Dan's hand and her eyes on Kendrick. He'd pinched her rather hard at Rainer and Emily's wedding over the summer, and she was timid. Dan kept an eye on Kendrick as well as keeping his body and his powerful shield between his baby girl and the demon child.

"Your first PTA meeting and you're already the head of a subcommittee," Wes teased.

Dan rolled his eyes and shook his head. "I'm not sure where that came from, but I will not be heading any committees. What the hell is up with that school board woman?"

Wes grimaced. "She's been up here for several years, and it's been a disaster. She wants to tell the teachers what to teach, ban books, turn the kids into robots. The teachers all hate her, but no one knows how to get rid of her. She keeps getting elected because she runs unopposed. It got so bad last year, Mom was thinking about retiring early."

Dan hated to hear that. He had no idea what to do or how to help.

"Dad told me you spent the summer in Hawaii. That sounds amazing." Wes was clearly trying to mend fences.

"It was perfect." He took Fionna's hand as Aida willed bravery and let Mrs. Willow show her around the classroom.

"I'm really happy for you." Wes gestured from Fionna to Aida and back to the baby.

"Thank you."

"Hey, but that's a mess at Venton. I saw you on the news this morning."

"I somehow seem to keep stepping in hornets' nests."

"It didn't sound like you had anything to do with it."

"No, I certainly didn't."

"Still a disaster though. That's our alma mater. I hate to see it tarnished. What the hell was Wilshire thinking?"

"I've been asking myself that daily for weeks."

Dan realized that it wasn't only him and Fionna that were disappointed. Venton held a piece of every single graduate—a piece of their souls, a piece of their past, and their innocence. The scandal hurt community wide.

"I don't get it. Why not get divorced or separated? Why do it that way?" Wes was careful to keep any of the kids from hearing.

"Daddy, look!" Aida gasped. Mrs. Willow was showing Aida an electrostatic arc she was producing with her hand. She was letting Aida touch it, which made Aida's hair stand slightly.

Dan laughed. "Pretty cool, huh?"

"I'm going to have my very own baby sister," Aida announced to Mrs. Willow.

Mrs. Willow beamed. "I see that. Do you think maybe you and Mommy will bring your baby sister to our class after she arrives and is big enough to visit?"

"Can Halia come to school with me, please?" Aida begged Fionna.

"Sure, but she'll need to be a few weeks old."

Turning back to Mrs. Willow, Aida reiterated, "When she's a few weeks old, we can bring her!"

"Perfect." Mrs. Willow winked at Aida.

"How far apart are the boys?" Fionna asked Wes's wife.

She chuckled. "Uh, well, they're nine months and two weeks apart."

Dan shook his head at Wes who'd squeezed his eyes shut for a moment.

Fionna nodded. "They look just like Wes."

"For Lauren's sake, we're hoping they don't *act* just like Wes." Mrs. Willow made everyone laugh.

"You're a dog, you know that," Dan goaded Wes under his breath. The old friendship rekindled quickly.

Laughing, he nodded. "I know, but look at her." He stared longingly at his wife.

Wes and Lauren had met the summer of their junior years. The Willows had vacationed on Hilton Head Island. Lauren Kendrick lived in North Carolina and attended Gutner, the Gifted Academy in Raleigh. By the end of their family's vacations, Wes was pleading to transfer to Gutner, which his parents refused. Lauren and Wes kept their long distance relationship going and married right after they both graduated.

Dan had attended the wedding with Amelia. Lauren was fairly average looking to Dan. But he was happy to hear after eleven years of marriage and two boys, Wes was still drooling over his bride.

"She nearly choked me when we went back for her checkup," Wes admitted.

Dan joined Wes's laughter. He shook his head at him. "Did you make use of the hospital bed, or did you at least take her home first?"

Wes seemed thrilled that he and Dan were reconnecting. "Even Governor Haydenshire harasses me. He loves to remind me that even Will and Garrett were eleven months apart. And if I may offer you a piece of advice, the old wives' tale that you don't have to cast her if she's nursing would be total shit."

"No joke."

"Hey, so Aida will be in Mom's class on Fridays with Clayton. Maybe we could all go out sometime. I would love to hear the story of how Dan Vindico scored Fionna Styler."

"Aww, cause he's such a stud," Fionna joined in the teasing.

Dan shook his head at her.

"He did just inform the entire PTA that you're always busy." Wes cracked up.

"Okay, we need to go now," Dan insisted. Aida moved back to him and laid her head against his waist.

"Are you tired, baby girl?"

"A little bit."

"Do you want Daddy to carry you?" he whispered. Aida blushed and shook her head, but she did want that. Dan could read it in her pleading rhythms that soothed when she fell against him.

Wes chuckled. "Dad's cool and all until there are other kids around."

"Aida, come watch what Grandma can do," Kendrick urged. Aida moved to him. She watched as Mrs. Willow held a potato and harnessed the energy store in the starch. She made the conversion and lit a light bulb.

"Mom's great for parlor tricks," Wes offered wryly as Dan chuckled his agreement. "Hey, how's she doing?" Wes gestured his head to Aida discreetly. "I saw your ad on adoption. That's really cool. The softer side of Dan Vindico."

"She's done amazingly well. Hawaii helped. It wasn't a smooth ride before that," he admitted. "But she's perfect. We see an Auxiliary counselor once a month. So far so good."

Fionna was listening intently to Lauren's birth stories.

"Another girl?" Wes gestured to Fionna's stomach.

"Yeah." Dan grinned.

"Dan Vindico and a house full of girls." He laughed. "If you ever get tired of Polly Pocket, you can come hang out with us."

"Polly's old-school," Dan scoffed. "It's all about unicorn princesses and light-up dance mats now. Come on, get with the times, man."

Wes smirked. "Say Ken or Clay want to date Aida at some point in the future. What will that be like for them?"

"Very, very painful," Dan assured him.

"Figured that." Wes shook his head. "Okay, so say in a few years, one of the little Haydenshire twins wants to go on a campout with the newest baby girl out on the farm like we used to. I don't suppose that will be happening either."

"Do I look stupid to you? Keaton and Henry Haydenshire might outdo Will and Garrett."

"Damn," Wes gasped.

As they headed back to the car, Aida extended her arms up to Dan. It seemed she no longer cared who saw her. She was tired and wanted her daddy, much to Dan's delight.

"I'm jealous." Fionna chuckled as she kissed Aida's cheek when she laid it on Dan's shoulder.

"Mommy wants to be carried too," Aida informed Dan with a yawn.

Dan nestled her between his chin and his shoulder. "I'll carry Mommy once we get home."

Dan eased back down the steps after laying Aida in her bed. Fionna was exhausted and lying on the couch.

With a sigh, Dan pulled the newest duplicated cell phone from his briefcase.

"Dad needs a little more research done. Do you want to help, or maybe you could give me an excuse to tell Dad that I'm sorry but I had to take my wife to bed because you know we're busy all the time."

Fionna laughed again over the debacle in the McCarron Healthy

Bears Eat Beary Well Lunchroom. He sank down on the couch, and Fionna squeezed him tight.

"We can do whatever your dad needs. I'm all keyed up after dealing with the alpha mom squad anyway. Might as well make an evening of it."

While wondering if Fionna might want to talk about the bitch patrol, Dan switched on the phone. "Other than Wes and his family, the entire night was kind of a disaster." He tried to give her a place to jump in.

She knew him far too well. "It's a really difficult world for moms right now."

"Keep going," he urged.

"You have to understand what it's like to have opinions constantly forced down your throat at every turn. Work outside the home. Don't work outside the home. Nurse. Don't nurse. Your baby is coming into *your* world, and she has to understand that she has to adapt to you. Let your child dictate your entire world. You're all she knows. Your baby should be sleeping with you until they're one. If you co-sleep, your child will still be in your bed when they're in high school. Use this schedule for your newborn to help them sleep. How dare you try to use a schedule for a newborn? It's constant, and there is no consensus.

"It makes everyone desperate for approval because no one is confident in what they're doing. And it makes moms act that way because they're so insecure *they* act like children. Everyone is desperate to do the *right* thing. There is no right thing for everyone." She tucked herself under his arm and into the safety she needed to feel from him. "Everything feels like the stakes are so high that you might ruin your kid if you choose wrong. It's overwhelming and exhausting."

Dan brushed a kiss on her forehead and set the cell phone on the couch. "Is there anything I can do to help?"

"Not really. It's like being in middle school all over again, only worse because I don't want to be friends with people like that, but now instead of girls just hating me, they make their daughters be mean to my baby and that kills me. I miss Malani."

"Less than two weeks. I'm taking you home."

"I know. I can't wait." Fionna gestured to the waiting phone. "What did your dad want us to look for?"

"He wants to know if Wilshire and Bryant ever went on one of these seminars but then didn't attend any of the classes. I doubt something like that would be in an email. If they discussed skipping, I think they would text that."

"Definitely."

"If I need to dig further, I'll see if Jeff can help me figure out which classes they'd registered for from the convention databases. Right now, I'll take a, 'Hey, how about instead of Techniques of Teaching, we play in my room.'"

"Do you think they still talk?" Fionna tucked closer to Dan. "How does a relationship that was never supposed to happen, one that you go on for years pretending doesn't really exist, how does that end? Or did it end?"

"No idea, baby doll. Wretchkinsides had dozens of mistresses stashed in every freaking seaport, but if they got on his nerves or wanted out, he had them offed. This is my first civil case, so I have nothing to go on."

"Look." Fionna pointed to a text that was still displayed on the lock screen when Jeff re-cloned the phone. It was from Katherine Bryant *Dean, you have to stop texting me. I have to put my life back together. This was a huge mistake. Don't talk to me anymore.*

Dan nodded. "When her daughter informed her that she'd ruined her life and that she hated her, I think everything fell into place for her."

"No." Fionna shook her head. "Remember, he cloned this copy right after the custody trial, so that means she must've sent it before the trial began."

"Maybe it was the custody hearing itself that put everything in perspective for her," Dan considered.

"I wonder if she ever even allowed herself to think about it ending, or if she just sort of kept living for that attention. I wonder if she thought she'd just get him out of her system and that no one would ever find out."

"I don't have any idea, but it sounds like she wants it over with." He began scrolling through the pages and pages of texts for years that Wilshire kept on his cell.

He halted at one of the first sets of texts of nothing but room numbers. If they'd planned to play hooky together, that would be when it would have been discussed.

Care to have a late dinner a little farther away from the convention center, sweetheart? was a few texts below the number 512.

You always know just what I need. I don't think I've been on a date in ten years. Should be fun was Mentor Bryant's response.

"Do you think she's exaggerating?" Fionna asked.

Dan shook his head. "I doubt it. I don't think quitting work and staying home worked for Terry Bryant. He hung too much of his identity up in his job. When he quit and she stepped in as bread winner, I think he stopped doing a lot of things he should have done."

Well then, my love, you shall be wined and dined at the finest restaurants each and every night we're here, was Wilshire's response.

"Because he was getting lucky every night they were there." Fionna rolled her eyes.

"The question is—did he pay for those elaborate dinners or did the school?" Dan jotted down the dates of the texts to compare to the school credit card records.

"Do you think that could be it? Do you think he paid for stuff for her with his Venton credit card and then paid it back to the general fund?"

Dan shook his head. "There's nothing on the records that indicates that at all. I have no clue why he put so much money in the general fund. I can't seem to come up with a plausible reason why he would do that."

"We'll figure it out," Fionna assured him.

I might not know how to behave was the flirty response from Bryant.

I rather enjoy your misbehaving, but don't worry, my dear, it had been nearly that long since I enjoyed the pleasure of female company in my bed. You showed me everything I was missing and more, so I'll be more than happy to guide you through dinner as long as you'll be my dessert.

"Oh gross, gross, gross!" Fionna gagged.

"And there's what happened to the Wilshires," Dan concluded.

"Ten years?" Fionna rolled her eyes. "I highly doubt that. He's a horny old man. It was probably like ten days, and he thought he'd been denied food and water."

Dan laughed. "I don't think so." He didn't really want to give Wilshire an out, but something in the pictures he'd seen posted of Dean and Ellen Wilshire told Dan that they weren't close physically. There was distance that he suspected was there long before the affair.

"How do you not have sex with your husband for ten years?"

"It happens. Look at my sister and Tim. She'd been sleeping on the couch for weeks. He would just have let that go on. I really don't think he would have cheated on her, but he was going to go on letting that kind of distance exist between them."

Fionna nodded thoughtfully. "Tutu says that if women don't take time for themselves and take care of themselves, they can lose their drive."

"I'm not trying to be a prick, but that really is hell on a guy," he tried to explain.

"We're just going to keep having sex all the time," Fionna decreed.

"Sounds perfect to me, but I'd prefer that we space our second and third additions out a little further than Wes and Lauren did theirs. We're going to take off the time that Adeline says we need to after Princess Halia reigns supreme."

"Okay, but you'll tell me if something's wrong."

"I won't let this fall apart. Both of these couples should have talked and realized something very, very wrong was happening long before Wilshire and Bryant ended up in bed together. And you know what, even if Ellen Wilshire didn't want to have a physical relationship with him anymore or couldn't have that, there still needs to be intimacy."

They went through several pages of texts with Dan noting anytime a dinner was mentioned, but they never found any record that either Mentor Bryant or Chancellor Wilshire hadn't attended the meetings they were supposed to attend at the many varied conventions they traveled to.

CHAPTER 4

FIGHTING REVELATIONS

Knocking on his father's door once he'd arrived on campus the next morning, Dan waited. He nodded politely to Vivian Lamb, whose face had set in a permanent scowl in the last few days. Ron Clover was nearby. He appeared to be trying and failing at getting the financial report Governor Vindico had demanded on his desk. Frustration and fear weighted his Duco bands.

Governor Vindico threw open the door with fury simpering on his face.

Dan slid inside. "Problem?"

"Eighty-five emails," the governor barked.

"About what?"

"I just got off the phone with Stephen. Half of them don't want their kids in Bryant's classes. The others want to know when I'm going to fire Dean. No one seems to have considered that it isn't quite that easy. He has a wife and children not to mention a hefty retirement tied up in this academy. I'm tempted to send out a school-wide email saying, 'if you want things improved, shut up and let me do my job. And if you feel the need to complain, please proceed down to the Auxiliary Department of the Senate to volunteer somewhere to improve this Realm. Clearly, you need something to do with your time.'"

Dan laughed. His father's ability to cut through all of the crap had always deeply impressed him. It was something he tried to emulate on a regular basis.

"What did Governor Haydenshire say?"

"He had me forward her reviews and her students' final scores along with her semester-long project grades. Truthfully, she appears to be an excellent mentor. She's had one or two negative reviews in all the years she's been here. The students seem to respond to her well. They appear to really understand the material she presents. Stephen thought perhaps I could talk to her and then assure the parents that nothing about the affair will ever be discussed in her classes."

"That sounds fair," Dan allowed.

"I don't have time to deal with this every morning. There are things that need to be worked on, and as of right now, I have to go hear trials at the Senate at eleven. Then come back up here before you bring my baby girl to see her grandpa tonight, which, by the way, is the only thing I'm looking forward to doing today."

Dan smiled. "Aida's excited too. She wants to play checkers with you."

Chuckling, Governor Vindico looked very pleased to hear that. "Truly, son, I hope you get down on your knees every single night and thank the Lord for her, because she is your own personal little angel to go along with the taller version that's currently agreed to house your third little angel, and they all love you."

"Trust me, I know how blessed I am."

"Oh, on top of all of this,"—he gestured his hand to the computer monitor—"Governor Sherman's son, Fergus, was in my office bright and early." Dan rolled his eyes automatically. "Uh-huh, he was eager to tattle on you.

"It's been a long time since a little pip-squeak ran up to me to inform me that you were being mean." He shook his head. "Out of habit, I started to call Stephen, because if you'd done something, we were always certain Will and Garrett were in on it as well."

Dan joined his father's laughter. "What did he say?"

"He informed me that you and Fionna had not been to any of the team-building events for the faculty and staff here at Venton."

Governor Vindico cracked up suddenly. Dan's brow knitted as he waited on his father to continue. "I believe his exact statement was, 'Sir, Mentor Vindico is just too hung up on his baby and his kid. You'd think Fionna Styler was all that mattered to him.'" The governor doubled over laughing. He seemed to need to laugh more than anything else. Dan clenched his jaw and tried to let him have his moment before he began shouting.

"Anyway," the governor finally quieted, "I did correct him on Fionna's name, and I did assure him that your wife and your girls were most definitely the most important thing to you. I told him that's how I raised you. But, Dan, come on," the governor got to the part of the story that Dan was dreading. "You need to do the team player thing. If for no other reason, then please do it for me. Your mother and I are coming to this fall formal thing Sherman has planned Friday night. Why don't you bring Fionna and have dinner? It's supposed to be nice."

"Dad," Dan whined. "The last conversation I had with that moron, he informed me that he didn't know why everyone went on about how gorgeous my wife is because, and I quote, 'she has tanning booth skin, her breasts are too big, and she's getting fat.'"

The governor's eyes goggled. "I feel certain I don't want to know the answer to this, but what did you do?" He grimaced. "Please tell me you didn't hit him."

"I might've jerked him up out of his chair by the collar of those ridiculous shirts he wears and informed him that if he ever discussed my wife's chest again, I'd make it a very painful experience for him."

Governor Vindico shook his head. "You are aware that although no one would argue that Fionna is a beautiful woman, that she doesn't do for everyone what she does for you."

"I've been beating men back with a metal baseball bat since before we were dating, and Fi and I are too old to attend Venton formals."

"Just come Friday night. Fionna might have fun. It's a dinner dance. I'm certain that either of your sisters would watch Aida if either Garrett or Fionna's parents can't."

Dan's jaw clenched. He knew Fionna wouldn't really want him sharing this, but he went on with it anyway. "Fi's having a hard time,"

Dan choked out, watching his father's face fall. "She's having relatively normal Braxton-Hicks contractions, but Adeline says they're too intense. They're affecting the gunshot wound. She's worried that Fi will need to be induced early if she doesn't rest and take it easy for the next few weeks. Adeline and I have both tried to talk her into going on to Kauai for a few weeks and letting her energy reset, but she's refusing to go without me and Aida. I don't think making her get all dressed up and coming to some ridiculous Venton fall formal is what she needs right now."

"I'm sorry she's struggling, but I'm going to go ahead and filter that through your shield that tends to jump to the worst possible scenario whenever one of your girls is involved. See what Fionna wants to do, please. If she's not feeling up to it, then you certainly don't have to come, but she might have fun. Women tend to like having a nice meal with their husbands and then dancing in his arms."

"Fine," Dan sighed. "I'll ask her, but I'm also going to tell her that I would much prefer her home on our couch with me waiting on her hand and foot."

"I would be shocked if you didn't."

A knock sounded on the door.

"Would you?" the governor requested. Dan stood and opened the door.

"I'm sorry to interrupt, Mentor Vindico, but there's a fight in an Adminis classroom, and it's bad," Jeff panicked.

Dan raced out of the room with Jeff and his father hot on his trail. Shoving people out of his way, Dan eventually realized that he was in Mentor Bryant's first period class. He pulled a sophomore he recognized off of a similarly sized freshman that was already bleeding from the mouth, while he was having his skull pounded against the ground. The freshman was still swinging as Jeff and Ben Cobson, along with Gerald Meere, held him back. His infuriated adrenaline upped his energy.

"What the hell?" Dan spat.

"In my office, now!" Governor Vindico snarled.

Dan grabbed the sophomore by the scruff of the neck and shoved him forward. The kid turned and spat at the freshman in hate-driven wrath. Dan was vastly quicker. He summoned and used his powerful shield to ricochet the saliva back in the sophomore's face.

"Ugh!" He wiped it away with the back of his hand.

"Do it again, genius."

Jeff and Ben shoved the freshman forward and tried not to laugh.

"Now," the governor menaced as soon as they were all back in his office. "Would you care to tell me why you decided to use your first period class to try and kill one another?"

The boys scowled and refused to look at each other. They also refused to speak.

"Has to be a girl," the governor guessed.

Seeing that this was going nowhere quickly, Dan turned to Jeff and Ben. "Who are the two stooges we have here?"

"That's Brodie Quentin." Jeff pointed to the sophomore who was attempting to move his broken hand.

"That's Kellan Morris," Ben supplied. "We were next door in the study period for testing out of history of defense. When Mentor Bryant came into the room, they were already arguing. She tried to stop them. I think she got hit."

"Yeah, it's about a girl," Kellan confirmed just a little too quickly.

"Yeah," Brodie agreed.

"Dan, please go make certain that Katherine Bryant isn't hurt." Governor Vindico sighed.

Making a return trip back to the nearby classroom, Dan peeked through the window in the door. The students were glancing around nervously, and Mentor Bryant was seated at her desk, rubbing her temples. Dan knocked. She waved him in.

"Could I speak to you for a moment?" Dan asked.

"I suppose." Mentor Bryant rolled her eyes.

He stood several feet from Katherine Bryant in the hallway and kept the door open. Rumors started with frightening speed.

"Ben Cobson said he thought you might have gotten in the middle of that. I was just making certain you were all right." He wasn't certain how Fionna would feel about his checking up on Katherine Bryant.

"I don't have the plague, Mentor Vindico, and contrary to popular belief, I'm not looking for a boyfriend, nor am I attracted to every man on campus."

"You appear to be just fine, so I'll leave you to your martyrdom then."

If she wanted to take out her self-created frustrations about her life on someone, she could find another candidate. Dan wasn't going to join her pity party.

"Of course, because I'm certain Fionna Styler would somehow be concerned with you talking to a woman like me. I certainly can't be a trusted coworker without any ulterior motives. And everyone knows whatever the Vindicos want, they get."

Dan narrowed his eyes, though he was intrigued with everything she'd just admitted without even being aware. "What the hell is that supposed to mean?"

"I told Dean not to hire you, but Glenn Sullivan insisted you were the man for the job. He refused to even interview anyone else, but you know, *Mentor* Vindico," she drawled her disdain, "not all of us spend the summers vacationing in Hawaii and refusing to do anything involving the academy. Most of us work through the summers and participate in activities for the academy outside of our classes. We don't threaten teenage boys that happen to let their hormones get the better of their mouths. But woe be unto anyone that compliments Dan Vindico's queen. Now, you've got daddy up here running the school. That must be convenient."

Dan shot a menacing glare into Mentor Bryant's malevolent eyes. He laughed in her face. "It seems to me you spent your summers and off hours in another man's bed. What exactly did that *do* for the academy? Trust me, Mentor Bryant, my wife is most definitely the queen of my castle and there will never be another. I happen to keep my vows. And my father is here trying to clean up the shitstorm that you and Wilshire created together, so take it from me, if you lie with dogs, eventually you will get eaten alive." He turned to stomp back to his father's office.

"Wouldn't you like to know why they were fighting?" she retorted.

"Not if it means talking to you. I used to be the Chief of Elite Iodex, and I am still the best damn detective in the Realm. I believe you saw just a few of my skills recently. I don't need you to tell me why two students were fighting."

As his fury began to ebb, Dan considered everything Katherine Bryant had just admitted. Despite her illicit affair with a doting lover, she didn't believe herself to be anywhere near as attractive as Fionna, and was admittedly jealous of Dan and Fionna's relationship. She and Wilshire had concerns about Dan coming to work at the academy. His reputation as a detective had certainly preceded him. As so often happens, the rats with the most to hide are the first to scurry when the cat lands on the ship.

"Is she all right?" Governor Vindico asked when Dan returned to his office.

"Oh, she's just fine." Dan rolled his eyes.

The governor's brow furrowed. "Their parents are on the way. We'll be seeing Mr. Quentin and Mr. Morris in two weeks. After that, they'll be working for me after school each day from then until Christmas break."

Dan didn't want to make it appear that he disagreed with the governor's decision, so he nodded his understanding. He'd wanted a chance to interview the boys separately and find out what the fight was really about. It definitely wasn't over a girl. That much had been obvious when they'd leapt on the offered excuse.

Dan returned to his office to grab his things for his first class.

"Mentor Vindico." Jeff followed him into his office.

"What's up?" Dan settled at his desk as Jeff took a seat.

"I know we were working on the affair thing first, but Logan and I had a little time at work yesterday. So, I showed him a few of the websites that those tests were being posted on. I swear I thought they were exams from a few years ago that the mentors were giving out to help us study. Now, I feel like I've been cheating."

"I believe you," Dan assured him. Relief etched Jeff's features as he went on.

"Logan and I found these other websites where the exams are being sold, and they have the answer keys with them. I've never used one like that. I've only ever studied the exams by looking up the answers."

"If I'd had any access to exams to study with when I was here, believe me, I would have been all over that. Please don't worry about it."

Jeff nodded. "We didn't buy any, obviously. When this breaks, I still need to graduate, and I know how easy it will be to link the students that bought tests. I showed Bec the stuff we'd found when I got home last night. She kind of thinks it's cool or whatever," he admitted sheepishly.

Dan tried to hide his chuckle. "Showing off for your wife is also completely acceptable."

He laughed. "But get this, when I was showing Becca last night after work, a bunch of new tests had been posted. I mean, like, tons. Wasn't yesterday when the mentors had to turn in new tests to your dad?"

"Yeah. Yesterday at noon."

"That's what I thought. So, between noon and last night at six o'clock, all of the new tests were already online. How are they getting in the test vault? They have to be coming back after everyone has gone home."

"I don't see how that's possible."

"Most of the mentors and office staff leave by 4:00," Jeff pointed out.

"Fi and I have birthing class tonight. Do you think you and Becca and Logan and Adeline could come over tomorrow and show me all of this? I'll grill burgers. I still don't want Fionna doing anything but resting."

"Yes, sir. I think so."

"Great. Now, we have to get to class."

"Tomorrow, do you think you could tell me what birthing class is?" Jeff asked as they rushed down the corridor.

Dan laughed. "Will do as soon as I know myself."

CHAPTER 5

TIME IN A BOTTLE

Much to Dan's delight, Fionna was standing outside of his classroom at the end of third period. "Hey there, baby doll. My day just improved dramatically."

She gave him his smile. "Your dad called me and asked if he could pick Aida up from school because the trial he was supposed to hear was settled out of court. I thought maybe we could have lunch and register for all of Halia's stuff. The Angels want to have my shower before we go to Kauai."

At that moment, Katherine Bryant released her class and followed them out of the room. With a dramatic eye roll, she took in Dan and Fionna. Dan moved closer to his wife. He stared into her eyes. "I'm about to kiss you, and I want you to really get into it," he urged under his breath.

Delight lit her eyes as she nodded. Dan leaned and began slowly and sensuously kissing his wife. He added to the intensity with each pass until he was devouring her mouth. He laced his hand through her hair and pulled her closer.

"Daniel," he heard his father scold. Breaking away, Dan's eyes snapped open. "Do you think you could refrain from making out with your wife in the corridor? The students really don't need any encouragement."

"She's gorgeous, and I have a score I need to settle," Dan admitted.

"I suddenly feel very used." Fionna shot Dan a smirk and made her father-in-law laugh.

"Why don't you two take that on home or at least to your office?" the governor ordered.

"We're leaving. Thanks for getting Aida. She'll be thrilled."

"Not as thrilled as I am. I thought maybe Grandpa could swing her by the toy store before we head home."

Fionna shook her head. "Between you and Daddy, she's going to rot."

"Hey, that's my job."

Dan walked Fionna to the Ferrari, ecstatic to be spending the afternoon with his wife away from Venton.

"Are you sure you're up to lunch and shopping?"

Fionna nodded. "I called Adeline, and she had me come by Georgetown to do an ultrasound. The scar tissue is some better. I sat down all morning. I'll be sitting at lunch. I'm sure the birthing class will be us sitting down. I can do a few hours of registering. Adeline said it was fine."

The pent-up air released from Dan's lungs. He laced his fingers through hers. "What was looking like a horrible day just took a dramatic turn for the better."

"You mean your wife showing up outside of your last class didn't do that?" Fionna harassed him. Dan was thrilled she was in such a good mood and that he was going to have hours to spend with her and Halia in blissful happiness.

He lifted her hand to his mouth and brushed a kiss on her knuckles. "That definitely did, but you just iced the delicious cake with the fact that my littlest princess is just as perfect as her mama."

Fionna gave him a knowing grin. "When your dad called about picking up Aida, he mentioned that there's a formal Friday night."

"I would've thought having my dad at school when I was a student would've been bad, but it's not really any better now." He reveled in her laughter. "All right." Dan released her hand. He pulled his cell phone from his pocket. "We have to do this right." He touched her name on his favorites list.

He changed lanes to avoid a car broken down on the side of the road. Cracking up, Fionna answered her phone when it began ringing in her purse.

"Uh…hello?"

"Oh, uh…" He cleared his throat for effect. "Is Fionna there?"

Fionna lowered her phone. "Okay, are you calling me for a date?" she whispered.

"Obviously," Dan teased.

Nodding, she held the phone out, and in a perfect imitation of her father's distinctive mix of Spanish and Hawaiian dialect she called, "Maylea, there is a boy on the phone. I don't like boys calling you. Why is he calling? You tell him you're not old enough to date," she quoted, and Dan howled with laughter.

"Daddy," Fionna gasped. "Stop yelling into the phone." She feigned embarrassment to perfection. "Boys are bad, Maylea."

"I know, Daddy," Fionna continued. "Uh…hello, this is Fionna."

Trying to breathe, Dan cleared his throat again. "Uh, hey, Fionna, this is Dan Vindico from creative writing."

Giggling, Fionna put her game face back on. "Oh, okay. Which one are you again?"

Dan clutched his chest. "Ouch," he mouthed, making her laugh. "I sit a couple of rows behind you."

"Oh, right. You're the cute one," Fionna feigned realization. Dan shook his head at her.

"I was just wondering if you'd like to go to the fall formal with me Friday night if you don't have other plans," Dan pretended to stammer nervously.

"Let me check my calendar," Fionna hemmed, and Dan cracked up again.

"Uh…you know…I could probably drive my Ferrari."

"Okay," Fionna agreed instantly. "But my dad's kind of a pain. My curfew is ten."

"Ten, wow, that's really early."

"I know, but if you can hang out for a few, I can sneak back out," she informed him with a great deal of sass.

"Really?"

"Yeah, and then I can stay out all night."

Dan groaned in the phone. "All night, huh?"

"Mm-hmm."

"I have my own place if you want to come over after you sneak back out," he assured her as she began giggling again.

"Really?"

"Yeah, you can stay as long as you want," he assured her.

"Okay, I'll see you Friday night."

"I'll pick you up at six." Dan ended the call as they both began laughing again. "I love you."

"Wow! We haven't even been on our date yet."

"That's about how quickly I knew," Dan reminded her. "Where would the lady like to dine?"

"Halia wants Granddaddy to make her a chicken salad sandwich, and we could ask them about Friday night."

"Now that your dad seems to like me, since I did, in fact, marry you and give him grandchildren, despite his adamance that I was only after one thing, then I don't mind going to see your dad and Gretta."

Fionna leaned and kissed his cheek. She grunted as she fell back into the seat. "I'm now too big to lean across the car and kiss you," she whimpered.

Chuckling, Dan pulled to a stop light and kissed Fionna's cheek. "Then I'll lean and kiss you until my baby lets you have your stomach back."

Rolling her eyes, Fionna rubbed her hands over her bump that was expanding each and every day. "Remember when I leaned across the car and did a little more than kiss you?"

The real estate in his trousers was suddenly nonexistent. Dan gave her a cocky smirk. "Hell, yeah, baby doll. I still don't know how I managed to drive the car home that night."

Dan glanced back at her discreetly as he turned into Styler's bakery. The time she'd given him a blow job while he drove her home was the night he'd gotten her pregnant the first time. At least, that was the approximate timing. Though Fionna would occasionally recall a few of the terrifying lonely weeks when she knew she was pregnant but was afraid to tell him and had sunk into a depression so badly it consumed her, they'd never discussed the awe-inspiring sex they'd had that night.

"Don't tell Gretta we're going to register," Fionna said as Dan opened the door for her.

"Okay." He locked the pain away deep in his shield and decided to rejoice in the life she'd given him instead.

"I can tell she wishes that she knew more, so she could help me."

"There's my Maylea. You haven't been in for a week," Mr. Styler scolded as Fionna entered the bakery. Dan fought not to roll his eyes.

"Hey, Daddy." Fionna went on with the eye roll. They embraced, and then Mr. Styler immediately demanded that she sit and relax.

"Chicken salad?" Since that had been one of Fionna's most common cravings, he'd guessed correctly. He used to offer his delectable Hawaiian chicken salad, with chunks of pineapple and macadamia nuts on one of his freshly baked croissants, on Thursdays, but he'd begun making the sandwiches every day just in case Fionna stopped by.

"Dan." Gretta moved out from the kitchen and hugged Dan and Fionna. "Chicken salad as well?"

"That'd be great." Dan seated himself across from his wife. The Stylers went to make their sandwiches and to help the steady flow of customers coming into the bakery.

"Want to tell me why we were putting on a show for Katherine Bryant?" She studied Dan closely. "I had a weird dream last night, and she was in it."

Dan's brow furrowed. "What happened in the dream?"

Fionna's pregnancy dreams had at times been quite humorous. At other times, she would wake up trembling and gasping for breath from nightmares so vivid Dan would have to cast her to get her back to sleep.

She'd dreamt repeatedly that something was happening to Emily and that Rainer was unable to save her when the Lawsons had been on their honeymoon and were being filmed unknowingly. The pictures were being sold to the papers. She'd often dreamed about their terrifying trip to Paris and the Fitzroys' home being attacked while they were inside.

She had dreams of her moments of consciousness from when she'd been shot. She often dreamt of her mother. Those made her sob so fiercely Dan's heart would ache as he held her and tried desperately to soothe his precious Maylea.

But she also had dreams about Supernova getting it on with his hot pink assistant, Wavelength, from Aida's favorite cartoon. So, Dan had learned to take them with a grain of salt, but he always paid close attention to them.

Fionna's all-encompassing powers as a Receiver coupled with her added hormones and Halia's energies meant that just like with Rainer and Emily, her mind was trying to warn her something was wrong.

"It was crazy weird, but all of my dreams have been weird," she confessed dejectedly. "I told you a couple of nights ago I dreamed that Chloe started dating Dick Van Dyke from *Mary Poppins* and that Garrett finally got jealous and proposed. Chloe broke up with Dick because she said she didn't like the way he kept jumping to the side and clicking his heels together." She giggled, and Dan laughed outright. "I do keep dreaming about Garrett proposing to someone. That is truly a wild idea, so they're probably all that insane.

"Anyway, Mentor Bryant kept yelling at people, only she sounded like she was far away. I couldn't make out what she was saying. Then you were there, and you kept taking students to Felsink, and I kept crying. It was so bizarre."

Unable to even begin interpreting that, Dan explained what had happened with the fight that morning and then what had spewed from Bryant's mouth when he'd been sent to check on her.

"You said that to her?" Fionna beamed as her father supplied their sandwiches, his phenomenal sweet potato chips, and a pile of tiny, sweet pickles. He added two Dr Peppers, just the way they preferred. "Thank you!" Fionna kissed his cheek.

"Anything for my Maylea and my moʻopuna," he assured.

Dan's brow furrowed and Fionna smiled. "Grandchild or loved one," she whispered when her father returned to the cash register. They inhaled their lunch and discussed what they wanted to do that afternoon. "I'm kind of nervous about class tonight," Fionna explained.

"Don't be nervous. It's for new parents."

"I know, I just try not to think about how much pain I'm going to be in." She shuddered slightly.

Dan didn't like to think about that either. Part of the reason he was so eager to attend the Gifted birthing classes given at Georgetown was so that he could learn how to cast Fionna and take on however much of the pain his body could acquire. He hoped to be able to take on more than half, but he knew that was difficult to do.

"Do you think we'll hurt everyone's feelings if we don't let them in the delivery room?"

"Sweetheart, no," Dan assured her. "We'll do whatever you want."

"When Amber had her baby, she had all of the Angels in there cheering her on, but I really just want you."

"Then it will just be me and probably Adeline and a few nurses." He winked at her. "I know how to deliver a baby, but I really don't want to."

"How do you know how to deliver a baby?"

"Part of basic training for an Iodex officer, but I never put the knowledge to use. I would definitely not be of much help."

"So, you mean Garrett Haydenshire knows how to deliver babies too?"

Dan nodded as he swallowed down the last of his Dr Pepper. His mother-in-law immediately supplied him with another. "The service in this bakery is phenomenal," he teased. Gretta shook her head at him.

"Garrett's delivered two," Dan explained.

"You're kidding me. I can't believe he never told me that."

"I don't recall what happened with the first one he delivered, but the second one, he got called out to a car accident. No one was seriously hurt, but the woman was in active labor. Her husband was flying to the hospital when he rear-ended another car. Garrett ended up delivering the baby."

"I bet he was freaking out." Fionna cringed.

"Garrett's a hell of an officer. If something needs to be done, he gets it done."

CHAPTER 6

COMMODITIZED INTIMIDATION

They hugged Fionna's parents goodbye, and Dan drove them to the mecca of all things baby in one of the nicer shopping centers in Arlington. His mouth hung open as he walked in the gargantuan store.

"Do we need one of everything?" he gasped.

Fionna giggled. "Surely not."

The store provided them with an electronic gun to scan the bar codes of the things they wanted on their registry. Dan immediately casted the gun to make it function more efficiently.

They were given a recommended items list that consisted of twenty-seven sheets of paper. Until that moment, Dan hadn't really been nervous about having Halia in his arms. All of his worries had been over Fionna's health and her being pregnant so soon after suffering a gunshot wound and a miscarriage. But as he stared around the store in dumbfounded awe, he began to understand just how much he didn't know.

Fionna reached for his hand and drew from him. She was clearly a little overwhelmed as well.

"Hey." Dan pulled her close. "We'll figure it out, okay?"

"I read a bunch of stuff online and tons of books about what to register for, but now I can't remember anything I read."

"Let's just take it one area at a time."

Fionna let him guide her to the shelves closest to the desk where they'd set up their registry. They stared up at a wall that must've contained three hundred kinds of pacifiers. Dan swallowed hard as he tried to take them all in.

Then, like a heavenly angel gliding toward them, Lillian Haydenshire appeared, pushing a cart with little Abigail asleep in her car seat. Dan was convinced a celestial light shone around her as she smiled and greeted them.

"Mrs. Haydenshire!" Fionna startled her with an exuberant hug.

"We're…just trying to register." Dan held up the electronic scanner.

"Do we need all of this stuff? Please help us," Fionna begged.

Mrs. Haydenshire bit back her laughter as she nodded. "Of course, sweetheart."

"I mean, if you have a few minutes. We don't want to take up your afternoon with Abigail." Fionna suddenly remembered her manners.

Dan offered nods to the Iodex officers assigned to Mrs. Haydenshire as her security detail.

They looked less than thrilled with their afternoon assignment but offered Dan polite smiles. "There was supposed to be a trial this afternoon, but it was canceled so Stephen and Connor took the twins out to the T-ball fields to play. I have a little while, at least until Abigail wakes up. We just stopped in for diapers."

"Yeah, Dad's picking up Aida," Dan explained.

"Diapers. We need those." Fionna still sounded completely overwhelmed.

With that declaration, Mrs. Haydenshire seemed to understand the gravity of the situation.

She chuckled. "Why don't we get started?"

Dan took Fionna's hand and led her behind Mrs. Haydenshire. Fionna settled down and began listening.

"If you're certain you aren't going to nurse, then I would pick your bottles. Then if you're registering for pacifiers, I would pick ones that are similar to the bottle nipples you choose," Mrs. Haydenshire guided.

"Oh, I read about these." Fionna picked up a box of bottles. Her confidence returned slowly, and Dan relaxed as his wife began to come around.

"Those are what we use for Abby Hope."

"How many do we need?" Dan asked.

"Far more than you think. The small ones." Mrs. Haydenshire pointed to the newborn bottles. Dan scanned the bar code. "Oh, several more." She chuckled as Dan continued to add to their registry.

Fionna located pacifiers made by the same brand of bottles they'd chosen.

"She may not take them," Mrs. Haydenshire explained. "But better to have them and not use them than sending Dan out at three in the morning for some while you stay at home crying with the baby."

"Yes." Dan did not like the sound of his babies crying without him there to help. They moved on to bottle cleaning brushes, drying racks, and formula dispensers.

"I'm not going to tell you that having some of these things wouldn't make your life easier," Mrs. Haydenshire soothed, "but you do not *need* them all. You can heat a bottle with your hand. I would get the cleaning brushes though. I'm sure I'd be burned at the stake if I told anyone else this, but I have always put my kids' bottles in the dishwasher, and they seem to have survived."

"Halia needs her own laundry detergent?" Fionna looked truly defeated as they made their way to the next aisle.

"No." Mrs. Haydenshire shook her head. "By all means, if you want to wash all of her clothes separately, then you're welcome to, but I had eleven children, eight of them in about a twelve-year span, so if I got laundry washed, dried, and folded, it was a great day. That's why Will and Garrett learned to do laundry when they were in kindergarten." She winked at Dan.

Dan's shoulders lowered as he began to understand. "A lot of this stuff is to make companies wealthy by making new moms and dads feel guilty if they don't buy it."

"Which would mean that this experience is built to make you feel…?" She gestured to the scanner in Dan's hand.

"Intimidated," Fionna huffed.

"See, you know more than you gave yourselves credit for knowing. She needs to know she's loved and that she is allowed to explore her new world within reason. She needs to know you'll be there no matter what and that her home is a safe place for her to express her emotions. Everything else is gravy."

Fionna visibly relaxed. "I use the laundry detergent Tutu makes. It's unscented and organic. There's really no reason that wouldn't work just fine."

"Smart girl." Mrs. Haydenshire winked at her. "Anything unscented will be fine unless the newest little Vindico has sensitive skin."

They made their way through blankets, bassinets, and digital baby monitors. Then through bath tubs, car seat stroller combos, jogging strollers, all kinds of devices for Halia to sit in before she could actually sit up on her own, diapers, a hot-pink-and-leopard-print cover for grocery carts and restaurant high chairs that Fionna had fallen love with, along with tiny fingernail clippers, and hair brushes.

She assured Mrs. Haydenshire that she'd already sewn all of Halia's bedding and that they would be using diaper rash cream, bath wash, shampoo, and lotions grown on the farm in Kauai.

"You should get an infant fever reducer." Mrs. Haydenshire patiently guided them to the medications area of the store.

"We can't lower her fever? Do babies have fevers a lot?" Dan started to panic again. "I lowered Aida's when she got an ear infection in Kauai." He was suddenly desperate for someone to assure him that he was a good father.

Fionna wrapped her hand around his forearm, soothing him at once. Mrs. Haydenshire politely ignored the faint purple glow moving from Fionna's hand into Dan's arm as she gave him a reassuring smile. The same one she would give Dan and Will when they played together as children.

"The only way you wouldn't be able to lower it is if you happen to have a little Ioses in there. If she's half as powerful as her daddy and she gets fussy, she might shield you out," Mrs. Haydenshire explained. "We had Garrett, Cal, and Logan at the medio's office more than any of the others. Most of the time, the kids would let me hold them until I got it lowered just like Aida does with you. Emily would always let

Stephen lower hers when she was sick," she recalled with a reminiscent smile.

Still feeling a little overwhelmed and irritated that he was being manipulated by the system, Dan sighed as his cell rang in his pocket. "Hey, Dad, is everything okay?"

"I do not know what on earth happened to McCarron Elementary, but it took me fifteen minutes to convince them to let me have my own granddaughter," he fumed.

"Let me guess—the school board liaison."

"Yes. Tell me, what does she have to do with the inner workings of the school itself? She's just up here to throw her weight around and make herself feel important. Let me tell you something, it ticks me off when people do that in general, but when they're doing it and it affects my grandbabies, I come out swinging."

Dan grinned. "I know, and I promise you're on the list of people approved to pick Aida up. Fionna even called to tell them you were going to be getting her."

"You apparently should have sent in a note two days ago letting the front office know that I would be picking my baby girl up. The secretary has been here since Lindley was in fourth grade. She knows me and even knows what I do for a living. She and Leah Willow assured them that I was not kidnapping my own granddaughter. Aida pointed out that if she was afraid to go with me, she would tell them that. It broke my heart. She thought this McBeechum woman wasn't letting me have her because she's adopted. I let her know precisely what I thought when Aida went back to her classroom for a minute. I showed her my license, three credit cards, even my Senate Governor ID. I mean, my word, does she need to see the deed to my house?"

Dan ground his teeth. "I'm sorry. Do you have her now?"

"She's playing on the playground with Olivia for a few minutes before we head home. Oh, she's coming over now." His tone changed to one of pride-filled elation from seeing Aida rushing toward him.

"Tell her I love her, and you two have fun."

"Talk to you later, son."

"What now?" Fionna looked exhausted. "McBeechum wouldn't let Dad have Aida until Leah Willow vouched for him. Aida is starting to think that all of this nonsense about who's picking her up is because she's adopted," he spat furiously.

Mrs. Haydenshire's mouth fell open as she shook her head. "I used to pick Rainer up constantly, long before Joseph passed and we became his guardians."

"That was before the school board representative from hell took over."

Mrs. Haydenshire shook her head. "At some point, surely the Non-Gifted people will understand that their government should work for them."

"It's set up to keep them from demanding that." Dan rolled his eyes.

She nodded. "I think you're well on your way to having everything your little one will need. And, Fionna, please trust your heart. You're going to know what your baby girl needs, and you have a wonderful, caring husband who loves you more than life itself, so just decide right now that no matter what, you're in this for the long haul. I promise you will survive the days that aren't so great because not all of them will be. You'll find that adding to your family is a wonderful process even if you feel a little lost or overwhelmed sometimes."

"But how do I know that I know?" Fionna asked.

"If it feels right to you and to Dan, you'll know. There is no perfect mother, and as much as you'll want her life to be perfect, it won't be. No one's is. I remember when Stephen and I brought Will home to that studio apartment downtown." She laughed. "My mother came and helped us for a week, but then she left. I had this little boy I had to take care of and a husband who was just as lost as I was.

"Stephen would hold me on the couch while I cried, and I would hold Will while he cried. Then, a few months later, I was pregnant with Garrett, so I decided I better figure out what was going to work for us. Two things I found that always helped—if it will take less than fifteen minutes, go on and do it. And if you can do it ahead of time, do that as well. If you have the energy, go on and make bottles, make meals, schedule appointments. Putting it off costs way more time, and there will be days when you do not have the energy to do much. You'll be thankful for everything that's already done. Thirty-three years and eleven kids later, I think we'll manage."

"Thank you for everything." Fionna hugged Mrs. Haydenshire again.

"You're welcome, sweetheart. Try to relax and enjoy it because one day you're registering for bottles and the next you're watching your academy graduates walk down the aisle and then move out of your house. The days are long but the years are awfully short."

Dan and Fionna nodded their understanding, but he suspected that it wasn't something a parent really understood until they'd lived the experience.

"You'll come to the hospital when I go into labor, right?" Fionna asked.

Mrs. Haydenshire looked truly honored. "Of course. You know Stephen would be devastated if we read about it in the paper." Relief eased the tense set of Fionna's rhythms. "My littlest princess will be up soon, so we're going to head back to the farm because she's going to be wet, hungry, and irritated when she wakes up. If you need anything at all, I'm a phone call away."

"Thank you so much."

"Thanks, Mrs. Haydenshire," Dan echoed as he was embraced by the woman that had mothered him while he grew up just like she had all her own and several others.

Dan guided Fionna around the rest of the store. They tried to take it just a little at a time, and Dan encouraged Fionna constantly to listen to her heart when it came to something she wasn't certain of.

As they made their way to the large section of infant clothing, Fionna relaxed completely. She seemed to be in heaven as she gazed at rack after rack of tiny dresses, sleepers, and outfits complete with tiny hair bows and bands.

"Oh my goodness," she gasped as she moved to a rack of matching sister outfits.

Dan chuckled as she picked out Aida and Halia several matching outfits for having their pictures made and for Christmas. Overjoyed, Fionna added several ruffled sleepers for Halia, matching them with hair bows or bands which thrilled her.

Dan pointed to a long-sleeved white knit shirt in Aida's size with a princess crown embroidered on it. The words "I'm a big sister and my Daddy's princess" were sewn in pinks, greens, and purples. Fionna added it to the cart. They continued shopping, each of them letting the sheer volume of items the store contained work through them. They remembered that most of it was unnecessary.

"Dan?"

"Yeah, baby doll?"

"I really don't think I like that stroller that Mrs. Haydenshire suggested. Is that okay? I mean, surely she knows what's best."

"I think the point of everything she told us is that we have to figure out what works for our family, and we're not them. As much as I love the Haydenshires, I don't want to have eleven kids."

She laughed and nodded.

He guided Fionna back to the aisle containing several dozen strollers in every shape and color combination. "As much as I wish I could be with you and the girls constantly, I just can't. I want you to have what you need to get Halia around comfortably."

"It worried me that I had a hard time folding up the one Abigail uses."

"That worried me as well."

"It seems like I might need to be able to fold it up with one hand kind of quickly," Fionna hemmed. "You know, if Halia's screaming and Aida's having trouble getting in her car seat or something. I'm going to literally have my hands full." She was grinning and rubbing her hands tenderly over Halia's bump. She looked thrilled by the prospect and ready to deal with the wonderful world of motherhood, aware that not everything was going to be grand.

Dan pulled the assembled model of the one Fionna was pointing to off the store shelf. "I wondered about the other one not reclining all the way back. If we get lucky, Halia will sleep occasionally, right?"

"Yeah, I thought that too." They tested out several models with Dan guiding Fionna in how to fold and unfold the stroller and then watching her do it on her own.

In the end, the one that was the easiest for her to maneuver was a hundred dollars more than the stroller Mrs. Haydenshire suggested. Fionna fussed over the price.

"Fi, baby, if you don't want to put it on the registry, then I'll buy it now, but I'm not putting something on here that you don't want and that we don't like." He added the one she liked to the registry.

Fionna added a box of nursing pads to prevent leaking to their cart as they made their way to the checkout.

"Don't say anything," she commanded.

"I'm saying nothing," Dan vowed. She giggled as he winked at her.

CHAPTER 7

BLOOMING CONFUSION

"I've never been so exhausted after shopping," Fionna confessed as Dan pulled her seat out for her at Truluck's, near Georgetown.

The waiter approached with a kind smile. "What can I get you both this evening?"

Dan placed an order for Fionna's requested trout amandine and ordered himself a filet.

"Fi," Dan eased as the waiter went to get their waters. "Should we really talk about Kauai?" They'd discussed moving to Kauai permanently with more regularity, but neither of them were certain what they should do. Dan hadn't brought up the fact that he did not really want to be a farmer full-time. If she really wanted to move back to Kauai, he decided that he wouldn't say anything. Maybe there was some other job there he could eventually find.

"Maybe is all I can give you right now." Fionna shrugged.

"Okay. We don't have to decide anything anytime soon."

"How did I get lucky enough to marry a guy that's really willing to move me and my girls back home? And what about everything and everyone here that we love?"

Dan noted that she'd called Kauai home. He extracted that piece of information from the rest of her worries.

As they began discussing the childbirth class, a woman at least ten years their senior moved to their table. Startled, they both turned toward the woman. Her hair was cut short around her neck, and she had tight curls on top of her head. Her eyes were wide and her lips pursed like she'd just licked a sour lemon.

"Well, you're Fionna Styler," the woman informed Fionna like she was somehow unaware. "I've been trying to find someone who'll give me your phone number, but everyone at the hospital is so hush-hush." Dan narrowed his eyes. His shield sizzled in his palms.

Fionna sighed audibly. "I'm Fionna Vindico, actually."

"Oh right, right, right, well," the woman tsked, "I'm Linda Barge." She didn't seem to mind the fact that she was interrupting Dan and Fionna's rather intimate dinner.

"It's nice to meet you," Fionna lied.

"I saw your name on the Georgetown registry for the same birthing class that we're taking tonight."

"How great."

Chuckling under his breath, Dan searched the restaurant for the woman's husband but didn't notice anyone fitting the bill.

"I had to come and tell you that you really just cannot be eating fish. It's dangerous for your little girl."

Dan cocked his jaw to the side and glared.

Fionna patted his hand, trying to soothe him discreetly. "This is actually lake trout, so it's a freshwater fish. No mercury. It's perfectly safe."

Linda's eyes narrowed in indignation. "I told Bob we wouldn't be having fried catfish anymore with our little Aakerman Robert on the way."

"Actually, catfish is also safe for pregnant women," Fionna informed her.

Linda didn't even acknowledge that Fionna had spoken. "I always tell Bob you never know about those places that don't fry their fish. What if it isn't cooked?" She spat all over Fionna in her exuberance.

Fionna nearly gagged as she backed away.

"Also, I went ahead and added your name to the nursing seminar after our birthing class on Thursdays. I noticed that you hadn't registered." She sounded like she'd just saved Fionna's life and should be duly rewarded.

Fionna's eyes goggled at Dan. He could hardly believe what he was hearing.

"Why would you sign Fionna up for anything?" he demanded. "You don't even know us."

"You should be thanking me. Spots in the nursing class fill up quickly."

"I will not be attending the nursing class, but thank you," Fionna spoke through her clenched teeth.

"Aren't you concerned about nipple confusion?" Linda rolled her eyes at Fionna like she wasn't capable of making a decision on her own. Dan tried to envision what on earth nipple confusion might be.

"Not really."

Dan's mind was still preoccupied with nipple confusion. He was absolutely certain that he could pick Fionna's nipples out in a lineup. They were just as perfect and luscious as the rest of her, but he had no idea what that would mean for Halia.

"I took the liberty of signing you up for the co-sleeping seminar on Saturday." Linda sounded highly put out.

Drawing a deep, steadying breath, Fionna grasped Dan's hand and pulled calm from him until a semblance of a smile returned. "The only person I will be co-sleeping with, Mrs. Barge, is my husband, but thank you for thinking of me."

Linda huffed, "I certainly hope that once your little precious arrives, you'll actually begin to understand that you're a real mother now. Then you'll be wishing you'd taken all of these classes."

Fionna erupted suddenly, shocking both Dan and Linda. "Oh, so you mean that I wasn't a real mother before now? Are you saying my seven-year-old didn't make me a real mother because I didn't give birth to her? Is that it?" she shouted.

"Fi." Dan tried to soothe her, but she'd clearly had enough.

"Let me tell you something," she roared. Dan grimaced as the entire restaurant turned their direction. "I was a mother the moment I signed Aida's adoption papers. And whether or not I nurse or bottle feed, or work or stay home, or sleep with my girls or with my husband, or eat fish, or sign my babies up for football, cheerleading, hula, and softball while they play their violins and pianos and then sell cheese for the PTA on the side does not make me a mother," she screeched. "I don't like you! Go away!" Fionna commanded, and Dan almost doubled over laughing. He was certain that was the cruelest thing his baby had ever uttered to someone she'd just met in her entire life.

Linda looked appalled, and Dan regained his composure. "My wife asked you to leave," he growled.

"Well, I never." Linda spun and stomped out of the restaurant. She met a man Dan assumed was her waiting husband on the sidewalk. Blood pooled violently in Fionna's cheeks as Dan gazed at her.

"Can I ask you something, baby doll?" She appeared to be on the verge of either hysterical laughter or horrified tears, but she managed a nod. "What the hell is nipple confusion?"

That did it. She cracked up and laughed uproariously.

"Oh my gosh, I feel terrible." Fionna began to cry through her laughter. "I've never told anyone I didn't like them."

Dan moved his chair beside her and wrapped his arms around her to let her hide in him. He considered his words very carefully. "You've been under a lot of pressure lately."

"You think I've gone insane," she whimpered.

Certain that hormonal fits of rage were completely normal, Dan assured her that he did not think she was insane. "I think you're adorable, and I'm so damn proud of you for speaking up." He wiped away her tears with his thumbs as he cradled her face in his hands.

"People do that to me all the time." Her breath shuddered from her fury and her tears. "They think they know me because they came to an Angels' challenge four seasons ago, so that must mean that I want to hear all of their opinions about pregnancy and children."

"I know, baby. I'm sorry."

Linda returned suddenly. She grabbed two Styrofoam take-out boxes from her table that had been forgotten, and then made another dramatic exit with her nose in the air.

After finishing their meal and leaving a generous tip, they walked hand in hand to Georgetown, which was only a few blocks away. Dan stopped by the car to get the pillows and Fionna's yoga mats that they'd been instructed to bring.

"If you want to nurse and pump and use bottles or use formula sometimes, some people think the baby can get confused and stop nursing because bottles are easier to use or something like that. It's called nipple confusion," Fionna explained as they moved through the DC sidewalks.

"Even little boys?" Dan effectively cracked his wife up again.

But Fionna whimpered as they entered Georgetown Hospital. "That woman is going to be in this class with us."

Adeline spotted them in the hallway. "Are you here for Medio Lenson's class?"

"Yeah. I'm kind of nervous," Fionna admitted.

Adeline gave her a reassuring smile. "Don't be nervous. She's great, but she won't be here tonight. Her daughter is on the third floor giving birth, actually. I'm not sure who they have covering for her, but I'm sure she'll be back for Thursday's class. But class or no class, you're going to do great, Fionna."

Certain that there wasn't a better medio anywhere, Dan gave Adeline a deeply appreciative smile. They moved into a kind of auditorium and viewed numerous other couples taking seats near the front of the room.

Linda and Bob were already seated near three other couples. Linda was whispering heatedly, and Fionna received scowls as Dan led her to a pair of chairs as far away as he could get her from Linda. The couple seated in front of them turned and smiled.

"I'm Scott Abrams, and this is my wife, Lisa." The man offered Dan his hand.

"I'm Dan Vindico, and this is my wife, Fionna," he offered politely.

"When are you due?" Lisa asked.

Fionna's internal shield began to ease away. Whatever emotion she was reading off of Lisa, she began to relax.

"Toward the end of November."

"Us too." Lisa studied Fionna for a moment and then seemed to decide to go on. "I know it's probably really weird or annoying that people you don't even know, know so much about you," she eased hesitantly. "I swear I'm not one of those crazy fans that wants to stalk you or whatever," she explained as Fionna chuckled. "I really was so sorry to hear about everything that happened last spring. We're huge Angel fans, so I'm thrilled you're here and devastated that we lost the best Receiver in the Realm."

"That's so sweet. Thank you." Fionna looked truly touched. "You're gonna make me cry."

"See, honey, you're not the only one," Scott teased his wife.

Lisa shook her head at him. "He came home from work yesterday, and I was sobbing because I watched one of those underprivileged child sponsorship commercials."

Fionna looked excited that she might have found a friend.

"Fi did that before she was pregnant." Dan kissed the side of Fionna's head.

"Are you coming to the co-sleeping seminar on Saturday?" Lisa asked.

Fionna's face fell. "No, I don't really want to do that too often."

"I'm not sure I want to either. I just thought we'd come and learn about it. I think you have to do what works for you and your family." Lisa seemed to have realized she'd unsettled Fionna.

Before more questions could be asked, a woman dressed in a green leotard with black leggings and gauzy scarves fluttered into the room performing spins and leaps as she moved to the temporary podium. She looked like some kind of deranged fairy.

Dan and Scott shared a concerned expression while Fionna and Lisa's eyes goggled.

"Good evening, little mommies and daddies of the Realm, or, as I shall call you for the rest of our time together, my gallant stamens with anthers so fierce, and delicate but mighty pistil stigmas." Dan fought the urge to let his head fall into his hands as the woman continued.

"Medio Lenson has gone to grandmother her little flower of her garden, and I've been called to present you a class on alternative childbirths for your consideration. If you would like to consider the natural way, then my classes are here each Wednesday night and at sunrise on Saturday mornings."

Suddenly, the woman squatted into a tight ball form on the stage. Her feet were bare. "You may call me Lotus," she announced as she began slowly standing and extending her arms up and out.

"Dear God," Dan huffed under his breath as Fionna bit her lips together to keep from laughing.

"For I am the gardener who will bring your blooms to fruition after our stamens with anthers so fierce have fertilized and ripened the seed," she continued, keeping her voice in a low echo.

Scott leaned back to Dan. "Dude, what the hell is an anther?"

Instantly deciding that he liked Scott, Dan shook his head in disbelief.

As Lotus stood, she twirled around and then leapt dramatically off the stage. Certain she'd meant to land on her feet, Dan tried not to crack up as she missed the mark slightly and stumbled into an empty chair.

"Now," she continued. "Let us begin by examining our beautiful flowers."

"I am not doing that in here," Fionna whispered as she and Dan bit back laughter.

Lotus moved to a large box and emerged with a life-sized plastic replica of the female reproductive organs. There was a pull string on the side.

"Honey, I think you may need to go back and see the medio. Your string is missing," Scott teased as Lisa and Fionna laughed.

Then to everyone's shock, Lotus tilted the model upward and began pulling the string which served to open the cervix. She began moving around the room saying, "Hello, this is how your flower will open to allow your bud to blossom," to each and every couple. She spoke through the model, looking down from what would be a woman's waist through the uterus, cervix, and vulva.

Fionna was horrified as Lotus pulled the string repeatedly to make it seem that the model was talking to her as she informed the class that Fionna's flower had accepted Dan's pollen even after her much-reported miscarriage.

Lotus returned to the front of the auditorium, and Dan tried to determine how noticeable it would be if he and Fionna ran from the room screaming.

"Now, let us begin our journey from seed to the glory of full bloom by going around the room and telling everyone your names and the story of your fertilization," Lotus urged with a replete smile.

"Okay, we are leaving." Dan grasped Fionna's hand.

Fionna shook her head. "We can't just leave," she pled under her breath.

"We are not telling everyone in this room how we conceived."

"I'm sure that's not what she meant. Everyone here knows who I am. I can't just get up and walk out."

During their distraction, Lotus had decided to start with the Barges.

"My name is Linda Barge, and this is my husband, Bob Barge. We own Bob Barge Used Cars and Automotives." Linda beamed proudly.

"Let us call him the mighty anther," Lotus guided.

"Oh, uh, well, okay." Linda looked momentarily confused. "This is my mighty anther Bob Barge," she corrected.

Fionna's hand flew to her mouth in an effort to keep from laughing outright as Dan shook his head. Bob was almost a foot shorter than Linda and appeared to have no neck. His entire being glowed red from being called her mighty anther.

"And how did Bob the mighty anther fertilize Linda's receptacle and her delicate stigma?" Lotus urged.

"She has got to be kidding," Fionna gasped.

"I'm not entirely certain I understand the question." Linda looked concerned.

"But I don't know exactly when," Lisa whispered to Scott.

Scott appeared lost somewhere between stupefied disbelief at what he was going to be asked and trying to soothe his wife who was concerned over not having the correct answer to the horrifying question. "This is insane. We're not telling people that," he tried to console.

"Tell us, dear cockscomb, when did you allow the mighty anther to penetrate your garden?" Lotus asked with a breathy sigh.

"Fionna!" Dan demanded in a low growl. Before Fionna could respond, Lotus was upon them. "It seems that Anther Bob and Stamen Linda wish to remain inside of their garden walls. So, my delicate, moon orchid, tell us how you were implanted. When did you allow your mighty anther to fertilize your tiny budding seed?" she urged Fionna.

Unable to speak, Fionna sat in the chair, shaking her head and trying to formulate words. Dan ground his teeth.

Lotus turned to Dan. "Introduce your flower, mighty anther."

"No," Dan spat.

"Dan!" Fionna cringed.

Rolling his eyes, Dan drew a deep breath. "I'm Dan Vindico, and this is my wife, Fionna," he begrudged.

"This is your flower, Anther Dan," Lotus corrected.

"She doesn't self-fertilize, and I've never watered her, so I'm gonna go with wife."

Scott and Lisa began laughing. Fionna slunk down farther in her chair.

Ignoring his quip, Lotus continued. "And mighty Anther Dan, tell us how your anther and stamens have brought your delicate moon orchid to bloom."

Abject fury coursed through Dan's veins. He tried desperately to keep his temper at bay. "I do not have a moon orchid. I have a wife named Fionna, and I will not be sharing anything about how we became pregnant. That is between us and no one else."

Lotus gave a disapproving tsk as she moved to Lisa and Scott. "And how about your garden story, my delicate Peruvian lily?"

"Uh…" Lisa began to hyperventilate.

"I'm Scott Abrams," Scott stepped in to try and save his wife. "This is my wife, Lisa."

"And tell us when you plucked Lisa's blooms and brought your garden to fruition," Lotus sang.

"Well, let's see here, I'd just gotten my license, and we were out in her dad's golf cart."

"Scott!" Lisa shrieked. Dan doubled over laughing.

Winking at Lisa, Scott shook his head. "I think we're gonna join the Vindicos and go with we'll be keeping that between myself and my Peruvian lily."

"So many secretive gardens this evening. For we must open our garden gates if we want to embrace the natural way for our garden to expand. Does no one want to share their germination story?"

No one seemed interested in going over their conception, so eventually Lotus moved on.

"The first thing we'll be going over this evening will be what I call flower visualization birthing." She began moving around the room with her arms in the air and her fingers tensed wide. She waved her hands together and then apart rapidly. "Close your eyes, delicate stigmas. Envision your pistils fluxing and releasing, fluxing and releasing, as you birth your little orchids.

"Pain comes from lack of visualization. Picture your flower producing and filling the world." She gained fervor. Fionna stared in wide-eyed confusion as the women in the room began letting their eyes close hesitantly. "Picture the mighty anther upon you pounding and germinating, pushing and tending your soil, pulling and urging your bloom. You are bringing to fruition the next bud of the celestial garden of our mother earth," she announced in a dreamy orgasmic lull.

"Fionna!" Dan seethed.

"You see, my blooming pistils," Lotus soothed, "we must envision our tiny buds pouring forth from our bodies. There is no pain. There is no stress or tension. We must remove the weed of contention and fear from our garden and embrace birth. Just as the sun awakens our blooms and our mighty anthers prod our seeds, for it is natural and beautiful. Pain means that your garden has not been properly weeded of apprehension," Lotus declared while standing in front of the assembled class, holding her arms out, lifted toward the ceiling.

"Now, my delicate pistils, we will begin birth rehearsal imagery," Lotus commanded. "Allow your mighty anthers to guide you toward the sun and find a gardening space around our fertile fields." She gestured her hands out to the auditorium at large.

"Fi, baby, please. This is insane," Dan pled under his breath.

74

"That Bob Barge Used Cars woman has half the class thinking I'm a total bitch. I can't just leave," Fionna begged.

With a huff of defeat, Dan helped Fionna up. They joined Lisa and Scott as they spread out toward the back of the room.

"Now, my dear cockscomb, would you and your mighty anther join me here in the epicenter of our garden." Lotus guided Bob and Linda to the center of the couples. Lotus produced what appeared to be a blood-red, knitted stocking cap.

As Dan studied it closer, he noted that the bulb-like item had a large opening on one end and then a slender tube on the top that was also open.

"Now my cockscomb, we will simulate the birth of our new blossom," Lotus announced grandly. Linda looked extremely proud to have been selected as the example.

With that, Dan choked back hysterical laughter as Lotus handed the strange cap-like item to Linda Barge. "Place this on your anther's head, for he will be our ripening bloom."

Before Bob could protest, Linda promptly pulled the knitted representation of a woman's uterus and cervix over her husband's head. It became stuck near his ears. Dan pulled out his cell phone and snapped a photo. He winked at Fionna. She tried to turn her giggles into coughing without much success.

"If she doesn't leave you the hell alone, Jeff and I are putting this up on Bob Barge's Used Cars' website—on every freaking page."

"Now, my burgeoning blooms, I would like for you and your mighty anthers to help us arrange our bouquets," Lotus urged. "Mighty anthers, please move behind your pistils."

With a complementary eye roll, Dan moved behind Fionna. He wrapped his arms over her swell and kissed her cheek. Maybe this part of the class wouldn't be too bad. Fionna laid her head back on his shoulder and let him cradle her. It always astonished him that it didn't matter where they were—if she was beside him, he was happy.

"Now, delicate pistil, we will allow our mighty anthers to enliven our flowers so that our buds may pour forth for his garden." Lotus performed a cartwheel in the middle of the classroom.

"Now, your stigma has been stimulated and fertilized by your anther. You are a blossom of beauty about to give birth. Visualize, visualize, visualize. There is no pain, only deep rapturous pleasure! We will practice allowing our mighty anthers to speak to our womb to encourage our opening so that our flower may burst forth."

With that, Lotus dropped to her knees and began speaking between a bewildered looking woman's legs.

"Fionna, this woman is insane," Dan whispered in Fionna's ear. He kept his head near her cheek. He felt her bump shake slightly as she began giggling again. "If you'll let me take you home, I will go by Mae's and get you a milkshake, any flavor you want, and then I will put you in our bed. I will show you how I stimulate your flower, and I swear I will bring you rapturous pleasure. No audience necessary, just please."

Fionna's entire body was shaking from her trying desperately not to laugh out loud. Lotus moved to Fionna, and she stopped laughing abruptly. Dan narrowed his eyes. The woman needed to be planted in a blooming mental institution.

"Delicate moon orchid and Anther Dan, please move to the garden epicenter," she directed. Fionna looked horrified, but she led Dan to the center of the room.

"Now, Anther Dan, your moon orchid will lean forward." Lotus placed her hands on Fionna's shoulders and pulled her forward at the waist.

"Do not touch my wife," Dan snarled. Fionna looked back from her bent position and shot him a pleading glare.

"Mighty anther, place your hands on your wife's waist." Lotus grasped Dan's wrists. He had to consciously remember not to throw his shield from his wrists, which would have knocked her off of her blossom.

"Now, you will massage and stimulate your wife's peduncle,"—she gestured to Fionna's lower back—"and rub and ripen her petals."

Dan's eyes goggled as Lotus motioned for Dan to begin rubbing Fionna's ass in front of twelve other couples. He was standing behind Fionna who was bent over. His crotch was right in front of what Dan was certain was a portion of heaven, making it an extremely uncomfortable position when there were prying eyes. Fionna shot back up. Her face glowed crimson.

"Honey, I don't feel well. Maybe we should go," Fionna lied relatively well.

Dan grabbed her hand. "Come on."

"Oh dear, moonbeam. Allow me to blossom your petals toward the sun for they will heal your discomfort," Lotus immediately vowed. "Anther Dan, perhaps help dear moon orchid to recline in a comfortable position whilst you rub and ripen her perineum. This is an area that can be massaged during your bud's emergence to guide your flower to fruition."

Fionna's mouth hung open as Dan tried to convince himself that the woman had not just instructed him to massage Fionna there in front of the class. "The perineum is the flower petal between your moon orchid's vulva and her—" she began.

"I'm well aware of where everything is located on my wife. We are leaving."

"You mustn't be afraid to ripen your moon orchid." Lotus shook her head.

"Now!"

"Alas, moon orchid and Anther Dan. Class, let us wave to our garden blooms as they are plucked and exit our garden." Lotus waved her arms in front of her, simulating the wind. "Be the wind, class," she instructed as other couples began mimicking the wind with their arms. "Goodbye, Moon Orchid. Goodbye, goodbye," she sang as Dan and Fionna raced out the door.

As soon as they'd made their escape, Fionna collapsed against Dan, laughing uproariously.

"Oh my God!" She wiped away tears from her hysterical laughter.

"If that's the best Georgetown has to offer, then I *will* deliver Halia." Dan shook his head in astonishment.

Fionna tried to breathe. "I was there when Malani had little Lanie and when Amber had Jensen. Believe me, I don't care how much you visualize and weed your garden, it hurts, like really, really bad."

Dan drew a deep breath and kissed the side of her head. "Let's go get your car. Then we'll drop off my car and go get our baby girl."

"I believe I was promised a milkshake if we left early." She giggled.

"All right. First Mae's, then your car, then our baby girl." They exited the hospital hand in hand, still stunned over their evening.

"Does this mean that I shouldn't scream out, 'oh, Anther Dan, oh, Anther Dan,' when you bring me to fruition?"

Reveling in his wife's laughter, Dan shook his head. "Whatever you want, Moon Orchid."

CHAPTER 8

ROSES AND THORNS

"You're early." Governor Vindico welcomed Dan and Fionna inside.

"Daddy!" Aida trilled. She rushed to Dan. "I beat Grandpa in checkers three times!"

Fionna shook her head at Governor Vindico. She'd figured out just as quickly as Dan that Aida might've had a little help from her grandfather in her success.

"Wow!" Dan feigned shock making Aida beam. Mrs. Vindico moved into the entryway carrying a notepad with a pencil over her ear.

"Daniel, Fionna, I've ordered the invitations for Ryan and Lindley's wedding, and I want to go ahead and order the birth announcements from the same company. That way I'll only have to provide the digital copy of the Vindico crest once."

Rolling his eyes, Dan decided to engage his mother in this insanity in order to get a little information. "When are Ryan and Lindley getting married, Mom?" He knew his sister and Ryan Tuttle were actually planning to get married at some hedonist resort in Jamaica. His mother, however, was going about planning a full Senate-affair wedding without so much as consulting his sister or her fiancé.

"I've decided February eighteenth. We'll do red roses set off by the snow, but not overtly a Valentine theme."

"How do you know that it will snow?" Dan spared her another eye roll.

She ignored him as usual.

"Why am I not surprised she's now ordering around God?" he whispered to Fionna.

She patted his leg.

"How was class?" The governor gestured Dan and Fionna into the living room.

"One of the most bizarre experiences of my life, and you know just a few of the cases I was called out on when I was Chief of Iodex."

Confusion etched the governor's face. "Your mother and I took a class before you were born. All I remember is that I nearly hyperventilated trying to get your mother to breathe."

"I really just want to know how to cast her. I want to try to make this as comfortable as I possibly can," Dan admitted to his father as Aida went to gather her things. Fionna gave him his smile.

"Talk to Zach. He did a remarkable job of keeping Kara calm." Dan nodded his agreement. He thought it was a brilliant idea. "They wouldn't let the dads do that when you four were born, but I imagine Stephen could help you as well."

Aida returned to the couch. She snuggled up beside Fionna.

"How was school?" Fionna kissed the top of Aida's head. Dan recognized the concern on her face. She'd picked up something in Aida's rhythms.

Tucking closer to Fionna, Aida's face fell as she shrugged.

"What's wrong, baby girl?" Dan asked.

His parents both moved in. They looked just as worried as Dan and Fionna.

"She didn't say anything to me," Governor Vindico mouthed.

"Jessica said that Haley and I couldn't go through the tube on the playground because we can't be in her club," Aida confessed dejectedly. "So, then we couldn't get to the slide."

"Did you tell Mrs. Powell?" Fionna wrapped Aida up in her embrace.

"Yes, ma'am."

"What did Mrs. Powell do?" Dan asked.

"She told Jessica that we could go through the tube," Aida sighed. "But then, when she went back to the teacher's bench, Jessica called Haley a mean name and said that no one liked her. Haley started to cry. I said that I like Haley, and that she's my friend, and it isn't nice to call people names because it hurts their feelings," Aida explained. Dan braced as Fionna's eyes betrayed her heartbreak.

"Then Jessica said I was a baby, and she and Saran started making crying noises," she concluded before tucking herself under Fionna's arm.

"Aida, sweetheart, you just tell Jessica who your granddaddy is and that if she can't be polite, then we'll have to have her moved to another class," Mrs. Vindico decreed.

"Mom." Dan shook his head.

"I'm sorry Jessica isn't being nice," Fionna soothed. "But you know that Haley is your friend and that the way Jessica is treating both you and Haley isn't the way we're supposed to act. I'm so proud of you for standing up for your friend. That lets her know that she's not alone, and that's so important."

"It makes my tummy hurt."

"I know," Fionna assured her. Dan's heart ached. This was how a Receiver's internal shield developed. This was how their energy and their spirits learned to cope with the fact that they could feel all kinds of emotions all around them—the hurtful, the pained, and the haunting. Dan knew that, but knowing something and watching it happen to his precious baby girl were two entirely different things.

Friday afternoon, Dan was feeling distinctly odd as he climbed in his Ferrari to go home and get ready to attend a Venton fall formal. The last fall formal Dan had gone to was when he was a junior. Amelia had been his date.

His senior year he'd been far too busy between his defense classes and then special ops training to attend any of the dances. As he drove the winding lanes leading off campus, he took in the bold stunning fall foliage of the maple and cherry trees that lined the lanes of the academy and the highway.

He let his mind review the information Jeff and Logan had shown him Wednesday night. There were at least twenty websites with multiple exams from Venton classes. They'd located all of Dan's that he'd turned in Monday. The websites selling the exams with the answer keys were heavily encrypted.

Jeff had worked for hours and only ended up in loops that ultimately linked to faulty scripting. Whoever was stealing and selling the exams knew what they were doing. Jeff explained that every time he tried to hack into the hosting servers, it triggered them to be automatically moved to different servers to make certain that no one caught them. The credit card accounts where the money was being held were from all over the world, largely in Aruba, where Dan and the American Realm had precious little say.

His faith in Georgetown had been restored the night before. Medio Lenson had seated the couples in a semicircle. She'd started with what Fionna would likely experience in the beginning stages of labor. She'd gone over how Dan could help ease Fionna's pain, when he should call Adeline, and when he should take Fionna to the hospital.

He was so caught up in his reviewing the first signs of labor, he almost missed the interstate exit to Arlington. Fionna's parents were coming over to the house to keep Aida for the evening.

Dan eased into the garage with a sigh. He still didn't really want to attend the formal that night. Trying to discern why his shield was so resistant, Dan moved up the stairs and into the house.

For ten long years, he'd hated to be home. He only went home when he was too exhausted to continue working. Now, it was the only place he wanted to be.

"Hey good lookin'." Fionna gave him her sweet sexy smile. She was standing at the kitchen island making sandwiches.

Dan moved to her with magnetic need. She drew him in and soothed his soul. "Hey, baby doll."

"Lunch?" she offered after he kissed her cheek and inhaled deeply of her.

"Sure. I'm starved." He carried her roast beef sandwich and chips to the table for her, while she fixed him an identical plate.

"How was work?"

"It's the day of a formal." He chuckled.

"Ah." Fionna nodded. She swallowed down a large bite of her sandwich with a sip of her Dr Pepper. "So, everyone was talking about who they were going with, what they were wearing, what that bitch so-and-so said to that other girl who's going with the guy she likes, who's riding with whom, who has a hotel room afterward, and there were a dozen girls in the bathroom crying because they don't have a date."

"You forgot the dozen or so guys who were debating whether or not so-and-so would still go with them if they asked today and whether or not they might get lucky," he added as she rolled her eyes.

"Are Jeff and Becca coming?"

"I'm not sure. Becca was sick this morning. Jeff missed part of class." He was still trying not to panic over that fact.

Concern etched Fionna's beautiful features. "I was worried they may not come because she wouldn't have a dress."

"I never thought of that." Dan stood to make himself a second sandwich.

Aida burst through the door at three fifteen. Fionna was in the shower, so Dan made her snack and snuggled his baby girl on the couch. He watched several *Supernovas* with her while Fionna got ready for the formal. The time together seemed to delight Aida as much as it delighted Dan.

At five, he took a quick shower while Aida watched Fionna apply makeup and pull the clips from her hair to release the waves she'd created. "I have to hurry. My date's supposed to pick me up at six," she teased.

Kissing her cheek, Dan pulled on a suit and tie and then returned to the Ferrari to acquire the wrist corsage he'd left in the front seat.

The Stylers arrived at a quarter to six carrying dinner in with them to begin their evening of doting on Aida.

Fionna moved down the stairs a moment later.

"You look phenomenal, baby." He leashed the lust and hunger from his voice, in front of her father at least.

She was wearing a coral, halter-style cocktail dress. The top put her heaving cleavage on jaw-dropping display. There was a delicate rhinestone detailing just over Halia's bump, and the hem was shorter in the front than in the back. It showed off her luscious legs.

Dan wondered how long she would last in the heels she'd chosen, but she looked phenomenal. He also wondered how long she would want to stay at the formal before he could bring her home and work her out of the gauzy dress.

He pulled the white orchid and ginger corsage he'd chosen from its plastic container. Fionna beamed. Those were the flowers she'd put in the lei Dan had placed on her at their wedding.

"You look beautiful, Maylea." Gretta hugged Fionna.

"Thank you."

"I miss everybody calling Mommy Maylea," Aida said thoughtfully. "It makes her smile."

Dan winked at Aida. "I'll call Mommy that more often."

"You wear your seat belt, Maylea," Mr. Styler ordered. "And you go straight to this dance and straight home. No stopping and no staying out late." Dan tried not to laugh as he and Fionna shared a wry glance.

"Daddy, I'm thirty years old, married, and pregnant. I'm not certain what you're trying to prevent now."

Gretta rolled her eyes. "Samuel, please. Maylea, you and Dan have a wonderful evening, sweetheart." She turned to Aida. "I brought some pictures of your mommy when she was a little girl that we can look at." Gretta produced several photo albums and offered them to Aida. This visibly delighted her.

"Oh no," Fionna lamented.

Aida crawled up on the couch and spread an album out in her lap.

"That is Mommy's other mommy." Aida pointed to a photo of newborn Fionna. Gretta smiled and nodded. "And, you're her mommy just like she's my mommy, and I love her so much and I love my other mommy so much even though she went away." Aida seemed to be testing Gretta.

"That's right, my sweet girl. I think you and Mommy are very special girls because you have so many people that love you so much." She squeezed Aida.

"I'm going to need to see those when we get home," Dan teased.

Rolling her eyes, Fionna seemed to accept her defeat as Aida giggled. "Mommy, you have noodles in your hair." She pointed to a picture of Fionna's first time having rice noodles.

"She still does that whenever I take her out for Italian," Dan mocked lament. The Stylers laughed as Fionna popped Dan's stomach with the back of her hand.

"All right, we're leaving. You be good, my sweet girl, and don't let Pops and Abuelita spoil you too much." Fionna leaned to kiss Aida's cheek.

Dan opened the Ferrari door for his beautiful wife before joining her on the other side.

"Are you gonna try to get me to go to Great Falls Park with you after the dance?" She laughed.

Dan shot his wife a cocky grin. "I don't know, baby doll. Your dad said we weren't allowed to stop anywhere on the way home, so, to me, what he was saying was, bring my little girl home, and take her straight to bed. I wouldn't want to break your dad's rules."

CHAPTER 9

EN GUARDE

Dan pulled into the main parking lot of Venton. Déjà vu shuddered through him as he worked through the memories he now found haunting. He opened Fionna's door for her, while trying to halt the memories of Amelia entering the Venton banquet room on his arm.

"Are you okay?" Fionna's soothing cast worked through him. Her warmth and her love moved through his hand. She knew the memories that flooded through him, and to his utter astonishment, she truly didn't mind. She was the most amazing person in the world.

Shaking himself slightly, Dan guided his wife through the entrance doors. "Been a long time since I walked under a balloon arch."

Fionna nodded as they moved under the plastic archway that had been covered in yellow and orange balloons. The room was lit by the candles on the tables and by a rented mirror ball complete with a spotlight. Students and faculty were meandering around the room decorated with balloons and cheaply crafted paper leaves.

Dan's jaw clenched as Fergus Sherman approached them.

"Here we have two Venton alumni," Sherman drawled stupidly into the pink orb held in his hand that he'd summoned to project his voice. "Mentor Vindico, tell everyone how you met Fionna Styler here at Venton and then, after dating for years, finally married her."

"Uh...we didn't," Fionna stammered as Fergus held his orb of sound energy in front of her mouth.

"No." Dan scooted Fionna away from Fergus and guided her to a table in the back of the room.

Dan's parents approached and gave him a disappointed glare.

"Daniel," his mother admonished.

"Mom, I'm not really in the mood to go over my life story with Sherman and the entire Venton student body, all right?"

Fionna wrapped his right hand up in both of hers and soothed him instantly.

"All right, all right." Governor Vindico tried to ease the tension between his wife and son. "May we join you?" he asked politely.

"Of course." Fionna gestured for them to sit down.

Students that seemed to travel in packs entered in steady streams.

"Fionna, you look lovely this evening," Governor Vindico said.

"Thank you." Fionna beamed.

Dan kissed her cheek. "Stunning," he corrected under his breath.

She chuckled as she took in a few students passing by their table. "Well, hello, Spencer," she called with more than a note of sarcasm in her tone.

"Oh, uh..." Spencer Coker's eyes goggled as Dan chuckled under his breath. "Hi...uh...Mrs. Vindico."

"Ah, Mr. Coker." Governor Vindico turned in his chair to view Spencer. Dan couldn't quite hide his smirk as his father narrowed his eyes. "Tell me, how is that little bet of yours going, son?"

Choking back laughter, Dan watched Spencer Coker cringe.

"I'm sorry, sir."

"Find a seat," the governor commanded.

Spencer fled the scene as quickly as he was able to maneuver through the seating area of the banquet room.

Mentor Sherman moved to the dance floor to welcome everyone. "I want to thank everyone for coming to the Fall Ball." He laughed at his own joke although he was the only person laughing.

Recovering quickly, Fergus continued. "I'd like to thank my lovely fiancée, Tilly McIntyre, for attending this evening with me. I won't tell you how I'll be thanking her for that later." He leered her direction. Dan rolled his eyes, and Fionna's mouth fell open.

The governor shot Fergus a glare. Picking up on Governor Vindico's scowl, Fergus's eyes goggled momentarily. "Uh, we'd like to thank Auxiliary Order for putting our formal on this evening. Please remember to be respectful of your dates and those around you as is Venton's policy." He managed to get through the required speech before he hightailed it back to Tilly.

With that, people began lining up at the buffet tables located on the west side of the large room.

Still concerned that Fionna really should be home on their sofa with her feet up instead of dressed in a cocktail dress, wearing heels, and trying to dance, Dan offered to get her plate for her.

"Thanks." She shot a nervous glance around the room.

"What's wrong, sweetheart?"

"I…don't know."

"Fi?"

"It's fine. Lots of emotions." She gestured to the hundreds of people standing around the room.

"Do you want me to stay with you?"

"No. I'm fine. I promise."

He supplied her with a large glass of water first and then moved to the food line for the mentors and staff.

The governor followed Dan, while Fionna and her mother-in-law began chatting amicably. Dan nearly dropped the two plates he was balancing when he reached the end of the line and studied the table he was returning to.

"Oh good grief," Governor Vindico spat. "She's got nerve. I'll give her that."

"That's what was wrong," Dan spoke to himself. He shook his head. "Dad, if she's making Fi uncomfortable, I'm taking her home. Fair warning."

"Of course." They both watched their wives edge closer together and away from Katherine Bryant, who'd taken it upon herself to sit at the table with the collective Mrs. Vindicos.

"Here, baby." Dan set her food in front of her and grasped her hand to let her draw from him.

"Mentor Bryant, how are you this evening?" the governor offered politely though he shot her a look that said to tread carefully.

"I'm fine, I suppose. Since this is my week with my children, I'm sure you understand that I'd rather not be here chaperoning a dance."

The governor nodded, and Dan braced. He was certain his father would have something to say to that.

"It seems to me that you didn't have too much trouble taking time away from your kids to attend educational seminars out of town, so I'm certain they'll manage for a few hours one evening." He narrowed his eyes.

Dan draped his arm over the back of Fionna's chair and kept her tucked closely to him as they ate. The mentors who volunteered to be official chaperones at Venton formals were paid for their time. Other mentors attended to try and communicate to their students that they wanted to be a positive influence in their lives.

Dan wondered if Bryant volunteered so she would be at the dances with the chancellor. Their affair wasn't outed until school began, and the dance chaperone sign-ups were sent out in June.

As they ate, Dan watched his mother work. After all, she was the wife of a Realm Governor. She could make small talk with anyone, and generally made people feel that she cared about them. Mrs. Vindico considered it part of her job to paint her husband and family in the best possible light for the Realm.

Although her tenacity irritated Dan, she was the model governor's wife, he supposed.

"We're having a lovely fall, don't you think? All of the rain over the summer was worth it now. The trees are just beautiful," she urged the table.

Fionna smiled. "It is beautiful. Dan raked the back yard when he got home yesterday, and Aida jumped in the leaves. She had a ball."

Chuckling as he recalled his baby girl's exuberance over something as simple as leaping in piles of leaves, Dan pulled his cell phone from his pocket to show the pictures of Aida buried in fall foliage.

The governor beamed at the pictures as he handed the phone to Mrs. Vindico.

"She'd never done that before," Dan added as his mother grinned. Mrs. Vindico politely turned the phone to Katherine Bryant.

"This is Dan and Fionna's little girl, Aida. She's almost eight," she explained kindly. The governor stared Mentor Bryant down. He almost dared her to make a derisive comment.

"Yes, we all heard about her. She's very cute," she offered half-heartedly. Fionna narrowed her eyes and bit back whatever comment begged to spill from her mouth.

"Yes, she is," the governor commanded as Dan's phone was returned to him.

Fionna started to stand. Dan helped her up and offered to walk her to the restroom. He didn't have to ask where she was going.

She shook her head, and Dan watched her walk down the short corridor off of the banquet room.

"Mentor Bryant, what classes are you teaching this semester?" Mrs. Vindico tried again.

Mentor Bryant's rhythms tensed in irritation. It appeared she'd been ready for a fight. Dan shook his head as he realized that's why she'd seated herself with Dan and the governor. She was out for blood. Polite, civilized dinner conversation hadn't been her plan, but she was cornered by not only a Realm Governor's wife but her boss's wife no less.

"Oh, uh..." She drew a deep breath. "I teach three Adminis freshman and sophomore classes and several sub and pre-freshman level creative writing classes. Dean let me move to more advanced levels," she fired. The governor nodded but didn't comment. "Someone has to teach the entry level classes. We can't all pick and choose the senior level simply because the students are easier to teach." She glared at Dan.

"Well," Mrs. Vindico chuckled, but her expression said that she had Bryant's number as well. "When you're as talented and work as hard as Daniel, I suppose you get first choice." Her tone was laced with menace. Fionna returned as Dan gave his mother an appreciative grin that seemed to delight both of his parents. Dan and the governor stood as Dan seated Fionna. Katherine rolled her eyes dramatically.

The meal dragged on with Mentor Bryant making snide comments occasionally. Fionna and Mrs. Vindico discussed the weather, Aida's upcoming birthday, Dan and Fionna's trip to Kauai, and Halia's baby shower.

A group of students took to the stage carrying guitars. One fell behind a drum set and began playing. Dan was impressed. They weren't half bad. A slow song began, and Fionna gave Dan a hopeful glance.

"Would you like to dance, sweetheart?"

"I guess, unless Spencer asks," she teased. Dan scowled, and the governor laughed heartily.

Dan led Fionna to the dance floor. He chuckled as a few of his favorite upper level Ioses students offered them wolf whistles and several rather overtly dirty comments.

Dan wrapped Fionna up in his arms with Halia between them.

She rubbed one hand on her belly. "Okay, but in a few months, just I get to dance with you."

"Or I could dance with all three of my girls separately."

Fionna tucked as closely to him as she could. He kissed her cheek.

"I've never been to a formal and had my date's parents sit with us."

"Yeah, I'm going to have to put a stop to this nonsense."

"You mean you weren't planning on showing up on Aida's dates?" Fionna continued to tease.

"That would mean that at some point I allowed her to go out on a date," Dan feigned confusion. Fionna laughed as he swayed her around the dance floor among Venton students.

"Somebody else wants your attention," Fionna whispered as Halia moved between them. Slipping his hand discreetly to Fionna's bump, Dan rubbed his hands over her until Halia responded to the pressure.

"You know the first time you asked me to dance at Anglington's, you slipped your hand somewhere else," Fionna flirted.

"I'd been staring at your gorgeous ass in that tight leather skirt all night, baby doll. A man only has so much restraint."

"Look at where your roving hands got us." She gestured to her bump.

"Let me see if I can remember everything I said to you that night to get you to leave that bar and take me back to your place. We can go home and do it all over again."

Fionna's heartbeat picked up pace in her rhythms, and the familiar longing he always felt when she was near took up residence in his groin. He'd never get enough of her. He would always want her, and as he shifted his eyes slightly to the left to determine who was glaring at them, he found that reassurance very comforting.

"She hates us so much." Fionna shuddered slightly.

"She doesn't hate you, baby," Dan immediately vowed.

She lifted her head off his shoulder to stare him down. "Emotion is *my* thing, remember?"

"Right. Sorry." Dan grimaced.

"She's angry at the world. I don't have to be a Receiver to figure that out, but she seems to particularly hate us." She continued to glance around the room nervously.

Fury coursed through Dan's shield. Fionna didn't deserve hatred from anyone. She was sweet, good, and kind. "I told you what she said to me when Dad sent me to check on her after that fight. She's angry and jealous of you. She blames me for getting Wilshire suspended and her kids taken away from her. It's easier to blame me than to try even a modicum of introspection."

Hatred led to many places and none of them were good, and people that felt they had nothing else to lose were the most dangerous.

He recalled Fionna sobbing in their bed, lying against him, pleading with him not to get himself in a situation where he could be in danger. His reassurances that he'd never put her or his girls in danger again mocked his shield. Katherine Bryant's daughter screeching that she hated her mother and that she'd ruined her life shattered through Dan's conscience.

"Don't think I don't know who found all of that for them." Wilshire's implicit threat formed a knot-like enclosure around Dan's throat as he wrapped Fionna up tighter in his arms.

"Fi, baby, please let me take you home," he begged. He had to get her away from Katherine Bryant. The fear was palpable in his gut.

"We can't leave yet, but I don't have a good feeling."

"If you don't have a good feeling, we *are* leaving."

She soothed him with her energy. "We're going to be fine. I promise."

CHAPTER 10

LENS FLARE

The song ended, and she guided him back to their table. Keeping his glare leveled on Katherine Bryant, Dan tried to stop the thoughts of Wilshire alone in a cheap hotel room asking his wife for money and what vengeance may surface from living that way for too long.

Fionna's hands moved to her bump. "She has the hiccups," she whispered with an adoring smile.

"When I was pregnant with Daniel, he had them all the time," Mrs. Vindico recalled. Dan was reminded of the fact that his mother loved him and his wife, even if she was often overbearing.

Mentor Bryant had rolled her eyes with Fionna's announcement, and Mrs. Vindico bristled. She reached for the governor's hand. Dan was suddenly aware that Bryant didn't just frighten his wife. She frightened his mother though she would never admit that. She watched her husband go off to work each day and interact with a woman that certainly hadn't shown good moral fiber and appeared to have a thing for older men in powerful positions.

Dan had seen the disgust in his father's eyes when he'd shown him evidence of Katherine Bryant and Dean Wilshire's affair. Governor Vindico would never cheat on his wife, but Dan supposed he understood the concern.

The governor laced his fingers with his wife's. He'd seen the fear as well. In that one simple move, Dan realized the depth of love that his parents held for one another and how much he deeply admired his father.

"It's been a long time since we danced at a Venton formal, but I'm game if you are." The governor offered his wife his arm.

"We didn't dance quite like that." Mrs. Vindico threw a disapproving glance at the dance floor. Everyone turned to see numerous Venton students grinding into their dance partners provocatively.

"Mentor Bryant, I believe your name was at the top of the list of chaperones for this evening, and that isn't appropriate," the governor commanded.

With an audible sigh, Katherine stood and moved to the students. She shook her head.

Dan watched them tone it down slightly, but the derisive eye rolls from the majority of the students she'd reprimanded after her back was turned spoke volumes. She reseated herself.

"I guess Jeff and Becca aren't coming," Fionna lamented. Dan glanced around the large room once again. He hated they were missing out on being seniors because of the baby.

After several faster songs, Fergus approached the dance floor again. "All right, students, it's time for the faculty to teach you a thing or two. All faculty members and your dates, please make your way to the dance floor."

Fionna chuckled at Dan's disdain. "Come on, Mentor Vindico. Dance with me and then I'll let you take me home for a few private tutoring sessions." Her flirting made him ache.

"Is that a promise?" He helped his wife out of her chair.

His parents joined them on the dance floor as the band began playing.

Fionna glanced back at the table where Katherine Bryant was seated and pouting with her arms crossed over her chest. "I feel kind of bad that no one's going to dance with her."

The majority of the staff was married, and certainly no married man was going to ask the chancellor's former mistress to dance unless he was looking for divorce papers himself. The single male portion of the staff was significantly younger than she was, and no one was looking to start the rumor mill.

"She had a choice, and now she's going to have to live with her choice whether she likes it or not."

"I know, but it's easier not to like her when I can't feel how miserable she is."

"Hey, look at me." His wife's beautiful sienna eyes gazed up into his own. "I love you." His vow made her beam. "Dance with me. Just you and me, and then I'm taking you home, baby doll. I plan to spend all night making love to you. I want you to forget about everything else." Dan cradled her as close as he could get her on the dance floor. He wrapped his long, muscled arms around his beautiful wife.

She laid her head on his shoulder and tucked her face into his neck. She wanted to be shielded from the world, wanted to hide away for just a little while. She wanted and needed her husband to stand between her and the cold, cruel, corrosive world around them. Dan would never let her down. He would be her rock and her protection forever. He was her Shield.

They began to sway, and Dan kissed her temple. "Think about it for me, baby doll," he guided as her breath picked up pace. "Think about my hands all over your luscious body. Think about me tasting you, drinking you, then laying you out in my bed, and filling you so full of me all you can do is scream out my name and beg me for more," he murmured softly and made certain she felt his strain against her.

Dan slipped his hand down her side, letting his thumb just barely caress the side of her swollen breast. He made certain no one saw his quick move.

He tempted her, building the need, kindling the fire that he planned to let consume them for the next several hours.

Fionna panted. The storm of passion and desire swam in her eyes as she lifted her head to stare him down.

"Is that what you need, honey?"

Fionna discreetly brushed his strain with her hand. She moved it away a split second later. Giving a heavy nod, her eyes begged and tempted him.

"Good, because I'm gonna make you take it," he assured her as she trembled in his arms. Dan pulled her back in so he could continue building the passion inside of her. "I'm gonna make you feel it, and suck it, and then I'm gonna bury it so deep inside of you that you come undone for me over and over again."

With that, Fionna lifted her head. Her eyes were dark and filled with ardent need. She leaned, and Dan met her swollen lips with his own. He dipped his tongue in her mouth, pulling the erotic energy from her as she began to suck his tongue. She was showing off her skill and making white-hot fire ignite from his groin, eager for her mouth to pull him deep and her tongue to lap at his need. She needed to consume the fire she'd lit.

Dan laced his hand in her hair and pulled her in harder. He devoured her mouth. But suddenly, a spotlight landed on them, shining brightly in their face. Fionna jerked away to shield her eyes.

"What the hell?" Dan spat.

"You've been caught on the kiss cam," Sherman chanted.

A picture of Fionna sucking Dan's tongue was projected up on a blank wall in the room. The students went wild as Fionna blushed violently. The governor shook his head, trying not to laugh, but Mrs. Vindico looked appalled.

As Sherman was the one running the kiss cam, Dan glared. "Take that down now," he demanded.

"Dan," Fionna pled, but suddenly everything went pitch black. Not only was the picture off of the wall, but every light in the building was out along with the speaker systems.

Panic charged through the room now only lit by tiny votive candles on tables. Dan immediately lit a glowing light from his hand and wrapped his powerful shield around Fionna. Students and faculty followed suit, and Dan searched the room. Terror settled in the pit of his stomach.

Katherine Bryant was nowhere to be found.

"What happened?" Fionna panicked. It was a Gifted university.

Although there was certainly public electricity run to the school, to keep the Non-Gifted from being too curious, every light was casted, every breaker held a drawing charge, every fuse held the power of energy around it. The power did not go out at Venton Academy.

CHAPTER 11

ORDERS

Sirens from the security system began blaring.

"Dan, get her home. I don't know what's happening, but you need to get her out of here," the governor commanded. Panic etched his tone. His father was absolutely right. If panic set in and people began fleeing, Fionna could get caught up in the mob. She couldn't move very quickly.

"All right, everyone, let's get all of the chandeliers casted," the governor ordered the students and staff.

"Come on." Dan guided Fionna out of the room. Iodex SUVs were flying into the parking lot.

"Dan, what the hell happened?" Portwood rushed toward them.

"I don't know. Something must've tripped the security alarm, but even that shouldn't have knocked out the power."

"We'll get everyone out. Get Fionna out of here," Portwood commanded. Dan let the order wash through him.

It was distinctly odd to have a man that had been his subordinate giving him orders, but life had changed, and he'd clearly trained Landon correctly. Getting a pregnant woman in her last trimester out of a tense situation that could turn dangerous was precisely what was to be done first no matter who was running the show.

Landon turned to Mike Ericcson. "Get in there and get the governor out now."

Mike took off.

"Fergus probably broke Venton," Logan huffed as he met Rainer. They both raced from their cars. Rainer nodded as he laughed his agreement. They both halted at Dan and Fionna.

"I'm gonna go with the assumption you can get her safely to your car?" Rainer was clearly not certain how to both follow protocol and not offend his former boss.

"Yeah, take your baby mama home, Vindico." Logan tried to soften the blow with a joke. Fionna giggled in spite of everything.

"I've got it," Dan assured them.

"You know I had to ask." Rainer hesitated.

"I know." Dan guided Fionna into the parking lot. He heard Portwood's voice project throughout the banquet room. "We're going to get the students out first. Please proceed to the nearest exits. Make certain that you give your name and grade to one of the officers posted near the doors, so that we know we've gotten everyone out."

Dan opened the door to the Ferrari and tucked Fionna inside.

"How on earth did that happen? And where was Katherine Bryant?" she demanded as soon as Dan started the car and pulled away from the school.

"I don't know, but you're going home and away from this."

"It's kind of nice to have all of Iodex so worried about my sweet Halia," she admitted hesitantly.

"They love you, sweetheart. Not as much as I do, but they love you." He winked at her.

"They only love me because you mean so much to them," she reminded Dan.

Supposing that was probably true, Dan racked his brain. What the hell had happened?

"Dan?" Fionna whispered a few minutes later.

He lifted his eyebrows. "What, baby doll?"

"It means a lot to me that you left. I know that was really difficult to do, and I'm sure they could have used your help."

Pleased that he was beginning to show her that he could walk away from a job if it was for her, he smiled. "You come first. I keep telling you. You and my baby girls—nothing else even matters."

"I love you." Her voice was suddenly rough from her plea.

"I love you too. Would my baby mama like a milkshake?" He hoped to get her mind off of their disconcerting evening though he could think of nothing else.

She blushed, and Dan immediately moved the car to the exit ramp near McLean where Mae's Milkshake Shack was located.

"I'm just gonna get bigger," she fussed.

"You are not big, and Halia likes milkshakes. She told me."

"Did she?" Fionna laughed.

"What? She can tell you she wants coffee but not tell me she wants milkshakes?" Fionna cracked up. If she would just keep laughing, then everything would be all right. The plaguing confusion of all that had happened would drown out in light of one of his favorite sounds.

He led Fionna to a booth inside of Mae's and wondered if he should call his father. He was certain Ericcson had gotten them out first, so he wasn't certain his dad would know anything. Ordering Fionna's strawberry milkshake and a chocolate one for himself, Dan tried to focus on his wife.

"Halia says, 'Thank you, Daddy,' for her milkshake," Fionna teased.

"Tell my baby girl anytime."

"What do you think happened?" Fionna asked as they both slurped down their shakes.

"I don't have any idea." Defeat pulsed in his shield. As they were finishing, Dan's cell rang. Relief flooded through him.

"What happened?" he demanded of Logan.

"Where are you?"

"I brought Fi to Mae's for a shake."

"Be there in a sec. Is Fi up for a little reconnaissance?" Logan sounded perturbed.

"What?" Dan demanded. "Fionna is not doing reconnaissance." The line went dead.

Haydenshire Farm was only a mile from Mae's. Dan wasn't surprised that Logan was nearby, but he had no idea why Logan thought Dan would ever allow Fionna to be in harm's way. Before he could explain the conversation to Fionna, Logan was entering Mae's.

He slid into the booth beside Fionna.

"A few little problems," Logan sighed.

"What?"

"Let's talk in the truck."

Standing, Dan grabbed Logan's shoulder. "Where are we going? You've lost your mind if you think I'm putting my wife and my baby girl in danger."

"Dan, come on. Would I take her anywhere that there was even the possibility of her getting hurt? Give me a little credit, please. I can't say anything in here, and we need to hurry."

"Come on," Fionna agreed.

"I'll sit in the back." Dan climbed in the back of Logan's extended cab pickup. He wedged himself inside, allowing Logan to help Fionna up into the passenger seat. "Now what is going on?"

"Obviously someone caused the power outage at the academy," Logan stated as soon as he'd cranked the truck. "Some genius sent a major electric pulse through the advanced lock on the test vault. I'm talking enough power that it took more than one person to send that much through that system."

"Which means several people broke into the administration building," Dan gasped.

"Why would they do that when there were so many people at the school?" Fionna asked. "And I didn't feel anyone with intentions like that. I would've felt that."

"We weren't anywhere near the admin building, sweetheart," Dan reminded her. "And we were in a constant sea of people. You did keep telling me something was off."

Fionna nodded, but she didn't seem like she believed his reassurances.

"Their cars were easier to hide for one thing, and they knew that even though there were tons of people there tonight, it wasn't likely that anyone would be in the admin building," Logan explained.

"Where are we going?" Dan asked.

"We're going to the Holiday Inn in Arlington."

"Why?" Fionna was immediately intrigued.

"Before we started getting the students out, just as Tuttle pulled in, he saw a navy blue Lincoln circle the back lots. They stopped, and someone got in the car. Tuttle knew your dad had asked you to look into Wilshire's affair, so he didn't report it to Portwood. But he got the tag. It was his car."

"I guess I owe my future brother-in-law quite a bit," Dan admitted.

"Mentor Bryant's car was the only one left in the Venton parking lot after we got everyone out." Logan shot Dan a knowing glance. "If she's at that hotel with him, I have to tell Portwood. If either of them had anything to do with that level of damage to a secured vault, we're going to have to open this up to a full-on Iodex investigation."

"That's fine, but neither of them did it." Dan shook his head.

"How do you know?" Fionna turned back to study him. "She was so angry."

"Yeah, she was angry and hurt enough to drive her back into Wilshire's arms, but she wouldn't have wanted anyone to know where she was going or who she called. Causing a big disturbance would have been the last possible thing she would have wanted to do."

"That's what Rainer and I thought too," Logan agreed. "But then Jeff wondered if she didn't mean to do anything more than shut down the power, so she could slip away. I thought about that. Jeff doesn't have as much training as I do or as Rainer does, and none of us have as much as you do. We all know the best way to get out of wherever you are is to just slip away quietly. You of all people know that the best place to get lost is right in the middle of a crowd.

"You're the guy that got your wife and kid out of Paris without anyone in the world knowing where you were taking them, when the entire world wanted to know where you were."

"Okay, so what?" Dan agreed.

Fionna had been listening intently. She nodded. "Jeff is thinking that Katherine Bryant wouldn't have known how to get out of Venton without anyone seeing her. She thinks people are paying more attention to her than they actually are. She would've thought she needed a distraction."

"Jeff Strenton is going to make one hell of an officer," Dan admitted, with Logan nodding his adamant agreement.

"He and Rainer are hanging out in the Porsche, hidden at Venton, waiting to see who brings her back to her car in case we don't find them at the Holiday Inn." Logan took the exit into downtown Arlington and headed toward the hotel just off the interstate. He parked the truck in the back of the Holiday Inn near the dumpsters.

"How do we figure out if they're in there?" Fionna sounded intrigued. To Dan's astonishment, she appeared to be enjoying her first stakeout.

"I can't believe she asked him to come get her." Logan shook his head.

"Oh, I can," Fionna assured him. "She's completely miserable. Think about it. No one wants to be near her even if they've done the same thing or have considered doing the same thing. Everyone is treating her like she has the plague. Her husband is hurt and furious, obviously, but she knows that's her fault. Her kids hate her for how this disrupted their lives. I really think she sat with us tonight trying to pick a fight just so someone would speak to her, acknowledge her existence. When you're that depressed and all alone, I'd bet the other person that probably feels exactly the same way is better than nothing."

"And her husband filed for legal separation, which was granted, so technically she's not breaking the law anymore," Dan pointed out.

"Well, I gotta tell you, I'm not interested in busting in that room even with you as my partner and seeing what's probably going on in there. What do we do if they stay all night? My wife's going to freak when she finds out that it's my fault her favorite patient isn't at home with her feet up." Logan gestured to Fionna.

She beamed. "Aww, I'm her favorite patient?"

"Hell yeah. We love you guys. You know that."

Dan chuckled but then allayed Logan's fears. "We're not going to have to go in there. This is her week to spend with her kids. I'm sure she's desperately trying to prove herself to them. She'll stay here only until the time that she would have headed home from the dance. That's how she's justifying taking time away from them. That's how their relationship has always worked. It's always been under the cover of darkness and in the shadows because ultimately everything about it began as a lie."

"Okay, but how does them being here together prove that they sent the pulse through the lock on the test vault?" Fionna asked.

"I've taken to calling her Catwoman," Dan stated in answer to Logan's deeply impressed expression.

"No joke, man." He grinned. "It doesn't really, but it does prove that he picked her up from the school. Dan's dad told him not to be on Venton property unless he had written permission from Governor Vindico, which he does not have. We're building a case. You were there on the night this happened. You weren't supposed to be there, so what else did you do or see?" Logan concluded.

Dan tried to sort through everything that had happened. If Katherine Bryant was there with the chancellor, they would most likely be arrested and taken in for questioning. Iodex would take over the case. Dan couldn't continue to play personal detective in order to save his father's reputation in light of property damage of that magnitude. Deep regret worked through him. He just couldn't let his father take the fall for Wilshire's doings.

"But Wilshire didn't even get out of his car," Fionna began again. "He's kind of a coward. I personally think that men that cheat are all cowards, but I just don't believe that he has the ba..." she began but then blushed violently.

Logan cracked up. "You don't think he's got the cojones to go in a Venton building."

"Right, and you said it was probably more than one person that sent that pulse. She didn't do that alone."

Everyone was thoughtful for a moment.

"Did you see whose passcode was used to enter the building?" Dan asked.

"Yeah," Logan sighed uncomfortably. "There were six codes used to access the building this evening, but the time stamps on the codes were within seconds of each other. Obviously, they're fake because the security system takes three minutes to reset once someone has entered after hours legally. Whoever sent the false codes must not have known that." Dan braced. He knew what was coming. "Of the six codes that were used, one was yours, one was your dad's, one was Mentor Bryant's, one was Fergus's, one was Jeff's, and one was created on the fly but doesn't belong to anyone.

"But," Logan added quickly, "we do have you two on the kiss cam at the exact same moment that your code was used in the building. Yours was the last one entered." He lifted a pair of binoculars to his eyes to check the front and back exits to the hotel. He'd parked strategically where he could see both.

"Everyone that anyone is suspicious of," Dan concluded.

"Who could have made up their own code that would work?" Fionna shifted uncomfortably.

"Baby, what's wrong?" Dan no longer cared who set a new passcode.

"Oh...nothing really," Fionna assured, but Logan and Dan were both aware she was lying.

"Fi?" Dan urged.

"Do we need to go?" Logan asked. Dan was immensely thankful for Logan's concern and his willingness to take care of Fionna over taking care of the case.

A blush creeped up Fionna's neck and pooled in her cheeks. "I just kind of need to take off these heels because my feet are swelling around them," she whimpered.

"Take them off," Dan and Logan insisted simultaneously. Neither of them saw this as a problem, but Fionna was thoroughly embarrassed.

"Baby, it's fine." Dan leaned and laced his fingers through his wife's.

"You're not going to offend me," Logan assured her. "I grew up with six older brothers. One of them is Garrett, so I'm pretty much un-offendable."

Logan's cell rang suddenly. Dan saw the name as Logan lifted the phone. "Hey, what's up?" he asked Rainer. "How the hell?" he gasped. "No, not yet." He shook his head. "I'll see you tomorrow." Logan ended the call. "An Uber just dropped Katherine Bryant back at her car."

"But how?" Fionna demanded.

"Don't know. She must've left here just before we pulled in."

"Is Rainer arresting her?" Dan hadn't seen the chancellor's car on Venton property, and he couldn't make the calls anymore.

"No, not yet. Let's see if we can't figure this out. Dad doesn't want this falling in your dad's lap any more than you do."

"Okay, but before we try to figure this out, I have to go inside and pee," Fionna finally admitted the source of her greatest discomfort.

"Sweetheart." Dan shook his head, but Fionna started to open the door to the truck.

"NO!" Logan and Dan both reached for her.

"Please," she begged.

"Okay, but not here. That's Wilshire's car." Logan pointed out the navy blue Lincoln parked in the lot. "How about McDonald's?" He gestured across the street.

"I'm thinking anywhere that we can get quickly," Dan instructed.

In under two minutes, Logan had the truck parked near the side entrance closest to the ladies' room.

"Dan, I can't get my shoes back on." She was on the verge of tears, and Dan's heart fissured. He racked his brain but couldn't come up with a way to help her other than to carry her inside, which he knew would do nothing to soothe her nerves.

"Here." Logan reached into a pocket on the back of the passenger seat and pulled out a pair of flip-flops. "They're Ad's. She certainly won't care. I keep them in here for when she goes out with me to check the fields barefoot. Sometimes the back of the farm gets a little swampy."

"Logan Haydenshire, I love you." Fionna pulled the flip-flops over her swollen feet and flung the door open.

"Here, I'll take her. She's gonna wet her pants before you get yourself wedged out of my truck." Logan chuckled as he quickly escorted Fionna inside.

They returned several minutes later with Fionna looking vastly more comfortable.

"I'm sorry, honey," Dan apologized.

"You're sorry? I'm the worst detective ever. Swollen feet and peeing constantly. I'm so embarrassed. Catwoman probably never has swollen feet."

Chuckling, Logan shook his head. "I'm the one who dragged you out here. His kid is dancing on your bladder or whatever, right?" he reminded her kindly. Dan wasn't accustomed to another man—other than Garrett—taking such good care of his wife. He wasn't certain how he should feel, but he didn't really care for it. "Trust me, I have a wife, two little sisters, and several sisters-in-law at this point, so stopping at public restrooms is something I'm very familiar with." Logan continued to try and quell Fionna's embarrassment. "Rainer and Em and me and Ad rode to the beach over Labor Day weekend with Patrick and Lucy. Good God, I swear we stopped at every exit so Lucy could pee. It took us, like, ten hours to get to Virginia Beach. But Patrick's kid is dancing on *her* bladder, so nothing anyone can do."

Logan headed back to Dan's Ferrari in the parking lot of Mae's.

"Who could have made up a working code to get into the Venton admin building?" Fionna asked again.

Deep concern continued to tense in Dan's shield. He'd already put the pieces together, while he waited on Logan and Fionna to emerge from McDonalds. "I think somebody must suspect Jeff is helping me out," he admitted.

"Oh my gosh! That's why they used his code. They're trying to frame him?"

"I still say it looks like Mentor Bryant," Logan added quickly. "Think about it. You know she hates you and your dad. She told Wilshire not to hire you. She just typed in all of the codes she could think of who were people she'd like to get into trouble or who people are suspicious about.

"Everybody's talking about Fergus because of Tilly. If she has any idea that Jeff is how you showed your dad all of the stuff about Wilshire putting money back in Venton, she'd be pissed. She added hers trying to throw us off."

"That's precisely what I was thinking as well," Dan agreed. "She had Becca in one of her classes last year. Maybe Becca said something about how good Jeff is at casting electronics."

"What a bitch," Fionna spat.

As Logan pulled into the parking lot, he smirked and offered Dan his hand. "You married well, my friend."

Fionna laughed as Dan nodded. "That I did."

"I have to make certain there's no way Jeff could be implicated in any of this," Dan lamented as soon as Fionna was in the Ferrari and he'd headed toward home.

"He wasn't even there…" Fionna's argument died out as soon as she realized what Jeff's not being at the dance would mean to someone that was trying to frame him. "I bet she heard me say something about them not being there at the table."

Dan recalled Fionna's worrying out loud at their table while Katherine Bryant was seated nearby.

"But how did she know how to make up a new passcode that would work?"

"Wilshire," Dan spat. He was hardly able to believe that the chancellor and a mentor would stoop low enough to frame a student just to cover up their affair.

"You think he told her how the passcodes are set? He helped her try and frame Jeff? I don't know, Dan. That seems really far-fetched."

"He was putting hundreds of thousands of dollars in the Venton general fund to cover something up, baby."

She shook her head. "Is there anything they won't do?"

"Remember, Officer Hot Lips, we don't have any proof yet. Nothing other than Wilshire's car on the property, and that isn't enough to do anything. He could say one of his kids borrowed his car. Hell, he could say it was stolen, and unless I want to hand this off to Portwood, the fact that we know his car was at the Holiday Inn does us no good. Wilshire and Bryant don't have to tell me anything. I'm not an officer anymore." He sincerely wished that weren't the case, but he tried to shake off that feeling. "We have to have more to go on."

"Do you think they slept together again?" Fionna sounded disgusted by the thought.

Dan nodded. He refused to lie to her even if it might've lessened the burdens held in the truth.

"She didn't want to think anymore."

Dan's heart sank as he watched his wife grapple with truths of the cold, cruel world. She was his light, his warmth, his wildflower. She was his Maylea, able to brighten any area she was in, able to make everything around her beautiful. But there was no beauty in an affair. There was only pain and scars that could never be mended. Irreparable damage to everyone involved.

"And you know what? That's a perfectly fine way to feel. It's fine for you to want me to make it all go away for a while or vice versa. If she'd sought her husband or at the very least divorced him when she realized she no longer wanted him to be the one who shared her burdens, then it would've been fine. But she didn't. She wanted someone else to take on the pain and the feelings she couldn't comprehend, and now, she's going to let him do it all over again."

"She was there less than two hours," Fionna whispered in harrowing disbelief.

"They can't be seen in the light. There is no holding her all night long or even taking their time. She has to go home to her kids. She'd never allow it to take away from them again. That was the negotiation she decided on."

Dan pulled in their driveway as Fionna nodded her understanding.

"She must feel all alone and like he's the only person that understands."

Dan kissed her forehead sweetly. "We can't save them now." He guided her into the house.

Their very groggy little girl was dressed in her pink frog pajamas and lying in Gretta's lap awaiting their return. "She wanted Daddy to tuck her in," Gretta explained.

Dan lifted Aida up into his arms.

"I missed you." She yawned and tucked her head into Dan's neck.

"We missed you too," Dan assured her as he carried her up the stairs.

CHAPTER 12

REPARATIONS

The following Friday, Jeff came by Dan's office before heading to work at Iodex. "Hey, I got your text." He closed the door behind him.

Dan pulled an envelope from his laptop bag. "I wanted to give you this, and I wanted to give you a few reminders for while I'm in Kauai."

Sinking down in one of the chairs in front of Dan's desk, Jeff took the envelope.

"You're planning on working all week next week, right?"

"Yes, sir, and Becca's going to pull her first full week at the Gifted daycare, so we might be able to actually, like, order a pizza or something," Jeff tried for a joke, but Dan caught the exhaustion in the quip.

"Have a slice for me." He gestured to the envelope and pretended he hadn't noticed the apprehension.

"What's this?" Jeff asked as he removed the check.

"Your bonus." Dan chuckled as Jeff's eyes goggled over the amount that would easily cover two months of Jeff and Becca's rent and several nice dinners out.

"For what?"

"You've cloned laptops and cell phones, hacked into the academy's most secure files, you made my dad a duplicate copy of the books so that he could compare his to Wilshire's, showed me all of the sites where the exams are being sold, you helped Logan figure out who probably sent the pulse through the new vault security system, went on a stakeout with Rainer, and last night, you and Becca kept Aida so Fi and I could have dinner and go to childbirth class."

A deep flush stained Jeff's cheeks. "Yeah, but I mean, you're training me, and Becca loves playing with Aida. You let us have all of your furniture. You let us live with you and Fionna." He shook his head and set the check back on the desk. "And that wasn't a stakeout. I sat in Rainer's Porsche for an hour, and after she left, he let me drive it."

"Sweet ride, isn't it?" Dan allowed with a wry grin. He'd driven Rainer's loaded Boxster convertible a few times, and it was definitely a rush.

"I'll say."

Dan handed the check back to Jeff. "That's not just from me. That's from my dad and Governor Haydenshire and myself. We really couldn't have done this without you. You earned every bit of that."

"Sir, I can't..." Jeff shook his head, but Dan wasn't taking no for an answer.

"You either deposit that, or I'll call Will Haydenshire and have it direct-deposited in your account. The choice is yours."

Jeff gave him a begrudged nod. "You have way too many friends in high places."

"That's probably true." Dan chuckled. "How's Becca doing? Fi said she was a little tired last night?"

"She's okay, I guess."

Concerned, Dan grabbed a Dr Pepper from his shelf, chilled it, and handed it to Jeff before duplicating the process for himself.

"Could I ask you something?" Jeff popped the top of the Dr Pepper.

"Of course." Dan knew there was something eating at him. He'd been distracted for most of class and their lab.

"It's just..." Jeff seemed to be reconsidering.

"Come on, I haven't let you down yet, have I?"

"Becca's kind of..." Jeff hesitated.

A gnawing concern began to swirl in the pit of Dan's stomach. "The baby's all right?"

Jeff's grin relieved him. "We saw Adeline Tuesday. She did an ultrasound. I couldn't tell much, but she said he looks healthy. Everything looks good."

"Good," Dan echoed. "What's going on then?"

An audible breath escaped Jeff's lungs. "It's just that the Sapmans kind of were able to give Bec whatever she wanted, and I really want to do that too. I just can't right now. And she kind of doesn't understand..." he choked in defeat.

"How little money you have right now," Dan concluded for him. He didn't need Jeff to finish. He could feel defeat rolling in his energy.

Jeff looked utterly relieved to have shared his burden.

"How bad is it?"

"It's not her fault," Jeff declared adamantly.

Dan smiled. "Okay."

"Her parents never made her pay bills or anything. She really didn't even understand how credit cards work. When I tried to explain it, she thought I was mad at her, and she started crying..." He gushed out the heartbreak, clearly hoping that Dan could offer him some peaceable solution. Drawing another deep breath, he continued. "I wasn't mad at her. I swear. I would never be mad at her. I was just frustrated. It's like to Bec, shopping at Target is saving money because it's so much cheaper than, like, shopping at Nordstrom. I can't seem to make her understand that Target is still too much."

Dan felt truly sorry for him. He didn't want to tell Becca no, but he was going to have to start.

"Do you have a budget?"

"Kind of. I showed her how to balance the checkbook and how to pay the bills. She'd never even logged into a checking account." He sighed as shock washed through Dan.

"But when I said, 'this is what we have left over for food and stuff,' that seemed to depress her more. You have to understand. She had three gas cards, a card to all of her favorite department stores, a gold card, and a debit card linked to her parents' checking account. Her dad paid them every month. She had no idea how any of it worked. I just don't want to disappoint her." He finally attached what he clearly considered to be the most harrowing piece of the puzzle.

"Believe it or not, I do completely understand," Dan began. Jeff's brow furrowed.

When Dan had quickly worked Fionna Styler from a one-night stand, to his girlfriend, to his fiancée, to his wife in just a few months' time, she'd been the lead Receiver for the Arlington Angels. When they'd met, she was bringing in ten times what Dan made in a year. But it wasn't Fionna Dan was referring to.

"The most important thing is that you keep talking. Amelia and I fought about money constantly. She wanted a big house out near where we'd grown up. We signed the papers once we both had jobs. The deal was that if we bought the house, we couldn't afford to do other stuff. But my idea of not doing other stuff and her idea were very, very different." Raw regret washed through him.

"How'd you make it work?"

"We didn't. Not really. That's what I'm telling you. Talk don't yell. Really talk about each and every bill. Try to be patient with her. Like you said, she doesn't understand. Didn't she have to take the banking and budgeting class here as a sub-freshman?"

"She did, but she didn't really do that well. I don't think she ever thought she'd need it back then. They should teach that class more often, not just in the prep school."

Studying Jeff closely, Dan drew a deep breath and decided to go on. "I've never told anyone this," he admitted. "Not Fi, not my dad, not even Fitzroy. He's my—"

"He was your partner in special ops, and you worked the task force in Paris with him when you first started at Iodex," Jeff supplied.

"Yeah." Dan found it odd that he was chuckling. "Anyway, like I said, we fought about money all the time. And it certainly wasn't Amelia's fault that I was damned and determined to catch Wretchkinsides, but the money was part of it.

"I guess I figured being out making more money was better than my being home fighting about not having enough. I wanted the recognition and the fame. I wanted Wretchkinsides, don't get me wrong. I was a complete ass, but the money was part of why I worked so many hours for so long." The confession eased the tense set of Dan's shield.

"But that wasn't the answer. We needed to talk and work on the relationship and the budget and the bills. Instead of me just shouting and then walking out and slamming the door behind me, I should've stayed home and really talked it through with her. You'll find something that works, and Becca will learn. She's young. Try to give her some time, and try to be patient. Explain it to her carefully." Dan willed Jeff not to make his mistakes.

"I will. I promise. And thank you for this." He held up the check.

"Just keep up the good work, and one more thing before you go. Remember that we suspect that Katherine Bryant knows you're helping me out. Make certain that over the break you don't do anything on the cases we're working. I know you're planning on working at Iodex all week, but maybe you and Becca take a night off from budgets and bills and just be seniors. Enjoy being newlyweds. I'm not taking any of this with me to Kauai. I'm gonna give myself a break and Fi as well." Dan fought not to tell Jeff about the offer he knew Portwood was going to make as soon as he got to work. It wasn't his offer to share, but he was certain it would ease at least some of the constant strain Jeff was carrying.

"I promise to only work on cases that are *on* the books."

"Text me if anything significant happens," was Dan's final request.

"I will," Jeff assured him. "Have a nice trip."

"Plan to."

CHAPTER 13

WOODPECKER

Dan made it home just a few minutes before Aida's bus.

"Hey!" Fionna rushed into his arms.

"Hey, sweetheart." He kissed the side of her head then leaned to kiss Halia's bump. "Are you ready to go home, baby girl?"

"She's ready, and Aida's ecstatic. I packed everything. I just have to get ready for the shower and then tomorrow morning we're going home," Fionna tittered on the brink of elation.

"And you're sure you want me at this thing?" He secretly wished the Angels baby shower for Fionna wasn't coed.

"I know you don't want to go, but it's a couples shower."

"I'm just not entirely certain what to do at a baby shower," he admitted.

"Chloe's throwing it, so it could be entirely inappropriate. You know, like instead of rubber duckies floating in the punch bowls, it could be spiked and have plastic sex toys floating in it."

Dan scowled. "That's just disturbing."

Fionna pulled off the knit maternity top and stretch pants she was wearing. Dan gave her a hungry grin. "I'm not sure we have time for that, baby doll, but I'm not above trying."

"I'm getting ready for the shower, Mr. Vindico," Fionna drawled flirtatiously as she wrapped her arms around his neck. Dan slid his hands from her shoulder blades to her backside. Her back arched from the motion.

"And what shall we do after this shower, Mrs. Vindico?" His voice was low and reverent.

Giving him a breathy moan, Fionna's eyes flashed as she gazed up at him. "We should start our vacation a little early."

Dan dipped his hands down the back of her panties. He kneaded her backside, cupping it and pulling her closer into his hungry embrace. "And how shall we do that?" He let his breath caress her neck before his lips began tasting her skin.

"I have several ideas." Fionna shivered in his arms, making Dan ache.

"Mommy, I'm home!" Aida called from downstairs. "I need you."

"I'll look forward to hearing those ideas after the shower." Dan opened the bedroom door. "I'm coming, Aida."

He blew Fionna a kiss before heading downstairs to welcome Aida home.

To his shock, she wasn't alone.

"What the hell are you doing here?" he demanded of Cindy McBeechum, the school board liaison and the most annoying woman on the planet.

"You and your wife failed to sign up for our McCarron Meet Your Beary Helpful Staff conference. I did mention at the open house meeting that I would be stopping by all of our new little bears' homes if you didn't make an appointment for us to get to know each other."

To Dan's horror, at that moment Fionna descended the stairs. As he turned to take her in, his eyes goggled. She crested the bottom of the steps wearing nothing more than a low slung pair of short knit shorts that fell under Halia's large bump.

"I forgot my dress is in the laundry room," she explained before she turned to see Cindy McBeechum staring at her on full display in their living room. Fionna screamed as she covered her breasts. She spun her back to Ms. McBeechum, and Dan floundered around in his mind to figure out what to say.

"What are you doing here?" Fionna screeched. She kept her back to their uninvited guest. Dan moved in front of her.

"We're trying to get ready to go on vacation. This clearly isn't a good day, and I would appreciate it in the future if you could call before you just show up in our home," Dan ordered.

"I informed you that I would be visiting the homes of our little bears that were new to McCarron this year. I must say, Mrs. Vindico, I do not believe in any way that Mama Bears should walk around their home unclothed in your state. I will be mentioning this to the school counselor."

Dan's jaw clenched in fury as Fionna spun around, keeping her hands over her breasts.

"I don't walk around like this when we have company. I had no idea you were here."

"Sweetheart, why don't you go get dressed?" Dan soothed but then turned on McBeechum with infuriated gall coursing rapidly through his veins. Fionna began marching up the stairs as Dan glared at the woman standing in his living room.

"I do not appreciate your showing up here uninvited, and how dare you tell my wife what she can and cannot do in her own home? There is absolutely nothing wrong with my wife's state. She is pregnant. That *is* how we get children here, is it not?" Dan gestured to Aida who was staring up at him in shock. "You want to get to know my family, Mrs. McBeechum? Great. Listen up." Dan's fervor gained in intensity as he thought about everything his family had endured at the hands of the school board.

"Aida is our pride and joy," he vowed, and Aida beamed. "That being said, I do not appreciate the school board deciding when I can pick up my little girl, nor do I appreciate her grandfather being denied access to her when he has permission to pick her up anytime per the documents we signed when we registered Aida for school. I do not like and will not stand for you trying to ban books or for you scolding my daughter because she reads above her grade level, nor will she be selling any kind of cheese or wrapping paper to fund your committee on bigotry. You showing up in my home uninvited is not only incredibly rude, it's also intrusive. Just how did you get in here?" Dan demanded.

"Aida let me in. I just followed her bus here," Mrs. McBeechum informed Dan. She sounded highly put out.

Aida was shaking her head vehemently.

"What really happened, baby?" Dan asked.

"I know I'm not allowed to answer the door if Mommy or Daddy aren't with me, and I didn't. You have to say, 'who is it,' and then wait and go get Mommy or Daddy. I'm not allowed to open the door. You said that my mommy said you could come in. I said I have to ask permission. You said that my parents wouldn't mind because you were from school. She wouldn't let me come get Mommy or close the door."

Fionna made it back down the stairs fully clothed in time to hear Aida's explanation. She pulled Aida to her and let her rest her head against Halia's bump as Dan's eyes flashed in acrimony.

McBeechum drew herself up into a monument of righteous indignation. "You do understand that we consider your family part of our family. We feel we need to know what kind of homes our students come from in order to best serve our community."

Forcing a mirthless chuckle, Dan shook his head. "You consider my family your family, do you? Aida has a family, Mrs. McBeechum. It took my own father the better part of half an hour to gain himself access to his granddaughter. This is after, as I've already informed you, my wife and I filled out the necessary paperwork to make certain that he was approved to pick her up. And after my wife phoned the school to inform you that he would be picking Aida up from school that day. Now, you've gained yourself access to my home by way of a child, which is against the law. I will be pressing charges."

Glowing crimson, Mrs. McBeechum's face contorted into an infuriated scowl. "Aida, dear, perhaps you should run along and play. I need to speak with your parents," she commanded.

Tears pricked Aida's eyes as she nodded her understanding that she was being sent away.

"Come with Mommy, sweetheart."

"Mrs. Vindico, it is pertinent that I speak with you," Mrs. McBeechum demanded.

Fionna's eyes narrowed to dagger slits. "My daughter is scared. I don't understand how you don't see or feel that, but she is. You can say whatever it is you came to say to my husband. Aida has two parents. I'm going to go upstairs with our daughter to try to calm her down as you have frightened her and made her feel uncomfortable in her own home."

With that, Fionna guided Aida into the kitchen, grabbed her a granola bar and a Capri Sun, then led her upstairs.

Dan crossed his massive arms over his chest and glared at the woman in his living room.

"What is it you came to say?"

"Well..." Mrs. McBeechum began to pout as she adjusted her large black felt vest that was decorated with cutouts of one-room schoolhouses and stick-figure children in primary colors.

"I have some grave concerns about Aida. You know, often times *adopted children*, especially those that aren't from here..." She said the phrase as if being from Brazil was a failing on Aida's part. Dan's blood boiled. "Those kinds of children don't fit in the way we'd like for them to," she sneered.

"Those kinds of children?" Dan snarled. He vibrated in his hate-fueled fury. His shield flared red.

Mrs. McBeechum's eyes goggled as she shrank under Dan's glare. Seeming to decide to speed up her speech, she drew a deep breath. "I've been observing in Mrs. Powell's classroom, and I have to tell you that Aida seems to be overly empathetic with the other children. She's just a little too helpful. Do you understand?" she quizzed in a tone that said she thought Dan was unintelligent.

"NO," he growled.

"Aida tends to worry about the other children. She wants to help them even at her own detriment. That's not normal for a child her age."

Dan ground his teeth as he tried to discern how to explain to the Non-Gifted woman in his home that his daughter was a perfectly normal Gifted Receiver. "It seems to me that there are far worse things my child could be other than overly empathetic. The world could use a great deal more empathy."

"I feel it would serve Aida well to speak to a child psychologist about her desperate desire to care for other children. I'm certain you know that growing up in a place like an *orphanage* probably affected her deeply," Mrs. McBeechum clucked out her mocked lamentation.

"Aida does see a counselor," Dan menaced. "And I will be more than happy to speak with both Mrs. Powell and Mrs. Willow, Aida's Gifted teacher. If they feel that Aida might need to see the counselor more often, then my wife and I will determine how we'd like to handle that, but for right now I would appreciate it if you would stay the hell away from my little girl. See to it that Aida never feels your deep-seated prejudices against her because she wasn't born in Arlington," he shouted.

"Other than that, I think that my wife and I will continue to make certain that Aida knows just how much we love and adore her and that we couldn't care less where she came from because she is our child."

"I just don't feel that you're listening, Mr. Vindico. Aida doesn't seem to be like the other children in her class."

"I've met several of the other little girls in Aida's class, and I cannot tell you how pleased I am that she isn't like them. And I just don't feel that you're understanding that I am now politely asking you to leave my home. But please know that I'm rapidly losing patience, and very soon, I'm not going to be so nice."

"Your family's inability to follow rules seems to have already affected Aida, even if she isn't really your child." Mrs. McBeechum huffed out the words that Dan was certain might be her last.

Fire seared through his veins. His shield lit all around him. "Get out of my home!" he growled. "You seem to be under some great misapprehension that my wife and I care at all what you think. You are nothing more than a pompous, racist bitch, and I won't have you standing in my home near my children saying things like that," he shouted furiously.

Dan caught the flashing blue lights as they turned into his driveway. He ran his hand over his mouth to try to hide his grin. His wife was not only sweet and beautiful, she was a genius.

"I have never been spoken to so rudely when I am doing nothing more than showing my deep concern for Aida," Mrs. McBeechum scorned.

Waiting until Garrett was far enough up the walkway to hear him, Dan spat, "Did you or did you not follow my child home from school and then use her to gain yourself access to my home?"

"I did inform you I would be dropping by. There was no reason Aida shouldn't have allowed me in your home. You've obviously frightened her not allowing her to even open the door."

Dressed in full uniform and sporting a very convincing scowl, Garrett stepped onto the front porch.

Dan feigned shock.

"Are you Mr. Vindico?" Garrett quizzed as both he and Dan made a concerted effort not to laugh.

"Yes, sir. Is there a problem?" Dan replied as Mrs. McBeechum's mouth hung open.

"You tell me. I just got a call from Mrs. Vindico stating that someone from your daughter's school had followed her home. They entered your home with your seven-year-old, frightening her and your wife? Is that correct, sir?" Garrett played his part well.

"Yes, she's right here." Dan gestured to Mrs. McBeechum.

Garrett narrowed his eyes hatefully. He no longer had to playact. If anything scared Fionna or Aida, he would see to it that it was ended violently.

"Officer Haydenshire, ma'am." Garrett flashed his badge. "Let me go ahead and warn you, the commonwealth does not take child endangerment or abduction lightly."

"I am not abducting her."

"I just heard you admit to Mr. Vindico here that you entered his home with his daughter without his permission. He is the homeowner, correct, Mr. Vindico?" Garrett turned back to Dan.

"Yes, I am."

"I'm the school board teacher liaison," she spouted.

Garrett feigned deep concern. "So, you're telling me that you have access to young children on a daily basis?"

"I have never been treated so rudely," Mrs. McBeechum decreed. "I am leaving."

"Just a minute." Garrett halted Mrs. McBeechum on the porch.

"Is that your Explorer in the driveway?" He gestured to the tan-colored Ford in Dan and Fionna's drive.

"Yes," Mrs. McBeechum huffed.

"Are you aware your tag's been expired for three months now?"

"I haven't had time to get to the tag office. I have a very demanding job on the school board. I do very important work."

Dan rolled his eyes.

"You mean like forcing your way into the Vindicos' home uninvited and frightening Mrs. Vindico and their little girl?"

Her face was pulsing purple. She was on the verge of apoplexy.

"I'm going to have to write you a ticket for that tag and demand that you leave the Vindicos' home." With that, he pulled the metal clipboard from his belt and wrote the ticket that Dan was certain would cost her several hundred dollars. "You make certain you take care of that, and get your tag up to date," Garrett ordered. "And I'm gonna go ahead and tell you that if I were you, I'd stay away from the Vindicos' home and their children."

Mrs. McBeechum jerked the paper from Garrett's hand and stomped toward her car.

Dan and Garrett watched her try to maneuver around Garrett's squad car and then drive away. They doubled over as she made her way down the street.

"Garrett!" Aida cheered as she raced to him. Fionna chuckled as she followed behind her.

"Hey, baby girl." Garrett lifted Aida up into the safety of his embrace.

"Very nice," Dan complimented as he offered Garrett his hand.

"Hey, I do what I can, and you do not mess with my girls." Garrett tickled Aida's ribs. She giggled and contorted in his arms.

"That woman is just…" Fionna halted, not wanting to call Cindy McBeechum all of the words that were clearly coming to mind in front of Aida. "How'd you get here so fast?"

"I'm not even on duty, baby." Garrett laughed. "I got off a half hour ago. I took off tonight to prove that I love you so much I have actually agreed to attend a baby shower," he feigned disgust.

"Halia appreciates your being Chloe's date," Fionna assured him.

"She better." Garrett gestured his thumb toward the driveway. "What are you going to do about McBusybody?"

Aida lifted her head off his shoulder and grinned. "Mrs. Powell told Mrs. Willow that 'she's like a woodpecker on the ark,' but I don't know what that means."

Everyone bit back their laughter as they debated how to explain the quip.

CHAPTER 14

RESIGNATION, RELIEF, AND REBUTTALS

JEFF STRENTON

Sinking nervously into the chair in front of Portwood's desk, Jeff swallowed hard. He wasn't certain why his boss had called him in his office, but he prayed that he hadn't done anything wrong.

Portwood ended the call he was on and offered Jeff a kind smile. "Man, don't look at me like that. You have no idea how nice I am. If one of us got called in here when Dan was running this ship, we'd usually try to cast sound barriers over our eardrums to keep them from rupturing."

Jeff managed a nod, but he still wasn't certain he wasn't getting reprimanded.

"You're doing amazingly well. I just wanted to see if I could take a little of the pressure off," Portwood eased, and Jeff allowed himself to breathe.

"Thank you, sir."

"Let's just keep this inside of Iodex for now, but Ramier told me yesterday that he and Kendra are thinking of moving back to Boston to be near her family." He sighed.

Hope and fear fought for dominance in Jeff's mind as he nodded.

"They're looking to move their kids closer to Kendra's parents. There's a position opening in the Boston Iodex early this spring that he'll most certainly get if he applies. They have to sell their home first. So…" Portwood chuckled. Jeff assumed it was from his very visible exuberance. "I'd like you to replace Ramier as our Elite Technology Specialist."

Unable to halt the broad grin that stretched across his face, Jeff was certain he must be dreaming. "Are you serious, sir?!"

"I am serious, but you have to graduate. I can't hire you without that diploma. And I not only need you to graduate, but to work almost full-time from the time Ramier has to report in Boston through your graduation. But get that diploma and stay out of trouble, and you're hired onto the Elite Squadron."

"I will. I swear," Jeff vowed. "Thank you! I mean, I'm married and have a baby on the way, so my days of even potentially getting into trouble are over."

Laughing, Portwood nodded. "I'm in the same boat, remember, and I know that Becca's due in April. If you sign a contingent contract in March, that will guarantee you a four week paid paternity leave through the Senate. I can only give you two as an intern."

"Yes sir, I know. Thank you," Jeff continued to gush.

"I do have one other carrot for you if you're interested."

"I'm definitely interested."

"Governor Willow approved a training addition for me. You'll have to see how you could work this, but if you can take your exams early and keep yourself in the top ten percent of Ioses, then I'll make you a full Elite Squadron member as soon as you've taken your last exam."

Jeff fought the urge to jump up and down. "I don't think I can take them all yet and still stay in the top ten."

"I assumed that. One other thing,"—Portwood was still grinning over Jeff's exuberance—"Ramier's got his hands full with this hacker that keeps shutting down the Senate Bank's website. He's trying to get access to the accounts. Thus far, he's only managed to shut down the entire site repeatedly. John's been watching him work and thinks he'll be making another attempt this weekend. John's premise is that this guy thinks fewer people will be watching the site then. If you'll work this weekend and you catch this asshat, then I'll give you a thousand-dollar bonus."

Jeff tried to remember how to close his own mouth as Portwood went on. "I want this taken care of. He's making us look like fools. The site's been taken offline four times now. Governor Haydenshire isn't happy nor is Buffett." He pulled an envelope from his desk drawer.

"Here's half of your bonus. Go home and spend a little time with your wife, but by Monday morning I would really like to be done with whoever JSly4361 really is. Figure out where he is and how he's doing this. Send out Iodex in the nearest city. Arrest him and the rest is yours."

"You've got it," Jeff assured him.

"Just remember, once you're full-time, you don't get bonuses like that." Portwood chuckled.

"I know, sir."

"Ramier's planning on staying up here all weekend."

"I'll be here."

"Good man. Go on. Tell Becca I promise not to do this to you too many weekends."

"Thank you, sir. You have no idea how excited I am."

"Just remember this feeling a year from now when all of the governing board asks you to look up whoever it is that their teenagers are dating and report back."

"I'll do that too. I'll do anything they need."

"Get out of here. I'm sure you can think of some way to spend a few extra hours this evening before you spend the next two days staring at a computer screen."

Feeling lighter than air, Jeff laughed. "I'll think of something." He was thrilled to actually be joking around with the Chief of Iodex. Jeff rushed to Rainer and Logan's desks. "I want to take Bec somewhere kind of nice tonight, romantic or whatever, but not overly expensive. I'm too excited to think." They both laughed.

"I'd go with The Tavern. It's out on the riverfront," Rainer suggested.

"Yeah," Logan agreed. "It's nice. Ad and I have been there a few times. It has all the stuff girls like—candles, quiet, wine, whatever, and it's like thirty bucks a plate."

"Perfect. Do I need a reservation?"

"Nah, they don't get too crowded until around seven. Just go early," Rainer said.

"Great, thanks!"

"I take it we're celebrating?" Logan quizzed with his signature smirk.

"Definitely." Jeff was still unable to believe the day he'd had. "I just got two bonuses and a guaranteed spot on Elite as long as I graduate."

They both stood to congratulate Jeff. As much as he appreciated them sharing in his joy, he wanted to get home before Becca.

"Okay, go home and let Becca congratulate you," Logan teased.

"I'm hoping."

Much to Jeff's chagrin, he nearly raced headlong into his father-in-law as he headed toward the exit doors. Jeff's stomach clenched uncomfortably. He never knew what to say to Governor Sapman when Becca wasn't around.

"Have a nice weekend, sir," he offered hopefully.

"It's barely four o'clock. Did you just decide to leave early? I doubt very seriously that you can afford that," Governor Sapman huffed in disdain.

Before Jeff could argue, Portwood came to his defense. "I was bringing Jeff copies of the information we have on the project I just assigned him." He handed Jeff a thick file folder. "He's working all weekend. I told him to go home early and have a nice night with Becca," Portwood goaded the governor, and Jeff tried hard not to smirk. "Thought they could celebrate his appointment to Elite in the spring."

Jeff was astonished that his boss had come to his defense so readily and so adamantly.

Governor Sapman looked stunned. "Well...uh...congratulations."

"Thank you." Jeff reveled in his father-in-law's shock. He was sick and tired of the governor upsetting Becca on a weekly basis with some other rudeness directed toward Jeff. She'd been in tears two nights before because her father had requested that she come to dinner with her parents and brothers without Jeff.

She'd refused and had been given a lengthy guilt trip which had simply been more than she could take. She'd dissolved into puddles of tears on Jeff's shoulder.

She still wasn't feeling all that well. She'd been sick a few times and was nauseous every day until well after lunch. School was taking its toll. She wasn't used to going to school, then going to work, then coming home and doing homework, and starting all over again the next day.

Growing up, whenever Becca was upset, she generally soothed herself with shopping. As that wasn't really an option anymore, Jeff had been feeling like an utter failure as a husband as he watched his pregnant wife grow more and more depressed.

He just wanted one night to let her forget about all of that. He wanted to try and make everything up to her.

"You and Becca can come over to the house tonight then. Since you're leaving early, I know that would make Sarah happy," the governor insisted.

Jeff narrowed his eyes. "We can't tonight, sir. I'm taking Bec out just the two of us." The impressed look on his boss's face bolstered his determination.

"You are aware, Officer Strenton," the governor sneered, "that she is my daughter."

Fury swirled in Jeff's shield. He'd had enough. He was going to make something of himself. Nothing was going to stop him, and he was tired of being looked down on by Becca's family.

"I am aware of that. I'm also aware that she's my wife."

Portwood's eyes goggled as he slapped Jeff on the shoulder.

The governor seemed momentarily unable to speak.

"Tell Ramier I'll be here early in the morning," Jeff requested of Portwood.

"No problem. Have a nice night." Portwood edged himself between Jeff and his father-in-law.

"Sir." Jeff gave the governor a slight nod before moving out into the parking deck.

CHAPTER 15

PARTY LIKE AN ANGEL

DAN VINDICO

Dan noted the momentary longing as it worked through Fionna's rhythms. He guided her toward the Angels arena ballroom. "Are you okay, sweetheart?"

"Yeah." Fionna gave him a sweet smile as she ran her hand over her bump. "I'm just still trying to figure out how to hold on and how to let go."

He stopped outside the door and folded her into his arms. "Want to talk about it?"

"Maybe while we're in Kauai."

He nodded. "Whenever you want. Just know that I'm always going to hold on to you."

The ballroom was full of Angels setting up for the shower. Rainer, Logan, and Portwood all made their way over to them as the Angels surrounded Fionna.

"You missed a showdown at the office today." Portwood laughed. Rainer and Logan both looked thrilled as they nodded their agreement.

"What happened?" Dan was extremely intrigued.

"I offered Jeff the spot on Elite as long as he graduates."

"I'm sure he was thrilled."

"You pretty much made his entire year," Logan assured Portwood.

"He's a freaking genius. I honestly don't even care if he graduates. I'd take him full-time right now, but I can't tell him that. But yeah, he was definitely feeling his oats after we talked, and I gave him the afternoon off."

Logan picked up the story. "So, Governor Sapman makes his appearance. I swear he comes by just to intimidate Jeff." He rolled his eyes.

Portwood nodded. "He pretty much ordered Jeff to bring Becca over to the Sapman Mansion for dinner. Jeff was polite, but he told him that he was taking Becca out."

Logan leapt back in. "Yeah, so Sapman asks Jeff if he's aware that Becca is *his* daughter, and Jeff Strenton actually stood up for himself. He said, yeah, and I'm also aware that she's my wife."

"Damn," Dan drawled to nods from the men surrounding him. "But good for him. I knew he had it in him. He just needed his fire lit."

"He's a great kid, and he's had a hell of a life. He takes care of his wife and his mama and he works himself to death. It was high time he knew somebody believed in him," Portwood immediately vowed.

Fionna returned to Dan, and he wrapped his arm around her.

"And how is Mama V?" Portwood grinned.

Fionna giggled, but Dan felt the tension in her as he draped his arm over his wife. "I'm all right. Just full of baby, and exhausted, and I pee every five minutes."

"Something to look forward to." He nodded to Julie, who kept her hand lovingly on her own much smaller bump and looked thrilled to be at the shower for Fionna.

"Something like that."

Dan eased Fionna away from the crowd of people gathered to celebrate their upcoming addition. "What's wrong?"

She laid her head on his chest. "I have a bad feeling." She sounded weary.

"About what?" Part of the reason Fionna was so exhausted was that with Halia's energies coupled with her own phenomenal powers, she felt emotions much more strongly than she ever had before she was pregnant.

"I don't know exactly. It's like Venton, and Jeff and Becca, and…I don't know. Something isn't the way it's supposed to be."

While thinking over Jeff's biting remark to his father-in-law, Dan nodded. "I talked to Jeff just before he left the academy. I gave him the check, and then he went to work and Portwood offered him a spot on the Elite Squadron once Ramier leaves. I'd say he's having a great day, but he also kind of told off his father-in-law, so there might be some tension from that. And Venton's been bothering you for a while," he reminded her gently.

"I know. It just feels worse." She gained strength as Dan held her. She drew from his hand, and Dan felt his own energy move into her. It was still just as remarkable as it was the first time she'd done it. He'd never get enough.

She was smiling and more relaxed as they moved back to their guests. Dan shook his head as he noted that Chloe Sawyer had ordered petit fours decorated with pink icing sperm. There was also a hanging whiteboard where the guests could vote on which sexual position they thought Dan had used to impregnate his wife.

"Honey, are we going to be naming winners in this?" Dan gestured to the board.

Fionna laughed and shook her head. "This is what happens when Chloe uses TikTok to plan baby showers."

"Nice." Rainer pointed to the whiteboard.

"Yeah." Dan rolled his eyes.

"I heard you're the new owners of your own island in the Keys." Fionna wrinkled her nose.

"Why, yes we are." Emily gave her a weary sigh.

"They settled out of court this morning," Fionna explained to Dan.

"I had a feeling that was going to happen." Dan offered Rainer his hand.

"I was really hoping it would. I had no interest in watching my father-in-law and the governing board look at those photos that Jack was going to use as evidence." Rainer shuddered.

Numerous photographs of Rainer and Emily on their honeymoon had been published in newspapers all over the Realm. When Dan figured out who was behind it, Rainer had been out for blood. He'd sued the rental company, the man who owned the island, and every employee that had a hand in the betrayal.

"Are you going to keep it?" Dan asked. He'd been impressed with Rainer's driving determination to end the men that had plastered photographic evidence of their intimate honeymoon all over the news.

"I don't know." Rainer shrugged. "I can't say I ever want to go back. Kind of leaves a bad taste in my mouth. I'd have to talk for a long time to get Em to vacation there again. I'm hoping to talk her into us using the fifteen million in compensatory damages to up her security team." He gestured to Emily. "She'll probably maim me for suggesting it."

"It's hard to think like a Shield when you're not a Shield," Dan reminded him. He tried not to recall the photos he'd seen of Rainer and Emily naked on the beach with her on top of him in the surf going for a ride. No one should have to endure something like that.

"Owning my own island seems a little excessive anyway. I just want to see the headlines in the papers for a while. You know, if you mess with my baby, I will quite literally *own* you."

"Hear, hear."

Fionna gasped suddenly. "Look!" she squealed as she moved to a fake white Christmas tree that was situated in one corner of the room. "Oh my gosh!" She was overjoyed.

"We all know how Fi loves shoes." Emily giggled.

Fionna was moving around the tree that had pairs of baby shoes, one from each couple in attendance, hung with pink ribbons all over the tree.

"Look, little Mary Janes." Fionna was on the brink of jumping up and down. Dan chuckled as he watched her. She was applauding as she studied each tiny pair of their child's shoe wardrobe.

"Oh my gosh! These are adorable!" She lifted a tiny pair of sandals with a red grosgrain flower on the toe. Her mouth hung open in delight as she took in a pair of tiny houndstooth boots from Rainer and Emily.

The tree was beside a mountain of unopened presents. Dan was overwhelmed by their friends' generosity.

"You all are the best." Fionna swooned as tears formed in her eyes.

∽

Jeff Strenton

"We can really do this?" Becca was overjoyed, and Jeff felt the customary ache in his heart begin to ease.

"Yeah, baby." He pulled her close and wrapped his arms around her. She'd been getting ready for their dinner, and Jeff was simply unable to keep his hands off of her. "Let's just forget everything tonight." He cradled her face in his hand and guided her lips to his own. He felt her heartbeat fly in her rhythms as her energy eased and then began to spin in waves of elation.

He let his hands move over her bare shoulders and down her back. He traced the top of the panties she was wearing and forced himself not to move his fingers to her slit. They had all night. "Just you and me and nothing else—not the money, or the baby, or your parents, or work. Just be with me, okay?"

Becca's breath panted deliciously as she nodded her agreement.

Jeff leaned and kissed her again. He began to suck her tongue. He wanted her so badly he could taste it. Nothing else even mattered.

"What are we doing after our dinner?" Becca giggled as she pulled away and studied him. Her eyes were excited and eager. Her cheeks were pink from the lust coursing through her body, and Jeff's trousers became uncomfortably tight.

He was elated that she was feeling better and even flirting with him again. The past few weeks had been tough. "I thought maybe we'd go out to eat and then walk around the city a little if you want. Then I thought I'd bring you back here." He let his breath caress over her cheek as he whispered in her ear. She was panting, and he fought not to strip her and lay her out immediately. "Maybe I'll give you a bath if I can stand to wait that long," he admitted and delighted his wife. "Then I want to take you to bed. I want to feel you, just you and nothing else. That's all I'll ever want. And we'll figure everything out, I swear. All I have to do is graduate and then we can get a house way bigger than this, and I'll take care of you and of our little guy." He slipped his right hand from her shoulder to her stomach. She tensed under his caress.

"You are taking care of us," Becca soothed. "I'm sorry I got all confused about the money. I'll do better, I swear."

"Don't worry about it. With the bonuses I got today, we can pay off the card. It's fine." He wanted her to relax and for the rest of the world to slip away for a little while. "Let's go eat." He hoped the change of scenery might get her mind on more pleasant things.

She pulled on a pair of jeans and then moved to the bathroom. She looped an elastic band she normally used to pull her hair up in a ponytail through the button hole of the jeans and then over the button. She pulled the sweater down to cover her makeshift fix.

"Uh, baby,"—the guilt began to consume him again—"how about after dinner, we go by the mall or wherever and get you some maternity clothes?"

"Can we afford that? I really just want some jeans."

Reminding himself that he'd just deposited two thousand dollars in their bank account that he hadn't been counting on, and that he was determined to get the other five hundred Monday at work, after catching the idiot that was trying to hack the Senate Bank, Jeff nodded. "We can't get you tons of stuff, but we can definitely get you enough to get by for a while."

She threw her arms around him which effectively broke his heart. "Thank you, thank you, thank you!"

"Okay, now I feel really awful."

"Don't feel bad. I kept thinking that I wouldn't start to show until after the Vindicos' baby was born. Fionna's going to let me use her maternity clothes, but our little guy sort of had other plans."

"Let's go get some dinner and you some clothes."

Before he could lock up the house, Becca's phone rang in her purse. She extracted it, showed Jeff the screen, and rolled her eyes. It was her father calling. Jeff's stomach turned uncomfortably as he watched her.

"You know what? Not tonight." Becca delighted him by leaving it on the kitchen counter.

He walked her to the Volvo and opened her door for her. Focusing on the fact that he was actually going to take her out to a relatively nice restaurant for a real date that he was going to pay for and then take her shopping, he settled into the car.

"It's going to be kind of sad when we pick out a name and stop calling him little guy." Becca grinned. She gazed up at Jeff with a look he hadn't seen in many weeks. She adored him. He could tell from the look in her eyes.

"Little Guy Strenton seems like it might get him beaten up though," Jeff teased just to hear her giggle. The sound made him feel like everything might really be all right.

"I know, but he is my little guy." She stared down at her barely existent bump.

"He's *our* little guy," Jeff corrected her.

CHAPTER 16

GIFTS

DAN VINDICO

"Very nice, Chloe." Fionna laughed hysterically. She held up a maternity T-shirt that stated, "Eight Months Sober." The box also contained a pink onesie for Halia that said, "I got my good looks from my mommy. You should see her rack." Dan fought the urge to roll his eyes as he handed Fionna the next gift box. She shook her head as she quickly stowed Chloe's gifts back in their box.

The other gifts were much more appropriate. Rainer and Emily had purchased the stroller Fionna wanted. Adeline gave Fionna loads of things for her and Halia to use as soon as they came home from the hospital. They were all to help with Fionna's discomfort or Halia's newborn issues. Most of the Angels had a ball picking out adorable outfits for Halia, all well aware of Fionna's love of fashion. Dan was relieved that Rachel Carson, the Angels' new junior Receiver, seemed thrilled to be at the shower for Fionna. She'd purchased Halia several outfits and matching receiving blankets.

Sasha Cohen, one of the Angels' Shields, gave them a pad to put in a sink to bathe Halia. It was shaped like a huge, hot-pink hibiscus flower, and Fionna was thrilled. Angels that had retired before Fionna, most of them to have babies of their own, supplied things like blankets, bottles, burp cloths, pacifiers, and diapers.

The smirk on Garrett's face had Dan concerned as he handed Dan his gift. Dan started to give the gift bag to Fionna, but Garrett instructed him to open it. Everyone chuckled as Dan shot him an incredulous look.

"I thought someone should get you something. I mean, you did all the hard work."

The women in the room began throwing wads of wrapping paper his direction.

Dan pulled the tissue paper out of the gift bag.

"Chloe wrapped it for me," Garrett explained how it had gotten tissue paper in the first place.

Dan reached in and pulled out a bra, holding it by his fingertips.

"Did you seriously get me a nursing bra, Garrett?" Fionna rolled her eyes.

"No." Garrett laughed. "I got it for Dan, not Halia."

With that, he grabbed the bra from Dan's hand and demonstrated how the front flaps opened easily with the pop of a hook and eye closure. "When she wears this, you have really easy access."

The room exploded in laughter as Dan shook his head. "I taught you years ago how to pop the back with one hand. Did you forget or something?" Dan brought on more raucous laughter.

"He already has easy access." Fionna stuck her tongue out at Garrett as she began laughing.

As the men consumed more beer, Garrett eventually donned the nursing bra over his Iodex T-shirt with the cups open. He stayed in costume for the remainder of the shower.

Jeff Strenton

Although Jeff had never been much for shopping that didn't involve a video game store, he thoroughly enjoyed watching Becca's face light up as she tried on clothes that actually fit her. True to her word, she only purchased two pairs of maternity jeans, a few long-sleeved knit tops, and a dress. Jeff encouraged her to get more, but she insisted that she had plenty.

They walked farther down the mall, and Jeff ordered himself to man up. "Hey baby, do you want to get a couple of bras that actually fit?" He was well aware that as soon as she got home, either from school or work, she dispensed with her bra altogether. She'd have deep red grooves in her skin from the straps. He was certain they were painful to wear.

"You are just way too sweet. Are you sure that's okay? Bras are expensive."

"You need new clothes. You're having our baby, and I want you to be as comfortable as you possibly can be. I want to take care of you. I know I can't buy you everything you'd like or that I'd like to, but those are actually two of my very favorite things. I don't want them to hurt," he teased, deciding that might be the best way to get her to loosen up. She laughed as she turned, and he followed her into a large lingerie shop.

Jeff tried to convince himself that it was perfectly normal to be in the store with his wife and not look like a total perv while he waited on her outside the dressing rooms. He sincerely wished the saleswomen would stop asking him if he needed any help picking something out.

Becca finally emerged carrying three bras. She looked like Jeff had just given her precious jewels. She was biting her nails and obviously debating something.

"What?" he asked. Her blush had his heart picking up pace.

"I was just wondering if I could make you go away for a few minutes and if I could get something to wear tonight. You know, to surprise you since we're celebrating, but since I had to ask it's not a surprise," she lamented.

Jeff didn't want to give her a budget or tell her she couldn't buy things, but he also didn't want to miss a rent payment to the Haydenshires. "You don't have to wear anything for me. You're beautiful just the way you are."

Disappointment cast her features as she nodded and tried to force a smile.

He changed his tune. "If that's really what you want to get, go ahead. I'll go get us a Dr Pepper." He shut down the plaguing murmurs in his mind. It was one night, and it was what she wanted.

"Are you sure? I won't spend much. I promise."

"I'm sure. What guy in his right mind turns down lingerie for his wife?"

Becca's broad, beaming grin and her energy lilting in excitement made it worth it in Jeff's book no matter what it cost.

Sitting in the food court waiting on Becca, Jeff tried to mentally determine when he thought he'd be able to take his exams and still keep his ninety-eight average. He didn't feel right using the posted exams anymore, since he now knew they weren't being posted by mentors. That was going to make it much more difficult. He decided he'd ask Mentor Vindico about tutoring him when they returned from Hawaii.

"Dinner was delicious. I've never eaten there before." Becca still sounded thrilled as Jeff drove her home.

"I'm glad you liked it." The hefty paycheck that would come with being an Elite officer would afford them meals out at places like the Tavern much more often. He couldn't wait.

"I never thought I would be so excited to buy jeans." She was beaming. Her fingers were laced through Jeff's as he drove just the way they always used to ride before they'd gone from relatively happy-go-lucky kids to full-fledged adults in one afternoon when they'd let their libidos overrule their brains.

"I'm going to miss you tomorrow though," she added hesitantly.

"I hate I have to work, but that's a pretty hefty paycheck for one weekend."

"Oh, I know. I don't mind you working. It's just been a little tense lately, and I miss you. I miss us."

"I'm sorry. I let everything get to me this week. Now that I know I made Elite and that I can start as soon as I take all of my exams, I feel like we can handle this."

"I know. I'm so proud of you. You've worked so hard." Her praise made him feel like a king.

Dan Vindico

"All right, Mrs. Vindico, we have to go pick up our baby girl and then be on a plane in about nine hours," Dan urged Fionna to leave their shower. She was torn. He could feel it in her energy. She was thoroughly enjoying hanging out with all of her friends and helping clean up, but she was also exhausted, and their flight to Kauai left at six o'clock the next morning.

"Okay," she sighed. "Thank you guys for everything." She held out her hands for a collective group hug from the Angels past and present.

After many goodbye hugs and lots of help loading up the presents, Dan helped Fionna into the Mercedes. She was asleep when he pulled into his parents' driveway. Debating for a moment, Dan decided to leave her asleep and retrieve Aida quickly. He left the car running and raced up the stone walkway to his parents' front porch.

"Where's Fionna?" the governor quizzed as he gestured to another of Dan's sleeping beauties curled up on the Vindicos' couch. She was under the blanket that had always resided on Dan's bed growing up. Swallowing hard, he gazed at her. It always took him a moment to readjust whenever his old life, the one with Amelia, crashed headlong into his current life.

"She's sound asleep in the car," Dan finally answered his father. Chuckling, the governor nodded as he retrieved Aida's things and put them back in the bag she'd packed to take to her grandparents'.

"How was the shower?"

As he scooped Aida up into his arms, Dan laughed. "We ate petit fours with pink sperm iced on them, and Garrett ended up wearing a nursing bra for most of the evening, so I'd say par for the course."

The governor tried not to awaken Aida with his laughter.

His mother appeared wearing the pea-green bathrobe she'd worn for as long as Dan could remember. Her face was covered in cold cream. The scent instantly took Dan back to his childhood. It was distinctly odd to be carrying his sleeping child in his arms and feeling like he was suddenly ten.

"You and Fionna have a nice trip, but you really shouldn't be out so late since you have an early flight," his mother scolded.

Refraining from comment, Dan thanked his parents for watching Aida and carried her out to the car.

CHAPTER 17

REBEL YELL

JEFF STRENTON

Jeff flipped through the folder of information Portwood had given him before he left work, while Becca put away her new clothes.

She picked up her phone from the counter where she'd left it. "Any idea why my dad's called eight times?"

Grimacing slightly, Jeff prayed she wouldn't be mad. He didn't want anything to ruin his plans for the evening. They needed to reconnect. They'd talked all through dinner and then at the mall. So far, everything was perfect.

"Kind of," he admitted.

She raised her eyebrows.

Jeff grimaced. "I pissed him off as I was leaving work today."

Though the delighted grin was not what he was expecting, Jeff was overjoyed to see it form on Becca's face.

"What did you say?" She sat beside him on the couch. Her eyes lit with intrigue, defiance, and rebellion. Jeff had to remind himself to think with the head above his belt line.

"He all but demanded that I bring you over there tonight since I was getting off early." He wrapped his arm over Becca's shoulders as she cuddled into him. She rolled her eyes at her father's demands. "I was nice at first," Jeff assured her, but that clearly wasn't what she wanted to hear, so he went on quickly. "I said that I was taking you out tonight. And then he did his whole 'you are aware that she's my daughter,'" he mimicked her father's voice derisively. The grin returned as she nodded. "I said that I was aware of that, but that you're my wife."

The hungry storm swirling in her rhythms lit explosively, and Jeff was woefully unable to look away.

"Wow," she whispered as she turned slightly and then eased her hand over his crotch. Since what she was after was on prominent display, she moaned as she grasped him firmly. That was it. He was done for. He didn't give a damn about her parents or whom he'd pissed off. He wanted her, and he was going to take what belonged to him.

He devoured her lips. His hands grasped her breasts, squeezing and groping her, as she moaned in his mouth.

"That's it, baby, grab me. Feel me. You make me so damn hard." He kept his kisses deep and penetrating. "I need you. I need to be inside you. I want you wrapped tight around me."

"Oh god, yes," she gasped.

Their energy began to roll together, filled with rebellion and craving need. The world had taken too much, and he wouldn't allow that anymore. It could just wait outside the door because he had other plans for the next several hours.

Whatever she'd purchased to wear for him that night could wait as well. He wanted her naked and on top of him. He needed to feel her hot flesh meld with his as he made her his own.

He pulled the sweater over her head and had her bra off in seconds flat. A deep, shuddering groan escaped his lungs as her breasts spilled, fevered and heavy, into his waiting hands. Her nipples were puckered and swollen cherry red. They begged for his attention, and he was only too happy to soothe their aching need.

Lowering his mouth to her breasts, he listened to her needy moans as he spun his tongue over them. She arched her back, and he pulled her right breast in his mouth and sucked her forcefully. He drew the erotic energy from one of her storehouses. He let it fill him before he moved to the left.

Becca was on fire. Her moans were unending, and desperate desire swam in her energy. She shoved Jeff back on the couch as she shimmied out of her jeans and panties. He growled as she straddled over his crotch buck naked. She hoisted her cleavage in his face.

"My god, you are so damn sexy." Apparently, telling off her father tapped a vast well of rebellion that she wanted him to indulge in before he soothed. He stripped as well and then reclined on the couch.

"Come here, baby," he commanded. "Do that over my face."

A hungry, gasping moan quaked from her as she followed his instructions. He grasped her backside firmly and then let his tongue lap at her swollen lips. They were dripping wet with voracious need. He sucked her and licked her swollen lips before dipping his tongue deeply between her folds, listening to her moans of ecstasy.

It had been too damn long. She needed to come undone, and he planned on seeing to each and every one of her needs repeatedly.

"In my mouth, baby," he ordered. "Give it to me. I want to drink you. Right now." He'd never been quite so demanding, but she sure as hell seemed to like it. His cock strained and vied for her attention.

Her breath caught. Her body tensed. Her temperature spiked, and she groaned out his name. Her energy arced high and then unfurled.

When she regained the ability to move, she slid back down his body as he sat up and rid himself of his jeans and boxers. He positioned her over his lap. She grabbed his cock. He throbbed in her hands. "Is that what you need, baby?" He groaned from the heavenly sensation.

"Now." She began making demands of her own, and Jeff was quite certain she'd never been sexier.

He wrapped his fingers around her waist and thrust hard up into her. He was unable to wait any longer. She gasped from the force and then moaned her adamant approval as she began to ride him. He caught her left breast in his mouth and sucked her as she rode him hard. She came almost instantly.

Her release pulsed around him fiercely, and he had to fight with everything in him not to give in to the desperation to fill her full of his energy. He wanted her to have more. He wanted another one, and he was determined to give her relief.

He began to buck. He pressed himself in deeper. Her head fell back as he pumped her full.

"That feels so good," she moaned. It drove him wild. She began to move faster. She wanted more as well.

Suddenly, she fell forward. Her breasts were in his face as she spiraled undone, and he lost it all. He flooded her with his energy, and she took it all. Her muscles cinched tightly around him, milking him. He couldn't tell where she stopped and where he began. It was the way their world should always be. He held her tight, unwilling to withdraw until he had to.

A little while later, Jeff held Becca in their bed. He was playing with her hair and feeling her energy roll through him in languid satisfaction.

"You know, if I'd known telling your dad off was gonna get me that, I would have done it a long time ago." He reveled in her abashed giggles.

"That was really hot. And you telling my dad off was really, really hot. Can we please just not fight anymore, because I need more of that?"

"I'll tell you what—no more credit cards, and I'll stop freaking out about money. And we'll do a whole lot more of that."

"Deal," she vowed. "I love you." She traced her fingers over his bare chest.

"I love you too. So much."

He cradled her on his chest as she fell into a deep sleep. He lay awake in the moonlight thinking of all he needed and wanted to do over the next few months. He was going to make this work.

CHAPTER 18
STICKS...

"Jeff," Becca gasped. "Wake up!" She was sobbing.

Shaking himself from his deep sleep, he tried to determine what was wrong. "What, baby?" He sat up and ran his hands over his face.

As he moved, the blankets fell away from her and he saw. She was lying in a pool of her own blood.

"Oh my God!" He'd never been more terrified in his life. His Predilection took over instantly. His shield surrounded her without being summoned. "We have to go to the hospital. I'm calling Adeline."

Nodding, Becca tried to stand, but her eyes spun slightly, and she sank back down. He released his cast, grabbed his cell phone and a pair of her sweatpants, and phoned Logan as he helped her dress.

She clung to him as he quickly explained what had happened, first to Logan and then to Adeline.

"I'll meet you at Georgetown. Leave right now. Tell Becca to wear a pad to keep the blood from getting everywhere. I need you to tell me if you can still feel the baby's energy," Adeline eased.

With impending doom and loss settling on him harshly, Jeff guided Becca back to the bed.

"Just try to relax for me," he soothed.

"What are you doing?" Terrified tears leaked down her sweet face.

"Adeline wants me to see if I can lock on to him." He tried to suppress his own energy as well as he was able.

Becca tried to help him, but her rhythms were jagged and terrified. It broke his heart. She was trembling and weak from all of the blood she'd lost, but suddenly, hope sprang in the depth of his harrowing fear.

"I feel him," he gasped in the phone to Adeline.

"Okay, good. Now get her to Georgetown. I'll meet you there."

The line went dead, and his focused drive took over his brain. "Adeline says to wear a pad to the hospital. She's going to meet us there. It's going to be all right." He hoped against hope that he wasn't lying to his wife.

Feeling the need to move pulse constantly through his shield, Jeff eased Becca from the car and into the emergency room. Adeline was waiting on them. Logan was standing nearby and offered him a soothing smile. Adeline and a team of other medios guided Becca into a wheelchair.

"We're going to take her upstairs. As soon as we get her in a bed, I want you to cast her to see if we can't get her a little stronger while I figure out what's going on," Adeline instructed Jeff.

"No problem."

"Becca, would you like Logan to call your parents?" Adeline asked.

Becca clung to Jeff's hand as he ran beside her. "I guess so."

"I'm on it," Logan assured as one of the nurses casted the elevator, and it shot to the third floor.

Jeff tried to steady his own heartbeat as he helped Becca change into a hospital gown. Blood was still pouring down her legs, and tears cascaded down her cheeks. He guided her into the bed and set his shield over her immediately.

"Soothing and a little heat," Adeline instructed.

He filled his shield with as much soothing energy as he was able. Becca eased, and her muscles relaxed slightly.

"Okay, lower it," Adeline guided a few minutes later. He dropped his shield.

She pulled the gown up, and Jeff clenched his jaw. He didn't even know the two men standing in the room staring down at his wife.

Suddenly, Adeline's hands were on Becca's abdomen, and there was a picture on a computer monitor by her head.

A nurse moved to the other side of the bed and began reading Becca's energy waves.

"She has a UTI. It's pretty bad," the nurse informed Adeline.

"What is that?" Jeff demanded.

Adeline offered him a kind smile. "It's a bladder infection. That's part of the problem, but that's not causing this amount of bleeding. We'll get that healed up in just a minute," she soothed.

"It's the placenta," Adeline explained. The other medios grimaced. "I think I can move it, but we need to get her stable."

"What's happening?" Becca pled.

"The Sapmans just arrived, and the Crown as well, along with the Lawsons, and the first lady," a nurse informed them as he moved into the room and closed the door back.

"You're going to be all right, Becca. The placenta has moved over your cervix. That's causing you to bleed. I'm fairly certain I can lock on to the energy in your womb and readjust everything, but a few things are going to have to change. I need you to really relax for me. I'm going to go outside and talk to Jeff and then your parents and then we're going to take you in to surgery."

Terror flooded through Becca, and Jeff tried to hold her in the bed.

"I'm not leaving her." He shook his head.

"She's going to be fine. Medio Metzger is going to cast her, heal the UTI, and get her calm. You're just too frantic. I need to talk to you, and she's a governor's daughter so she can have twenty-four-hour care. We're going to get you both through this, but I need you to come out in the hallway with me and let them work." Adeline's tone was soothing, but Jeff sensed that he didn't have a choice.

"I'll be okay," Becca whispered.

"Baby." He just couldn't leave her. She looked so small and weak and terrified.

"Just for a minute. You need to sign some papers, and then you can come right back. I'll let you go into surgery with her. She should only be in for a half hour or so. Then we'll bring you back in here and you can stay with her constantly," Adeline insisted.

"Go on. I'm okay," Becca assured him.

"I'll be right back." Jeff kissed her forehead and squeezed her hand. His heart pounded in his throat as he followed Adeline into the hallway.

"George, you are insane. You have got to get over this. I will do nothing of the sort." The Crown Governor was furious as he snapped at Governor Sapman.

Mrs. Sapman rushed to Jeff. "Is she okay?"

Jeff wasn't entirely certain what the correct answer was. "Yes, ma'am. I think so."

"Becca is going to be fine. Right now, our concern is the baby," Adeline explained to Jeff's mother-in-law. "I just need a moment with Jeff."

Logan offered him a hopeful smile which Jeff tried to return.

"Alone," Adeline ordered Mrs. Sapman away.

Governor Sapman glared at Jeff, who turned his attention to Adeline and turned his back on his father-in-law's glare. His mother rushed into the hospital. She offered Jeff her kind, soothing smile. It was the same smile she'd been giving him his entire life. Drawing from that feeling, Jeff focused on Becca.

"This is going to be husband trial by fire, I guess." Adeline sighed as she took in Governor and Mrs. Sapman.

"I don't care what they think. Just tell me what we need to do," Jeff commanded. The deeply impressed looks he received from the Haydenshires, Rainer, Logan, and his mother strengthened his resolve.

"She has some thinning of her uterine wall. I'm going to try and repair that as well. I do think we can repair everything, and that she'll be able to carry him almost full term, but it's not going to be easy."

"I'll do anything she needs."

"She's going to have to stay here until I make certain she's not going to miscarry. I'm going to insist that she miss the next week of school and work. I'll check her again on Friday. If there is significant improvement, she can resume school the following week. But this is quite serious. I'm not certain she's going to be able to work. She can't be on her feet so much."

"We're out of school this week anyway," Jeff tried to ease her worry. "I was going to pull a full week at work, but I won't. I'll stay home and take care of her."

"Hey man, you don't have to do that. We can help," Logan offered.

Emily nodded. "The Angels don't practice on Tuesdays and Thursdays. I'll stay with her then."

"I'm off Monday, sweetheart, and I can take off another day this week as well," Jeff's mother reassured.

"I'll come over and stay with her, Jeff." Mrs. Sapman moved away from her husband to reassure her son-in-law.

Adeline didn't look as shocked by the outcry of support as Jeff certainly felt.

"She really just needs to rest and stay off her feet." Adeline lowered her voice so only Jeff could hear her. "And I'm going to recommend a week of pelvic rest as well."

Jeff assumed that meant that they couldn't have sex, but he decided he would ask about that after he was certain Becca and the baby were going to be okay.

"That's fine," he assured Adeline.

"This is ridiculous. Obviously, this just wasn't meant to be. Just get rid of it and heal my daughter. Let's get this divorce over with and get on with our lives," Governor Sapman demanded.

Fury rocked Jeff to the core. His body spasmed from the governor's words.

Mentor Vindico rushed to them. He looked exhausted, but Jeff could hardly see his favorite mentor's face through the red haze of his own infuriated energy that pulsed from his shield as it surrounded him.

"Jeff," he heard Mentor Vindico's warning tone.

"We are not getting divorced," Jeff snarled. "Whether she loses the baby or not, we are married, and we will be married forever. I can't fucking believe you actually want her to lose our child." The realization felt like he'd been hit in the face with a brick. "That you want her to go through that kind of heartache and pain. What is wrong with you?" He shook his head. "You know what,"—he focused on Adeline solely—"I'll do anything you need, just get my wife and my little boy taken care of. Make them okay. That's all that matters to me."

He threw a hateful glare back at his father-in-law. "Because I love them." He turned on Governor Haydenshire next. "That's what he wanted you to do, isn't it? He wanted you to start the divorce papers?" He realized suddenly what had upset Governor Haydenshire. Shaking his head in abject disbelief, Jeff gave a final order. "Just keep him the hell away from Becca."

With that, he stormed back into Becca's room and slammed the door behind him.

Dan Vindico

"He cannot order me away from my child," Governor Sapman challenged.

"Actually, he can," Adeline informed the governor. She looked almost as disgusted as Dan felt. "He's her husband, and he's the father of their child. Now, if you'll excuse me, I'm going to follow Mr. Strenton's requests that I take care of his wife and his little boy."

Dan stared Governor Sapman down. He let the hate Jeff certainly felt work through his body as well. He'd been up packing until midnight. He let the exhaustion and the fury pour from his mouth. "You know, I've been where he is." He pointed to the obstetrics intensive operating room that Becca had been assigned. "And I've watched my wife go through surgery, and then I've held her and helped her heal from a miscarriage. It was one of the most horrifying things either of us will ever live through."

Governor Haydenshire nodded his adamant agreement as he slapped Dan's shoulder in a show of infuriated solidarity.

"To actually be willing to wish your daughter go through that kind of pain because you can't see what a tremendous guy she married is criminal."

"I can't believe you said that." Mrs. Sapman seemed shocked as well. "Becca may never forgive you for this."

Everyone watched a surgical team move into the room and seal the door shut quickly.

~

Jeff Strenton

"I'm right here." Jeff kept up his constant reassurances as he watched the medios drain Becca's energy. Her body convulsed in fear.

"I heard you yelling." She clung to him with all of her might, which was rapidly diminishing. "What did Daddy say?"

Jeff caressed her face and brushed her hair away from her eyes. He would never tell her what her father had said. It was too awful, and it would hurt her too much.

"Go ahead with your soothing energy, Mr. Strenton. The baby has picked up on you. He's responding." Medio Metzger showed Jeff the baby's rhythms on a monitor beside Becca.

"It's going to be okay. I'll be right here the whole time," Jeff pledged as Becca's eyes closed and her body went limp. Adeline's glowing blue orb moved over her womb.

CHAPTER 19
AND STONES
DAN VINDICO

"Hey, baby," Dan answered his phone quietly. "She's all right. Adeline and the surgical team just came out of the room. Jeff's keeping her casted for now. Adeline stopped the bleeding, but she's put Becca on bed rest for the next week."

"How long does she have to stay in the hospital?" Fionna sounded every bit as tired as Dan felt.

"I'm pretty sure they're going to keep her here over the weekend. I'm leaving in just a few minutes. I'll pick you up, and we'll head to the airport."

"Okay, I'll get Aida up. Give Jeff and Becca my love."

"I will." Dan ended the call.

Adeline took the vacant seat beside him. She was scrubbed clean of Becca's blood but looked worried.

"You were amazing. She's gonna be great," Logan immediately stepped in to reassure his wife.

"I hope," Adeline admitted in a pained whisper. Drawing a deep breath, her defeat seemed to overwhelm her rhythms. "She's not going to be able to work. I'm not certain she's even going to be able to go back to school for a while. Can they afford for her to stay home?"

Logan shared a quick, concerned glance with Dan. "Jeff's going to be an Elite officer. He'll make plenty. She can stay home with the little one if that's what she wants. All he'll want is for Becca to be healthy. He's her Shield. They'll make it work, and we'll help out as much as we can.

"I need to call Portwood. Jeff's supposed to work this weekend, and obviously he can't." He gestured to Becca's room. Dan sincerely hoped Jeff and Becca were sleeping, but he doubted Jeff would allow himself the rest.

Adeline turned to Dan. "If I give you Fionna's latest test results without her here, will you sue me or have me fired?" she tried to tease, but she sounded deeply concerned.

"No," Dan assured her.

"Her rhythms are better…"

Dan waited for the inevitable "but."

"But she's still very stressed. I've never had a Receiver as strong as Fionna. I should have realized how strongly she would feel everything at the end of her pregnancy." Dan's mind raced as he tried to think of how to reassure Adeline and take care of his wife. "Her blood pressure spikes whenever she starts worrying, and the gunshot wound is constantly agitating her uterus as it expands so rapidly right here at the end. The blood pressure spikes are a normal stress response, but it isn't good for the baby. And she can feel everyone around her. The baby has made her filters weaker because she's made Fionna stronger if that makes sense."

"I know."

"I was wondering if you thought you might convince her to stay another week or two in Kauai. I'm comfortable inducing labor early if we need to, but I'd like her to be another two or three weeks along."

"I think it might be time for me to insist." Dan hoped it wasn't going to come to that.

Adeline offered him a smile. "Tell her that I'm insisting too."

Dan stood. He had to take care of his own family, as much as he'd like to stay and help Jeff and Becca. He had to get home, get his girls, and get them to the airport.

"Let me know what happens," Dan commanded Logan. He gestured his head toward Becca's room.

"Will do," Logan agreed with a deep yawn.

"And hey, if there's any way Jeff could drive by my house a few times over the next two weeks without it adding anything else to his load, I could pay him for that. If you think it will work, just tell him I asked." He tried to think of any way he could get Jeff and Becca to accept money they were clearly going to need if Becca wasn't going to be able to work.

"Are you taking an extra week off?" Logan picked up on the timeline immediately.

"Probably."

"And you think Jeff will buy the fact that Dan Vindico needs his house checked on when you and I both know you're going home to cast the hell out of it before you leave?"

"Just try for me."

An hour later, Dan was casting the Mercedes, carrying his very sleepy little girl on his shoulder, and dragging their luggage behind him.

Aida rallied as they entered the airport with the busy hubbub around her.

"Can I hold Lanie when we get there? Is she going to pick us up at the airport with Aunt Malani?"

"We'll have to see, baby girl," Dan soothed.

Deciding to wait and try to ease Fionna into staying an extra week or two while they were on the flight, Dan didn't change her ticket at the counter. They headed toward the gates for Gifted flights as the shops and newsstands in the airport were opening for the day.

Fionna pointed to the latest edition of the *New York Times*. "I want to see what they're reporting about Rainer and Emily's lawsuit."

Curious himself, Dan picked up the paper and a few of the tabloids that had run the pictures back in the spring. He paid for them and then guided his family to the seats where they were to wait to board the plane.

Flipping open the paper, Dan summoned and locked on to the heat energy used by the printers on the papers and with a quick move, it read *The Realm Times*.

"The Lawsons Get Their Way Out of Court" was the headline.

There was a small picture of Rainer and Emily heading into the Pentagon to sign the papers settling the multiple lawsuits. It then listed the sheer amount of money Rainer and Emily had gained in compensatory damages and the worth of the island in the Keys that they now owned, as most of the owner's assets were tied up in the island.

Fionna continued to glance through the story while Dan casted one of the tabloids. He wondered what ridiculous spin they would put on the victory.

His eyes goggled and his stomach clenched as he read, "Not Vindico's Baby," on the cover. "Divorce proceedings begin tomorrow for former Chief of Iodex Daniel Vindico and famed Angels Receiver Fionna Styler."

They'd photoshopped a picture of Dan stalking out of the Senate looking furious, from months before he'd even met Fionna, and a terrible shot of Fionna leaving Georgetown. Her eyes were half closed in a blink, making it appear she'd been crying.

"Why does it say that?" Aida panicked. Heartbroken tears pricked her eyes as her chin began to tremble.

The blurb informed the Realm that Fionna had admitted to Dan that the baby was actually Garrett's, and that Dan had filed for divorce.

"It's all lies," Dan assured Aida as he quickly threw the papers away. Fionna was on the verge of tears as well.

"Why did it say Halia isn't your baby?" Aida pled. Terrorizing fear perforated her tone. "I'm your baby girl, and she's going to be your baby girl too because she's my baby sister."

"As long as you know that, then that's all that matters to me," he soothed.

"I don't want you to get divorced." She trembled in hi's arms.

"We are never getting divorced. I promise," Fionna vowed. It appeared to physically injure Fionna to watch Aida cry.

The flight began boarding, and abject panic seized his shield as he realized that Fionna's blood pressure had absolutely spiked from the article. He had to get her to Kauai and figure out how to convince her to stay there without him until it was safe for Halia to be delivered.

Fionna had lost some of her mass-media appeal when she'd stepped out of the Angels limelight, and the press had backed off some. It appeared instead of telling their readers that the Lawsons had drawn a line in the sand for themselves, they'd decided to dredge up the old stories about Garrett being Halia's father instead of Dan.

A flight attendant approached Aida. "Hi there, would you like to sit by the window so you can see? You'll be right beside your mommy and daddy." She seemed concerned that Aida was crying because she was afraid to fly.

"My mommy and daddy aren't getting divorced," Aida announced to the flight attendant.

She grimaced as she nodded her understanding. "I saw the paper," she mouthed to Dan and Fionna. "But I mean, who really believes any of that?" She patted Aida's back.

"Thank you," Fionna sighed.

They spent the first hour of the flight trying to explain why someone would print out-and-out lies in a paper and then why people would spend money to read it. As there really wasn't any logic to it, Aida continued to tell them that she didn't understand. She cheered a little as Fionna and Dan cuddled up on the flight after reassuring her constantly of their undying love for one another and for both of their daughters.

CHAPTER 20

EQUAL REACTION

JEFF STRENTON

Jeff gasped and shook himself awake. He'd fallen asleep again. Resetting the cast over Becca, he rubbed his eyes.

"Jeff," Becca whispered as she fought to awaken.

"I'm right here." He kissed her forehead. She looked so pale it terrified him.

"The baby?" She panicked instantly.

"He's fine, sweetheart. Adeline stopped the bleeding, but you're going to have to take it easy for a while, okay?" He brushed her hair away from her face. He loved her so much it hurt him to watch her be frightened or in pain. His shield sizzled against his skin.

"Listen, that's his heartbeat." He quieted so she could hear the monitors he'd been listening to for the past few hours.

Tears leaked from the sides of her eyes. Her chin trembled as she clung to his hand. "What time is it?" she finally managed as she rubbed her hand tenderly over her midsection. Altering the energy of her womb had caused her to swell. She looked like she was several months more pregnant than she was. Jeff tried to blink his watch into focus. "It's just after six."

A quiet knock sounded on the door to Becca's room. Adeline tiptoed inside. She gave them both a kind smile.

"Feeling a little better?" She read the printouts on the monitors by Becca's bed.

"Kind of. What happened to me?"

"I'm not entirely certain. Your body is having to adjust to being pregnant, of course, so that's really the best explanation I can give you. You don't have placenta previa, but you do have a few spots that are thin in the walls of your uterus. That's why I'm putting you on bed rest for a few weeks. It looks to me like your Gifted rhythms have been under a lot of stress lately."

Guilt washed over Jeff in a tidal wave when he thought of their heated discussions over money in the last few days.

"I already explained all of this to Jeff, but you're going to have to really take it easy this week. I want you either sitting or lying down at least twenty hours of the day, and let's do a week of pelvic rest. The baby responds easily to Jeff's energy, so I do want him to cast you a few hours each day though."

"What's pelvic rest?" Becca asked. Jeff was relieved he wasn't the only one who wasn't certain about the terminology.

"Sorry, medio speak." Adeline chuckled. "No intercourse for a week."

"Please tell me that's not what caused this," Jeff pled.

Adeline shook her head. "Actually, the fetus drew from your energy while your ejaculate was inside Becca. I think you saved him." Color returned to Becca's features by way of her own deep blush. "That's why I want you to cast her each day for the next several days." Adeline didn't seem like knowing that her patients had sex just hours before rushing to the hospital was odd.

"You're supposed to be at work," Becca remembered suddenly, and panic set in her weakened rhythms.

Jeff shook his head. "I'm not leaving you here. Work will wait. This is where I need to be."

"We're going to need that money, especially if I can't work."

"Baby, please, just relax. We'll figure it out. I'll make it work. I just need you and our little guy to be okay."

"He's going to be an excellent daddy," Adeline vowed. Becca nodded as she blinked back another round of tears. "Actually, Logan called Chief Portwood while you were casting her. He told him you wouldn't be in today. I think they came up with a plan if you want to try it."

"I'm staying right here beside her."

"You can still do that."

"What's their plan?" Becca asked.

"Would you mind if they came in for a minute?"

"It's fine," Becca said before Jeff could stop her.

Adeline left the room, and Jeff pulled the sheets and blankets up to Becca's chin. It made her giggle.

"They both have wives. We have all the same parts," she teased him. He reveled in how strong her voice sounded.

"Yeah, well, your parts are mine, and I'm very protective of my baby. You know this."

"I really like that," she admitted with a grin that soothed Jeff's soul.

"You know, if you didn't want him to work this weekend, you could've just said something. The whole, *now I have to go to the hospital* routine gets so overused." Logan winked at Becca as he led Portwood inside.

"I promise I didn't mean to." Becca laughed.

"Sure, sure." Logan continued to harass her.

"Man, you do not have to do this." Portwood held up one of the high-powered Iodex laptops from the Senate. "I completely understand. You won't ever get in trouble with me for being a good husband."

"Thank you, but what was your idea?" Jeff wondered if there was any way he could stay right beside Becca, take care of anything she might need, and catch a hacker on the side.

"We figured you weren't gonna leave Becca boo and little Jeff-y Jr. there." Logan pointed to the approximate location of Becca's stomach under the layers of blankets Jeff had covered her in.

"Good guess." Jeff chuckled.

Portwood rolled his eyes and shook his head at Logan. "Can you imagine if I let him do the rundowns on Monday mornings?"

"Dude, I would be awesome at rundowns." Logan cracked everyone up.

"Oh, it hurts to laugh." Becca's body contorted, which effectively halted the laughter.

Portwood offered Becca a sorrowful gaze. "We'll get out of here so you can rest. Ramier loaded all of the files on our little hacker friend on here." He lifted the laptop again. "I don't care where you are when you catch him. If you want to sit right where you are and hold her hand and keep this in your lap, it's fine with me. If we have a guy in the holding cells Monday morning, the money is yours."

Hope welled in Jeff's mind, but he wasn't going to ignore his wife for money. If she was uncomfortable with him working and taking care of her, he wouldn't do it.

"You should do that," Becca immediately urged. "I know you can catch this guy, and I'm just going to be lying here."

"Are you sure?"

"Yes. I'm hurting and exhausted, so I'm just going to sleep."

"And if you need anything or you need me to cast you, you'll tell me no matter what I'm doing," Jeff defined the terms of him agreeing to this. Portwood gave him a pride-filled smile.

"I promise."

"Okay." Jeff took the laptop from his boss. "Thank you. I'll do my best."

"You always do, man, and take care of her first."

Immensely appreciative of his boss, Jeff gave a silent prayer of overwhelming gratitude that his son and wife were all right for the moment and that he was being given another opportunity to prove himself.

Adeline moved back in the room with a breakfast tray. Logan brushed a kiss on her cheek before he and Portwood headed out. She beamed at him.

Logan spun back at the door. "Rainer and I will supply you with as much food and Dr P as you need. You just catch this guy."

"Thanks." Jeff gave him an appreciative smile.

"We're going to keep you on the fluid drip, so this food is for Jeff," Adeline explained to Becca as she pushed the cart past the bed.

"Good, because I don't think I can keep much down," Becca sighed.

"I'm going to give you something for that and make certain we got rid of your UTI. Then I'm going to give you a light sleeping pill. Your body will heal when you sleep. I'll keep you casted while you're out, and we'll let Jeff work," she explained the morning plans for Becca. "But before we start all of that, both of your parents would like to see you." She glanced at Jeff uncomfortably.

Becca turned to Jeff. "That depends on what you were yelling at my dad about." He'd hoped that she would forget or think it was a dream as they were putting her under, but that didn't seem to be the case.

He set the laptop on the counter and tried to discern what to tell her.

"He was just worried about you." Jeff hoped that wasn't a lie.

"I don't think I've ever heard you yell at anyone." She shook her head. "You weren't upset because my dad was worried about me."

"I'm going to let you two talk for a minute. Jeff, you eat, and then I'll bring in the pill to help you sleep, Becca." Adeline whisked from the room.

Jeff moved back beside Becca and took her hand. He was still stalling for time.

"Just tell me."

"You need to rest. I just want you to be better."

"Do you remember on our wedding night? You made me promise not to keep things from you because you said it scared you worse when I didn't tell you things. It scares me too when you don't tell me what's going on. You're my husband. I want you to tell me everything."

Defeat settled on him harshly. "I don't want you to be mad at your dad."

"You're mad at him, so I'm already mad at him."

Jeff brushed another kiss on her forehead. "I think your dad sort of thought you were going to…" He couldn't say the word miscarry to her when that was still a very real possibility.

"Lose the baby," she choked and then promptly began crying again.

Jeff nodded as he wiped away her tears.

"Is that why you got so mad?"

"That was part of it," he choked.

"What else did he say? Just tell me."

"He said for Adeline to just get rid of it, so that we could go on with the divorce," he managed, though the words felt like poison as they fell from his lips.

"What?!" Becca gasped. "Why would he think that? Even if something horrible happened, I'm not divorcing you. I want you forever. I want to have your babies even if it's a little earlier than we planned." She spewed out all of the things Jeff had already informed her father of.

"I know. That's what I told him, more or less, and that's exactly how I feel as well."

His vows seemed to steady her.

"I don't want to see him. I'm tired and it hurts." She effectively broke Jeff's heart.

"I'm so sorry." He summoned and sent soothing energy into her womb to ease her pain.

"That feels better, but you need to eat."

Jeff kept his cast on her and tore the wrapper off a protein bar with his teeth. He inhaled it as he worked his energy through his wife and child.

Dan Vindico

Dan relaxed as he pulled the armrest between his and Aida's seat up, and she laid her pillow in his lap just moments before she fell asleep cradled against him. He turned his attention to Fionna before he fell asleep himself. He was exhausted from his long night.

"So, Mrs. Vindico…"

"I know you're not telling me something," she informed him.

"I wasn't trying to keep anything from you. I haven't really had an opportunity to tell you." He gestured his head to their baby girl in his lap.

"Tell me."

"I talked to Adeline before I left Georgetown." Fear tensed in her rhythms. Dan wrapped his arm over her shoulders. "Everything's going to be fine."

She nodded but was fighting tears. "Is something wrong with Halia?"

"No, but you're going to stay in Kauai for at least the next two weeks." He wasn't taking no for an answer.

"Dan, no," she immediately argued.

He shook his head. "You *are* staying in Kauai for the next two weeks. It's not a choice anymore, sweetheart." He hated to tell her what she was going to do, but it had to be done. She scowled. "Fi, baby, please.

"I'll call Dad when I get there. I'll either take off an additional week or at least part of it. I don't think Aida missing a few days of second grade will be that detrimental, but your scarring is agitated, and your blood pressure and rhythms aren't good. Halia needs you to stay where the Hawaiian energy can regulate your rhythms and hers. Adeline says if you can do that for two or three more weeks, then she's comfortable inducing, but not until then."

"I don't want you to leave me there." Fionna began to cry.

"I don't want to leave you there, so let's see how you're feeling. Maybe I won't have to. But if you need to stay for three weeks, that's going to get tricky." He somehow knew his father wasn't going to like him taking off two additional weeks when rumors of nepotism were flying fast and free around the Realm. He just didn't know what to do about it.

Fionna buried her face in Dan's neck as he tried to cradle her to him and keep Aida asleep in his lap. He didn't want to leave his babies on Kauai with him five thousand miles away. Shutting down thoughts instantly of Fionna going into labor with him in DC, his heart seized.

She fell into a fitful sleep. Dan tried to conceal his worries, but she felt him more easily than anyone else. He was doing nothing to quell her fears.

As she slept, he debated. He would not miss his child's birth. But, Fionna was still eight weeks from her actual due date, and being back on Kauai would regulate her rhythms. That coupled with being on her family's farm and away from the majority of society would mean that her blood pressure and rhythms would remain stable. There was very little likelihood that she would go into labor early as long as she remained in Hawaii.

He shuddered. He just didn't want to think about doing nothing but work and then going home alone. He'd lived that life for ten long, hard years, and that was doing a job he loved not one he hated. He'd spent two nights in the last ten months since he'd followed her home from a bar alone in bed. The night before their wedding she'd stayed with her best friend and her grandmother.

Dan had laid awake for hours. He needed her, needed to know she was safe in his arms, needed to feel her rhythms rolling through his skin as he cradled her closely.

If she improved dramatically in the next week, he could fly back Tuesday. He was giving several tests Thursday and Friday. He was teaching defense against multiple attackers in his lab classes. He knew he shouldn't leave that to a substitute or cancel all of his classes the next week. Dan swallowed back the dejection of leaving Fionna behind. If she continued to improve, she could bring Aida home Saturday. They could spend all day Sunday tucked up in their house together. Then they would need to get everything ready for Halia to make her arrival.

If he decided to stay in Kauai, he knew his father would take the heat for his decision. It would be painted to appear that Governor Vindico had allowed his son an extra week of vacation in Hawaii. No one would ever believe a Hawaiian vacation was a need instead of a want.

Clearly, the other mentors were already gossiping about Dan's not working for Venton all summer. Mentor Bryant had pulled that information out of her hat quickly. He was certain she wasn't the only one who felt that it was an injustice.

As Governor Haydenshire often said, "People only ever see what they want to see and hear what they want to hear." Dan knew it was true. No one wanted to remember that Dan had taken down a massive criminal organization or that the love of his life had been nearly fatally shot in the process and then suffered a violent, excruciatingly painful miscarriage. People wanted to ignore that their daughter had very nearly been kidnapped while in Paris.

No one was willing to take any of that into consideration. No one wanted to know the real circumstances of another man's grief and responsibilities. They would much rather whine and complain that Dan had spent four months on a beautiful Hawaiian island instead of attending faculty meetings and seminars that were nothing more than a cover-up for the chancellor's affair. It was far more appealing to complain about what they didn't have than to appreciate what they did.

CHAPTER 21

THE TIDES

JEFF STRENTON

Jeff held Becca's hand and watched over her obsessively as she slipped into a deep, drug-induced sleep.

"She'll be out for several hours. I need to regulate her rhythms. We're going to have to figure out some way to ease her stress levels. If we don't, she's going to lose the baby," Adeline explained as she lowered the lights in the room.

"This is all my fault," he admitted in a choked whisper.

"No." Adeline shook her head. "It's not anyone's fault. Now we know we have a little complication, so we'll deal with it."

"I'll do whatever she needs."

"Right now, she just needs to sleep, and for the next week, she needs to rest. After that, we'll see what we can add back in."

A timid knock sounded on the door. Jeff moved to open it. The Sapmans weren't coming in. He would be her Shield for everything, even from her own family.

"Oh, hey, Mom. I'm sorry. I meant to come back out and see you." Another layer of guilt added its crushing weight.

"No, it's fine. I'm heading to work, but I'll come back this evening and bring you some supper." His mother gave him her reassuring smile.

"You don't have to do that."

"I want to." Jeff hated to admit that knowing that his mother was coming back to check on them brought him a great deal of solace. His mom could fix most anything. "Sweetheart, I know you're upset with the Sapmans…" He bristled but didn't argue. "I just don't think he meant that quite the way it sounded, maybe."

"That's exactly what he meant. He doesn't want her to be married to me, and he certainly doesn't want us to have a baby. That's precisely what he wanted to happen."

His mother gave him a consoling nod. "I just…don't want you to carry that around with you. Being mad at someone really only hurts you, and being mad at her parents will hurt Becca. I don't ever want either of you to hurt." She blinked back tears of adoring love, the kind a parent was supposed to have for their child.

"I know, but right now I am mad. I'll get over it," he tried to reassure the one woman who had made him everything he was, that had loved him with all of his flaws and had been there his whole life.

"Tell Becca how much I love her, and if she wants anything from your house, just make a list. I'll pick it up on my way back tonight."

"Yes, ma'am. Thank you." He hugged his mom tight. Her love worked through the anger and volatility he'd felt for most of his harrowing morning.

Becca was sound asleep. She looked replete and peaceful. The color began to come back to her cheeks as Adeline worked over her.

When she finally dropped her healing cast, she smiled. "I'm going to check on a few of my other patients. She's already much better. There are her rhythms, and those are the baby's." She showed Jeff the printouts on the scans of Becca and the baby. They were steady and healthy. Relief washed through him. "It really is amazing what rest will do for the body. She'll be out most of the day, but maybe cast her for a few minutes in a couple of hours. Let the fetus know you're here."

"Of course." Jeff nodded. He'd always be there. They were his, and he would always take care of both of them. He would never do what his father had done.

With a sigh, Jeff moved to Becca's bed and placed a gentle kiss on her forehead. "I love you so much," he whispered. He didn't know if she could hear him, but he needed to tell her. "I'll take care of you and our little guy. I swear I'm going to make this work."

After he carefully heat casted all of the blankets over her languid body, Jeff moved to the bench seat in the back corner of the small room. Drawing a deep breath and letting stubborn determination work through his veins, he opened the laptop and summoned it on.

Dan Vindico

It was always distinctly odd to fly a Gifted commercial flight from DC to Kauai. The six-hour flight coupled with the six-hour time difference meant that they arrived at the same time they'd left.

The Senate flights flew faster, so they arrived in four and a half hours instead of six, but with the cries of nepotism and favoritism floating around his father, Dan hadn't wanted to ask his dad to get them tickets on a Senate jet.

Dan rubbed his eyes as he heard a coolant officer's voice project through the plane, announcing that they would be making their arrival in Lihue in a half hour.

Aida was sitting up and coloring on her iPad color app. Dan grinned as he took in the neatly colored picture of Ariel and Prince Eric's wedding. She labeled Ariel as Mommy and Eric as Daddy, still coping with the tabloid she'd seen that morning. Dan's heart ached to think that something like that had frightened her so badly.

"We'll be there in just a little while," he tried to reassure her. She loved Kauai and Fionna's family farm. They'd lived there all summer, and Aida had healed and grown just as much as Fionna and Halia. Dan included himself in the list after consideration. It had offered them the respite they so desperately needed.

Aida turned to gaze out over the mighty Pacific so far below them. Her eyes lit in worry as she turned back to Dan. She looked panicked.

"What's wrong?"

"I forgot to remember something! I'm so sorry."

"It's okay, sweetheart. What did you forget?"

"Maybe I still have it." She threw her doll, Sophie, in Dan's lap along with the iPad and began going through her backpack. "I hope I didn't lose it."

"Baby, what are you looking for? I'll help you," Dan offered. She looked terrified, and the way she took responsibility for everything always made him worry.

"I found it!" She sounded utterly relieved.

With all of Aida's jostling, Fionna awoke with a deep yawn.

Dan kissed her forehead before he took the folded piece of yellow paper from Aida's hands.

"What is this, baby girl?" Fionna looked pleased to be so close to home.

"Grandma said for me to give it to you last night, but I fell asleep. I'm sorry. I think it's things she wants you to bring back for her from Tutu's store."

Fionna began giggling, and Dan turned back to her. His brow furrowed as she bit her lips together to keep from laughing outright.

"What?" Dan was delighted she was laughing.

She showed him his mother's handwritten list. He shuddered slightly. "She couldn't just order that so I don't have to play delivery boy?"

"I promised we'd get more for Meredith and Tim too," Fionna informed him.

The lubricant that Fionna's grandmother grew the ingredients for and then spun into a liquid lotion that was made to enhance the sexual experience was something Dan was extremely fond of as well. He and Fionna used it regularly. It caused their energy to bond more readily. It not only felt incredible when Dan joined their bodies together, but it allowed him to pound into his wife just like she liked it without any fear that she might be rubbed or sore the next day. It even made their orgasms more intense.

The friction was perfection, and Dan found himself eager to get to their cottage on the farm and to spend a few hours caught up in their bedroom, just the two of them deeply enjoying an erotic night.

But his mother's list requested three large jars of the ʻŌhiʻa lehua lube, and Dan couldn't seem to get his face to return to its normal shade. He was momentarily lost in a sea of desire and repulsion.

"I can't believe your mom wants stuff from the farm."

His mother certainly had several less than kind things to say about the farm that meant everything to him and Fionna and the girls, but it appeared she'd come around when she'd seen that the products Fionna's grandparents grew and produced actually worked.

"Is it okay that I just remembered?" Aida asked

"It's fine, baby. We have all week to get these things for Grandma," Fionna assured her. "Why don't you get Sophie and all of your things all packed up because we're about to land."

With that, the coolant officer requested that everyone prepare for landing.

"Two weeks," Dan reminded her gently. "I'll take off the first part of next week as well. Then if you want Aida to stay with you we'll do that, or I can bring her home and pick you up Saturday. We'll spend all day Sunday together. If you need to stay another week, I'll fly out Friday night and spend the weekend with you. Then I'll bring her back home with me for the next week." He explained the plan he'd settled on while she'd napped.

"I don't want to talk about it until next week."

"Okay." Dan didn't want to think about it or talk about it either.

"Will you take a nap with me on the porch bed this afternoon?"

"Of course." That was their custom after all.

A little while later, Dan, Fionna, and Aida spilled out of Malani's Jeep. Dan drew a deep breath of the Kauaian air. It stirred and soothed his soul. He never wanted to leave.

"Tutu, I'm here!" Aida trilled.

Fionna's grandparents appeared instantly. They were both thrilled that Aida was so excited to be back on the farm

"You *are* here!" Tutu hugged Aida fiercely.

Fionna handed Kai and Malani's little girl, Lanie, to Dan so she could hug her grandparents. Dan was shocked at how much the baby had grown.

It felt quite natural to cradle her on his shoulder and brush kisses on her sweet head that she was able to hold up on her own now.

"Maylea." Tutu shook her head as soon as she embraced her granddaughter.

"I know," Fionna sighed. "I'm staying an extra week if that's okay." Her grandmother, who was a Receiver with even more power than her own, immediately picked up on Fionna's harrowed emotions and her chaotic rhythms.

"You say that like I didn't already know." Tutu chuckled.

"And you should know you don't even have to ask," Papa reminded her. "But from the look on your Tutu's face, maybe you better stay longer."

"Let's see how I am by the end of this week."

"And I know Dan isn't staying an extra week." Tutu gave Fionna's arm a reassuring squeeze.

"I'll stay 'til next Tuesday or Wednesday, but then I need to go back to work."

"It doesn't feel like that's really what you want to do or what your rhythms are telling you to do, Daniel," Tutu informed him.

"No, they aren't," Dan agreed. "Maybe we should talk a little more about moving out here permanently after graduation." Fionna's entire body lit with glee.

Malani began jumping up and down. "Yes! You should definitely talk more about that."

Tutu smirked. "Oh, how the tides are changing…"

In the midst of her celebrating, Malani slipped a burp cloth on Dan's shoulder under Lanie's head. He was patting her back gently, and she was almost asleep. Suddenly, she reared her head back and spit up. It completely missed the protective cloth and oozed down Dan's chest. He mopped himself up and cleaned up Lanie's mouth.

Malani cringed. "You still have to love her because Kai and I want you and Maylea to be her godparents. I wanted to have the blessing while you're here this week. And if you do move back, you are never, never moving away again!"

Fionna was thrilled. She gave Dan a pleading gaze.

"Of course, baby," he agreed.

Kai pulled up in his truck a moment later. He'd been out on the back fields planting from the looks of it.

"There's my baby girl," he sang to Lanie who had a drooly smile for her daddy. Dan handed her to him.

"Ah, she got you." Kai shook Dan's hand and gestured to the spit-up mark on his shirt. "She's quick with that."

"All right, Miss Aida, Auntie Malani is going to make breakfast. Do you want to help while Mommy and Daddy unpack?" Malani offered.

"And Papa made you some *Pani Popo*." Papa winked at Aida.

"I want to help." She raced into Tutu's kitchen.

Though Aida was most certainly not conceived on the island of Kauai and didn't carry the Kauaian rhythms like Halia would, Dan noted that her trepidation over the tabloid article seemed to melt away in light of being back on the island.

Papa loaded Dan and Fionna and all of their luggage in his truck. He drove them to the guest cottage on the farm where they stayed when they visited.

"You know, if you're gonna move back out here, we're gonna have to build you something bigger when my little Halia comes and then your next two," Papa commented.

Fionna shook her head. "Maybe next *one,* but it won't be two."

If Tutu had already informed Papa that there would be other additions to the Vindico family, Dan was certain that was true. She was never wrong, and her powerful Predilect coupled with her ability to read the rhythms of Kauai made her a force to be reckoned with. But they'd only ever discussed having three children.

Tutu would never have let that slip. Emotions certainly changed, and she never wanted her feelings to shadow others' decisions.

Papa chuckled. "We'll see, now won't we."

After Dan helped Fionna unpack and then ate the breakfast prepared in their honor, he cornered Tutu in her kitchen. Fionna and Malani had taken Aida to see her garden.

"Can I ask you something?"

Giving him her wise, knowing smile, Tutu chuckled. "Of course."

"I know that you don't always like to tell people what the island rhythms tell you, but I need to know that Fi isn't going to have the baby while I'm gone. Before I set all of this up, I'm not leaving if that's even a possibility."

"Maylea will be fine," Tutu assured him. "Your *girls* will not be born here on the island," she explained with a twinkle in her eye as she placed heavy emphasis on the plural word girls. "Halia will be born in Virginia."

Dan's brow furrowed. "But my boys will be born here?" He tried to envision that.

Tutu gave him a grin as she patted his hand.

"You said that, not me."

"Just how sure are you about that?" he demanded. Tutu laughed at him outright. "Do you mean, like, boy-s like plural boys, like more than one boy?"

"Daniel, relax," Tutu soothed. "The island will guide you, and right now Maylea is a mess. We have one week to make her whole. She will feel lost when you leave, but it is still better than what she's experiencing in DC."

Feeling like he was being rent in two, Dan nodded his acceptance of the next few weeks of his life.

He let everything he'd just learned stir in his mind as he moved back to the cottage. Hooking up his laptop, Dan set to work. He switched Fionna and Aida's return tickets, then his own, then he emailed Mrs. Powell and explained that they'd decided to extend their vacation. He asked if she would mind sending Aida's work via email.

He checked his voicemail and was relieved to hear Logan's message that Becca was doing well, but that Adeline was keeping her sedated for the rest of the day. She would be released Sunday night as long as her condition continued to improve.

With that, he shut his laptop and turned off his cell phone. He wanted to absorb the island with his wife and his girls.

CHAPTER 22

WHITE HAT RED CAPE

JEFF STRENTON

Becca stirred, and Jeff left his work immediately. Laying the laptop on the bench, he brushed tender kisses along her forehead and cheek and then let his shield move out over her body. His heart flew as he felt his little boy's rhythms pick up on his own. Jeff flooded his shield with soothing warmth, and Becca fell back into a deep sleep.

While caressing his hand over her abdomen, Jeff noted that the swelling seemed to be going down.

"Hey, little guy," he whispered as their little boy's rhythms spun and began to lilt. "Please be okay. Just please," he choked. "We love you so much. I swear I'll keep you safe and be there for you always."

He kept Becca casted for a while but then returned to his work. She needed to sleep, and he needed to prove his worth to Portwood and to Iodex. He planned to take his exams soon. He needed to convince his boss to hire him even if his GPA slipped because he needed a real full-time job with a real full-time paycheck. If he could catch this idiot quickly, he was almost certain he could convince Portwood to hire him even without his 4.0.

Jeff concentrated on the screen before him. He felt the energy of the machine in his lap. He could see the data moving all around him. He'd always understood the energy inside electronic machines almost as well as he understood his own shield. It made sense to him. He casted and threw the data up into his shield so he could study it all around him.

Rolling his eyes, he chuckled quietly at the hacker's self-assigned screen name. As he typed it into Google just for kicks, something struck him.

JSly4361 had been bragging rather pompously on numerous websites about his skills and that always irked Jeff. Being angry at the guy made his Predilection stronger, which he needed now. He was exhausted and he wanted to catch this guy. 4361, 4361… That number seemed familiar, but it took Jeff a minute to recall where he'd seen it before. JS4361—he remembered suddenly.

He accessed his email on his own laptop at home. His brow furrowed as he opened a logged email from Venton from before school had begun. It was an electronic copy of Jeff's schedule they'd sent out for review.

Student Name: Jeffrey Aaron Strenton
   Class Rank: Senior
   Predilect: Ioses - Lieutenant Commander of Order
   Student Number: JS4361

He tried to tell himself it was a coincidence, but an ominous sense of dread worked through his shield. He shut down the information on his own laptop and went back to the task at hand. Student numbers only ever appeared on schedules and report cards. He hardly remembered his own. He was never asked to give it for any reason. He didn't even know Becca's. He tried to pacify himself as he continued.

Throwing himself into his work, Jeff summoned and casted the laptop. He logged in with his Senate security account via his Iodex badge number and kept a close eye on the traffic moving back and forth over the firewalls of the Senate Bank website.

Criminal hackers generally liked to access multiple accounts with vast amounts of money in them. Skimming a little off of the top of numerous accounts could make a hacker quite wealthy, and if they were smart, they could keep doing it without the account owners getting wise to the missing funds for some time.

Jeff began watching accounts that had been compromised in the hacker's last attempts. The banking board of governors had immediately reset the security on those, but it was a decent place to start. He skipped over several of Rainer and Emily's accounts. He wasn't trying to spy on people, and he didn't want to know how much money his friends had. He preferred to work anonymously. The people's accounts he was watching were really nothing more than numbers on a screen.

Nothing seemed unusual as Jeff stared at the information. He decided to start at the beginning. He archived and then reset all of the security logs on the accounts he was interested in. He began watching the feeds along with the firewalls.

Rubbing his eyes, Jeff forced himself to focus. He popped open one of the Dr Peppers Logan had left chill casted and downed it in a few sips before he inhaled another protein bar.

"Jeff," Becca whispered. She sounded terrified. Jeff half tossed the laptop on the bench seat beside him as he rushed back to her side.

"I'm right here."

A timid smile formed on her beautiful face as she reached for his hand. Jeff laced their fingers together and leaned to kiss her sweetly.

"You're supposed to be asleep, Mrs. Strenton." He gave her an adoring gaze. Her blinks were heavy as she managed a slight nod.

"I had a weird dream." She coughed. Jeff lifted the plastic cup of water Adeline had left and held it for Becca to sip through the straw.

She inhaled the water, and Jeff refilled the bottle and supplied her more.

"Thank you."

"How do you feel, baby?" He set the bottle near her and then set his cast over her once again.

"Better when you do that." She relaxed as she felt him permeate the very air she breathed in. "I think we should name the baby Aaron, after you and after your grandfather."

"We don't have to decide today." Thinking about naming his son after his grandfather had a rock-like enclosure cinching around his throat. It would mean a great deal to him and his mother, but he wanted Becca to choose.

"I like Aaron. It's perfect," she insisted.

"Okay." He let his hand caress over her stomach again. He breathed a sigh of relief to discover that the swelling was reducing.

Aaron must've sensed his father's shield. His rhythms picked up again.

Becca felt it as well. Tears leaked from her eyes.

A deep yawn overtook her. He kissed her cheek and released his cast. "Go to sleep, sweetheart. Adeline wants you to rest, and it's really helping." Her color was returning, and her body seemed to be healing before his eyes.

Becca eased to her right side and tried to get comfortable. "I wish I had my pillow...or you," she fussed.

As he tucked her back in, a sense of contentment worked through him. It didn't matter what her father thought. She was happy with him. He made her feel safe and loved and that was all that would ever matter to him.

"Mom said she'd go by the house on her way back from work. I'll get her to bring your pillow."

"I love your mom." She yawned as her eyes began to close again.

A hesitant knock sounded on the door. Logan poked his head in. "I brought you some subs from Big Mickey's and more Dr Pepper," he whispered.

"Thanks. Come on in."

Logan set the sandwiches from Iodex's favorite sub shop on the table and added several additional cans of Dr Pepper to Jeff's supply.

"How's it going?" He gestured to the laptop.

"Slow, but that's kind of the deal with stuff like this."

"Is she okay?" was Logan's response as he glanced at Becca.

"She's woken up a few times. She's been having these crazy dreams ever since she got pregnant, but she seems loads better."

"Yeah, I can tell." Logan seemed to know that he needed the reassurance. "I'm gonna go home for a little while, but Rainer and I will be back after we help Dad with one of the Gators he can't get to work. Ad's working all day, so she'll be by in a little while, I'm sure."

"Are my in-laws still out there?"

Logan nodded. "I'm pretty sure they think you'll eventually give in and let them see her. Ad keeps telling them she's just sleeping."

"They'll be waiting a while," Jeff huffed.

"Simmer down there, Strenton. Her mom's really upset."

Jeff refused the guilt that prodded his internal shield.

"Call me if you get anything or if you need me." Logan exited the room.

Jeff unwrapped one of the sandwiches and opened the laptop again. The meatball slathered with cheese almost came forcefully back out of his mouth as he took in one of the security logs that had numerous entries suddenly. It seemed to have withstood a brute force attack. There were over fifty thousand hits of random passwords on one account.

"Shit." He swallowed down the food and went back over the firewalls and logs. His mind raced as he tried to determine how to take care of his wife and little baby, catch this idiot, and score himself a job all at the same time.

He needed to go on the offensive instead of playing a passive defense. Jeff quickly coded an enhanced trojan. He casted the laptop again and forced his own energy into the detection trojan device he'd just created. He attached it to the accounts under attack. If Becca needed him, he would be there. He could let the technology work for him.

The enhanced tracer would send back data from the hacker's computer. If he'd juiced it just right, it would supply him with location information on the IP addresses in use.

Glancing back at Becca, he drew a deep breath. She was sleeping peacefully, and Jeff moved his ardent gaze back to his work. Frustration set in as everything seemed to halt. He clenched his jaw and casted yet again. He moved his search outside of the firewalls.

Stunned disbelief rocked through him as he watched the password attempts continue but never make it to the firewall to be rejected. Expanding further, Jeff began to see page request after page request be redirected to a faulty script page. No one else was signed in to the Senate servers that could have been deflecting the attempts.

Studying the redirect page, Jeff gasped. Someone had taken it upon themselves to stop the bank hack—a white hat. Jeff ground his teeth. *Can't I just be the hero today?*

If he was going to use his trojan device and actually find the guy doing this instead of just keeping him from the sites, he was actually going to have to help the hacker to the firewall.

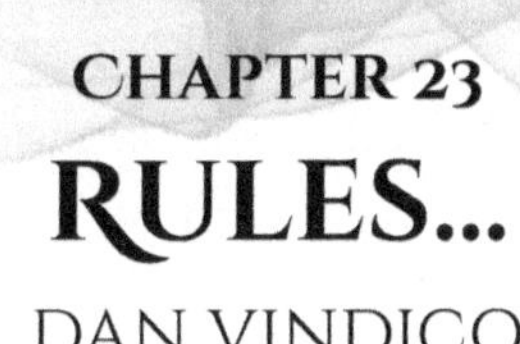

CHAPTER 23
RULES...
DAN VINDICO

Dan lifted Aida into his arms and spun her around as he listened to his baby girl squeal with delight as they played in the gentle ocean water. Fionna watched them from her chair on the sandy shore. She beamed. After a few more spins, Dan sauntered back to his wife and her grandparents.

"Now, I was serious this morning," Papa began. "If you're bringing my girls back to me, then I think we need to either build you a house on the farm or give you ours."

"We can't take your house," Fionna insisted.

"And why not?" Tutu asked. "There are going to be four of you for a little while then maybe more, and there are only two of us."

"Because your house is your house."

Dan understood that to his Maylea, Tutu and Papa's house was an institution that would remain forever in her mind. He debated bringing up the one significant complication with the idea of moving back. He wasn't so sure he wanted to be a farmer, and he had no idea what kinds of jobs were available on the island. He decided to bring that up later.

Fionna was already better. Her color and rhythms were stronger. The stress and worry had ebbed from her features just as the makeup on her face had been replaced with nothing more than sunscreen.

191

Contented relief washed through him as he studied her, relaxed and at peace. He'd talk to her about wanting a different job later.

Jeff Strenton

Clenching his jaw in defiant determination, Jeff prayed Becca wouldn't need him for the next few minutes as he set about shutting down the helper's servers. He flooded them with a denial of service attack. He casted each packet of information, expanded it, and sent it in rapid transmissions. He let his fingers fly. He needed to win today of all days.

Suddenly, the account he was watching was accessed, and Jeff halted his attack on the white hat instantly. His heart pounded as he casted and activated the homing beacon on the trojan he'd set.

Jeff wiped the sweat from his hands on his jeans as he watched the relays begin. It worked! Every cell in his body rejoiced as he watched the trace route light up on his screen. He called Logan.

"I just got something. Can you and Rainer get back out here, like, right now?"

"We were already on our way back up there. We'll be there in just a few," Logan assured him.

Indonesia, Brazil, Myanmar… Jeff stared at the screen and prayed his tracer would lead him wherever the hacker might be. Costa Rica, then California. Jeff's heart hammered. He was afraid to even blink.

Rainer and Logan flew through the door without knocking. They stood behind Jeff and watched the laptop screen silently as Becca slept on.

Wyoming, New Jersey. Everyone leaned in as the tracer beacon slowed.

Virginia, Arlington flashed on the screen.

"What the hell?" Logan whispered as they continued to watch.

Jeff's heart sank as he began to realize that perhaps JSly4361 was not a coincidence.

The signal homed in just as Jeff had programmed it to do. His cast held. The laptop glowed green with the signatures of his casts.

Virginia, Falls Church was next.

Logan's mouth hung open.

"No way." Rainer shook his head.

Virginia, Falls Church, Idylwood pulsed on the screen.

"No fucking way," Jeff gasped under his breath. Everyone stood in stunned silence as they watched the beacon halt and pulse on 79 Highland Estates Way. It took the enhanced mapping program on the computer a half second to show a satellite image of the Sapmans' multimillion-dollar mansion on the golf course.

"Why is it showing us that?" Logan demanded. Jeff shook his head in abject disbelief. He willed the laptop to say anything else.

"That's where the hacker is right now," he managed to choke.

"I was afraid that's what you were going to say." Logan rubbed his forehead as Rainer began to pace.

"Man, her parents are sitting out there. You understand that we now have to go arrest the Sap-asses." Rainer cringed.

"I'm...sorry." Jeff tried to locate the appropriate reaction.

Letting his training kick in, Rainer jerked his phone from his pocket. "Portwood, Jeff's got them, and you're not going to believe this. We're heading out. I'll give you the address in the car." Rainer and Logan sprinted from Becca's hospital room.

Jeff ran his hands through his hair as he marched in front of Becca's bed. A million thoughts vied for his attention. *It serves them right. Greg and Brent aren't smart enough to have done this. What the hell were they thinking? There is no way they know how to hack like that. Does Daddy not make enough money?* He couldn't believe what he'd found.

He returned to his laptop and continued to watch their attempts. "Unbelievable." He glanced back at Becca and tried to formulate what to say to her after her brothers were apprehended.

His cell phone vibrated in his pocket.

"We're here. We just busted in the front door. Ramier's got the computer, and he's extremely impressed, by the way," Portwood said. "But the Sap-asses aren't here. Did they get word we were coming?"

"Wait, what?" Jeff stared at the laptop again. "You have the computers?"

"Yeah, John's unhooking them. They're evidence."

"Sir, there's still activity on the servers. Someone hacked their computers. They're logged in remotely. It's not Greg and Brent."

Casting again, he reworked his trojan device and pushed it harder. He forced it to find where the Sapmans' computer was being controlled from.

"I've got it," he gasped.

"Okay, where is this prick, because I just broke in a governor's house," Portwood demanded.

"He's at the Starbucks right across the street from the Senate."

"We're on our way!"

Logan Haydenshire

"Why would this guy be spoofing the Sap-asses?" Logan demanded of Rainer as he flew back to the Senate.

"Got me." Rainer threw the Porsche into park and leapt from the car among the flashing blue lights and blaring sirens. A kid that looked younger than Jeff sprinted out the front door. He was clinging to a laptop.

"That's him! Get him," Portwood ordered, but the kid was fast. He threw the laptop on the pavement and dodged in and out of tourists, making his escape in the sea of people.

Tuttle and Ericcson raced into the coffee shop as Rainer saved the laptop from an oncoming bus.

Tuttle emerged a second later, sporting quite a smirk. "Wonder how long it'll take him to realize he might've left something behind?" He held up a forgotten cell phone.

"Haydenshire," Portwood commanded.

"Sir," Logan answered.

"Take the phone, and you and Lawson find this kid. Bring him to Georgetown. I'm bringing in the Sapman boys as well."

"You got it." Logan and Rainer took the phone and flew up to the Iodex office.

It took them approximately thirty seconds to have a name and address to go along with the cell phone number. Logan called Garrett at the Non-Gifted police precinct to meet them there.

An hour later, Garrett escorted a scowling, belligerent teenager into Georgetown Hospital.

Portwood dragged Greg and Brent Sapman in. They were also in cuffs. "I sent Ramier up there with Jeff. Adeline got us a conference room."

Rainer and Logan followed Portwood to the room.

As the Sapman boys were escorted by their parents, the governor was visibly stunned.

"Landon, what is the meaning of this? Are you looking to lose your job?" Governor Sapman spat.

"Let's talk in here, Governor." Portwood never lost his cool and never looked frightened. It was quite impressive. It was also something he'd learned from Dan Vindico.

Logan and Garrett tried to hide their smirks as the scowling Sapman brothers shot Portwood infuriated glares.

Jeff Strenton

"I'm really sorry, but I need to get back to Becca," Jeff pled with Ramier as he paced in the Georgetown Hospital conference room that Portwood had ordered everyone to.

"Just give me a second," Ramier soothed. "Adeline's with her, and you casted her five minutes ago."

Suddenly Ramier booted Greg Sapman's computer and intrigue got to Jeff. He stared at the screen as Ramier opened the browser history.

Jeff gagged. "Man, my pregnant wife is lying in a hospital bed. That is wrong on so many levels." He turned away from the website that loaded as Greg's home page.

"Agreed, and you're a smart man to be saying that now, but I thought Governor Sapman might like to know how their home computers and network were compromised." He pointed to the webcam and then to the web addresses of numerous live chat programs listed in the history repeatedly.

Ramier casted the computer and brought up the women available for chatting. Jeff convulsed. It appeared that Greg had multiple conversations with a brunette that called herself Tammy Tangston.

"They cannot be that stupid." Jeff shook his head.

Ramier laughed. "Here's your chance. Why don't you show the good governor what idiots his sons are? Might make him change his tune about you."

As appealing as that sounded, Jeff didn't want to look his father-in-law in the eye and explain how his moronic sons had compromised everything from their own home to the Senate Bank.

The door to the conference room opened. Logan and Garrett shoved a kid through the door with Sergeant Sorenson, the Non-Gifted police chief, behind them.

"I'll be with you in just a minute." Portwood directed Governor and Mrs. Sapman along with Greg and Brent into chairs in the waiting area outside the conference room.

"Tuttle, keep an eye on the Sapmans for me, would you?" Portwood directed.

"You got it," Tuttle agreed. Jeff watched his father-in-law burn with acrid fury.

"Why am I here? What are you gonna do to me?" The guy that Garrett Haydenshire had by the shoulders appeared terrified as Garrett shoved him down in one of the rolling chairs in the room.

"Here's what we're gonna do." Portwood leaned inches from the guy's face. Jeff tried not to look shocked by his fury as he watched his boss work. "You're gonna shut the hell up and then we're gonna figure out who you are and why you decided to be a genius and try to hack the National Bank's website?" Portwood spat and Jeff understood.

The guy seated before him wasn't Gifted. There were so many Gifted people currently in the room Jeff hadn't yet realized that there wasn't an energy stream coming from the suspect. That's why they'd called in Garrett. He was the Gifted liaison to the Non-Gifted police precinct in DC. The American Realm Senate Bank would not be acknowledged by anyone in the room until they figured out what the guy they'd arrested knew.

"His name is Christopher Reynolds, nineteen years old. He's a Hokie," Garrett sneered with a chuckle.

"I swear I wasn't gonna steal any money from the accounts," Christopher pled.

"Uh-huh, you just wanted to see if you could get in just to do it, right?" Ramier rolled his eyes.

"No, I swear. I'll tell you everything. Just don't arrest me."

"Do you see the cuffs on your wrists? Those aren't for looks. You've been arrested. What are they teaching you at Tech?" Garrett quizzed with a smirk.

On the verge of tears, Christopher seemed to decide that he could talk his way out of the cuffs. "These guys emailed me and asked if I could make it look like this other guy was gonna hack this, like, big bank or whatever," he began. "I said sure, for the right price. The next morning there's five thousand dollars in my checking account. I was supposed to use this guy's student number, Strenton, or whatever, and make it look like he was gonna pull a bank job online."

No one spoke as nervous glances shot around the room.

"Who were these guys? What are their names?" Portwood demanded.

"I don't know. I never saw them, but I mean they already had my checking account number, and I just kept getting paid. They said they'd cut me in on a big score they were taking if I got the guy into trouble for them." Christopher couldn't get the words out fast enough. "They gave me his address. Told me to make it look like everything was coming from Strenton's computer. So, I did, but I swear that's all I know. How did you even find me?"

"Get him out of here," Portwood commanded. "Take him in, print him, and call his parents." He gave the order to scare the shit out of the guy but not to lock him up.

"Yes, sir." Garrett jerked Christopher out of his seat and shoved him forward.

The latch of the door gave an ominous click as Jeff tried to remember to breathe.

"Any idea why you're being set up?" Portwood studied Jeff closely.

Sharing a quick glance with Logan, Jeff prayed that Mentor Vindico wouldn't hate him for telling the truth. "Maybe, sir."

"It's not his fault." Logan stepped up for Jeff immediately.

"It may not have anything to do with that. A lot of people at school are pissed at me," he reminded Logan.

Drawing a deep breath, Portwood threw back the chair Christopher had previously occupied. "You two sit and talk, and Jeff, if you want the Elite appointment, you better start at the beginning and not leave anything out."

"Yes, sir." Jeff and Logan took seats.

"Everyone else wait outside but don't go anywhere," Portwood ordered.

As the rest of the team filed out of the room, Rainer offered Jeff a hopeful smile.

Jeff began speaking as if his very life depended on it. "Becca told me she was pregnant like a week or two before school started." Portwood seemed to visibly soften as Jeff continued. "I freaked, of course." He was still disappointed in himself over his initial reaction. "I guess I never really hung out with a bunch of people or whatever." He hoped that Portwood understood that he was trying to say that he'd never had many friends. "I hung out with Logan and Rainer mostly, and then after they graduated, I just sort of worked all the time or hung with Becca.

"But I needed to talk to somebody about the baby. I didn't know what to do. I knew Mentor Vindico would kind of understand because everyone knows what happened back in the spring. So, I went to see him. I told him everything, and for some reason he helped me. But you gotta understand, people at school haven't ever really liked me. You know my dad or whatever, and I always had to work so I couldn't really just hang out and mess around," he regurgitated the way his life had been for as long as he could remember.

"I got the appointment to Iodex as an intern, and a bunch of people are still really angry about that. With everything that happened to Becca, they thought it wasn't fair. No one has any idea how hard I've worked to keep my grades up and try to make enough money to help my mom with rent and groceries and pay for my clothes and everything. I worked my ass off, I swear."

"I know," Portwood assured him. His gentle tone gave him hope.

"Anyway, so Mentor Vindico is tough. I mean, like, the hardest teacher Venton's ever had." This brought about a genuine chuckle which furthered Jeff's hopefulness. "But for some reason, he believed in me, and he didn't care that I don't know my dad or have even half the amount of money most of the kids at school have. But outside of his upper level Ioses defense classes, people don't like him. He doesn't take their shit, and he doesn't really seem to care." Jeff was still in awe of his favorite mentor.

"People not liking Dan has never bothered him, but what does that have to do with people trying to frame you for hacking the Senate Bank?" Portwood demanded.

"You told him not to skip anything," Logan reminded him gently. Portwood nodded for Jeff to continue.

"People obviously heard that Becca was pregnant and then that I got the Iodex appointment and then I guess Mentor Vindico kind of took me under his wing. He's been giving me extra training sessions and he lets me hang out with him." Jeff's cheeks blazed as he considered how lame that probably sounded. "People are furious, and they do the whole mentor's pet crap. But I don't care. I just want the hell out of school. It's so stupid. I'm tired of hanging around with people whose biggest concern is who has the newest version of some freaking video game and who banged who Saturday night. I've learned more in the last month from you and from Vindico than I've learned in the last five years at Venton. Stuff that I'm actually gonna use in my life. I'm going to have a kid. I need to grow up." His boss appeared deeply impressed, and Jeff was able to draw a deep breath.

"Anyway," he moved on quickly, "Governor Vindico asked Mentor Vindico…" Jeff didn't want to out either of the Vindicos.

Logan stepped in quickly. "Dad and Governor Vindico asked Dan to figure out what the hell was going on at Venton. They didn't want it all falling in Governor Vindico's lap with the press. They didn't want to open it up as an official Iodex investigation. And here's the missing piece to this puzzle that Jeff doesn't know—Fionna's not doing well," Logan's voice lowered even though they were the only three people in the room. "Ad's making her stay in Hawaii for the next few weeks because she's from there and something about the volcanic energy of the islands regulates her energy. But what happened to her back in March is affecting the baby. You know Dan." He gestured his hands out to Portwood. "He's a disaster, so he asked Jeff and me to help him help his dad with Venton. He knew if we opened it up as an official Iodex investigation, the press would eat Governor Vindico alive, and that would also affect Fionna.

"We suspected that Mentor Bryant knew Jeff was helping Dan and that she was trying to make it look like he sent that electric pulse through the lock on the test vault, but maybe that isn't it. But don't be mad at Jeff. You know he's not gonna turn down Dan." Logan shared a knowing glance with Portwood that made Jeff uncomfortable. Clearly, his admiration of Dan Vindico was known throughout Iodex.

Drawing a deep breath, Portwood nodded. "And when Dan presented his findings on the affair to his dad and Governor Haydenshire, Wilshire figured out that you were helping him. I take it he knows of your tech skills." Portwood gestured to Greg's computer still on the table.

"After what just happened, sir, I'm not sure that either Chancellor Wilshire or Mentor Bryant know anything about me at all. Dan asked me to get him the stuff on Wilshire's affair first. That's what the governors wanted most, so that's what I did."

Portwood nodded. "Before we get into what just happened, I need you to listen to me. I don't give a damn if you and Logan want to play detective for Dan or the Crown or whomever. If Governor Haydenshire or Vindico had asked me to look into Venton, I would have done the very same thing. So you can breathe, Jeff.

"But let me tell you a few things about Dan Vindico. Know that I love Dan like a brother, and I admire the hell out of the guy. There's not much I wouldn't do for him, but Dan's never been all that good at playing by the rules when it came to getting what he wanted. When it comes to Fionna or his girls, stand back, because he's like a man possessed. When they started dating, he somehow got better and worse."

Logan nodded adamantly.

"He was almost human again instead of the shell he'd been for years, but then he had a prize and he was going to get her come hell or high water. He would quite literally kill anyone who stood in his way," Portwood elaborated, and Jeff understood the Wretchkinsides reference only too well. "I need you to let me do your training instead of Dan. It sounds like he's got his plate full with his girls, and you *have* to learn to play by the rules. Dan has never had to."

"Yeah, that's what the other mentors are saying too," Jeff allowed.

Portwood drew a deep breath. "So, if you want to be on the Elite Squadron, then here's one of your final exams. Do you think whoever the people are that paid that idiot to make it look like you were trying to hack the Senate Bank are just trying to get you into trouble, or is there more to this? And why are they doing this? What did we just learn?"

Jeff swallowed down his fear. "No sir, I don't think they're just trying to get me into trouble. I think whoever is stealing the exams and putting them online are the same people that did this. I think they're the same people who sent the electric surge through the test vault. They're trying to pin it *all* on me. It would be perfect. They know that I would know how to get the exams on the Internet. They know I could run enough servers to handle that load. They could get back at me, make me lose my job, and embarrass Becca." Jeff shuddered slightly before going on.

"But not only that, they could make Mentor Vindico look like a joke for asking for my help, and that would really make Governor Vindico look like a fool. There are a bunch of kids that don't like Governor Vindico being up there. The last few years, Wilshire hasn't done much, so everyone liked that no one cared what they wore to school or if they had soda in class or whatever.

"But whoever did all of this must not know me that well, because they thought I was living at the Sapmans'. Clearly, they thought I'd be home today, so it's no one that had any idea that Becca is in the hospital. I think we're looking at students, not mentors. They sought out a college kid because they *are* college kids. That's why I don't think it's Wilshire or Bryant. If these are the people who are posting the exams online, then they know how to hack. They were setting that Non-Gifted kid up as their fall guy in case they got caught. Ramier is Ramier. He could've found the IP address the same way I did. Whoever is doing this doesn't want to be anywhere near it." He stated everything he'd deduced from the last few minutes.

"Excellent detective work," Portwood complimented. His deeply impressed grin eased the tense set of Jeff's shoulders. "Now, I think we're going to ask Dan to help you. You're going to school with kids who are willing to put you in Felsink. That tells me that neither you nor Becca are particularly safe at Venton Academy.

"Let's go yell at the Sap-asses, take the governor down a notch or two, and let him see what an incredible officer his son-in-law is going to be. And hell, you two finish helping Dan with Venton. I don't want Governor Vindico going down for this either, but just remember what I said. If you want to be one of my top officers, then we're going to do this the right way, by the book. No more rogue missions or ones you're keeping from me."

"Yes, sir," Jeff and Logan answered.

"Is there anything legal on that machine?" He gestured to the Sapmans' computer.

"It's nothing but porn and pirated video games," Jeff sighed. "But, sir, please let me go check on Becca before we do this."

"You've got five minutes, and then you're going to watch me chew the Sapmans' asses. Then we're gonna discuss how I and a few of your Elite teammates will be tutoring you and getting you through your exams. You're right. You do need a real job in the real world. If you're willing to step up to the plate, then it shouldn't just be Dan who stands beside you. We're going to catch the guys trying to set you up. We're going to figure out what the hell is going on at Venton Academy, and then we're going to make you an Elite officer."

"Thank you!" Jeff gushed. "You have no idea how much that means to me. I'll do anything."

"Go check on her," Portwood ordered.

"I'll be right back."

CHAPTER 24

AND CONSEQUENCES

He met Adeline coming out of Becca's room. She looked relieved. "Becca just woke up. She's asking for you. I was coming to get you. She's much better. I still want her to stay overnight, but if we can keep her rhythms regulated, and she takes it easy, I think you're going to be a daddy in April."

"Thank you for taking care of her. She means everything to me." Jeff swallowed back the emotion that had him in a sudden chokehold. He was not only going to make this work, but he was going to have help.

"Go see her."

Jeff was astonished at how much better Becca appeared. She gave him a weak grin as soon as he entered.

"Hey, baby." He rushed to her side.

"Where'd you go?"

"Long, long story, but things are definitely looking up." He wondered if he should tell her about her brothers but decided to wait until the story had an ending.

"Relax for me. Let me cast you because I have to get back to Portwood, but I'll tell you everything as soon as we're done."

Becca studied him as he set his shield over her. "Your rhythms feel like you again. I haven't felt you like this in so long."

"I'm sorry. I let everything get to me."

She grasped both of his hands with more force than she'd had in the past twelve hours. "I'm just glad you're back."

"I have to go in just a minute, sweetheart. I'm sorry." He pushed the guilt away. This was part of being a good husband and a good father. He had to finish this job so that he could be there for her and for their little boy.

"I didn't mean right now. I meant you feel like you're here with me. Like we're going to take care of our little guy together and figure out everything." She tried to explain, but she was still weak and tired from the blood loss and her surgery not to mention the medication she'd been given.

After sitting with Becca for several minutes, staring at her stomach as he felt Aaron's energy soothe under his own, Jeff kissed her forehead and promised to be back as quickly as he could.

Emily and Mrs. Haydenshire had come back to check on Becca. They'd gone home after Becca's surgery. Governor Sapman had apparently called the Crown Governor about his sons being arrested. Governor Haydenshire was waiting with Portwood. Jeff thanked Emily and her mother for sitting with Becca while he worked up the courage to explain what had happened to the Sapmans and the Crown Governor.

He raced back in the conference room to expectant faces. Rainer and Ramier had returned to the room as well.

"This ought to be good," Governor Sapman huffed indignantly.

"George, your sons have been arrested. Why don't you simmer down and let's figure out what exactly is going on?" Governor Haydenshire commanded.

Portwood nodded. "Although that is true, Jeff proved that Greg and Brent were not actually hacking the Senate Bank. Had he not done a phenomenal job and performed feats of technology today that I've rarely seen, we would be taking your sons to Felsink right now, Governor." He stared Governor Sapman down.

"What?" The governor gasped.

"I believe *thank you* is the phrase you're looking for," Governor Haydenshire ordered.

"We didn't hack the Senate Bank." Greg rolled his eyes. "I wouldn't even know how to do something like that."

Governor Sapman turned his glare back on Jeff.

"Someone hacked your home computers, sir," Jeff patiently explained to his father-in-law. "They were able to log in remotely and make it appear that Greg and Brent were attempting to steal account numbers and passwords from the Senate Bank. I figured out where the guy doing it was actually located, and he's been arrested. But your files and any other information on any of your computers have been compromised. You're going to need to update all of your security measures, and I would recommend new networking as well."

"I imagine if you apologized for being an ass earlier and asked very nicely, your incredibly talented son-in-law might be willing to help you with that." Governor Haydenshire was clearly just as furious with Governor Sapman as Jeff and Becca.

"I don't understand. How did this happen? How did someone hack our computer or log in remotely or whatever you said?" Governor Sapman asked Jeff. His tone was concerned but much more kind.

Jeff grimaced. Ramier gave him an encouraging nod. "Well,"—Jeff swallowed down his disgust—"anytime you use an online service, or a pirated game or book, or any kind of illegal software, you're opening yourself up to viruses and worms. This was a worm, and it appeared that it came through a program that was being used frequently." He glanced at Greg who was slinking farther down in his seat.

Portwood stepped in. "The majority of this particular computer's hard drive space"—he gestured to the desktop machine on the table—"is full of pornography and illegal video games. The hack came via a webchat program Greg was using. It would appear that he and a busty brunette named Tammy Tangston have been getting nice and chatty lately."

Governor Sapman looked mutinous as he glared at both of his sons.

"What, 'cause you don't do shit like that?" Greg rolled his eyes at Jeff.

"No, I don't do stuff like that!" Jeff was defensive instantly.

"Right."

Fury pulsed in Jeff's shield.

"And why don't you have things like that on your computers, Jeff?" Governor Haydenshire asked calmly.

"Because, that's disrespectful to Becca. She's my wife, and I don't want to see other women like that. And that's not even real. That woman is getting paid to say and do whatever she's doing. She doesn't care about you." He threw his hands out toward Greg. "She shouldn't have to. I would never do anything that would make Bec think she wasn't enough for me. I have the most beautiful girl in the whole world. She's everything to me, and even if I didn't, I'm sure as hell not going to find anything worthwhile on an Internet porn chat room."

Governor Haydenshire shot Governor Sapman a derisive glare. "That is a very impressive thing to have realized at barely twenty years old."

Governor Sapman was rubbing his temples. His rhythms tensed with shame and embarrassment. "So, you put something illegal on your computer, and then it infected every computer in the house?"

"We're not certain of that. This is the only one we've booted and casted, but for safety purposes I would say that is probably the case. And if I may," Portwood continued, "some thought might be given to the fact that your son or sons were using a porn chat room with their webcams. There is video evidence of them doing or saying whatever it is they were doing or saying. If the press ever got ahold of that, I can't say that would be good for your governorship or your family."

The governor paled considerably as Mrs. Sapman's head dropped into her hands. But it shot back up a moment later, and Jeff watched defiance light a blazing fire in her eyes.

"You know, I think I've had just about enough, George," she declared. "Our sons clearly need more to do with their time. Therefore, you two will go out and find yourselves full-time employment next week. I would look hard because if you wish to stay at home then you will begin paying rent for your room and board. You have an outstanding education from the top Gifted academy, so employment shouldn't be difficult. Otherwise, it's time for you both to move out and make it on your own."

Turning on her husband, she narrowed her eyes. "You have treated our son-in-law with no more regard than you give a common housefly for the past four years that he has been with our daughter. He has loved and adored her and has taken care of her and he still does. But you can't see that, can you?" She began shouting much to Jeff's shock.

"Becca loves him, and now, after you let your childish temper get the better of you and said some absolutely unforgivable things, I can't even see my little girl who is lying in there in a hospital bed. I'm certain she's feeling many things right now, but I know that she's scared. She's scared for her child. She's a mother now, and you really just need to get over yourself and get on with life because, God willing, in a few months we're going to be grandparents. She is a mother, and she loves her little boy and she loves her husband. How could we ever ask for more than that? I've kept my mouth shut for far too long because the fact that she loves this man with all of her heart should be enough for you to love him as well." She gestured to Jeff.

Wanting desperately to melt into the floor, Jeff braced. She didn't appear to be finished.

"And not only that, but I really believe that we should be thanking him for being the kind of man that will always love and respect Becca and will always take care of her. This isn't going away. I honestly don't know why you want it to so badly. This is life," she shrieked. "Jeff and Becca are married, and they're going to give us a grandson. And you know what, if you can't support them and show them that you accept and love them and their children then we have a very serious problem. Not Jeff and Becca. You and me.

"Jeff." She turned to him with tears leaking down her cheeks. "Sweetheart, I am so very sorry for the way George and our sons have treated you. Please believe me when I tell you that I will not allow it any longer. I will not allow any of them in to see Becca either, and I don't blame you for keeping us away. That is precisely what you should have done. But please, please may I go see her? She's my little girl." She began to sob.

"Let me talk to Bec first." Jeff hoped that his mother-in-law wouldn't begin to cry harder. She nodded her understanding as she gave Jeff pleading looks.

Portwood gestured his head down the hall, and Jeff whisked quickly from the room.

An hour later, Jeff sat holding Becca's hand as she and her mother talked.

"I had the same thing when I was pregnant with you," Becca's mother reassured her. "I was on bed rest for several months. I was so scared I was going to lose you, but here you are—my precious little girl getting ready to have my precious grandson." Mrs. Sapman brushed Becca's hair away from her face.

"I never knew that." Her mother's words visibly comforted her ragged rhythms.

"If it's all right with you, I'd really like to come over next week and take care of you while Jeff is at work. You know, I started doing crosswords when I was on bed rest with you."

Becca's grin delighted her husband. Mrs. Sapman was very rarely without a crossword book. They'd always been a part of Becca's life.

"I won't let your father come, but I would really love to spend the week with you. We could look at baby books, and nursery catalogs, and get you ready to be a mom. I'll take as much time off as I need to."

Becca blinked back tears, and Jeff's heart fissured.

"Please," Mrs. Sapman begged.

"I would really like that," she managed as her mother began to cry as well.

CHAPTER 25

OLD HABITS

DAN VINDICO

"Dan." Fionna seated herself back on the swing bed where they'd been napping. "Honey." She shook him gently. Dan blinked his eyes open hesitantly and wrapped his arms around her backside. He tried to pull her to his chest, but she shook her head. "Landon's on the phone. He needs to talk to you." She held up her cell phone.

Dan sat up, rubbed his face, and willed himself to awaken fully. As he realized that he'd turned his cell off and Portwood had been desperate enough to call Fionna's phone, he panicked.

"What's wrong?" he demanded.

"Nothing immediate," Portwood assured him.

Dan sat in stunned disbelief as he listened to the long, sordid tale of how Jeff had located the Senate Bank hacker and the discovery that he was being set up.

"I know you want to help Jeff. We all do," Portwood began, and Dan's heart sank as he realized the kind of trouble he'd caused Jeff by asking him to help with the cases at Venton. "But I'm the Chief of Iodex now. He's one of my officers, and you've put him in quite a bit of danger."

"I know, and I really am sorry. I never imagined this would get so out of hand. Truthfully, he's so good, I've been relying on him too much. I wasn't careful enough, and clearly, more people than Wilshire and Bryant suspected that he's helping me."

"I'm not entirely certain either Wilshire or Bryant know anything. Jeff pointed out that both the test vault and what happened today are fairly sophisticated digital crimes. He thinks the same people are behind them, and he thinks it's students. I tend to agree with him.

"You are going to have to keep him safe and Becca as well," Portwood continued. "If whoever is after him is willing to go to these lengths to get him in trouble, I'm not certain where they'll stop. And these are kids that clearly have no conscience."

"I'll keep them safe. I promise you. I should never have agreed to doing this on the side, and I should never have asked Logan and Jeff to help me. I really am sorry. I'm not trying to intrude," Dan begged forgiveness he knew he didn't deserve. Customary guilt settled in the pit of his stomach. Fionna picked up on his distress, and her soothing cast moved over his body.

"Like I said, I probably would've done the same thing, but I think this may be more than you, or Jeff, or either of the governors were thinking. And now we have to get Jeff out and graduated and keep Becca safe. I want Jeff on Elite before graduation. He's clearly proven his worth, but he needs an Ioses diploma. I plan on helping him get that as soon as possible."

"I'm about to spend a week at home without my girls. Send him over. I'll get him through his Ioses exams. I owe him a hell of a lot more than that, and I promise you I'll teach him by the curriculum."

"I don't really think he could ask for a better tutor," Portwood tried to soften the dressing down Dan had just been given, but he didn't feel the comment was necessary. He deserved to be reprimanded.

He'd learned a great deal since he'd taken over Iodex, but asking two current Iodex officers to help him on the side certainly hadn't shown that he'd learned his lesson.

He needed out of DC. The reality of that was abundantly clear. It was too easy. He was too accessible to his father and Governor Haydenshire. They all had to rely on Portwood to do the job they'd appointed him to do. Dan couldn't be an option anymore.

"Landon, I really owe you an apology. This was all me, not Jeff and not Logan."

"It's fine. Honestly, I'm more worried about what other kind of shit these kids might pull. And call me a chauvinist, but I'd say Becca makes a very appealing target. And you and I and every other Shield on the planet knows that the way to get to Jeff is to hurt Becca."

"I won't let anything happen to either of them. According to Jeff, their little boy is set to make his appearance before exam time. We need to get both of them through their senior years before they become parents."

"Then let's get it done."

"I'll be home Sunday night."

Fionna's face fell.

"Is Fi feeling any better?"

"She was." Dan sighed over the truthfulness of his confession.

"Hey, it won't be too long until your next addition is here, and she can get a break hopefully."

"Yeah." Dan pulled Fionna back onto his chest. "We just need to get through the next few weeks."

"She'll be fine. She's tougher than you give her credit for."

"Yeah well, she's my baby," Dan vowed more for Fionna's benefit than Portwood's.

"I take it she's right beside you, so I'm going to let you go. Have fun in Hawaii."

Jeff Strenton

"That's pretty much how my morning went." Jeff concluded the long story about the hacker, and being set up, and catching her brothers for Becca. She was reclined in the bed with her mouth hanging open.

Her mother shuddered, but she promptly informed Becca what she'd told the governor on Jeff's account. All in the same motion, she refilled Becca's water bottle and then offered to go and pick up a few of her favorite magazines.

"Thanks, Mom, for everything, but especially what you said to Dad about Jeff. He's the greatest guy ever," Becca gushed. Jeff's cheeks burned once again as he shook his head in adamant disagreement.

"For you, my sweet baby girl, I think you're right. I'll be back in just a few minutes." She kissed Becca's cheek before she slipped from the room.

Governor Sapman prevented the door from closing.

"Jeff, may I speak with you, please?" he managed in a spiteful tone. Becca glared hatefully at her father. It seemed to physically wound him.

Jeff moved out into the corridor. He closed the door to Becca's room and stood in front of it with his arms crossed over his chest. His shield attempted to leave his body to cover Becca. The few times Jeff had felt the sensation before, it always startled him, but protecting his wife and his son seemed so natural, he felt nothing odd this time.

"Jeff, uh…" Governor Sapman forced, "I suppose I owe you some kind of apology." He sounded like the words tasted bitter on their way out of his mouth. "I am sorry for the way I reacted to you and Becca's telling me that she was pregnant. You have to understand this wasn't really how I'd seen her life going. It was a shock."

Jeff offered a nod as he waited on the governor to finish whatever it was he wanted to say.

Drawing an audible breath, Governor Sapman seemed to let some of his guard down. "It all just threw me. One day, I had the sweet little blonde-headed baby girl, and then all of a sudden she went off to the academy. She came home one day, and all she talked about was you." He tried to quell his anger but couldn't quite manage it.

"She talked to you about all of her problems and asked you to help her do everything. It was like she didn't need me anymore at all." His jaw visibly clenched. "I was resentful of you. But for what it's worth, I am very sorry for all I've said and not just this morning but for the past few years. My wife is right. I certainly never gave you your due, and I should have trusted Becca. Will you please forgive me?"

Jeff considered for a minute. "I will, but I don't know about Bec right now. That really cut deep."

"I've never been all that good at reining in my temper or at not getting my way. I still have a great deal to learn. Please tell Becca how sorry I am. I will try not to intrude on your and Becca's life, but I would like very much to be a part of it."

"She'll come around. She always does. She's pretty incredible."

"Yes, she is. Just please promise me you'll never forget that."

"Not ever."

CHAPTER 26

DRUMROLL ECHOES
DAN VINDICO

By Tuesday evening, Dan was overjoyed with Fionna's progress. She not only looked healthier, but her rhythms were steady and strong. She was relaxed and let Dan and her grandparents dote on her continuously. They'd napped on the bed on the screened-in porch each afternoon for several hours.

The exhaustive tension that had plagued Fionna's features melted away in the Hawaiian sunshine and in the love and adoration of her family.

Aida would nap for a little while in her bed after lunch, but then head off to play with Papa or Kai if he was working the farm.

Dan had given Fionna baths each evening, and her grandmother kept her in steady supply of homegrown herbal teas and tinctures to regulate her hormones and her rhythms. Halia felt stronger and more placid as Dan locked on to her and felt her kick in Fionna's womb.

Fionna and Aida helped Tutu in her workshop while Dan helped Papa and Kai work the farm in the mornings. Then the whole family would play in the ocean or in the waterfall each afternoon after their naps.

Malani and Kai wanted to take Dan and Fionna for an evening out, and Papa and Tutu were only too happy to keep Aida. Malani's parents were thrilled to have little Lanie for a few hours as well. Kai had mentioned that he had something he needed to discuss with Dan.

Dan guided Fionna into the restaurant and to the table where Kai and Malani were already seated. The views were spectacular, and Fionna was excited to be out for the evening with Dan and her friends.

They dug in to the delectable island meal they were served with discussion of Dan and Fionna's potential move back to Kauai.

"Are you going to let Papa build you a new house?" Malani trilled.

Fionna shook her head. "Nothing is official yet, okay? I am too hormonal to make major life decisions right now." She'd been saying that same thing every time Dan had asked her about it. He assumed she was picking up on his hesitations and didn't want to beg him to move them back, though he knew that was what she wanted.

She hemmed as she scooped up a bite of her quinoa bowl. "I guess our cottage might get a little tight with both girls running around, but they'll have the whole farm to play on."

Malani beamed. "Sounds to me like you *have* made a decision."

Fionna glanced up at Dan. "No, we haven't."

Unable to sit there and watch her try to pretend that's not what she wanted, Dan wiped his mouth. "I'd love to move them back. I just…I'm not sure how good of a farmer I'll make. I love helping out when we're here, but I've learned a lesson on taking a job I know I'm not going to like for the long haul."

Kai smirked. "On that note, the Gifted police precinct in Lihue is looking for a sheriff. It wouldn't be anything like running Iodex. This is Kauai, after all. Sheriff Beles is retiring, but not a lot of people know that yet."

Desperation to accept the job surged through Dan's shield. He tried to quell it. Fionna had never handled his job in law enforcement well, but being the sheriff of Kauai would be vastly different from running all of Iodex.

"The most trouble we get around here is some idiot breaking into hotel rooms or cars. Tourist crap and the locals getting irritated with the tourists. Some domestic stuff. It's not like DC," Kai continued to point out. His insistence had Dan curious if perhaps Papa was the person that had heard of the current sheriff retiring and had approached Kai about bringing it up with Dan. Papa was one of Kauai's Gifted Consul members.

Though he tried not to let the desperation to be involved in law enforcement seep into his energy, Fionna was simply too strong, her receptors were too potent, for Dan to hide any emotion from her. Certainly not excitement. That was a very powerful emotion.

Fionna turned and studied him. He offered her a shrug, still trying to discern what she might think of his going back into law enforcement.

"We are not talking about that until after Halia is born. I'm not able to think clearly at all," Fionna insisted.

Malani nodded. "Okay, but trust me, it doesn't get that much better after they're no longer holding prime real estate in your waist. But at least your receptors will be back to normal, I guess."

Quickly deciding to let it go until after his little girl was in his arms instead of in his wife, Dan kissed Fionna's cheek. "We don't have to talk about it at all," he assured her.

But as Dan focused on Fionna's energy, he noted there wasn't the normal flood of terrorizing fear that came whenever he'd had to go out with Iodex or even discussed the missions he'd been on in all his years as Chief of the Elite Squadron. She seemed excited that Dan was interested and able to access calm with Kai's reassurances that very little in the way of violent crime ever took place on the small island.

"If we *do* move, do you want to build a new house on the farm?" Fionna asked thoughtfully.

"I'll do whatever you want, but your grandparents seem pretty certain that my baby girl won't be our youngest. We might need more than two bedrooms."

"I don't want anything huge though. If we build, we're taking up prime gardening land."

"Yeah, but Papa and Tutu just bought that farm behind them," Kai reminded her. "I'm pretty sure they did that because they know you're moving back. It's gonna double our operations. There'd be plenty of room to build you a new hale. They close at the end of the month."

"And we can plan it all out and decorate it. It will be like playing house when we were little only for real," Malani gushed.

Fionna giggled, but Dan noted she seemed thrilled with the idea.

As they were talking and laughing, suddenly Malani's mouth fell open, and her eyes goggled.

"What?" Fionna's brow furrowed.

"Oh, this is going to be awkward." Malani's expression was a mix of panic and embarrassment.

"What?" Fionna demanded again.

"Mano Forsyth just walked in, and now he's coming over. I don't think he's seen you yet," Malani managed through her teeth.

"What?!" Fionna panicked. "I thought you said he moved to California."

"Clearly, he's back."

Suddenly, a well-built Hawaiian man that Dan had seen in a photograph in Fionna's childhood bedroom made his way to their table.

"Aloha, I haven't seen you in a while," he offered Malani and Kai. He turned to give a kind smile to their guests, but it bled instantly into a look of panic as he took in Dan and Fionna. "Maylea, is that you?" His voice shook slightly.

Fionna chuckled uncomfortably. "Mano, how are you?"

"I'm good. We're in town visiting my parents," he explained, though there was no one with him.

"This is my husband, Dan," Fionna introduced.

CHAPTER 27
REGRETS

Dan begrudgingly offered Mano his hand as he narrowed his eyes spitefully. Mano had been Fionna's first love and her first time. They'd dated all summer long when Fionna had stayed with Tutu and Papa. He'd been very attentive right up until the moment he'd taken her to the airport to fly back home. Then he'd never called again.

Dan ground his teeth as Mano shot him the customary male look when you ran into a woman you'd had a relationship with in the past. Everything about the cocky glare he shot Dan as he shook his hand said, *"oh yeah, well, I was there before you."*

Dan fought back the bile that flooded his throat as he leveled his own responsive glare. *"Yeah, and you were replaced, now, weren't you?"*

"There you are," Mano drawled as a woman joined him at the table.

"Uh…Maylea, this is my wife Keelee. These are some old friends of mine from school. Kai Coiner and Malani…" He seemed unable to remember Malani's last name.

"We're married," Malani gestured to Kai.

"Oh, right." Mano nodded and turned to Fionna. "And this is Maylea Styler. No, wait, what's your last name now?"

"Vindico." Fionna offered Mano's wife her hand. As she slid to the side, Mano's eyes landed on her bump. Dan shot Mano a cocky grin.

"Wow, look at you," he choked.

Keeping up their silently threatening conversation, Dan rubbed his hand over Halia's bump while narrowing his eyes at Mano.

That's right, she's all mine and so is this, so you can stop thinking about my wife being in bed with you, you prick. Every feature of Dan's entire body broadcast that message loud and clear.

"Oh gosh, I could hardly tell you were pregnant," Keelee offered. "When are you due?"

"In November, but I'm not sure I'm going to make it that far," Fionna explained.

"Congratulations," Mano forced.

"Thank you," Dan offered coolly.

"Is this your first?"

Dan knew instantly that he'd heard about the wedding. He wanted to know if they'd gotten married because they thought they had to.

"Oh no, we have a seven-year-old little girl," Fionna explained.

"Oh." Mano was now thoroughly confused. Dan chuckled.

"It was really good to see all of you. We'll be visiting my parents for the next few weeks. Maybe we'll run into you again." No one believed that he hoped that would happen.

"Why don't we go out for dessert or coffee or something? I'd say drinks but that seems like it might not be a good idea," Keelee offered Fionna with a slight laugh. "I went to school on the mainland at McMillan, so I never knew any of Mano's friends. I'd love to hear about growing up here in Kauai with Mano."

Mano shuddered slightly. "I'm sure they need to get back to Maylea's family. Or…uh…they probably need to get home to their little girl." His expression said he was pleased he'd come up with that quickly.

"Oh, well then, why don't we just join your table? We ordered at the bar so we can just have our food brought here instead," Keelee, who was very forceful, suggested.

With that, she swung a chair from an empty table nearby and situated one for Mano right beside Dan.

The waiter supplied Mano and Keelee their drinks from the bar and agreed to bring their dinner out quickly so they could eat with their old friends. Dan kept his arm wrapped around Fionna possessively.

Malani was visibly delighted though she played it off well.

"So, Mano, what do you do now?" She began showing off for Fionna.

"I'm a market researcher for a company in LA. Currently, I'm working with an investor who's trying to figure out what would draw tourists to the islands." He sounded like he was confessing to a brutal murder.

"Ah." Malani no longer seemed pleased to be dining with Mano. Dan knew that many locals didn't particularly care for Hawaii to be over-branded. They didn't want their lands filled with tourist traps and gimmicks.

Keelee, however, beamed up at Mano. "So, Maylea, do you stay home with your little girl or do you work outside the home?"

"I was the lead Receiver for the Arlington Angels until last spring. Now, I stay home with Aida and our new little one." She rubbed her hands over her bump, and Dan pulled her closer.

"I could never have left a career in professional Summation. I told Mano when we got married that if he wanted kids we'd have to adopt or something ridiculous like that because I wasn't getting fat. I just don't see how you could ever get your body back after that."

Fionna and Malani narrowed their eyes and closed ranks quickly. If Keelee made another comment like that, she was going down. Kai and Dan both shifted and glared at Mano.

Mano visibly panicked as he tried to cover his wife's gaffe. "So, uh…Dan, what do you do?"

"I was the Chief of Elite Iodex in DC until last spring. Now, I'm the head of Ioses Order at Venton Academy."

Mano's eyes goggled as he swallowed harshly. "Elite Iodex…wow." He slid away from Dan as much as he was able.

"Chief," Fionna added spitefully.

Keelee looked impressed. "Tell me what Mano was like when you were friends."

Dan wanted to vomit, preferably on Mano.

"I didn't know Mano that well." Fionna glared at Mano, daring him to tell his wife she was lying. "I didn't go to school here. I went to Venton with Dan."

"Oh." Keelee was now extremely confused.

"Mama wanted me to be a farmhand on Maylea's grandparents' farm one summer back in school. She didn't think I had enough ties to the land." Mano rolled his eyes. "Maylea lived with her grandparents that summer. I went to Magma with Kai and Malani."

Dan watched as several pieces of the puzzle cemented in Keelee's mind. She nodded and then visibly reappraised Fionna. She turned on Kai and Malani. "Then, you tell me about Mano in school."

"We didn't speak," Malani informed Keelee. Dan understood. When Mano had shown himself to be nothing more than a douchebag that had used Fionna all summer and then sent her home without a second thought, Malani had refused to speak or acknowledge his existence for the rest of their school careers. She and Fionna most definitely functioned under the female policy that if my best friend hates you, so do I.

Kai stepped in. "Mano and I had a few classes together, didn't we, but that was ages ago. We haven't seen much of him since."

Keelee grimaced. She seemed to be rethinking her choice of dining tables.

"How did you two meet?" She quizzed Dan and Fionna.

Dan glanced at his wife. He'd go along with whatever tale she might want to spin. She'd already alluded to the idea that they'd been together in school even though they'd barely spoken the years they'd attended Venton together.

"Dan came to a party the Angels were throwing, and it was love at first sight."

Dan nodded. "It definitely was."

"How about you two?" Fionna turned the questioning on Keelee as everyone began eating again. Dan winked at Fionna as he reheated her dinner for her.

"Mano was a contestant on this local reality show in LA. It's kind of a spin on those bachelor shows. I was chosen as one of the girls competing for the guy, and we fell head over heels."

"How nice," Malani offered with a slight eye roll.

"Did you take a season off when you had your little girl?" Mano seemed to decide to go with the catching up portion of their evening as they were seated with Dan and Fionna with no attainable nearby escape.

"No," Fionna sighed and drew from Dan. She wanted Mano to go away. He felt her energy drown in the desire and her internal shield set firmly. "We adopted Aida last April."

Mano looked faint. Dan assumed he was recalling his wife announcing that adoption was ridiculous.

"We're actually the spokesfamily for the Auxiliary International Adoptions Within the Realm program," Fionna added with a great deal of spite.

"Wow, that's great. I mean, getting sponsorships…that's probably a lot of money," Keelee announced.

Dan tried to think of some way to get Fionna out of the restaurant and back home in his arms.

"Malani and Kai had a little girl back in July," Fionna obliged.

"Yep." Kai nodded. He pulled his cell phone from his pocket and showed off pictures of Lanie.

"My little Leilanie Maylea." Malani narrowed her eyes at Mano again.

Tension flooded Fionna's energy, and Dan decided that he really didn't care if he pissed off the table at large. He was taking her home, and he was going to soothe her energy and make her feel his overwhelming and all-encompassing love.

"We should go, baby. We need to check on Aida before I take you to bed."

Malani couldn't quite hide her giggle.

"Are you staying on the farm?" Mano quizzed. Dan's body seized as he saw the wistful look in Mano's eyes.

Fionna saw it as well. She tucked even closer to Dan. "Yeah. We're just on vacation for a few weeks."

Mano nodded. "Yeah, us too, if I make it that long. I get crazy being away from the big city. You know how it is. DC must be amazing."

"Actually, Dan and I were just talking about maybe moving back. Papa expanded the farm."

"Oh." Mano downed a long sip of his drink. "So, your grandfather is expanding. I guess the business must still be doing well."

"Since Dan started helping out, it's exploded. He's got a real knack with the lands, and Maylea and Malani have been running the store." Kai got in a hit next. He loved Fionna almost as much as Dan and Malani, and he seemed to have picked up on her discomfort as well.

"Do you still work over there?" Mano quizzed Kai. Defeat tensed in his rhythms.

"Yeah, but I also help my parents with the market. We're thinking of putting Tutu's products in the market next summer since we've doubled our farmland."

"Ready to go, sweetheart?" Dan urged again.

"Yeah." Fionna gave Dan his smile. "Thank you," she whispered.

"Anytime." Dan kissed her cheek. He would step in and save his baby anytime, anywhere. It was what he'd been put here to do. He was her Shield.

"It was nice to see you again, Mano, and nice to meet you, Keelee," Fionna stated politely.

"You too," Mano echoed.

Dan threw down enough cash to cover their bill and then guided Fionna out of the restaurant. Malani and Kai followed suit as they offered Mano a quick goodbye.

"I'm sorry," Fionna fussed as they headed toward Malani's Jeep.

"You didn't do anything wrong," Dan assured her. He may not have been her first, but he sure as hell would be her last.

Suddenly, Mano was upon them. He'd followed them out of the restaurant and rushed to Fionna's side. That was several steps too far. Dan moved himself between Fionna and Mano and glared at him hatefully.

"Look, I just wanted to apologize." Mano held up his hands in defeat.

Not having heard Mano's declaration, Kai and Malani stepped in. Malani tugged Fionna back as Kai moved beside Dan.

"Mano, back off, bruh. She's married and happy, and you're

married. Let it go, okay? He's killed over her, and I don't think he'd hesitate to do it again," Kai urged.

"Maylea, really, I just wanted to say I'm sorry things ended between us. I was an idiot. I really am happy for you both," he offered Dan and Fionna.

"Good," Dan growled but Fionna grasped his hand. She calmed him.

"It's really fine. I hope you have a wonderful life because I certainly am."

Mano nodded his acceptance of that. "You deserve a great life. I'll see you around."

Dan helped Fionna up into the Jeep. He wasn't certain what to make of Mano's apology.

"That was weird," Malani announced as Kai started the Jeep.

"He does feel bad. I could tell," Kai eased.

"How big of him." Malani rolled her eyes.

Shaking her head, Fionna giggled. "Trust me, nothing about him was all that big." She and Malani then promptly cracked up. Dan and Kai tried not to join in.

"That's all it comes down to with you two," Kai teased. "And you say men are shallow."

"Aww, honey, you should be honored. I married you." Malani laughed as Kai turned the shade of an overly ripe tomato.

Fionna turned introspective. "He doesn't have to feel bad. I hadn't even thought about him in ages."

Dan pulled Fionna into their bedroom. He held her close and shielded her from the rest of the world. She was his, and he didn't like some other guy lamenting that their relationship had ended.

Dan let his hands caress down Fionna's curves. He massaged and grabbed what he wanted forcefully. She moaned as her breaths quickened. A slight shiver quaked through her body. It made him ache.

"What do you want, baby doll?" He edged his lips to her neck and kissed from her earlobe to her collar bone slowly.

"I want to be yours," she confessed in a choked whisper. He understood only too well. She wanted him to take it all away. Everything that had come before the two of them were together no longer mattered. It all fell away in light of their energy spinning as one.

"You're all mine, Maylea. All mine," Dan growled in her ear. "Every inch of your gorgeous body inside and out. I'm gonna lay you in that bed and take what belongs to me."

"Now." She shook in her need.

"Do you need it, baby doll? Do you need to be reminded who owns this pussy? You want me to fuck you so hard you know you're mine. Then, if you're a good girl, I'll slow it down, make you beg me for more. Then I'll pound into you until the only thing you remember is my name and the only thing you want is me to keep filling you full." He explained precisely what his plans for the rest of their evening entailed.

With that, he stripped her bare and let his hands work her out of the dress she was wearing. She moaned as he located her fevered flesh in the humid evening. He groped and pulled her breasts and then traced his hands down until he was kneading her backside forcefully. He edged closer to the slick wet space that he wanted to permeate.

"Grab me, baby doll. Put your hands on my cock and feel what you do to me," he ordered. She moaned out her appreciation. She let her hand move over his strain and then quickly dispensed with his belt and trousers.

Dan's eyes rolled back in his head as she grasped him. His need leaked from his head in preparation for her. She leaned down and swirled her tongue over him, drinking the liquid form of his energy.

"My good girl likes that, don't you? I'm about to fill you full of it."

Her eyes flashed in ardent desire as she panted for him.

"Now. I need it," she commanded.

"Be patient, Maylea. We have all night, and I'm gonna bring you over and over until you just can't stand it any longer. Then I'm gonna fill you full over and over again."

She gasped and shuddered from his promises, and Dan led her to their bed as he began to fulfill them.

CHAPTER 28
HORIZONS

Unable to believe it was already Saturday, Dan fought the urge to whimper as the sunlight peeked through the windows into their bedroom. He squeezed his eyes shut tighter and clung to Fionna. She was curled up on his chest with Halia's bump lying on his stomach.

A week didn't sound as long as the weight of being without her would feel. He'd booked a night at the villa where they'd spent their wedding night so many months before. It was a surprise he'd worked out with Tutu and Papa who were keeping Aida for the evening. He planned on spending all night worshipping Fionna's body and tending their relationship to make up for the time he'd be gone. Then they would come back to the farm, and he'd spend the morning with his sweet Aida. Then he would fly home and count the moments until all of his girls would be back in his arms.

His mind mocked him. He recalled the times he'd scoffed at all of the Gifted legends that stated that Receivers and their Shields should never be parted. He was then brutally reminded of how he'd thought it was ridiculous that Rainer had snuck out of the country to go to Brazil to see Emily when she'd only been gone a week. Now, he understood.

He'd woken up in the middle of the night to his beautiful Maylea wiping away tears and trying to hide them from him. She'd been sitting on the swing bed on the porch outside their room.

He knew she wanted to beg him not to go, not to leave her, but she knew that he had to go. He had to go back to Venton. He had to make certain that Jeff and Becca weren't in danger. Fionna hadn't wanted to add to his burdens, but he'd felt the plea in every wave of her energy. It had cut him to the core.

Dan's leaving had plagued their entire trip though they'd enjoyed their time together on the island. It had been the incessant murmur that had prevented his Maylea from relaxing completely and allowing the island to soothe her weary soul and her restless energy.

Debating again asking her to come back home with him, Dan forced his mouth to stay closed as he cradled her tenderly in his arms. *She will feel lost without you but it will be better than what she's experiencing in DC.* Her grandmother's vow echoed in his mind. *She needs to stay here. It's only a week*, he tried to tell himself, but the pain of leaving shut down the logic his brain tried to process. *It could be longer than a week.*

He moved on to his plans for their evening. They were to participate in Lanie's blessing that morning, and then they were spending the afternoon helping Aida finish the project Mrs. Powell had assigned for her week out of school. After that, he would try to make the night last forever, to force the sun he usually welcomed from the island for his last night in the only place he'd ever truly felt at home.

Tutu, Malani, and even Aida had promised Dan repeatedly that they would take excellent care of Maylea while he was gone, but Papa seemed to know better. Dan was inconsolable, so Papa only offered him a slap on the back and a promise that his spirit would rebalance when Maylea stepped off of the plane and into his arms.

As had become customary, Halia awoke before her mommy. Dan felt her shift against his skin. Smiling in spite of his depression, Dan slid his hands over his baby girl. He pushed his energy through Fionna's bare skin, and Halia responded immediately.

"Yeah, I'm going to miss you too, baby girl," he assured her.

His mind went back to their night in their honeymoon villa. He began listing the things he needed to pack for their passion-filled evening. He planned to pull out all the stops. He'd do everything he could think of to give Fionna a night that she could cling to throughout the next week when she couldn't cling to him. He needed that as much as she did.

Fionna whimpered as the sunlight refused to be ignored.

Dan kissed her forehead, letting her bury her face in his chest.

"I'm right here," he assured her tenderly.

"Yeah, but you won't be," she fussed. "I'm sorry," she apologized instantly. She could feel his heartbreak.

"We'll be fine," he assured her as he began running his hands over her curves. "I don't want to go. You know I wouldn't if I had any other choice. I can't stand to think about all of my baby girls being here without me, but we will survive this."

A timid knock sounded on their door.

Fionna smiled. "She can read me so easily. I keep trying not to be upset, but I can't help it. I'm just so hormonal." Dan handed Fionna one of his T-shirts as he slipped into a pair of boxers before letting Aida in their room.

"Mommy is sad again," she explained as she dragged her blanket into bed beside Fionna.

Dan joined them. He cradled all of his girls in the serenity of their bed.

A few hours later, Dan held little Lanie in his arms as they met the *Kahu*, a holy man in Hawaii, on the south shores of Kauai. Fionna stood with him right beside Kai and Malani as they participated in the blessing of Leialanie Maylea. Dan was surprised to learn that he and Fionna would actually play a bigger part in the ceremony than Malani and Kai.

Family friends surrounded them along with Tutu and Papa and Lanie's grandparents as well.

Lanie did well right up until the point that the holy water, pulled from the sea and blessed, was sprinkled on her little head via a large

Ti leaf. She didn't seem to particularly care for the water. Her face contorted in a deeply offended scowl as she began wailing.

Auntie Maylea took her from Dan and soothed her instantly. Aida looked on as she stood beside Malani for the ceremony.

They all went back to Malani's parents' home after the blessing for lunch. Dan kept in constant contact with Fionna, pulling her into his lap as she ate.

"Maylea, you will be fine. You will be here taking care of your precious little girls, and we will be here taking care of you," her grandmother reminded her.

"You might as well go talk to the banyans." Papa chuckled. "My Maylea isn't going to be soothed until she's back in the warmth of the fire." He gestured his head to Dan.

Papa had explained Dan and Fionna's relationship to perfection just before their wedding. Dan was the fire, a fierce blaze that could be impossible to contain, one that had on occasion consumed him until he'd met his quelling tide. She was the cooling water. The overflowing love of his beautiful bride was always the stronger force. She needed his light and his protection surrounding her, but she needed no help standing on her own.

After leaving Malani's parents' home, Dan drove Fionna and Aida up to the lighthouse. Mrs. Powell had informed Dan that she was certain that spending an extra week in Kauai would be an excellent educational experience for Aida. She'd asked that Aida compile a poster board of photographs of a few of her favorite places on the island and then tell the class about her trip upon her return.

Fionna had shown Aida the places most tourists would never see while Dan had taken pictures of their little girl learning about the island. Today's adventure was on most people's travel itinerary, but Aida was excited to go.

Evening fell much too quickly.

"You'll call as soon as you land." Fionna was pacing and frantic as she tried to help Dan pack his things. Stopping, Dan grabbed her hands, drawing her to him.

"Fi, come on, you know I will call you constantly. I will miss you so much I'm sick to think about leaving in the morning, but we have to do this for Halia. For tonight, just please try to relax. I want to spend the night taking care of you and just being together. For me, let it go. Let's think about tomorrow, tomorrow."

After dropping Aida off at Papa and Tutu's and assuring her repeatedly that they would spend the whole morning together, Dan helped Fionna up into Papa's truck that they were borrowing for the evening.

He'd quickly snuck into Fionna's suitcase and removed an item he planned to make use of that evening while Fionna had settled on the couch with a cup of her favorite Kauaian coffee.

The rest of the items he needed he'd acquired from Tutu and Malani.

"Okay, I'm not even going to think about tomorrow. I'm just going to pretend it's not happening," she announced as Dan cranked the truck.

"That's perfect." He lifted her hand to his mouth and kissed it tenderly. "In fact, my whole goal of this evening is to make you forget everything but you and me," he flirted shamelessly, but the delighted grin on Fionna's face gave him hope.

He made his first stop at the taco stand that sold their favorite fish tacos. After placing a large order, Dan guided Fionna back into the truck and drove her much farther out on the island.

"Where are we going, Mr. Vindico?" Fionna quizzed with a knowing look in her eye. She'd already figured him out.

Dan shook his head. "I have a feeling you already know, but if you'll wait a few minutes you'll see."

Her laughter soothed his soul, but he could still feel the tentative sadness that permeated her rhythms.

He pulled up to the cottage he'd rented on their wedding night. Fionna's energy lilted toward happiness as she gazed up at the villa where they'd made their baby girl.

"Why don't we see just how long we can make this night last?" Dan guided her out of the truck and up to the rustic romantic villa. They ate their picnic dinner on the deck of the chalet and watched the sun set over the ocean. Dan reclined in one of the large wooden lounges with Fionna seated between his legs.

"What are you going to do this week?" she asked.

"Portwood's going to make a big show tomorrow at Venton. He's opening the pulse sent through the test vault up as an official Iodex investigation. He's also managed to convince the hacker from Tech to keep in contact with whomever framed Jeff. He let him plea bargain his way out. There's a chance he could lead us to the kids causing this insanity. So, I'll be there early Monday for that. Then I plan on getting lots of work done because once you get home, I don't want to work. I want to spend every moment with you, and very, very soon I'm going to be a daddy again. I need to make certain that Jeff isn't in any danger before Princess Halia makes her much anticipated debut." Fionna beamed at him. It was the most precious sight on the most beautiful face in the entire world.

"After Jeff gets off work, he's coming over, and we're going to try to cram his entire senior year into a week's time. Becca still hasn't been cleared to return to school, so her mom's taking another week off to stay with her. Dad's agreed to having her school work sent to her to complete at home." Dan went on though Fionna knew most of this already. "I'll spend most of my miserable week counting down the minutes until I pick my girls up from the airport."

"I don't want you to be miserable. Landon and Garrett both said they'd hang out with you," she reminded him gently.

"I have to help Jeff. The faster we can get him out of Venton the better."

"Don't forget to give the stuff from the store to your dad Monday," Fionna reminded him.

"It's in my bag." Dan didn't really want to make that delivery, but he didn't see any way around it.

"Something besides leaving us for a week is bothering you."

Chuckling, Dan nodded. He'd thought her ability to read him had been incredible before she'd been pregnant with his baby. Now, his Gifted DNA was growing inside of her, and it was uncanny how she knew his every thought.

"I'm forgetting to remember something," he quoted Aida's redundant declaration for whenever something slipped her mind. Fionna laughed and leaned to brush a kiss across Dan's jaw line.

"Is it something important?"

"I think it's something at work. Probably a meeting or something that I forgot to put on my calendar. There's something going on this week. I just can't seem to remember what."

"You'll remember when you get there Monday," Fionna assured him.

He didn't want to think about work or their upcoming week anymore. He wanted to drown himself in her. He needed to feel her erotic energy surrounding and encompassing him. He wanted to make love with her for hours until they collapsed in each other's arms and cocooned away from the rest of the world.

Reading that emotion as well, Fionna tucked her head under Dan's chin, nestling her body into the safety of his embrace.

"Are we going to recreate our wedding night?" She sounded hopeful.

Dan inhaled deeply of the scent of her—the sultry island scent of coconut and vanilla that seeped from her pores and into his soul.

"No, baby doll." Dan shook his head. "I was too damn horny that night. I'd been without you too long," he whispered as he let his hands trail up her arms and then began to lightly massage her shoulder blades. "You had me spun so damn tight I nearly lost it all just watching you come for me in the bathtub. I was hung so fucking hard I hurt for you. I needed to own you too badly, and I plan to make up for that tonight.

"Tonight is all about you. I'm gonna make you ache and drip for me. I have so many plans for you tonight before you make me feel like I've died and gone to heaven," he explained in a low fervent whisper as he dragged his teeth over the sensitive spot where her neck met her shoulder blade.

A breathy moan escaped her lips. Her rhythms pulsed in need. Her eyes were dark and voracious.

"I'll be more patient tonight than I was then, but I'm tired of waiting." He let his hot breath caress over her neck.

CHAPTER 29
PATIENCE AND REWARDS

Fionna stood, and Dan took her hand. He guided her to the bed. He'd already arranged candles all over the small cottage that he lit as he guided her past them.

"You're wearing way too much." He began to slowly strip her out of the low-slung wrap sundress she'd fixed around her bump.

He traced his fingers in delicate patterns over her skin as he worked.

"Lie down on your side for me, baby doll." He guided her to the bed. He would take care of every single thing. He wanted to take away every fear, be everything she needed. He wanted her to let him push away the morning light in the ecstasy of the two of them together.

She reclined, and Dan slathered his hands in the coconut and kukui oil he rubbed all over her belly every night. He began at her neck and worked his hands over her soft supple skin. He massaged gently and then added to the intensity as he rubbed away the tension and the heartache of his leaving. He worked diligently down her back, keeping his hands covered in oil and gliding them over her luscious body.

She gave furtive moans, and her body writhed under his pliant touch. Dan let her feel him pulse against her back. A desperate groan quaked from her as she reached for his throbbing erection, but Dan caught her hand.

"Not yet. Be a good girl for me. Relax and let it build," he commanded.

He let his hands slide over her gorgeous ass but didn't linger there despite her slight frown. With a cocky smirk, he continued on to her feet as he joined her on the bed.

"Roll onto your back for me, sweetheart." He helped her reposition. As her feet perpetually hurt with trying to carry around an extra twenty-five pounds all in the front, Dan spent a great deal of time easing the muscles there as well. When her entire body was languid and her eyes were closed in her ecstasy, Dan moved on.

He pushed his hands up her calves and worked out the strain there as well. As he slipped his way up her legs, he would occasionally trace over her mound. A shuddering moan escaped her, and her eyes begged him to keep his hands on her lips instead of returning them to her legs. But driving her to distraction was part of his plan.

"Do you enjoy torturing me?" she teased.

"Trust me, baby doll, it'll feel even better when I finally give in and bury myself inside of you." Her back arched as she spread her legs farther, desperate for him to soothe her need. "Are you showing me where to touch, baby doll? Such a good girl," he growled as he slid his hands to her inner thighs and massaged, but he gave her no reprieve from his torturous moves. "I'm gonna take good care of you, but you have to be patient for me."

He worked her thighs until they were relaxed, and he could spread them easily. With a quick move, he dipped his fingers into the 'Ōhi'a lehua lubricant just before he traced two fingers just outside of her slit. She went wild just as he'd known she would.

He'd spent the last hour hot-wiring her body for him. As he finally touched the very heart of her, she vibrated in need and pent-up desire from the lightest caress. He began to draw slow patterns over her mound. The energy between her mound and his fingers pulsed over the tightly wired nerve endings that needed to be soothed.

He slid his hands up to her breasts. They were fevered and swollen in need. He grasped them firmly, lifted their weight in his hands, and gave her relief as he groped and massaged her.

Giving light twists and pinches to her nipples, he watched his beautiful wife convulse in her need to be filled full of him.

"You've been such a good girl for me, baby doll. I'm gonna touch you now. Are you ready?"

"Please," she begged in need acute to the point of pain.

With that, he slowly traced his hands down her body and then separated her lips until he could see the pink pulsing flesh aching for his touch. He slowly edged his index finger just in her opening. She couldn't remain still. The sensations were too much. Her need was too great.

Giving in, he slipped two fingers inside her, forcing a powerful orgasm from her almost instantly. She'd waited long enough. Continuing his build, he dipped his left hand in the lubricant while keeping his right hand working her over from the inside. With his left, he lightly traced her clit. Her back arched off of the bed as her energy spilled out all around him in heady waves of pent-up desire.

As she shook from the power of the orgasm, Dan stood and grabbed the item he'd borrowed from her luggage. Her eyes were closed as she reveled in the power of what he'd forced from her body.

Working quickly, Dan flipped Fionna's favorite clitoral vibrator to its lowest setting and heat casted it with his hand.

"There you go, baby doll." He set the vibrator against her clit and kept his fingers working over her G-spot.

"Oh my god." She began to claw the sheets underneath her.

"I know it feels good, doesn't it?" He watched her entire body respond to the overwhelming sensations he was bringing her. She spasmed and lost it all again. "My good girl is so fucking sexy. I'm about to pound into you, honey," he warned as her orgasms began to roll together one after another. "I know this feels so good, but it's just not as good as when I fill you full, is it?" Her body rolled and her head pressed back into the pillow as she allowed him to own her fully.

Simply unable to wait any longer, Dan tossed the vibrator to the bed. He paused a split second to stop its rhythmic pulses. He grabbed

Fionna's thighs and threw her calves against his shoulders as he spread her legs and pierced through her forcefully.

"Take it. Take it like my good girl," he ordered as he watched himself plunge her depths and then withdraw slightly, coated in the heavenly liquid he elicited from her body. He transitioned until he was taking her hard and fast as she screamed out for relief and called his name repeatedly. "That's it. You tell everyone who owns this tight pussy. You get so sloppy wet all for me. Say my name. You're all mine," he commanded as she continued to encase him in her perfection. "I want you to come for me again and then I'm gonna fill you full of me," Dan ordered. She lost it all once more.

"Such a good girl comes when I tell her to," he growled and then with one final ragged thrust, he lost it all, filling her full of his energy and of all of him. Forcing their energy to spin in one constant stream that wrapped all around them.

"I'm still going to be smiling like this next Saturday night." Fionna giggled in replete satisfaction.

"Good, but I'm not near finished with you."

He lifted her ass off the bed and took her again, every bit as hard, every bit as fast until he was thoroughly spent. He fell to the bed beside her.

"I love you," he whispered as he kissed her hair. It was damp around the edges from all he'd done.

"I love you too," she vowed. She fought the exhaustion, but she couldn't withstand it. Dan set his shield firmly in place over her and watched her fall fast asleep, wrapped up in his protective love.

They stayed lip locked for a solid five minutes as Dan heard the last boarding call for the flight to DC.

"One way or another, I'll see you Saturday." If she couldn't come home yet, he was coming back to Kauai. He glanced at Malani who'd come to the airport with a full box of tissues. Being lifelong best friends with a powerful Receiver had left her prepared. Dan lifted Aida into his arms and squeezed her tight.

"I'll take care of Mommy and baby Halia, and I showed Mommy

how we could put X's on the calendar to count down until Saturday," she promised Dan.

"I love you, baby girl, so much." He kissed her cheek.

Setting her down, he watched her grasp Fionna's hand and lay her head against her mother's arm.

"Bye, Daddy. We love you so much too!" She blew him a kiss as he waved goodbye. With one final blown kiss, he boarded the plane home.

CHAPTER 30

HOMEMADE WARNING

Dan drove the Mercedes home in a vicious mood. He'd called Fionna as soon as they'd landed. She didn't sound any happier than when he'd left six hours before. That coupled with the press meeting his plane to report on the fact that he'd flown home alone and screaming out questions about Fionna's whereabouts and if he'd filed for divorce had him feeling vile.

His heart seized as he turned into the driveway. After methodically scanning the yard, Dan eased his pistol from the glove box and tried to determine why there was a man lying on his front lawn.

He slid from the car and led with his gun. While keeping a sharp eye out, he eased toward the man. As he moved closer, he heard the man moaning.

"Sir, are you all right?" Dan studied him to determine what had happened. He reached for his cell phone. He assumed the guy needed medical attention.

The gentlemen eased himself into a seated position. As he didn't appear to be armed or in any capacity to injure anyone, Dan offered him his hand to help him up. He slipped the pistol in the back of his jeans.

The guy brushed the grass from his clothing and stared up at Dan in shock.

"I'm Dan Vindico. Is there some reason you're lying in my front yard?" His cautious mood turned back into irritation in a matter of moments.

"Oh…uh…yeah." The man rubbed his head as he shook himself slightly. He was rather short and paunchy. He sported a terrible comb-over and a thick mustache.

"I'm Fred Sheckles. We just moved in across the street." He pointed to the house. "I was just coming over to introduce myself. My wife made you some cookies." He gestured to the yard, which contained several shattered pieces of a pottery plate and cookie shrapnel. "I started to knock on your door, and it was the strangest thing. Like being electrocuted or something. Threw me backward. Maybe I got struck by lightning." He stared up at the clear blue sky.

"Maybe so." Dan swallowed down panic. It never occurred to him a Non-Gifted neighbor would touch the door while they were on vacation. The shield he usually set on his home or on their cars while they were away would most certainly have thrown the guy backward. It could have killed him. Dan began amending his policy on casting the house so thoroughly while they were away.

"Anyway, we just moved in, like I said. My wife, Betty, and our boys, Walter and Wendell. We just moved here from Pilmore."

Dan nodded and attempted a polite smile. "Dan Vindico. My wife, Fionna, and our daughters are visiting her family in Kauai this week, but maybe you'll meet them later."

Fred elbowed Dan's forearm and waggled his eyebrows. "Maybe we could fix up our kiddos. You know, your girls and my boys, girl next door and all." He gave a hearty horse laugh.

Dan narrowed his eyes. "How old are your sons?"

"Walt's sixteen and Wen's thirteen," he announced proudly.

"My oldest is seven." He glanced longingly at his house. "I need to get in. I have to get a few things done before work tomorrow."

"I'm real sorry about the cookies." Fred stared at the remains of the plate and the cookies his wife had prepared.

"Don't worry about it. I'm just glad you're all right."

"I'm sure we'll be seeing a lot of each other, neighbor."

Dan wasn't certain what caused it, but an ominous sense of dread tensed in his shield. He nodded his begrudged acceptance of what he considered to be a warning. He cupped his hand and pulled the shield off his home and back into his body. He opened the garage door and drove the Mercedes inside.

"I blew up our new neighbors' cookies," was the text he sent Fionna as soon as he threw his suitcase upstairs in their room and fell dejectedly onto the couch.

A second later his phone rang. A broad grin spread across his face as he answered to hear his wife's hysterical laughter.

Dan considered Googling how to deal with an annoying neighbor as he drove into work the next morning. The customary metallic rattle between his legs as he steered the Agusta onto Venton's campus soothed him.

According to Fred, he'd knocked on the front door at five thirty in the morning to deliver Dan his paper. Dan had gotten up long before that to go for a run, and when he hadn't answered, Fred had taken it upon himself to walk around the perimeter of the Vindicos' home in search of Dan.

When Dan returned covered in sweat and checking his watch to get the time on his seven-mile run, he'd entered the house through his front door and found Fred peeking through the back door into the kitchen. He'd nearly shot Fred as he saw his shiny head reflect off the glass on the back windows.

Dan had promptly informed his new neighbor that he and Fionna really just liked to keep to themselves and never ever to come in their backyard again unless they were invited. Fred had left with his tail tucked between his legs and a dejected frown on his face.

As Dan leaned and guided the Agusta toward the faculty parking lot, his stomach twisted uncomfortably.

"Oh fuck," he spoke into his helmet. "Oh, please no," he begged the merciless air around him.

Yanking off his helmet, he let his head fall as he took in a large display set up by Mentor Hannon denouncing amative energies week.

She was joined by a very small part of the student body that were holding up signs announcing that anyone participating in sex before marriage was doomed to hell.

Dan stomped to his office. He flung his helmet in the cushioned chair in the corner and marched into his father's office.

Governor Vindico was sporting quite a smirk as he took in Dan's expression.

"Please, for the love of God, tell me it isn't amative energies week," Dan pled.

This was what he'd forgotten. He hadn't put it on his calendar because he'd wanted to will it away.

"Not only is it amative energies week, son, but this,"—he held up a student request form—"is the one hundred and forty-seventh request I've received for you to be their health and wellness mentor for the week." Governor Vindico fought hysterical laughter.

Dan's eyes goggled as he took in the stack of requests. "What?! Why?"

"Well…" Governor Vindico was enjoying this entirely too much. "I would say seventy-five percent of these young men are really hoping that you might give them a brief overview on what it's like with the beautiful woman that you share your amative energies with, and the other twenty-five, I suspect, heard about your well-known reputation before you married and are hoping you might give them a few pointers."

Dan let his head fall into his hands. "I should have stayed in Kauai with Fi."

"The question is shall I just give you all one hundred and fifty young men and set you up in a lecture hall, or am I going to be nice and divide them up the way we've always done at Venton," the governor continued to harass.

"This isn't funny."

"I don't know. I find it rather humorous." Governor Vindico chuckled.

Dan stomped back to his office and pulled up the curriculum on amative energies for the junior and senior Ioses, Valeduto, and Vis Virres Predilects that he'd negotiated with his father to teach each afternoon all week long. The morning classes remained the same, not that his students would learn anything at all that week. Amative energy weeks typically had the students of Venton Academy extremely amorous.

The people with uteruses would be learning how to cast themselves to prevent pregnancy. The first three days, mentors and nurses would cast them to let them learn how it should feel when they were closed off. Thursday and Friday they would cast themselves. The female half of the student body being casted generally made the already overly hormone-driven heterosexual young men on campus fly into overdrive.

Portwood knocked on Dan's door a few minutes later. Jeff followed Landon in. He looked thoroughly annoyed.

"Amative energies week." Portwood shook his head. "I cannot tell you how happy I am that I do not have to deal with this week every freaking semester ever again," he offered Jeff. He'd grown up in Lexington, Kentucky, and had attending Benedict Academy, but every Gifted academy had amative energies week.

"Believe me, sir, this is yet another thing that I will not miss about being in school."

Portwood smirked at Dan. "Mentor Vindico, your dad says most of the male half of the academy is hoping you'll educate them in all of your well-known skills." He laughed.

Dan shook his head in defeat. "I swear if I'd thought about this week before I signed my contract, I wouldn't have taken the job." He checked his watch again. It was the middle of the night in Kauai. Dan fervently hoped his girls were sound asleep even if he longed to talk to Fionna before he tackled a horny group of academy upperclassmen.

"Rainer, Logan, and John will be here at eight. We're going to put on a big show of investigating the test vault. We'll be asking the staff to let us know if anyone acts nervous. We'll also let it fly that we're suspicious of Mr. Strenton here." He slapped Jeff on the back.

"I really am sorry about all of this," Dan offered. "This was entirely my doing, and I will make it right."

"No, sir, it's fine. I can take care of myself. As long as Bec's okay, then I'm good."

"How's she doing?"

The smile that formed on Jeff's face told Dan and Landon everything they needed to know.

"She's a lot better. Adeline let her be up and around a little yesterday. We went out for pizza. She was craving that Hawaiian pizza from Musconi's, but she was pretty tired when we got back home. I'm afraid to let her do much of anything." As all of the wives of the men currently in Dan's office were pregnant, this was something they understood only too well.

"Any idea if she'll be able to come back to school?" Portwood asked.

"After everything that's happened, I wish she could just finish at home. I'm worried sick about her."

"I won't let anything happen to her, and Dad's already approved her staying home the entire time I'm out after my little one comes if that needs to happen."

"I'm gonna go start going over the test vault. I think I'll see who turns up first," Portwood explained.

"Good luck." Dan waved his goodbye. "Have a seat," he directed Jeff. "Clearly, people already know you're a close friend of mine, so no need to hide out." Dan continued going over the information he was to present for his amative energies class that afternoon. He scowled as he landed on one of the items. "I'm supposed to teach twenty-year-old guys how to put on a condom."

Jeff gave him an uneasy chuckle.

"How the hell do I demonstrate that?"

"Uh, there's a model thing in there, sir."

"Please tell me you're joking."

Jeff grimaced but then shook his head.

"But most of you know how to do that, right?"

"Uh…" Jeff's face colored rapidly. He'd only ever been with Becca. Dan knew that he certainly knew how to cast his wife, but he probably had no idea how to prevent pregnancy or the spread of disease with a Non-Gifted woman.

"Never mind, it's fine," Dan offered Jeff an out.

"Hey, believe me, I'm with you. I have to lose twelve hours of work this week so I can take this class because it's required to graduate, and my wife is home pregnant with my son. So, it seems like sex ed might not be something I need a class in."

"Yeah, well, maybe I'll let you teach it."

"At least it's you this year and not Mentor Sherman. I don't think I could take that again." Jeff rolled his eyes.

"What's Becca's plan for this since she can't be in the class?" Dan sent copies of a worksheet for his first period class to the printer from his laptop.

"Your dad said she could just do that paper on the Gifted female body. She obviously can't be casted, and it seems fairly obvious to everyone that she's had sex, so I don't think she'll be missing too much." Jeff gave an abashed shrug. "I think she's thrilled not to be here. When we talked about amative energies week a while ago, she kept thinking that the mentors would use her as an example of what not to do."

Dan offered him a grin. "I heard your father-in-law finally grew a pair and apologized."

"Yeah." Jeff rolled his eyes.

"Seems like that would be a good thing."

"It is. I mean, I'm glad he's trying to be human or whatever because he was really stressing Becca out, and obviously that's a bad thing." He hemmed. "I know this is awful," Jeff finally began his confession.

"Want me to take a guess?"

Jeff nodded and sported a genuine smile as he relaxed before Dan's eyes.

"You're happy the Sapmans are coming around and that the governor has admitted that you're a great guy that loves Becca. You're thankful Mrs. Sapman is taking care of her so you can finish school and work, but you could do with seeing a lot less of them."

"How do you do that?" Jeff cracked Dan up. "It's way better like this though. Mrs. Sapman's been great, and Becca is a million times better. I shouldn't complain. I just wish when I get home that she'd go home."

"Believe me, you are not the first guy to feel that way and you certainly won't be the last."

CHAPTER 31

SHIELD AND SPAR

~JEFF STRENTON~

Jeff summoned and sent the required magnetic pulses through the lock on his gym locker. It sprung open as he continued the debate that had been going on in his mind ever since Portwood offered to hire him on as soon as he took his finals. Vindico was tutoring him that evening, but he wanted to look over the digital textbooks of all of his defense classes before he got to Dan's house. He had to figure out what he needed to know most. Strategy was the name of the game.

He shed his jeans and T-shirt and shoved them in the locker.

"Hey, Strenton, if you've got copies of the exams, you need to let a guy in on that," Liam Northrup joked.

It took Jeff a second to process what he was talking about. He grabbed his gym clothes for Ioses lab and slammed his locker shut. "What?" He pulled on his shorts.

Liam rolled his eyes. "Come on, man. We've been friends for years. I'm failing both of Vindico's shit classes. I don't know who he thinks he is, but we're not all freaking geniuses." He gestured toward Jeff and Ben Cobson. Ben rolled his eyes.

Ire pulsed in Jeff's shield. Liam was an asshole. The year before, he'd casted the referees' mics at the first Summation challenge between the Venton Vixens and the Volts. Every time one of the refs spoke, Northrup would tap into the cast and make it sound like the ref was saying, "Girls suck at Summation!" Since the Vixens were the only all-female Summation team at Venton, this was particularly awful.

When Liam had been caught, he'd sworn to the school governors that it was all Jeff's doing, that Jeff had casted the mics and taught Liam how to tap into the sound cast. Rainer and Logan had gotten Jeff out of trouble by swearing that they were with him at the challenge that night. They had been with him, just not for the entire challenge.

Becca had arrived halfway through, and Jeff had gone to sit with her. If Rainer wasn't Governor Lawson's son, Jeff could easily have lost his spot as Lieutenant Commander of Ioses Order at the very least. He'd known he had to have a leadership position in Ioses Order to work for Elite. Jeff would never forgive Liam for what he almost cost him.

Jeff narrowed his eyes. "I'm not a genius. I'm not cheating. I don't know anything about the test vault, and we are not friends." He stormed out of the locker room.

He took a seat on the bleachers away from the students who'd already exited the locker rooms to await Vindico for their lab. Throwing punches sounded like an ideal way to spend the next hour and a half. He was sick to death of everything and everyone except his wife, whom he now never got to be alone with because her stupid parents were always at his house.

Stop being a prick. He shook himself as Ben joined him on the bleachers. "Hey, man, don't let Northrup get to you. He has approximately four brain cells and half of them are perpetually asleep."

Jeff couldn't help but chuckle. "I didn't have anything to do with whatever happened to the test vault. Kind of sick of people thinking I did." That was the part of Portwood's plan that irked him most. Why did they have to lead people to believe he'd had anything to do with it? Somewhere in the recesses of Jeff's mind, he knew that was how they solved the case, but he just didn't care at the moment. He also knew it wasn't going to work.

"Yeah, I know," Ben sighed. "Maybe Chief Portwood will catch whoever really did do it and people will blow off about it."

"Hopefully."

"Hey, how's Becca doing? I heard she was in the hospital or something."

Great. Apparently that was out now. Jeff sighed. "Yeah, she was. She's better now. A lot better."

"Good." Ben smiled. "Tough gig you've got going. I figure you don't need it to be any harder than it already is."

Deeply appreciative that someone else understood, Jeff nodded. "Just have to get through the next few months."

"If I can help, let me know."

"Thanks."

Jeff was certain Ben was offering his help because he was the current Head of Ioses Order. It was his job to support the Shields, but his offer still soothed some of Jeff's frantic strains. He did have a few friends at the academy—people who knew he had nothing to do with the test vault.

Before any other discussion could be made, Mentor Vindico walked in from the mentors' locker room with Mentor Assistants Jackson and Freeman. They all set their phones and bags down on the bleachers in front of the students and pulled on sparring gear.

A smile finally reached Jeff's features. Mentor Jackson was his favorite assistant. He'd been helping Jeff for the past several years. His pre-freshman year, he'd taught Jeff to master object-oriented programming. Mentor Jackson had been raised by one of his aunts. He didn't really know either of his parents well. He was a master at *Call of Duty* and had been featured in PC gamer mags several times for his kickass *Minecraft* mods that had well over two million downloads. He and Jeff had a lot in common, and they'd always bonded over their childhoods.

Since Jackson was Jeff's favorite assistant and Vindico was far and away his favorite mentor, this lab class was going to be fun.

"All right," Vindico began and everyone shut up. "I know it's amative energies week, and we're all eager to get to those classes." He rolled his eyes as several chuckles went around the gym. "But what we're about to teach you could actually save your life one day. If that isn't enough, it will also be on your finals. Pick your motivator. Today we're going to begin learning how to fight against multiple opponents at the same time."

Jeff's focus sharpened. He'd been waiting on these lessons. If he'd had this training, Becca's idiot brothers and their asshat friends would've at least not walked away unscathed.

"We're going to demonstrate a sparring match. Then I want you to get in nine groups of three. We'll do three rounds each with all of you getting the chance to be both the aggressors and the defenders. Mentors Jackson, Freeman, and I will be the refs. If we pull you, take a seat back on the bleachers. In the next round it will be one on four or five. We'll spar until we name a champion."

Jeff knew most other mentors would usually incentivize the students with something in a class like this—no lab homework that night, extra time on an assignment, something—but that wasn't Vindico's style. The knowledge they'd gain would be the prize. Jeff admired that about the way he taught, but it pissed a lot of the other students off.

He watched intently as the mentors' assistants squared off against Vindico.

Freeman popped out his mouth guard and chuckled. "I don't know, man. This still doesn't seem fair." Jeff joined in the class's laughter.

Dan removed his mouth guard and smirked. "All right, let's start right there. As much as you all might think it puts me in a good position for them to already be intimidated, it doesn't."

Jeff's brow furrowed.

"How could they not be intimidated?" Ben whispered in awe. Jeff nodded his agreement.

Vindico went on. "I'll admit that I come with a bit of a reputation. But that means I have to live up to that reputation. That means my opponents are likely to decide right out of the gate that they have to bring their A game. Seventy-five percent of hand-to-hand combat takes place in the mind, not on the mat. Your ability to adapt, to read every sign and every energy shift, to think outside the box, will help you far more than your ability to throw a right hook. Strategic incompetence or sandbagging if we're talking pool or poker is never a bad idea. When you come into a match with a reputation like mine, I no longer have that option."

Jeff doubted he ever needed that option.

Dan popped the mouth guard back in and nodded to his opponents. Mentor Jackson and Freeman got close. Jackson opened with an attempted head shot. In an epic simultaneous counterattack, Mentor Vindico met Jackson's fist with his elbow, making him stumble away while he landed his own gloved fist on Freeman's cheek.

"Damn," Jeff gasped.

Dan stopped them again. "If your attackers decide to come at you together, think of them as one. Make sure every punch or kick you land kills two birds with one stone so to speak. But remember that they're learning your style every time you move. They're not likely to try that again, which is why adaptability is key in combat."

They all watched as Mentor Jackson and Mentor Freeman tried to bring Vindico down from a myriad of different positions and using a bunch of different strategies. They both came at him from behind once. That had ended with him spinning around at lightning speed and sweeping his right leg out, which had landed them both on their asses.

Mentor Jackson summoned and casted quickly after that. Dan did stumble back, but then *he* summoned and punched at the same moment. Jackson had landed on the mat again.

Vindico would stop after a few moves and teach them how and why he was doing what he was doing.

Finally, it was time for the student sparring. Jeff squared off against Xavier and Chance. He tried to remember everything Rainer and Portwood had been teaching him. They came at him together so he mimicked Vindico's move. He knocked Xavier back with his elbow and forearm and landed a punch in Chance's face.

"Nice, Strenton," Mentor Jackson complimented. "Someone was paying attention."

"Thanks, sir."

After a few more moves, Chance squared off against Jeff and Xavier. Jeff threw a low punch while Xavier moved to Chance's far right. But before he could swing, Arial, Chance's girlfriend and the most annoying human on the planet, burst through the gym doors.

She rushed to Chance. Jeff and Xavier both halted. Neither of them were certain how to proceed.

Arial was already talking, and Chance seemed to have forgotten entirely about the sparring match. "Oh, holy mac-n-cheese balls, Haven Carteris and Greg Bowman just broke up in the corridor like right in front of me right after Zoey Graham puked in the girls' restroom. She said she had bad calamari last night for dinner, but Eliana Mills totally told Claire Kennedy that Misha Jennings told Evie Adkins that Greg and Zoey got assigned as lab partners in Occamy Construction lab class. Do you think they're dating? Do you think Zoey is *pregnant?*" she mouthed the word. "Do you think that's why she puked? What are we going to do? We're supposed to go to the Iris MacClapin concert with Haven and Greg, and obviously, now, we can't go with them. Do you know how long I was online getting those tickets? But we can't go with a couple who's like not a couple couple anymore. You know? Like we just can't. Who are we going to go with? If Greg is dating Zoey maybe we could go with them, but TBH I like Haven way better than Zoey. Zoey is like *not* you know. Just not. And Haven has like a better vibe, not like a vibe vibe but more like a chill kinda vibe, kind of a cool detached not a cold like oh I'm freezing kind of vibe."

Xavier shot Jeff an exasperated expression. "I will pay you to take your glove off and just hit me in the face, so I don't have to hear any more of this." He spoke through his teeth.

"So, what are we gonna do?" Arial finally demanded of Chance.

He stared at her long enough that she naturally began talking again. "I mean, I guess we could ask Zoey if her and Greg are like a thing now, or if she's just like into him or not or maybe we could see if Haven and Greg get back together before the concert, but that's only in like four months. It's kind of a long time but also kind of not a long time because I mean think about it. Last November, it was like a year before my birthday, and now my birthday is all of a sudden in like three weeks."

Jeff shook his head and turned back to Xavier. "If we get on opposite sides of the gym, and both run toward one another with enough force, we could probably knock each other out of our misery."

"I'm down if you are."

"Miss Winters." Mentor Vindico sounded pissed. "You are not in this class therefore you should not be in this gym."

"Okay, I know, but like Haven Carteris and Greg Bowman just totally broke up right in front of me in the corridor right after Zoey..."

"Oh, fuck no. I cannot do this again," Xavier whimpered, and Jeff cracked up.

"...She said she had bad calamari for dinner last night."

Dan shook his head. "Chance, if this conversation is more important than your lab grade, take it outside. If not, spar."

Chance looked thoroughly confused, and Arial was still talking about Zoey's calamari. Arial grabbed Chance's hand and pulled him toward the gym door. Jeff and Xavier were both visibly furious. Their shields tingled red in frustration.

"All right, I've got you," Mentor Jackson stepped in as he shook his head at Chance. "Let's go."

Because of Chance and Arial's insanity, every other sparring group already had a winner. Fury continued to pulse in Jeff's shield. Now, it didn't matter how good he was or how much he'd learned. Mentor Jackson wouldn't declare himself the winner, which meant that it wasn't really a fair match.

CHAPTER 32

BATTLE ROYALE

Letting his frustration drive him, Jeff battled through a labyrinth of his classmates. He used every trick he'd learned from Vindico, Rainer, Logan, and Portwood. Finally, it was down to him, Ben Cobson, and Maya Kumar.

Jeff knew he could've outlasted Chance if he'd been given the option, so he refused to believe that he hadn't earned his place in the final three.

"All right, each of you can choose one of us to be your coach for this final match," Mentor Vindico explained. "Three rounds and we'll declare a winner. You've all done very well today. We'll keep practicing, so if you didn't end up in this match, you'll have several other chances."

Guilt prodded Jeff's shield as Mentor Jackson gave him a broad, knowing grin.

"All right, Mr. Strenton," Mentor Vindico called, "who's your coach?"

"I'm sorry, man," Jeff offered Mentor Jackson. "I'm going with Mentor Vindico."

Dan chuckled and nodded. Maya chose Mentor Jackson, Ben chose Mentor Freeman, and the battle was on.

Jeff was defense first. Maya lunged toward him and swung out her leg.

"Jump and swing," Dan ordered, and Jeff did. He leapt up over her leg and brought his glove down, but she ducked away before he made contact.

Ben swung and hit Jeff in the gut. Jeff tried to block him but he crouched into the blow. He swung but Dan shook his head. "Step with your lead foot, keep your hips and center moving toward your target, punch from low in your chest when he's expecting you to go high. Hide your tells." Jeff followed his instructions, and Ben fell back, but he didn't hit the mat.

Ben lunged forward with a harder swing as Maya did the same.

"Feint back," Dan urged. Jeff stepped back. "Again." Jeff eased back again. Ben made a longer lunge, and Dan shouted, "Swing now!" Jeff swung, and Ben stumbled back. Jeff knocked him off-balance. Before he could get his footing, Dan called, "Again!" Jeff threw another punch and Ben hit the mat.

He huffed, rolled his eyes, and went to take a seat on the bleachers.

Jeff willed more energy from the air around him. He was exhausted, and Maya could kick pretty much anybody's ass. She was a fantastic fighter, but Jeff always felt guilty for sparring with her. His mother had been very adamant that he was never ever to hit anyone but most especially women. Just like everything else his mom had taught him, he'd taken those lessons to heart.

Jeff was lost somewhere between being a chivalrous Shield and wanting to win.

It seemed Maya, however, was intent on winning. She leapt and swung. Jeff ducked but didn't retaliate.

Dan met his eyes. He seemed to understand the struggle. "Fight, Strenton," he demanded. "She doesn't need you to hold back."

Jeff tried to believe that. He really did. He swung, but only succeeded in making Maya laugh. Suddenly, she had him in a headlock.

Jeff struggled against her with Dan coaching him through. "Lean low and then into her. Flip her over your back and take her down."

Jeff tried but Maya overpowered him. She dropped to her knees, and he struggled to stay up off of his.

"You've got him, Maya," Jeff heard Jackson urge. "Keep him down."

"Tense your core, ground your feet, drive forward and up with your head, Jeff," Dan demanded. Clenching his jaw, Jeff tensed and drove forward. He managed to break free of Maya's grasp.

Jeff wasn't shocked to hear most of the class rooting Maya on. His exhaustion taunted his shield. Maya came at him again. She swung right. Jeff ducked to the left, but she caught him with a left hook.

He managed to swing, but she folded forward fast, and though he hit her in the stomach he didn't get much impact. She kept coming. Jeff tried to take her on, but his mother's voice grew louder in his mind with each passing blow.

He tried to shake it off.

"Come on, Strenton. Endurance," Dan urged. "Don't stop when you're this close. Dig deep."

Maya swung her right glove toward his face. Jeff leaned back, and she swept her leg out and took him down in a swift blow.

He slammed his hands down on the mat, but then got up and shook her hand.

Vindico, Jackson, and Freeman were all applauding.

"Nice work both of you," Dan complimented. "Hit the showers and change. You have to be in amative energies class in twenty minutes."

The class headed toward the locker rooms, but Vindico halted Jeff's progress. He directed him to the bleachers instead. "Important lesson you need to learn now—women can do everything we can do. Most of the time they do it better as you just saw. The fact that they can do everything means that they don't need us to believe they're incapable of either doing right on their own or of doing wrong. An opponent is an opponent no matter where they fall on the gender spectrum. You can get yourself and the people on your squadron in a lot of trouble if you go in making assumptions about what sex the bad guys are."

"Yes, sir. I know."

"Do you?"

Jeff nodded. "I was just tired."

"Don't make excuses. Own what just happened."

Jeff's eyes closed in defeat. "I didn't want to hit her."

"Now take that admission, get your head straight, and go on with your day. You can't change the past, but you can change what happens next time."

Dan stood and his brow furrowed. He picked up his laptop bag from the bleachers and began searching around.

"What are you looking for?"

"My phone."

Jeff stood to help. Something caught his eye. "Here it is. It fell off the bleachers." He handed it back to Dan.

"You know I'm only hard on you because you're a kickass Shield," he reminded Jeff. "I know you can do better."

"Thank you. I'll do better. I promise, sir."

CHAPTER 33

CURRICULUM, CONDOMS, AND CONVICTION

~DAN VINDICO~

Tearing the wrapper off a protein bar, Dan sighed as he began to chew. *She'll be home soon. Get it together.* His prepackaged lunch did nothing to quell the longing for his wife. *You're spoiled rotten.* He continued to lecture himself as he wished for any of Fionna's outstanding cooking. Forcing himself to open his laptop, he reread everything he was to go over in the amative energies seminar he'd be conducting for the next two and a half hours after lunch.

He marched into the expanded lecture hall prepared for battle. His father had laid it on the line for him. "These kids look up to you, Daniel. You need to show them respect, and you need to teach them. That's what you were hired to do. Suck it up and get it done."

Dan flung the door open and proceeded to the front of the class. He met many expectant stares as he tried not to see the plastic models of reproductive organs that had been placed near his desk.

Nervous energy flowed throughout the room. It was so palpable and coming from so many sources Dan felt it instantly. The varied Predilects' colors gave differing shades to the nervous energy, but every wavelength in the room was tight with apprehension.

With a sigh, Dan seated himself on top of the mentor's desk. Jeff was positioned near the front with other Ioses Predilects. The room was full of young people looking to Dan to make an uncomfortable topic a little easier to understand.

"Okay," Dan began in a more pleasant tone than he normally used whenever he began any class. "Obviously this is Junior Senior Amative Energies. Few things…" Dan stood and edged closer to the young men seated on the front row. "Some of the stuff we have to go over is a little uncomfortable, but I'm more than willing to give you some leeway if you'll extend me the same.

"Since you've been in attendance for these classes for the last several years, you already know there *is* information I have to present and there's a question and answer portion of each class this week. I'm fine answering your questions but,"—he paused to make certain every eye in the room was on him—"try to ask questions that pertain to what we are discussing. Try not to be crude when you ask, and here's my one rule, so listen up. I will not under any circumstances discuss my wife or our physical relationship, nor will I discuss any relationship from my past," Dan vowed adamantly. "Anything else, within reason, I will do my best to answer for you." Disappointment was evident on many faces.

An audible huff echoed from a guy on the front row. He was a Vis Virres Predilect, so Dan wasn't shocked that he was going to challenge the rule.

"Problem?" Dan narrowed his eyes. As Vis Virres Predilects were rarely afraid of confrontation, the guy looked pleased to take the bait.

"You're boning Fionna Styler and we're not allowed to ask you about that?"

Dan narrowed his eyes. "I just asked you not to be crude. Any physical relationship is an extremely important part of a union, so no, I will not discuss my relationship with my wife with any of you or anyone at all, for that matter. That would be incredibly disrespectful to Fionna, disrespectful to the things that we share together, and disrespectful to my marriage. Precisely the same way that it is disrespectful if you share something intimate with someone and then discuss that with anyone other than the person you shared that with," Dan brought the lesson to the class at large.

"So," he went on, driving the point home, "regarding my beautiful wife, the things that she shares with me I will quite literally guard with my life just as all of you should guard the things that are shared with you in any intimate setting."

"But as long as we don't ask stuff about a specific person, you'll answer?" rang from the back of the room.

"I'll do my best, but I think I will reserve the right to refuse a question as well, but you can ask anything you want," Dan allowed. "All right, does everyone know what this is?" He held up a wrapped condom that he'd been given as part of the curriculum packet.

"Condoms," Dan answered the question himself as he noted a few quizzical stares. "These are available to you for free from many locations on campus. If you decide that you are going to be sexually active with anyone who is unable to be casted or doesn't want to be casted, please, please go and get however many you would like. My personal opinion, if any of you care to hear it..." He watched every eye in the room raise quickly. "If you can't take your ass into a drug store and purchase yourself a box of these or walk into the clinic here at school and acquire them, then you should not be taking anyone to bed." He vaulted the challenge and watched several young men slither farther down in their seats.

"Now, I'm going to go over how to put this on. I think we'll go for a verbal explanation rather than my actually demonstrating this on the model there." He gestured to the plastic model.

"It's fairly self-explanatory, just remember to leave some room at the head. Pinch that portion off before you roll it on. Otherwise it will break and that can lead to many things that you weren't planning on thinking about for a while."

He saw defiance cast a few faces in the center of the room where the Vis Virres Predilects had congregated. A hand shot up. Dan nodded to the gentleman who decided to test the waters.

"What's your name?" Dan quizzed.

"Gabe," he supplied immediately.

"Your question, Gabe."

"Yeah, so what happens if you want her to put it on?" He sneered his challenge.

Dan smirked. "Then ask her, but make certain that if she agrees, she knows how to put it on. If she doesn't want to help you apply it, please don't take that to mean that you shouldn't use one." He'd meant what he'd said. He'd answer their questions as long as they were within reason, but that didn't mean they were going to like his answers.

Resolve strengthened around the room and another hand shot up. Steve Abrams, an Ioses junior, seemed to have had to work up a great deal of courage to ask whatever was on his mind.

"Mr. Abrams," Dan called.

"I swear I'm not trying to be a jerk or whatever, but it's gotta be way better without that, right? I mean, using a condom or whatever can't feel as good."

"Trust me, either way feels pretty damn good," Dan vowed and visibly shocked a few members of the class with his use of that verbiage. "And not having an STD or a child that you weren't planning on feels excellent. In light of that, I grabbed a few extra from the clinic, so take one, pass them back." He handed a full box of condoms to every row.

"I will not be needing that, and my wife would freak if she found that somewhere," Jeff pled as Dan handed him the box.

"You and only you have my permission not to take one."

He moved back to the front of the lecture hall. "I'm certain you've seen these before, but in case you need a refresher, here are the Gifted male and female storehouses of erotic energy." Dan opened his laptop and used his hand to project the diagrams up on the large whiteboard that ran the length of the wall. "I'd say it's a safe bet that you know yours. They are fairly easy to locate." He received a few chuckles as everyone settled in. "Not only are there way more of hers, but they are spread out, harder to locate, and a hell of a lot more fun to access if you're into women." With that, he had them. He watched the young men in the class decide to let down their guards and really listen.

"For those of you that were hoping I might could offer you some advice, hear me loud and clear. It doesn't matter how good you are at locating these storehouses." He grabbed a pointer and ran it up and down the female form on the board. "If you want to be good in bed, then you need to get inside her mind before you get inside her pants.

Figure out what she wants from the experience before you start trying to touch any of these." He gestured his head back to the board. Most of the students were writing down his advice verbatim.

A very serious looking Valeduto Predilect raised his hand. Dan gestured for him to go on.

"I was just wondering," he hemmed and glanced around. "For those of us in Valeduto, especially those of us who are going into medical professions, we know all about the storehouses and condoms and all of that. We've been looking at those slides for years now." Lots of heads began nodding their agreement. "Could we skip the whole bees and pollen and energy joining talk and just ask you real questions? You're the first mentor in six years that I've sat through this class who's actually willing to talk to us like we have half a brain."

Excited agreement went through the room in murmured waves, but one young man seated near the question-asker rolled his eyes.

Dan debated. "You have to take a test on everything we're supposed to cover next Monday."

"If any senior fails the same test they've been giving us for the last six years, I think they have bigger problems," a Vis Virres student announced.

"All right, does anyone have a problem with veering off the curriculum for a little while?" Dan glanced at the guy who'd rolled his eyes when the suggestion was made. His jaw visibly clenched. "I really don't want to do this if it's going to make anyone uncomfortable."

The kid made another dramatic eye roll and raised his hand. Defiance pulsed in his rhythms. Dan nodded to him. He was a Valeduto Pred. Defiance was not usually their thing.

"Honestly?" the kid asked.

Dan gestured to the room at large. "I thought that's what we were going for here."

"I guess…"—the kid lost a little of his defiant momentum—"what if I'm sick of the entire stupid class being about women? No offense, but I don't really want to hear about your conquests. Not all of us are into that. But everyone prefers to pretend we don't exist."

Dan nodded. "What's your name?"

"Jace."

"You're one hundred percent correct, and I know I haven't been teaching very long, but I really am sorry that the entire curriculum was written for cis-het males. That isn't fair. I have no intention of discussing anything about me personally." Dan shuddered slightly. "But I hear you. I'll tell you what. I don't have any personal experience outside of cis-het relationships, but being physical with anyone does have a fair number of commonalities. The foundational elements are the same. Love is love as the saying goes. If you're willing to ask questions, if there are any that I can't help with, I'll get you some answers. I have quite a few friends who I'd bet would help me help you. If you aren't comfortable asking questions, I get that too."

Eager excitement flooded the room. A genuine grin formed on not only Jace's face but several others. Jace's brow furrowed. "You're serious?"

"Absolutely. Are you good with this format?"

"Yeah." He was suddenly visibly eager.

Dan went to his desk to hold up the stack of scrap paper he'd been given with the curriculum packet.

"Do you want to do the questions where everyone writes one down and I see how many I can get through, or do you just want to go on with it, raise your hand, and ask? Go ahead and assume that at least half the class had that question as well."

"I'm not sure we want to man up that much, Mentor Vindico," Ben Cobson admitted sheepishly.

"No problem. Here, take two each and come up with decent questions. We have quite a while left. I'll get through as many as I can. But the rules I gave you for questions at the beginning of class still apply—I will not answer anything related to my wife or anyone I've ever been in a relationship with before." He would most definitely not call any of his hook-ups in the decade before he met Fionna *relationships,* but the verbiage worked for the class.

The scrap paper flew around the room, and every student began scribbling quickly. Dan couldn't help but grin as he tried to remember what it would have meant to him to have a mentor conduct this kind of amative energies class when he'd been a student.

He moved around the room collecting the questions at random, noting that some students had used three or four slips of paper. He gathered them all and then returned to the desk.

"All right, first question." Dan drew a deep breath as he unfolded the slip of paper on top of the pile. Chuckling, he read, "What do you say to get a girl you don't know that well to go back to your place?"

Dan considered. "There is no surefire answer to this question, but I will say this. If you don't have any desire to spend all day Saturday doing anything at all that might make her happy, then you shouldn't be trying to get her in your bed on Friday night. So, maybe the way to get her back to your place should be, 'hey, I'd love to see you again next weekend and the weekend after that and the weekend after that and then maybe we could go meet my folks, hang out for a while, and then if all goes well we could go back to my place.'"

"Yeah, 'cause you took Fionna Styler to meet your parents before you took her to meet your sheets." A scowling senior on the back row huffed.

"First of all, I would really appreciate it if you could call my wife Mrs. Vindico, and you don't have to like my answers, but I'm telling you the truth as I know it from my own experiences."

Dan picked up the next sheet of paper and tried not to grimace. He shook his head slightly. "I guess I promised to try and answer these," he reminded himself audibly and gained laughter from the class. "How do I get a girl to go down?" Dan held up the paper. "Uh well…" He tried to remove the heavenly sensation and the erotic show Fionna often put on for him from his mind. It was awe-inspiring. He often informed her that her tongue should be given awards. "First of all, you should most definitely not expect that." The first time Fionna had guided him to the bed in the guest house they were staying in and arranged herself seductively on her knees and then proceeded to drink him dry seared through his brain without him being able to stop the memory. He forced the erotic imagery from his mind.

He hemmed and tried to think of the best way to answer the rather overt question.

"How about this?" he finally allowed. "This may not always be the case, but I will say that more times than not the better you treat her outside the bedroom, the dirtier it'll be in the bedroom. If you want a head queen, gentlemen, then she better be your one and only queen in every other aspect of your life. You need to make certain she knows and feels like she is, in fact, your princess."

Abashed laughter echoed around the room as most of the men discreetly continued to write notes.

Dan moved on to the next question.

"On a similar note, and let me just say, fellows, that maybe you should get your head out of your girlfriend's mouths on occasion, but this question reads, if I go down, shouldn't I get head?" Dan shook his head. "No. Not at all, and just for the record, if this is the way you're thinking about your sexual experiences with some sort of tally sheet, then your girlfriend needs to find someone worth having.

"Next question, how do I make certain she gets off before I do? Here is an excellent question, and I would say to whomever asked this, if it doesn't work out with your current girl, talk to the girlfriend of whoever wrote that last question." Derisive chuckles spread around the room.

"This actually pertains to the curriculum, so let's take a minute with this one. Getting your partner where you want them to be and where they would obviously like to go has a whole lot less to do with these storehouses than you would think."

Confused expressions etched most of the class's faces.

"They need to feel something from you before you have your hands on them." Dan only furthered the confusion. "This goes back to what I said about her mind before her pants. Women are much less likely to give it all away for you unless you've made them feel like there's an emotional connection of some kind. You've made her feel safe and like you're not going to sell her out, and that what you're sharing means something to you. She needs to feel like her desires are safe with you. If she doesn't, it's not likely that she's going to let you have that moment of bliss where she's giving you complete control.

"You have to earn it, and you need to make certain that you deserve that before you try to take it from her," Dan vowed. "I'll just add on the heels of those last two questions that if you go into it making her pleasure your only concern, trust me, you'll be taken care of better than you've ever even imagined." He watched the intrigue flash in his students' eyes.

Dan opened the next question and forced himself not to look Jeff's direction. He'd immediately recognized Jeff's handwriting but didn't want to out him in anyway. Holding up the question for a split second, he read, "You said to figure out what she wants out of the experience before you get into bed. How do you do that?" Dan considered for a long moment.

"Talk to her, kiss her, extend foreplay until you've learned something, really home in on her energy if she's Gifted, note the slight changes, watch for the cues that tell you what she's wanting. Try to think with the head above your belt line for a little while. This goes back to me saying that maybe you should spend a few weeks or months getting to know each other before you jump into bed. And if you've been together a while but want to know if there's anything different she might like, you have to make her feel comfortable enough to discuss it with you. Tell her that you want to know and not to be embarrassed by her own desires. But you have to be mature enough to handle whatever she might tell you."

Dan set Jeff's question on the desk and moved to the next. "This says, when I'm with a guy the conversation about top and bottom can get awkward. Any advice?" He considered. "Excellent question. I'm sorry I don't have any personal experience with this, like I said. So, I'm going to beg your forgiveness and ask you to let me check in with some friends of mine and get back to you tomorrow. But, this really relates to communication. Just like I was saying about women, in order for the experience to be fulfilling for you and your boyfriend or bedmate, you're going to have to talk. Try to push the awkwardness aside. Make out. Pick up on every shift of their energy. Figure out what they want out of the experience. I imagine it would be much easier to discuss this if you get to know them first. But I will make a few phone calls and see if I can't get you some specifics."

Laughing outright, Dan read, "To lube or not to lube, that is the question? I can tell you that this did not come from one of my Ioses Preds. We just aren't that poetic." He brought on more laughter. "That is between you and the person you're lubing, but I'd say give it a try.

You might like it, and more importantly they might like it. If you're not man enough to pick up a bottle at the drug store, you're not man enough to need it."

He spent the next forty-five minutes answering questions about length of foreplay, vibrators, and ways to ease the pains of the first time for women.

"I think we've got time for a few more." He opened another question. "This says, help a guy out with anal sex info." Dan paused to consider. "Three things you need to know before you participate in anal sex. One, lube. So much lube. Two, communication. Make absolutely certain that the person you're in bed with wants that kind of penetration, and remember that sex is not always about penetration. Three, more lube. Try silicone lube actually. Make lube four through ten as well and lots and lots of buildup."

Dan was exhausted by the time he made it back to his office. He'd been thanked profusely by everyone that had sat through his class and begged to continue the question and answer format the next day.

Sinking down in his desk chair, he smiled as his cell rang in his pocket. "Good morning, baby doll."

"Hey," Fionna yawned out the word and made Dan chuckle.

"Did you sleep well, Mrs. Vindico?"

"Kind of, but I miss you."

"I miss you too."

"How was your day?" He heard her draw a long sip of her coffee after her question. He could see her still curled up in bed with her hair in loose tangles on her shoulders, her eyes slightly heavy with sleep, her lips pink from her slumber, and her luscious curves wound around the sheets and quilts. He fought the urge to groan.

"I discussed everything from how to put on a condom to anal sex with seventy-five junior and senior males for the past two hours."

"I take it it's amative energies week." Fionna giggled.

"Correct."

"Aww and I'm not there to be your mentor's aide." Her flirting made him ache.

"Don't worry. I'll let you help me out with several things when you get home." Dan earned himself a sexy moan.

"Oh…okay, hang on."

Fionna laughed and then Dan heard, "Hi, Daddy!" from the sweetest voice in the world.

"Hey, baby girl, did you just wake up?"

"Yes, I got to stay up late and watch movies with Mommy!"

"You did?" He loved how delighted she sounded.

"Yes, and today we're going to play in the waterfall!"

The waterfall—Dan let his mind wander as he kept up his end of the conversation with Aida.

Fionna at the end of the summer, with him pressing her up against the rock walls of the small waterfall on the farm. Her gorgeous body on full display only slightly obscured by the rapidly falling water. Him grasping her hips and burying his need deep within her.

"I love you and I miss you bunches," Aida's vow shook Dan from his reverie.

"I love you too." He drew an X on his desk calendar, marking off the day even if it wasn't over yet.

When he ended the call with Fionna, he called Mike Ericcson. Dan had hired him not long after he'd become Chief of Elite. Mike could outshoot Dan with his eyes closed. He was a fierce Shield and a brilliant detective.

"Hey, man. How are you?" Mike sounded happy to hear from him.

"I'm good. I need to ask you a somewhat awkward favor if you have time and don't mind."

Mike chuckled. "For you, most anything."

Dan explained what he'd agreed to do and the question he'd been asked.

Mike was quiet for a long moment. "You know if parents get wind of you doing this, you're going to get fired."

"Couldn't care less. Somebody needs to be real with these kids. Until this conversation with you, I never gave much thought to what men do in bed together. Why the hell would gay and queer kids want to hear about what straight people are doing in bed? The curriculum should be relevant to everyone."

"I agree. I just never thought I'd see the day when that happened. I'm too jaded, I guess. In answer to this kid's question, once you have a little experience under your belt, literally, it gets easier to tell. I haven't been with many guys who always want to be one or the other, but there are a few. Bad experiences always leave their mark."

Dan's heart sank. "I'm sure."

"Honestly, the best thing you can do is to be adaptive and talk. If you can keep your brain engaged, even in the heat of the moment, you can tell a lot about what the other person is needing."

"That's pretty much what I told them."

"But remind them that what they want out of the experience is important too. Emphasize that just because there are assholes out there who want to tell us who they think it's okay for us to be with, that doesn't mean that being with someone whose desires don't align with your own is worth it. If they're in the closet, it can get really rough, Dan. When everything has to be undercover, kids tend to take what they can get."

"Yeah, I'm sure. I wish I could tell you that someday people will get their shit together and this will always be okay. I kind of doubt that's the case though."

"You and me both. But, hey, you're doing this. That's something. You might be saving some kid's life in there, just making them feel seen when the world wants to erase them. Don't discount what you agreed to. It's huge."

"No,"—Dan shook his head—"it's the very least I can do, and it should have been done long before I got here."

CHAPTER 34

CLANCY, CUSSLER, VINDICO

Unable to remember the last time he stayed at an office anywhere until after five, Dan grabbed his things and headed out to the Agusta. He didn't particularly want to go home alone, but Jeff would be leaving the Senate soon.

Giving in to his own longing, Dan touched Fionna's name on his call list. He casted and piped his phone through the speaker in his helmet.

"Hey there," she drawled.

"Hey, baby doll. I just wanted to hear your voice."

"I was trying to be brave and let you work, so I didn't call, but I miss you so much."

"If you want to talk to me, I don't care what I'm doing just call. Of course if you call me tomorrow between twelve-thirty and three, God only knows what you might overhear."

She laughed, and the sound soothed Dan's soul.

"I really think it's great that you're talking to them. No one wants to be real with kids. They get in their heads how it's supposed to be, and no one will shoot straight with them."

"They all really seemed to respond. I don't know why they want to hear this from me, but this is one of the first days since I started at

Venton that I felt like I might be making a difference, like I might actually be getting through to these kids, you know?"

"You sound like you had a good day," Fionna assured him. "And they want to hear it from you because you're an amazing man, and they look up to you. And 'cause you're so freaking hot in bed."

Dan laughed and was glad she couldn't see the cocky smirk that he was unable to halt.

"But only you know that, baby doll," he teased her. It was a lie, at least in some part, but all of the women that had come before her melted away in the heat of their passion and the light of their love.

"I'm looking forward to seeing all of your skills when I get home."

A shuddering groan echoed from Dan as he began to formulate just what he and his Maylea could do when he got her in bed.

He bit back a string of curse words several minutes later. Fred Sheckles was standing with his arms crossed in front of Jeff, who was scowling and rolling his eyes.

"Honey, our neighbor has captured Jeff in our driveway. Let me call you back."

"Are you serious?"

"Yes. I may kill our new neighbor before you get home, fair warning."

"I love you." Fionna giggled.

"I love you too." Dan ended the call. "What the hell?" He threw his leg off of the Agusta. "Fred, this is a good friend of mine. He's coming over to hang out some this week. What are you doing at my house, *again*?"

"Saw this kid knocking on your front door," Fred tattled. "Now, I'd heard there was more crime here in Arlington than I'd ever even fathomed coming from Pilmore. I plan on keeping my eye out."

"I told you that I'm a police officer, sir. I showed you my badge," Jeff announced in righteous indignation.

"You know, you've got a lot of expensive cars and items in your home. I was just trying to be a good neighbor," Fred assured Dan.

"How the hell do you know what I have in my house?"

Realizing his mistake, Fred changed tactic quickly. "So, you said you know this guy?"

"Yes, I know Jeff." Dan narrowed his eyes. "I know him because I used to be the head of a special ops unit out of the CIA that he is currently an officer for. And let me just add that I am highly trained and very easy to piss off. To say I'm overprotective of my girls would be a significant understatement, and I do not take kindly to people butting in my life," he snarled.

Jeff stared up at him in awe. The deeply impressed gaze had Dan trying not to chuckle.

"CIA, you don't say. I've read all of Tom Clancy's and Clive Cussler's books. I know all about secret crime fighting organizations." He was suddenly exuberant.

Jeff visibly held back laughter as Dan rubbed his forehead.

"That's great, but right now, Jeff and I have a little work to do. Like I said, I really don't need you to keep up with my house. I've got it under control."

"Hey, do you have, like, secret spy stuff in your basement?" Fred asked.

Jeff covered his mouth to keep from cracking up as Dan shook his head in defeat.

"Sure, why not. For your safety, stay away from my house."

"Don't worry. Your secret identity is safe with me." Fred saluted. That did it. Jeff doubled over laughing.

"Hey, I bet Dan Vindico isn't your real name, is it?" Fred was teetering on the brink of elation. He turned on Jeff. "Do you know his real name?"

"Are you kidding me? Nobody knows *his* name," Jeff vowed. This time Dan had to choke back laughter.

"Wait 'til I tell Betty and the boys."

"Let's just keep this between the three of us," Dan ordered.

"Oh, right." Fred saluted again. "You got it. I won't tell anyone." He raced back down the driveway.

"Dear God," Dan spat as he opened the garage door. Jeff was still guffawing.

He followed Dan into the kitchen, shaking his head. "You and Fionna are going to wake up one night, and that guy's going to be in your basement."

"We don't even have a basement, but trust me, if that moron wakes up my wife or my girls in the middle of the night, I will not hesitate to blow his ass back across the street."

"Wow." Jeff shook his head.

"Yeah, he decided to bring over cookies while we were in Kauai, and he intercepted my shield. When I got home, he was face down in my front lawn surrounded by barely recognizable cookie remains," Dan managed before he and Jeff both cracked up. "Want a pizza?" Dan asked as he quelled his laughter. "I don't cook anything like my wife, so unfortunately I don't have much besides beer or protein bars in the way of food."

"You don't have to feed me. I just appreciate your help. I won't stay too long."

Dan called the local pizza delivery and ordered two large pizzas.

"Come on, I'm going crazy without Fi. At least keep me company for a while. Your mother-in-law's still camping out at your place, right?"

"Yes." Jeff rolled his eyes. "Are you sure you don't mind me hanging out?"

"We can just go through what will be on your defense exams. I understand if you'd rather go home or hang out with your friends."

Chuckling, Jeff blushed and shook his head. "I'm sure this is really lame, but hanging out here with you would probably rank right up there with, like, graduation and helping you out with the cases at Venton."

Laughing, Dan willed away his embarrassment. "Trust me, I'm not that interesting." He handed Jeff a Dr Pepper.

"Right now, you're the coolest teacher at Venton."

"Why?" Dan directed Jeff to the couch.

"Everybody is talking about our amative energies class. That was awesome. No one will ever tell us stuff. Tons of guys are planning on skipping the class they were assigned to and sneaking into ours tomorrow."

Not certain what to think about that, Dan's brow furrowed. "Why?" he asked again.

Jeff hemmed uncomfortably. His face colored again.

"Come on, I shot straight with all of you all afternoon."

"It's like…" he seemed to force himself to go on, "everybody starts sleeping around or with whoever they're dating, but no one knows what they're doing. So, guys start watching porn partly because you want to be good at it and that's obviously readily available. But you figure out pretty quick that it's crazy wild shit that most people don't actually do, so you're still confused and thinking that you'll never be any good at it. And no one real will ever talk to you about it. You hear bullshit from other guys, most of which isn't true either. I don't know." He shrugged. "It was great to finally have a teacher who gets that we have sex and is okay with it."

Dan let that settle on him as he nodded his understanding.

"It was the best amative energies class I've ever taken, and like I said, everyone was talking about it. Every guy in there is probably home right now coming up with more questions for tomorrow."

"Great," Dan sighed.

Jeff's cell rang in his pocket. He smiled when he saw who was calling. Dan excused himself to the kitchen to give Jeff a little privacy.

"Hey baby, are you feeling okay?" He sounded worried. "Yeah," he assured her of something. Suddenly, he was chuckling. "Did your mom just hear you say that?"

Dan tried to find something to do that would make noise.

"Yeah, but not with your mom there," Jeff offered sheepishly. "Like you wouldn't believe," he vowed. Dan cringed. He was certain he knew what Becca had just asked.

"Couple hours," was the next comment. Dan considered turning on Fionna's coffee grinder. "No, believe me, baby, I am all over that as soon as your mom goes home," Jeff couldn't get the vow out quickly enough. "Are you sure Adeline said it was okay?"

The doorbell rang, and Dan moved quickly to answer it. He paid for the pizza, gave a generous tip, and thanked the delivery guy.

"Okay, you've got to stop. You're killing me. Get rid of your mom, and I'll be home in a couple of hours," he promised. "Yeah, I love you too."

Setting the boxes on the coffee table, Dan pointed back to the kitchen.

"Do you want a plate?" he offered.

"I'm good. Thank you, sir."

Dan opened the box and they both pulled a piece off of the piping hot pie.

"Is Becca feeling better?" Dan asked.

"Yeah, she's much better. She went to see Adeline today for a quick checkup. Her mom picked her up so I could go to work. She still has to take it really easy, but she's hoping to come off of bed rest in a week or two, at least long enough for school."

"Want to study a little and then head home?" Dan gave Jeff a smirk.

"Are you that good of a detective or did I talk louder than I meant to?"

"Why don't I show you how to cast the sound waves around you to create a barrier."

"Sorry," Jeff cringed. "It's just…you know when you go, like, weeks and weeks before the one night and then another week and then that's all you've heard about all freaking day," he tried to explain though his face was glowing crimson, and he'd squeezed his eyes shut long enough to make his confession.

"Believe me, I get it. If Fi called me and made that request, I would not be here hanging out with you."

Jeff laughed and seemed to settle in.

"Did Portwood get anything today?" Dan asked.

"A bunch of curious stares, but not much besides that. I actually have a theory that I'm hoping he'll let me test. I'd need to be up there when there aren't other people in the school though."

"What's the theory?"

"What if the pulse was sent digitally, and that's why there are no fingerprints?"

"Is that even possible? Wouldn't that have to be rigged up?"

"Yeah, that's why I'd need to get in the admin building when other people aren't around. It'd be almost impossible to see the electronic energy residue, but I think I could do it. Think about it, sir. They hired that guy to try to make it look like I'm some villainous hacker. All of the crimes are data-driven. You taught us that criminals tend to do what they know best. I'm thinking technology is their specialty."

"I'll talk to Landon."

Dan spent a solid hour trying to teach Jeff the things they would cover after Christmas break. He feigned exhaustion when he understood that Jeff had no capacity with which to think with the head above his belt line.

"We'll pick it back up tomorrow night," Dan assured him.

"Okay, great, thanks." Jeff nearly tripped over the coffee table as he made his escape.

As Dan closed the door behind him, he chuckled. "That's going to last approximately three and a half seconds from the moment he gets her clothes off."

CHAPTER 35

PENDERGRATH PUZZLES

By Thursday, Dan was growing weary of discussing any and all aspects of having sex but not having any himself. They'd spent the day before in his amative energies class going over the actual curriculum with the agreement that Dan would answer more questions Thursday and Friday.

Dan spent twenty minutes teaching from the curriculum and completely understood why his class had grown from seventy-five to well over a hundred. The curriculum offered them no practical useful information. By the time you were a senior, everyone knew about the energy pass that occurred when Gifted people have sex and the storehouses of sexual energy along with where the Gifted cells were held to create Gifted children.

They'd heard that it was a beautiful, wonderful experience but shouldn't be shared until they were older. To Dan's knowledge, most of the men in his class were already active, and bees and pollen and rabbits in the spring didn't offer them anything.

He entered the lecture hall and found a huge stack of questions awaiting him. Most of the students had already located seats though lunch wasn't technically over for another five minutes.

Dan debated approaching Fionna again about doing a little more than talking on FaceTime, but she couldn't shake the images from her mind of Mentor Bryant in a negligee sweet-talking the chancellor.

She was insisting that she was coming home on Saturday. Dan had agreed as long as Tutu thought her rhythms had really truly settled. Tutu had declared her healthy enough to return home.

The buzz of the bell shook Dan from his reverie.

"I can't believe any of you still want to listen to me drone on, but if you're certain that's what you want to do today, bring 'em on up."

The entire class stood to add questions to the already large pile.

Dan lifted the first folded piece of paper from the toppling pile spilling on his desk. "This one says…" Dan had to force himself not to think about Fionna as he answered lest his crotch let everyone know that his baby liked to be marked. "I left a couple of hickeys on my girl. I tried to heal her, but I can't get it to go away completely." Dan was certain this was a question from a Vis Virres Predilect.

The Valedutos, who could heal most anything, certainly wouldn't struggle with a hickey, and the Ioses Predilects would have gone to any lengths not to have to ask a group at large this question. By their very territorial nature, they would seek to protect the girl they'd marked.

"You need to use soothing energy first, then cool it off for a few seconds. You want to drop the temperature pretty low, until the swelling is gone. Then add in heat to dilate the blood vessels you broke and then speed up her blood flow around the bruise to heal it up. Add in your own energy to speed up the healing."

Shaking his head, Dan grimaced as he read the next question. "I'm going to lose my job."

"None of us have told any of the other mentors or faculty about the class," Ben Cobson vowed.

"We'd never sell you out like that, man," Steve Bowers, a Vis Virres Junior, promised adamantly.

Dan didn't let on that he didn't particularly care. "And it reads, I suck at dirty talk. My girlfriend ends up laughing at me. It's horrible and embarrassing. What am I supposed to say that won't sound so stupid?" Dan negated to read the words *please help* written under the question several times.

"I know a lot of my answers have started this way, but again, it helps to have some context by way of knowing what she wants out of the experience. In general, I'd stay away from using scientific terms for body parts." He wondered if this was a question from a Valeduto Predilect who had trouble calling a penis something a little bit dirtier and therefore much sexier. "I'd ramp it up slowly. If she shies away, back it off. Some people like to be called names, but I'd steer away from that unless that's been communicated to you that she likes that. Try giving them an idea of what you're planning on doing.

"You could ask her if she likes it or tell her that she does if you're absolutely certain that you're correct." He smirked. "Pet names are good. Tell her what you feel or see happening to her. That lets them know that you're right there with them enjoying the experience. You can tell her what you want her to do or feel. Telling her how beautiful she is will always get you farther, and telling her that you love any particular part of her will serve you well."

Everyone frantically wrote down everything he'd said.

"Think about it like this," Dan urged. The entire class leaned forward, eager for knowledge. "People who respond positively and then erotically to dirty talk, and I don't know that you'd find many people who would say they didn't, if you're talking during a time when they've allowed you into the most private parts of their primal being, then whatever you're saying needs to let them know that you're into it and you're into them.

"Being desired is one hell of an aphrodisiac, so let them know how much you want them. Build confidence. I'm betting you would all agree that a sexual partner who's confident in bed is pretty damn sexy. So, whatever you're saying…and please, if all you're coming up with is random thoughts that occasionally involve the pizza you ate for lunch or what you got on an exam, then just keep it shut, fellows. Whatever comes out of your mouth should focus on making your bed partner think it's the best sex you've ever had. If you do it right, it might just *become* the best sex you've ever had."

Dan read the next question. He was certain the friends of whomever had written it would most certainly know, but he continued on. "Got caught by my girl's dad in her bedroom. I really love her. We've been together for a while. He freaked and wants us to break up. Her mom said we could keep seeing each other as long as we stop sleeping together, but we don't want to stop. What do I do?"

Dan's mind whipped from trying to envision this question coming from Aida's boyfriend and then recalling his parents' reaction when his mother had walked in on him and Amelia in his bed when they were eighteen. "My best advice is to shoot straight with them. Try to make them understand that you're a serious guy and that you love her." He held up the paper indicating the vow made in the question. "Other than that, you could get a job and move in together, but that isn't easy while you're still in school. For the most part, parents want to know that you're going to love and cherish their child. It's fear that drives the demands they made on you two. Try reassuring them and see where that gets you."

Scowling, Dan rolled his eyes as he moved on to the next question. "If I buy my girl a diamond necklace, will she let me give her a pearl one? If not, what do I have to do? She keeps saying no."

"First of all, stop watching so freaking much porn," Dan demanded. "Let me tell you all something. If she says no, that means no. I don't care what you're asking. I don't care if you're in the middle of having sex with her, if the word no comes out of her mouth then you stop whatever the hell it is you're doing and apologize immediately. Do not pressure her into anything. Do not tell her how hot you think it would be. Do not tell her that other girls are doing whatever it is you want to do. Grow up!"

Dan went on answering questions for two hours straight. Everything from how hard to bite if you're going to take a nip to what happens when the Receiver you've been with for a while cries after sex but tells you that it was a good thing.

That one had Dan laughing without meaning to, but he'd tried his best to answer honestly just like he'd been doing for days.

At the end of class, he was approached by two Valeduto seniors.

"Hey, Mentor Vindico, could we talk to you for a second?" a tall muscular guy with a dark face and kind eyes quizzed. "I'm Leshawn, and this is Alex." He gestured his head to the student beside him.

"Sure," Dan agreed.

"I have a theory about all of those faked drug tests, and I think it's a pretty good one."

"I'm listening." Dan studied the students before him. Their energy was calm, and they seemed quite sincere.

"A couple of years ago, Wilshire expanded the internship programs for Valeduto students at Georgetown. It used to be that only ten students got selected, but he made it thirty. It seems to me that's your suspect list. It's got to be one of us, and I'm on that list so if you could keep this between us that'd be great."

"How much access do the interns have to the lab?"

"It depends on what your specialty is. I'm a surgical intern, so I have none. But there are quite a few students who are looking to be lab scientist medios and technologists. They work in the lab a lot.

"I can tell you that Mindy Langer and a few of her friends have been using Veneque whenever they hook up for a while, but she's still here. And, uh..." He glanced back at the classroom door. "She hooks up occasionally with Brittany Meeger..." He lifted his eyebrows.

"I'm guessing Brittany is one of the lab interns."

"Yes, sir, but she's also super straitlaced, so I don't know. Just a lead, I guess. But Mindy's been using for over a year, and she hasn't gotten suspended or expelled."

"Why are you telling me this now?"

"Because you've actually taught us stuff all week, and you haven't freaked because we have sex or want to know more about it. You're really cool. We want to help you if we can," Leshawn explained. He never dropped his gaze. "Plus, it's one of us," he sounded disgusted. "So, it seems like one of us should be who tells you."

"Thank you," Dan vowed. "Will you let me know if you hear anything else?"

Alex nodded. "We will. No problem. We're still going to be able to ask questions tomorrow, right?"

Dan assured them that they would as he gathered his things. He was eager to get back to his office to use his detective skills. But as he approached his office, he halted abruptly. His shield began churning in rapid, jagged twists.

Governor Haydenshire was standing with his father along with Governor Willow and Portwood. They hadn't noted Dan's approach.

He slowed his pace and listened.

"I'm begging you, Stephen. Wait until Fionna gets back," Governor Vindico pled.

"He's right, Governor Haydenshire. I really think we should wait. Fi will soften the blow. She makes him tick," Portwood urged.

"When is she due back?" Governor Haydenshire fretted.

"I just called her. She can't get a flight out until tomorrow morning, and the closest Senate jet is at LAX," Governor Vindico explained. "I didn't mean to upset her. She's supposed to be relaxing for the baby, but if she thinks something's wrong with my son, she comes unglued. Of course, she already knew something was wrong. She felt it." Regret filled his tone.

"I don't think it would matter if there was a flight out of Lihue right now. I'm telling you they're casting him constantly to keep him alive until Clarence gets here. He's got hours not days," Governor Haydenshire explained hesitantly.

"What the hell is going on?" Dan demanded, unable to wait any longer and furious that something had upset Fionna enough to make her book an earlier flight.

"Dan." Governor Haydenshire grimaced as nervous glances shot quickly through the group of men.

"Why did you call Fi? What's going on?"

"Come in here." Governor Vindico gestured everyone into his office. Governor Willow offered Dan a consoling smile which only furthered his terror.

Governor Haydenshire drew a deep breath and paced in front of the large desk in the office. "Son, Candor Pendergrath was taken to Georgetown yesterday." Trying desperately to figure out what Candor Pendergrath's imminent death would have to do with either Fionna or himself, Dan nodded. He needed the Crown Governor to get on with whatever he'd come to say.

"Coriolis took its toll. He wasn't exactly young when he went in back in March, and I'm certain the fifty years of smoking unfiltered cigarettes didn't help. He's not going to make it through the night. I just went out to Georgetown."

Trying to draw steady breaths and process the fact that Candor Pendergrath would be no more, Dan nodded again. Pendergrath was the last of Wretchkinsides's top men that would no longer pollute the earth by drawing breath. He was the man who'd helped Cascavel take Amelia. He'd disappeared right after Wretchkinsides had killed her. Dan tried to be respectful of the dead and of the dying, but he could find no remorse for the man who'd done nothing but commit heinous, horrific crimes for most of his life.

"He has a death bed plea, Daniel," Governor Haydenshire choked.

"Of course he does." Dan let his eyes close for the length of one heartbeat.

"He asked that I clear Clarence's record. He wants him out of prison, and he wants him to finish school." Governor Haydenshire paused, and Dan suddenly understood. He tried to brace himself for the obvious conclusion. He needed Fionna. He needed her to come home. His soul and his mind pled for his precious saving grace while his lungs begged for air.

"He asked that Clarence be educated here at Venton." Governor Haydenshire said the words Dan knew were coming, but his voice sounded distant and echoed.

"You understand he tried to kill both Logan and Rainer last March at the takedown." Dan narrowed his eyes at the Crown Governor.

"He took a swing at Rainer," Governor Haydenshire reminded him gently. "Clarence is barely eighteen, and he never knew anything but what his father taught him. Candor killed his mother when he was just a few months old."

"You think I don't know that," Dan roared as he ran his hands through his hair in his volatile anger.

"Dan," Governor Vindico soothed. His voice took on a calming thrum.

"He helped Pravus murder Cal. He helped Cascavel take Amelia. He was right beside Pravus and Wretchkinsides when they killed my daughter and damn near killed the love of my life," Dan erupted in rage. His shouting echoed off the walls of the office.

Governor Vindico looked stunned. Dan realized that he and Fionna had never shared the fact that the baby they lost, the baby Pravus had murdered, had also been a little girl.

"No, Daniel," Governor Haydenshire whispered, "his father did all of those things. He hasn't done much of anything except try to prove himself to his father. And I'm sorry for what this is going to put you through, but I feel like he deserves the opportunity to turn his life around. He deserves the chance to be so much more than his old man."

"Fine." Dan stalked quickly to the door. He turned a savage glare on the men staring back at him. "If he comes near my wife or near my girls, I'll make damn sure he gets to rot in the cell his old man just left, so you just keep him the hell away from me. I won't be here next year. So, I sincerely hope you're right and that he does turn his life around because if he doesn't, I won't be here to clean up the mess for you." Dan flung the door open and sped to his own office.

"Hey." Fionna's voice soothed him. He didn't want to speak. He just wanted to listen to her talk. "I'm flying out first thing in the morning," she promised.

"You don't have to come home early."

"I'd really like to if it's okay with you."

"No, you need to stay there and rest," he tried, but he wanted her in his arms so desperately his plea held no substance.

"No, I need to be with you. I've been resting and relaxing and spending time with my girls, and now I need to come home. When you aren't here, it just isn't my home. I want to come home now. Aida wants to come home and so does our little Halia. When the time is right, maybe we'll make this our home, but it will never be our home unless we're all together."

"I just told my dad that I'm quitting next year."

"Okay. We'll figure it out."

Unable to continue insisting that she stay there, knowing perfectly well that she was the more powerful force, Dan let the feeling that she would be in his arms in less than twenty-four hours wash through him.

"If you're certain you're better, I really would like you to come home. God, I miss you, baby. I need you."

"Then that's where I'll be," she assured him. "Do you want to talk about it?"

"Not right now." Dan wasn't entirely certain why he was so furious that Clarence Pendergrath had been given an out, but he knew he hadn't sorted through his own emotions enough to try and discuss them.

"Okay, maybe when I get home," was her patient reply.

"Yeah, maybe. I need to get out of here." If he couldn't be with her, if he couldn't hold her and let her make everything in his world right, then he wanted to be all alone.

"I love you so much."

"Me too," Dan replied with the only response he'd been able to give her for so long even though he'd been in love with her from the very beginning. "I'll call you later."

"I'll be right here."

With his thoughts and his shield at odds, Dan let his head fall into his hands. Why was he so fucking pissed that Clarence was being given an out when he, himself, had also been given a way to make reparations for what he'd done last spring? That galling thought burned away all others.

The answer was both obvious and infuriating. He'd been so certain working for Venton would bring him some kind of absolution. Instead, all it brought was a certainty that this wasn't what he'd been put on the earth to do. The sheriff's job in Kauai was still so tantalizing and every bit as out of reach. He didn't know what Fionna wanted him to do, and until he knew that, nothing else mattered.

CHAPTER 36

PAST, PRESENCE, FUTURE

Dan let the fiery hot water from his shower beat against his aching muscles. He'd been out on the Agusta for hours, flying down everything from interstates to dirt roads.

Stepping out, he ran a towel through his hair and haphazardly dried his body. He shrugged into a torn pair of jeans and an undershirt then headed to the kitchen to grab a beer. He fell on to the couch and flipped on the television. He knew very little would hold his attention.

A knock sounded on the door. With a dramatic eye roll, Dan stomped to the front door prepared to tell off his new neighbor.

"Fi called me. How 'bout we go out for one of those?" Garrett gestured to the bottle of beer on the coffee table.

"Been a while, man." Will offered Dan his hand. "We even dragged this loser along." He elbowed Wes Willow.

A smile Dan couldn't halt spread across his face as he chuckled and nodded his agreement. Fifteen minutes later, Dan joined all of his closest childhood friends at a table in the middle of a dive bar not far from his house.

"My God, how is it that I'm the only one of us who was smart enough not to get married?" Garrett chastised.

"I'd say that means you're the only one of us not getting laid, but you're you, and you'll bang anything that'll lie still long enough so...." Wes brought on derisive laughter.

"So not true," Garrett huffed with a broad grin. "I have standards."

"Yeah, over eighteen, blonde, big tits, and lacking clothing," Will goaded.

"Right...standards. That's what I just said." Garrett feigned confusion bringing on more laughter. "So, Fi's coming home tomorrow, which means Danny boy won't be surfacing until sometime around Christmas," he harassed as they were all supplied beers and refill pitchers.

"Good we went out now." Will laughed.

"He will have to get his head out of there long enough for his kid to be born," Wes pointed out as Dan tried not to laugh but failed miserably.

"Says the guy that boned his wife on the delivery table," Dan came right back.

"Hey, if Lauren says 'you wanna,' I do not say no. I'm not an idiot."

"Yeah, I'm sure that was all Lauren," Will scoffed as Wes tried very hard not to blush.

"What? You mean Brooke didn't jump you two seconds after Lily Ana was born?" Wes turned the quip back on Will.

"Uh, my little hottie doesn't have to say you wanna, man. She shakes those hips and I'm all over that." Will waggled his eyebrows with a cocky smile.

"Okay, okay, I still haven't heard how our Danny Boy hooked up with Fionna Styler," Wes reminded them.

Dan refilled his beer. "You've seen her, right? She walked in the bar. I started drooling and was unable to formulate coherent sentences. I managed to buy her a drink. We talked. We danced. She walked out of the bar. I followed her home and held on tight."

"That is actually entirely accurate," Garrett pledged.

"And I'm never letting go." Dan glanced at his watch and willed the next day to come quickly.

"That was made clear when you knocked her up on your honeymoon." Will laughed.

"Hey, I get the job done," Dan bragged to groans from his friends.

"Fi's great though," Will pledged to Wes. "She sure as hell keeps him smiling."

"Fi's amazing," Dan vowed. "Oh, but you would know that, wouldn't you?" He narrowed his eyes in on Will.

He grimaced. "She told you about that, did she?"

"She did." Dan still hated the fact that Will had his hands down Fionna's jeans when she was sixteen years old, even if she hadn't belonged to him them.

"Wait, what?" Garrett's face lit with intrigue.

"It was forever ago. I'm fairly certain we would both agree that it meant nothing. She was trying to get to you, and hell, I was pretty much just horny, and like you just said, she's gorgeous."

"And what exactly happened forever ago?" Garrett looked like the cat that caught the canary.

"We made out—nothing more," Will lied and Dan nodded. He didn't really want to go into the details. It still made him slightly queasy.

"How old were you?" Garrett demanded.

"Seventeen," Will huffed in effort to prove how long ago the event had occurred.

"You had Fionna Styler in our room when she was sixteen, and I did not know about this?" Garrett stared at Will like he'd suddenly sprouted another head.

"Talk about something else. Dan's been without for a week. He may combust or something," Will urged.

"Whatever, man." Garrett lifted his phone from his pocket to answer a text.

His face fell suddenly as he glanced at Dan. All sense of playful banter was gone in an instant. "They just took Pendergrath off life support. He's gone," Garrett stated as everyone studied Dan intently.

Nodding, Dan drew a long sip of his beer. He'd been consumed with taking them all down for so long he wasn't certain what to feel.

Garrett lifted his stein. "Long hard fight, but it's finally over. So, how about to the future."

Dan toasted that. He needed that. He needed his life, his love, his soul, and his future, but they wouldn't be returning until the next day. So, for now, he'd have to settle for the present in a bar with men who'd stood by him for his entire past. Through all of the hell he'd put himself through, they were the ones who'd never lost faith that he'd find his way back to the life he'd left behind.

CHAPTER 37

AMOROUS EXHAUSTION

Dan glanced at his watch between every question the next day in his amative energies class.

"Come on, Mentor Vindico, just tell us the wildest sex you ever had," urged Russ Hampton, a Vis Virres Predilect on the front row.

"No, Mr. Hampton." Dan shook his head. "I'll just keep that between myself and my wife." He gave them a little something. Laughter and wolf whistles rang around the room.

"Next question," Dan called as he pulled yet another slip of paper from the pile. "How can I make it last a little longer with my girlfriend?"

Dan grinned. "Put her on top, gentlemen. Pretty much works every time."

He moved on to the next question. "I will answer this even though you're clearly trying to get more for your money. If you had to give us three key pieces of advice to make our girls think we're the shit, what would it be?"

Considering, Dan hemmed. "How about draw it out. Don't give in too quickly. That doesn't just apply to women either. That works across the board. If you tempt long enough, the buildup will generally be explosive. Be with her in the moment, whomever she is right then. There are many, many sides to women, and if you try to take care of each of them in whatever version of themselves they're in, they should be very, very happy. Most importantly try to be confident, gentlemen. If you act like you know what the hell you're doing, you can cover a myriad of awkward situations. Go with it and at least act like you know what you're doing. That and communication is always, always key," Dan concluded. "If you fail the test on Monday, do not come to my office crying." He received many assurances that no one would fail and that even if they did, it was worth it.

"We have time for a few more." Dan glanced at his watch yet again.

Laughing, he shook his head as he read the next question. "Isn't there something my girlfriend could take or do that would make her a little less bitchy when she's PMSing?"

"Try this, fellows." Dan rolled his eyes. "Be patient if she bites your head off for no reason. For the love of everything good in the world, do not comment. She pretty much feels like hell, and most women are in pain for all of that, so running a little heat through your hand and trying to ease the cramps or just holding her until she feels better are really thoughtful things to do. Chocolate will generally at least make her not want to kill you simply because you exist without a uterus and are within arms' reach," he teased. "Hormones can be bitches. Theirs are constantly fluctuating. That is not their fault. And remember that you can always be replaced and that she puts up with all of your crap twenty-four seven so...." he drawled his conclusion.

With that, the bell rang.

"Daddy!" rang from the back of the class as the door flew open.

"Aida, wait." Fionna tried to stop her but Aida raced headlong into Dan's arms.

"Hey, baby girl." Dan scooped her up and hugged her fiercely.

"Sorry," Fionna fussed as she made her way to Dan. Shifting Aida to his hip, Dan pulled Fionna in. He was desperate to feel her close to him, to feel her safely in his arms.

He ignored the slightly abashed chuckles and the eyebrow waggles being shared by his students as they recalled his earlier comment about the wildest sex he'd ever had.

"We can do a few more next week after your test if you want," Dan excused his class.

Aida turned to look out at the students. She immediately tucked her face in Dan's neck, embarrassed to discover that all of his students were smiling at her.

They began gathering their things and putting away their notes. Dan couldn't keep his eyes off of his beautiful bride. He slid his hand over her bump, feeling Halia's energy as well.

"I missed you so much." He pulled her in for a long-drawn kiss. He no longer cared who was watching.

"Let's go home," Fionna soothed. Dan set Aida down as he packed his laptop.

"Why are there only boys in your class? That's not fair."

"Normally, I have girls too. This was a special class. The girls got to take one too," he reassured her.

Aida nodded and took Dan's hand. She led him out of the room.

His heart seized. His breath caught in his lungs. He lifted Aida back into his arms and pulled Fionna close as he took in his father and Governor Haydenshire walking down the corridor with Clarence Pendergrath.

Fionna's soothing calm moved through Dan as he shuddered. He looked just like his father only thirty years younger. His months in a prison work camp in New Mexico had aged him. He scowled as he saw Dan.

Shaking his head, Dan rushed his wife and his little girl into his office and shut the door tightly behind them.

Fionna's hands rubbed over her bump suddenly as a grin formed on her beautiful face.

"Halia knows Daddy's here too," she informed Aida, who grinned as she reached her hand to feel Halia kick.

"Let's go. I want my girls home safe with me," he ordered.

Fionna raised her eyebrows and gave him a look that said to tone it down.

"Sorry. Been a rough week."

Fionna brushed a tender kiss along his jaw. That was all it took. He wanted her so badly his mouth watered. His pulse begged for her with every beat of his heart, every pulse of his rhythms. His shield tensed toward her in desperate need to envelop her, to penetrate her.

Garrett had picked Fionna and Aida up from the airport and loaded everything into the Mercedes for them. Dan helped Aida into her pink flower car seat and then drove them away from Venton's campus.

His father had been trying all day to get Dan to talk either about his declaration that he wouldn't be at Venton the next year or about Clarence, but Dan had brushed him off repeatedly.

He wanted to go home. He wanted Fionna to change into sweats and lie beside him on the couch while they watched *Supernova* with Aida. He wanted to feel Halia respond to his voice and his energy. He needed to feel his wife's swollen curves move against him as she drew breath. He was desperate to simply exist inside their sanctuary and pretend that the rest of the world was miles from their front door.

"And I went with Papa and got salt from the Salt Pond that's different from the ocean one. And then Mommy and Tutu used the bunches of salt to make stuff to scrub your skin. Mommy said it will make your skin soft when you touch it," Aida informed Dan of the things she'd been doing all week in Kauai.

He gazed back in the rearview mirror and winked at her. "It sounds like you had lots of fun, baby girl." He brought Fionna's hand to his mouth and kissed it tenderly. A knowing, hungry grin formed on her luscious lips. She wanted him as well. Dan picked up speed on the interstate as he envisioned a myriad of things he wanted to do with his wife.

"I had lots of fun, but I missed you so much. Sometimes I woke up and I wanted you and Mommy would come but I still wanted you," Aida confessed in a slight choke. Fionna beamed, and Dan was certain his heart couldn't take many stories like that.

They spilled out of the car in the driveway. Dan was eager to get his family inside and begin his weekend.

"Hiddy there, neighbor." Fred raced up the driveway carrying mail he was perusing. Fionna offered a polite smile as Dan scowled.

"Fred, this is my wife, Fionna, and our little girl, Aida," Dan begrudged.

"Hi." Fionna extended her hand and tried not to laugh at the expression on Dan's face.

"Ah, so, I'm finally getting to meet the little lady." Fred beamed as he took in Fionna. His eyes made a slow path up her long legs and then lingered entirely too long on her swollen cleavage. Dan seethed as he stepped between his wife and their new neighbor. "I picked up your mail for you." Fred seemed to have to shake himself forcefully from his reverie under Dan's infuriated glare.

"Uh…thank you," Fionna stammered. "You don't need to get our mail."

"I figured with the kind of work you do you wouldn't want just anyone picking it up."

"I'm good with myself or my wife getting our own mail," Dan huffed.

Ignoring Dan completely, Fred stepped to the side so he could keep his eyes fixed on Fionna.

He handed her the mail after he flipped through it yet again. He waggled his eyebrows and gave her a leering smirk as he released the catalogs, bills, and advertisements. Her face flushed as she and Dan both noted a large catalog from one of her favorite lingerie stores, a copy of both Cosmo and Vogue, along with a coupon from the online company where Fionna had purchased vibrators and the shaving cream she preferred.

"Looks like you're gonna give Dan another one there. That's what I always say—a woman's place is either pregnant or getting that way." Fred chortled.

Fionna narrowed her eyes, and Dan ground his teeth.

"Betty always hits me when I say that," he commented.

"Imagine that." Dan rolled his eyes.

"Daddy." Aida pulled on his arm. She wiggled and then crossed her legs with a frantic look in her eye.

"Come on, sweetheart." Dan guided her up the garage steps quickly.

"Goodbye, Mr. Sheckles. We'll see you later." Fionna turned to follow Dan inside as Aida raced to the bathroom.

"I told you." Dan pulled Fionna into his embrace and kissed her forehead.

"A woman's place is either pregnant or getting that way," Fionna spat. "He only has two kids!"

"Yeah, I get the impression that he talks a much bigger game than he's allowed to play." Dan shook his head as Fionna laughed. "I'm so glad you're home." He couldn't seem to stop telling her as her energy swirled around him.

"Me too." She gave him a contented sigh.

"Why don't you go put on something comfortable, baby doll? I'll order Chinese. We could just lie on the couch and watch TV with our baby girl."

"That sounds perfect." Fionna seemed elated. Her energy rolled in soothing waves. It was so much stronger after her time in Kauai. It allowed him to really relax.

"Want to come help me change?" She waggled her eyebrows.

A shuddering growl echoed from Dan's chest as he followed her up the stairs.

"I missed you so fucking much." Dan helped her unzip the sundress she was wearing.

"What exactly did you miss?" Her flirtatious grin spoke needy erotic volumes, ones he planned to indulge himself in all night long.

"I missed doing this." He kissed his way from her earlobe down her neck. And I really missed these." He popped the clasp on her bra, flung it off, and he lifted the weight of her breasts as he laved her nipples with his tongue. Fionna gave him an aching, needy moan. It drove Dan wild. "Are you hungry for me, baby doll? Needy for me?"

Working his way down, he slid his hands around her bump. "I missed my baby girl." He kissed his way down her extremely swollen midsection. Halia's hand moved across Fionna's stomach as she heard her daddy's voice.

Chuckling, Dan was overwhelmed as he watched. "I missed holding you in my arms while you sleep. I missed hearing you laugh, seeing you smile at me, hearing about your day. You make everything in my life good, and, my God, I missed laying you out and taking you hard. Hearing you call my name, those sweet sounds you make for me, feeling you drip for me, then making you take it 'til you just can't stand it anymore," Dan vowed in a reverent growl.

Her breath came up short as Dan dragged his index finger along her slit through the thin satin panties she was wearing.

"After our little girl goes to bed, I hope you're ready. I'm gonna fill you so full I'll watch it drip back out of you. I'm tired of waiting for what's mine."

"Yes," gasped from her in a throaty whisper.

Dan edged the crotch of the panties aside. "Already so wet for me just like I like it. Such a good girl." He hesitantly traced right where she wanted so desperately to be entered. Her lips clenched against his fingertips.

"Oh God, stop. I can't take it. I need you. I need to be full of you."

Dan eased his hand away and held her close again. "Be patient and let it build for me. Let me go spend some time with my little ones. Then, I'm going to spend a whole lot of time with their mama."

After several long impassioned kisses where Dan was simply unable to keep his hands from her luscious tits, Fionna dressed and they headed downstairs.

Aida giggled as they entered the living room hand in hand. "I know what you were doing up there," she informed them with a great deal of sass.

"You do?" Dan lifted her up in the air and then seated her in his lap, thoroughly delighting his little girl.

"You were kissing," she announced.

"And how do you know that, my sweet girl?" Fionna snuggled in beside them on the couch.

Aida turned serious suddenly and grasped Fionna's hand. "I know because you were crying last night and you missed Daddy, and he doesn't want you to cry so he was kissing you and making you feel better." She planted a sweet kiss on Fionna's cheek.

"I'm okay," Fionna assured her as Dan's heart sank rapidly to his stomach.

"Fi?" He studied her, but she shook her head.

Dan was willing to wait until Aida had gone to bed, but he wanted to make certain it was nothing more than hormones and being away from home that had her in tears.

After their dinner of orange chicken and fried rice, they snuggled on the couch and reveled in being home together until Aida was yawning more than she was talking. Dan helped her with her bath and her pajamas then tucked her into bed after a quick story.

He let the disappointment wash through him as he returned downstairs to find his wife sound asleep on the couch tucked under several quilts.

"Let's go to bed, baby," he soothed.

Nodding, Fionna let him help her up off the couch. He guided her up the stairs and pulled off the yoga pants she was wearing.

"I'm sorry. I'm just so tired." She sounded thoroughly defeated.

"You have nothing to be sorry about. I just want to hold you while you sleep." He was certain if she'd been more awake she would've felt that his words were an outright lie. He wanted much more than that, but she was home and she was safe in his arms and that was enough. She curled up on his chest and fell back into an exhausted sleep.

CHAPTER 38

FIVE THOUSAND MILES

Dan spent the weekend doing nothing but hanging out in sweats with his wife and his girls. He and Aida went to the store Saturday morning, and Fionna fixed a huge pot of her chili that was Dan's favorite. They ate on it all weekend while watching movies, cuddling, and shutting the world out for a while.

Dan was granted numerous opportunities to reconnect with his wife while Aida was still asleep Saturday morning, and then again while she went to play with Olivia for a little while Saturday afternoon. They took a long bath Saturday night which ended in a lovemaking session that had them both needing another shower after it was over.

The process continued Sunday, so by work Monday morning, Dan was feeling restored. He was ready to face Clarence Pendergrath and ready to give the amative energies exam. He and Fionna planned on spending every afternoon for the next few weeks getting ready for Halia's arrival. They were taking a tour of the maternity floor of Georgetown along with a newborn care class that evening. Garrett was keeping Aida, and she was thrilled.

Prepared for battle, Dan entered his father's office before he stopped by his own.

"I have a list of suspects on the drug test swaps, and I really think you need to do a surprise test today or tomorrow. If we catch someone, you could use that information to get closer to the person or people that covered the tests in the first place." He laid a printed copy of the thirty names of Valeduto students, all juniors or seniors, who had been given internships at Georgetown in the last year. The top five on the list were actively working in the lab.

Governor Vindico looked bereaved. "I take it you and Fionna are moving to Kauai." He sounded bitterly disappointed.

"Nothing's finalized yet, but this really isn't for me. And I know if we decide to move that I'd be taking the girls away, but it's only a five-hour flight for you. I can't work here year after year with him. I can't have him around Fi and the girls, not after what his father did."

The governor let his eyes close for a long moment. "I feel like I just got my son back, and now you're leaving again," he admitted in a heartfelt choke.

Stabbing regret washed through Dan. "We're not sure of anything yet, and even if we move it wouldn't be until after graduation at the earliest. We haven't even really finalized any details, and Fionna's not in any shape to be making major life decisions right now."

"Will you just do something for me?" The governor pled. Dan nodded. "I know Venton and you don't make a good fit. I'll get you a job anywhere you want—just please think about it. Don't take my grandbabies five thousand miles away, please."

Swallowing back a sudden onslaught of emotion, Dan drew a deep breath. "I can't promise you that. I know it's a long way, but that may be where my family is supposed to be. I don't know how to make that work out for you, but I also can't stay here."

"Just think about it," his father begged again.

"Fine. I will," Dan agreed. As uncomfortable silence drowned the office, Dan made his escape.

∼

The next morning, Dan downed a cup of coffee while he drove to the academy long before the sunrise. His father, Jeff, and Portwood were standing in the entry corridor when he arrived.

Governor Vindico offered Jeff a kind smile. "All right, Mr. Strenton, I'm ready to be impressed."

"I'll try, sir. I just need to follow the electrical lines from the test vault out to the relay station and maybe all the way out to solar field. I doubt we have to go that far though."

"What are we looking for exactly?" Portwood asked.

"I'm not sure yet, but any evidence that supports my theory that this was done digitally. I don't think there was anyone actually in this building the night of the ball. So, thrown breakers, char marks, the electronic residue that occurs when someone casts a grid, that kind of thing."

"Let's get out to the relay then." Governor Vindico gestured everyone back out into the cold autumnal air.

As Dan fell in line with Portwood, the early morning dew of the vast Venton quad soaked through their trousers. "If this was done digitally, what would that have gotten the kids stealing the exams though? They need to get in the vault to get the copies to sell them. Someone had to have been here," Portwood pointed out.

Jeff grimaced. "I haven't figured that out yet, but I'm kind of wondering if someone is setting up Mentor Bryant."

"Like who?" Portwood asked.

"No idea, sir."

Dan shook his head. "No. I don't think so. I don't believe she planned to leave the dance early that night. It was too spur-of-the-moment."

Governor Vindico's brow furrowed. "So, you're saying you think she slipped out after the power went out?"

"I'm not sure. She either did it then or when the rest of the mentors were dancing. Her leaving was all a coincidence and has nothing to do with the breach on the test vault."

"If I find something, maybe it'll tell us," Jeff offered hopefully. He carried one of the high-powered Iodex laptops with him.

"I did call her into my office and ask her about the vault," Governor Vindico explained. "She swears she had no idea anything had happened. Then she told me that her daughter called and needed her to come home. We know that's a lie, so I'm inclined not to believe that she didn't have anything to do with the vault either."

They reached the relay building that housed all of the electronic wiring and grids for the entire campus. Governor Vindico unlocked the door and summoned to cast the lights.

"Look." Jeff pointed to three breakers that weren't flipped but did have black soot marks on them.

"What do those go to?" Dan asked.

His father searched for the numbers on the key that was posted near the breaker box. "The admin building."

Jeff summoned and then projected his shield cast over the relay grids. Dan had no idea what he was seeing, but something visibly intrigued him.

He dropped his cast, sank down on the concrete floor, and opened the Iodex laptop. "I'm checking the logs for any overrides from the night of the dance."

Dan, Governor Vindico, and Portwood all leaned in to see the screen on Jeff's computer.

"These are the grid logs. They show the flow of electricity to and from all the buildings on campus all the time. See, for the most part they remain stable. Large draws during the school day and then much smaller after the maintenance staff leaves to go home at night. The dorms remain steady throughout the day and night."

He began typing again. "Here." He pointed to the screen. "This is the night of the dance. Breakers have thresholds they're set to, so if more voltage tries to move through the system than the breaker is set to allow, it shuts it down. That's what breakers do. But that night, someone hacked in and set all of the breaker thresholds to zero. It shut everything down. There's only one breaker that wasn't set to zero."

"The test vault." Dan said what everyone already knew.

"Yeah, but because that breaker was the only one open, all the power from the entire campus went to the test vault. It blew the ground connection. Three minutes after that occurred, they went in and reset the breakers back to their original thresholds. But I don't think anyone was ever here on campus."

"That's why Fi didn't sense them," Dan confirmed.

"What would that get them though? Why do it?" Portwood began pacing.

"Access to the tests and answers, I'm assuming." Governor Vindico rubbed his temples.

"But we've all been all over that vault, sir," Jeff explained. "We've looked at the security camera footage endlessly. No one that shouldn't have been near the vault has been near it."

Dan and Portwood shared a knowing glance. Dan nodded. "Then it looks like the person stealing tests is someone who does have clearance to be near the vault."

Jeff shook his head. "Not necessarily, sir. There's still something we're missing. I'm just not sure what it is yet. Give me a minute."

He went back to abusing the keyboard, and several minutes later, he turned the screen so they could see it. "It was a trojan."

"I'm assuming that is different from what Trojans were when I was attending here," Governor Vindico guessed.

Everyone chuckled and assured him that it wasn't a condom.

Jeff grinned. "Yes, sir. This is how they were able to hack into the grid. They cleaned most of it up but didn't seem to realize that the log recorded some of the changes they made."

"Can you trace that back to the person who did this?" Portwood demanded.

"No, sir. They're not that stupid. They cleaned up their tracks fairly well. I can just see evidence of the coding."

"How about when it was done?" Governor Vindico asked. "Can you tell me that?"

"Maybe." Jeff clicked several more keys. "It looks like it was done well before the dance actually." He hit another few keys. "This was all set up the Monday you started as chancellor, sir."

Dan's eyes closed in defeat. "Because whoever is doing this had to start using their contingency plans when shit got real. This isn't some kid looking to make a few bucks. This was all premeditated. It's a far more intricate house of cards than any of us ever thought."

ABOUT THE AUTHOR

J.E. Neal (aka Jillian) vastly prefers coffee to tea, guac to salsa, the beach over anywhere else, and the world inside her head over the one outside her front door. She also loves not having to choose.

Driven by the question 'what if,' J.E. Neal's world began to manifest. What if there were people with powers the rest of us couldn't see? What if the energy of our world could be summoned and used at their will? Characters with these amazing abilities took shape in her mind. She created—and continues to create—an endless number of stories full of delicious escape from our reality where emotions are visible, desire is palpable, and danger is universal.

Learn more about J.E. Neal at JillianNeal.com

ALSO BY J.E. NEAL

TANGLE OF MAGIC

Tangle of Magic Boxed Set (Books 1-6)

Tangle of Lies (Book 1)

Tangle of Chaos (Book 2)

Tangle of Desires (Book 3)

Tangle of Fates (Book 4)

Tangle of Trust (Book 5)

Tangle of Ruin (Book 6)

ENERGY OF MAGIC

Shield and Shattered Cages (Book 1)

Shield and Faltered Steps (Book 2)

Shield and Splintered Oaths (Book 3)

Shield and Humbled Crown (Book 4)

Shield and Vile Serpents (Book 5)

Shield and Coveted Splendor (Book 6)

Shield and Guarded Shadow (Book 7)

Shield and Worthy Sinner (Book 8)

Shield and Sacrificial Heirs (Book 9)